Before
The
Music

Marie Claire Peck

Order this book online at www.trafford.com
or email orders@trafford.com

Most Trafford titles are also available at major online book retailers.

Printed in Victoria, BC, Canada.

ISBN: 978-1-4269-1742-4 (sc)
ISBN: 978-1-4269-1743-1 (dj)

Library of Congress Control Number: 2009939482

*Our mission is to efficiently provide the world's finest, most comprehensive
book publishing service, enabling every author to experience success.
To find out how to publish your book, your way, and have it available
worldwide, visit us online at www.trafford.com*

Trafford rev. 11/18/2009

Trafford
PUBLISHING® www.trafford.com

North America & international
toll-free: 1 888 232 4444 (USA & Canada)
phone: 250 383 6864 ♦ fax: 812 355 4082

ACKNOWLEDGEMENTS

To God Almighty and the Author of the entire Universe, Jesus the Son and finisher of our faith, and the Holy Spirit who guides us daily...

You have given me all of the loved ones below to enjoy for the time I am on this earth. I love You, cherish You, and I bow my knee to You. My soul belongs to You, and I thank You for Your grace that is eternal.

To Kara Mallory, friend, confident, mother figure...

Without your help during my double knee replacement recovery, I would not have gotten this book done in such a short time. You prepared meals for me, edited for punctuation and sentence structure, and otherwise cared for this cripple! My heartfelt thanks for such a friendship and love as you have shown me. To Rand also who supported both of us while you were away from him for so long, a big hug and thank you for your kindness and agape love.

To my precious husband Cliff, my best friend and supporter...

I cannot express the wonder of the life we've had together, the ways we have both grown in our faith, me especially. I do love you, dear Cliff, with all my heart. Thank you for having two wonderful boys who love me. I could never have children, and Brett and Jason are a blessing I would not otherwise have had. I love them dearly. I cannot thank you enough for your encouragement and helpfulness in the making of my second story. My cup truly runneth over.

To Tracy Brazie, editor and friend...

Thank you, dear one, for your many hours of help on the writing and putting together of this work. I am so blessed to have you as a friend. Thank you for helping make this book a better read than the first one! We're a good team, I think!

To my dog, Cannon; frequent visitor, Gracie Hall; and two horses that have had to sacrifice so that I could spend all my time on writing rather than on you...

You have been stress relief for me. Thank you for the hugs you let me give and the treats you let me bestow on you. I love the times I can just sit and visit with you and curry, brush, and pet you. I love you four-legged kids.

To Trafford Publishing, the people who publish and sell my books...

Thank you from the bottom of my heart for your diligence and perseverance to see that my work gets done in a timely manner.

To sundry friends and family – Leslie, Trudy, Pastor Frank, as well as all those above...

I thank God that I have you in my life. I love you dearly. My prayers go out on your behalf every day. I thank you all for your support and encouragement. May God richly bless all you do each day, and give you peace knowing you are richly blessed and deeply loved.

And last but not least….

This book is dedicated to men, women, and children throughout the world who don't know how to better their circumstances. The author was a battered child, then a battered wife. She is writing her books to be able to bring awareness, and through awareness, help, to these suffering women and little ones. Child abuse is rampant in the world today. Every day millions of children are sexually abused and neglected. Beaten and left to fend for themselves, these children are frightened to the point of shutting down emotionally, allowing the abuse to continue. It happens oftentimes at such a young age that the child believes it is normal and what is to be expected of them. Nothing could be further from the truth. Three children die daily due to abuse and neglect in America alone.

Women, too, are abused and neglected by uncaring, unsupportive husbands, and even killed by men they think love them. I urge those women to move on. Get out when they can, while they can, and find help through women and children's agencies, police, and fire departments. Save your life, women. Save yourself. Save your children. Get out of abusive situations and stay out of them!

Woman, if you are an abuser, for goodness sakes, get help! No child should have to suffer because their mothers are too strong-willed and perfection-oriented, angry at life's circumstances that cause them to be hurting, and/or too impatient to want to deal with the small life they brought into this world.

If you, or someone you know is on drugs or alcohol and is abusive to their children, or you come in contact with a neglected child, turn them in and get them help. Don't stand by and watch a child being beaten, burned, and otherwise tortured. Thank you!

For Eli Creekmore, a little boy lost and whose last days I cannot get out of my mind; my mother, Cecelia McCory, and all the others out there who have endured tough times and were not able to overcome their tormentors. And to JC, the finisher of our faith.

PREFACE

THE AUTHOR wrote this book to share her personal experiences, and in the hope that it may help others, she has taken into consideration the affect abuse has had on women she interviewed. The days of her first marriage were stressful. There were few days filled with smiles, fun, and trust. Her husband was a controller. He dissected her wallet and purse, receipts, phone calls – everything. He told her what to wear and how to fix her hair. While she was never one to wear eye makeup, he dictated that she wear it and how she wore it. This author was not a happy wife. The couple had few friends but none who were close.

The author is dedicating this book to the millions of women and children who are killed yearly, due to the domestic abuse they live with. The mothers, who feel powerless to help themselves or their loved ones, need to know I understand and that there are ways to overcome the abuse. I say 'feel' because, like my biological mother, they have been so beaten down that they don't realize they have a voice, a choice, and people around them everywhere who will reach out and help them transform their lives. It's time to stop the abuse. It's time to save our children, ourselves, before it's too late.

Women, it's time to take over your own life. There is nothing about a man that it is worth losing your identity, your freedom, your everything. We were made to be helpmates for our spouses, not beating boards for them to take their insecurities and hatefulness out on. If you are in this kind of situation, get out! You will find freedom and respect somewhere else. You don't need the abuse, the degradation, the pain. The author has found happiness, true happiness, and you will too. Share her story with other abused women. They, too, can find peace elsewhere.

She would love to hear from you, so email the author. She promises to answer your correspondence. If you'd like a phone call, please leave your name and number and the best time to reach you! Our author is a good listener, and does her best to help. You can reach her at <u>Donttellbaby@q.com</u>

Synopsis

THE MANUSCRIPT, known as <u>Before the Music</u>, is loosely based on the life experiences of a young woman, Marie Claire Peck. This author has quite a vivid and active imagination. Good stories are often written because the author puts the words running through his or her head to paper.

Clint Bellham, in this sequel to <u>Don't Tell, Baby</u>, has helped our heroine, Marie Claire, grow up and toughen up. Her faith in God, the Christ whom she believed in as a young girl, grows and so does her circle of friends. Marie Claire has to endure a tough marriage to Francis Kingman. She opens her home and land to developing a horse training and riding academy for handicapped children and adults. She endures one final event that leaves her fighting for her life. Kindled for a time by circumstances beyond Marie Claire's control, an unusual occurrence brings the music of Marie Claire's laughter back. The friends and family around her are amazed and delighted by the blossoming of their loved one.

Marie Claire and her family make new lives in an ending that, though not an event of real life, is still a happy fairy tale come true.

Books by Marie Claire Peck

How to Write a Book, a how-to pamphlet for new writers
Available at <u>donttellbaby@q.com</u> for $4.95

Don't Tell, Baby

Before The Music

Rocking Horse Ranch – available December 2009

Bethany's Story – Available spring 2010

Before The Music

By Marie Claire Peck

R OY COPELAND took Marie Claire Peck to the Vancouver Bears vs. Seattle Civics hockey game one Saturday evening. It was the first time Marie Claire had been to any kind of sporting event outside of horse shows and rodeos. She thoroughly enjoyed cheering Seattle's team. The guys yelled at each other, people on the ice and in the bleachers were screaming at the players, and 'kill him, smash him, hook him' could be heard clear across the arena. Other things screamed out were 'hit him hard, and check him to the board (which is to say - 'knock him out!'). One player skated over to an opponent and gave him a 'face wash', where players will skate up to an opponent and, with gloved hands, try to reach through the opponent's barred guard to get to his face. It's a brutal and often times bloody game, much like football, and it can be boring at times, even uneventful, but it's well worth watching.

Marie Claire got so excited each time she saw the puck moving across the ice, she jumped up and cheered.

"You're only supposed to cheer our team, Marie Claire. That was a goal for the other team!" Roy had never seen a girl get this excited. With laughter in his eyes, he stood and looked at Marie Claire.

She kissed her friend on the cheek and shrugged her shoulders, then turned back to look at the game field. Roy sat down. The guys were getting off the ice for a few minutes, taking a break.

"This is fun," Marie Claire said to Roy. "I'm not much for sports, but I love this game. They are very competitive, aren't they?"

"Yes, they are. My dad got me hooked on hockey. I come as often as I can to see our team." Roy spoke quietly, looking between Marie Claire and the ice. "They're coming out," Roy said as one player appeared at the bottom of the stands to skate on the ice. They raptly watched him as he skated around the playing field, occasionally jumping and twirling in the air, skate tips pointed downward as though he were a ballerina. The enthralled crowd watching knew that this man loved the ice, and the captive audience smiled as the skater enjoyed his free time.

The teams came out ten minutes later. The Civics wore white jerseys, well padded in the shoulders, knees, elbows; and the red boots sported white trim. The red numbers stood out on the white jerseys. The Bears wore green jerseys with white numbers.

Plunging to be the first to hit the readied puck, players fell, got up, lunged at each other and tried to hit the black cylinder, and in their frenzy to be the first team to make a goal they would push, shove, and try to hook the stick around an opponent's knee or thigh to make him fall. Sometimes, after a mad dash to check someone, a player would slide into the goalie because the ice sometimes kept the players from stopping on those slender bladed skates. In the end, tears streamed from Marie Claire's eyes from all the excitement and laughter, though this sport was rough. She looked around her and the audience watched raptly, but didn't get as excited as Marie Claire did. She felt somewhat odd, but the couple appreciated and marveled at the skill needed in such a hard game to play, and the teams competed with eagerness and determination. Roy never said anything all night about her exuberance, other than her cheering earlier.

Civics player Number 99 had made most of his team's goals, and at the end of the game, he fought hard to, but never felt, the victory. It wasn't to be. The puck slid toward him. Player 99 got into position, slid into the opponent to keep him from making the puck, but just as his club hit the small round target to make it past the goalie for a score, Player 15 from the Bears checked him hard.

However, a hard loss for the Seattle Civics, in camaraderie the Seattle team bumped shoulders and headed for the showers. Their motto after losing was 'another game to come, another chance to win!'

Though the Bears won, the young couple wasn't disappointed. Marie Claire had fun watching the ice game. Roy had fun watching the joy on his girlfriend's face as the small hands squeezed his arm, and she squealed as another puck found its goal, no matter which team got the points. They held hands as they walked out to the car.

Marie Claire knew nothing about the game, but she was a pleasure to watch in herself. Always so quiet and shy ever since he'd first met her several years ago, amazement overtook Roy at the laughter coming from his girlfriend's mouth.

"You surprised me, Marie Claire. I have never heard you laugh. I've not seen you smile much either." Roy smiled beatifically at Marie, and she looked into his eyes, a bright smile of her own shining across the chasm.

Taking her face in his gentle fingers, he leaned into her and gave her a chaste kiss. He would have loved to deepen it, but Marie Claire gave a slight push against him. Roy straightened up behind the wheel, and still turning a smile to Marie Claire, he turned the key in the ignition, the engine purred, and he backed out of the parking space. In a few minutes, the BMW was on the interstate heading south and the couple made small talk about the game as the quiet car carried them towards home.

Roy stopped at the IHOP near the ferry dock so he could buy them each a banana split. The two really only had seen each other during school hours the past year, but they spent all the time they could talking while walking the school grounds, or sitting in the library when inclement weather set in. Roy enjoyed the game tonight. It was the longest they had been able to be together in quite a while.

*   *   *   *

Marie Claire asked her parents earlier in the day if she could go to the game with Roy that Saturday night. The Kingman's had something going with friends so the answer was 'yes'. Marie Claire could hardly wait for the minute that Roy would pick her up. So much was going on in her life that she couldn't wait to get away.

Roy talked to his mother about his feelings for Marie Claire and he told her he would like to propose marriage to the lovely girl. All smiles, Margarethe Copeland, Roy's mother, exuded her pride and happiness to her son. She thought Marie Claire a wonderfully nice young lady, and she would love to have her as a daughter-in-law.

"Oh, my son. That would be a pleasure. Marie Claire is so sweet. You said she doesn't have any hobbies but horses, so maybe I can teach her how to knit and crochet! I'd love to have a young lady helping me around here." Margarethe Copeland, much to Roy's delight, went on to tell how he needed to propose and when to do the thing. Roy's gentle heart made him take his mother's advice in the intention meant. She doted on her boy, and though not bossy, she tended to be overly protective.

Roy's mother was a sweetheart and often helped out in the community. Well known on the little island, people swarmed to her classes as she taught gardening in the winter and spring months. Other women sometimes went to Mrs. Copeland when they had concerns, and Margarethe, never one to turn away anyone needing help or advice, always made sure to be available to give aide, advice, or just be a sounding board for young and old alike.

"I'll like to talk to you and your father after she accepts."

"Mother, do you think she'll take me as her husband?" Roy was always calm and never nervous, but Margarethe could tell that her son seemed very much in love and wanted Marie Claire for his wife. Right now, he did seem a bit nervous, which was natural. Marriage was a big step, but Roy was well mannered and a very smart young man. He would do well in his life.

Margarethe and her husband, Roger Copeland, hadn't seen much of Marie Claire this past year. She and Roy used to be seen almost every day together, and she shared many meals with them, and even sailed with them a few times. They both thought her to be a good match for their son. She seemed, and according to Roy, was a proper young lady. Someone with good morals was getting hard to find in this day and age. Girls now were wearing miniskirts that, when they sat, their panties could be seen, and their blouses were getting shorter, showing some of the waistline. Parents knew because their children told them that make out sessions happened under the football stadium bleachers. They also knew the names of the kids involved. Being such a small place, everyone knew everything that happened on Vashon Island.

Roy's parents were in their sixties. Roy was born when they were in their forties, after having thought they wouldn't have any more children. He was their pride and joy. His mother doted on him. His dad taught him sailing, hiking, and encouraged him to join the Explorers in high school so he could learn to become a top rate officer should he join the navy. His father and his father's father had been in the navy, and Roger wanted Roy to follow in his forefather's footsteps.

"I don't know, Roy. She is so quiet and I can't read her well at all. Just ask and let the Lord lead the way. I know she's a Christian and a very nice young lady. You could do worse." She put her hands on her son's shoulders, kissed him on the cheek as she'd done when he was a young child, then she turned him and patted his back. "Go now, and have a good time." Margarethe, the sun shining on her snow-white short curly hair, became deep in thought as she watched her son drive away.

*   *   *   *

Marie Claire hadn't been to a casual restaurant like this. Inside, she smelled hot pancakes being cooked. The sweet aroma of maple syrup hung in the air. She loved breakfast, and hotcakes and waffles were her favorite. She wasn't really hungry so she just decided on a banana split and waited for the waitress to seat them.

There were quite a few people here tonight, at least a hundred. More came in the door each minute. *They probably all came from the hockey game*, Marie Claire thought. She marveled as she watched all the people smiling, laughing, and as the waitress seated them at a small table in the back that overlooked the ferry dock, Marie Claire and Roy both admired the happy, noisy people around them.

Over their sweetly decadent banana splits, Roy gazed at Marie Claire with love in his eyes. "I'd like to ask you something, Mare," Roy commented. Marie Claire, used to people saying what was on their mind without asking her opinion, felt surprised. She quickly lifted her head, a question in her eyes. She loved the fact that Roy gave her such a nickname. Her smile was sweet and her eyes lit up with pleasure.

"Sure, you can say anything you want." She put down her spoon and folded her hands in her lap. Her gaze stayed on Roy's shirt collar. Other than her grandfather, and out of deference to Francis Kingman, she looked everywhere but at anyone else's eyes when they talked to her.

"What would you say to marrying me?" Roy's gaze continued to stay on Marie Claire.

Sitting back in her bench, Marie Claire, a look of surprise on her face, stared at Roy as though she just received the biggest shock of her life. She never expected this question. Roy could see the wheels spinning in her head. Her fingers were kneading and entwining every which away. She glanced in his blue eyes.

Marie Claire looked away and, with remorse in her voice she said, "I want to finish school, Roy. I'm not sure what I want to do afterwards."

"Mare," Roy continued, disappointment tingeing his otherwise cheerful voice, "I will be in the navy. You can finish school and we can still be together." He explained how it all worked for servicemen and their wives and dependents. "You can be married to me and it will be just like you were part of the service. Nothing will change."

"No, Roy. I'm sorry. Thank you for asking - maybe later. Ask me again later." Marie Claire rose from her seat and walked outside. So many things were going through her head. So many reasons she wasn't good enough for anyone to marry, let alone her friend, Roy. She knew she couldn't marry anyone. She felt so unworthy. *Besides*, Marie Claire thought, *I don't know that I love Roy. I'm not sure I know what love is.*

Marie Claire wished she had someone to talk to, someone who would listen and understand. She wished God would just open up His arms and take her to Heaven. *I'm such a worthless person. I don't know why I'm alive*, she thought all the time. Things were happening to her that no one knew about. She tried several times to share with friend's mothers. No one would listen. She found hatred instead of understanding, lost friends, and just had nowhere to turn. Three women she thought would help her wouldn't. They just called her a harlot, or told her she was a sinner and they wanted nothing more to do with her. Her own biological mother just told her that she would have to 'live with it. Everyone else has to.' Marie Claire didn't understand that, but she let it be. She never again would talk to anyone about what was happening to her.

Roy walked up behind her, hugged her to his chest, and said, "You're worth waiting for, Marie Claire. I will ask you again. Count on that. Now, let's go home."

The ferry ride was quiet and the house more so when they reached her home. The back porch light glowed yellow, illuminating the carport and the steps up to the side door. The gravel of the drive caught a small space of the light, just enough to show where the gravel met cement of the parking bays. Only one car on the far side sat empty. It was Mom's new Mercedes. All the inhabitants would be away for another hour or two. Roy walked Marie Claire up the steps, gave her a chaste kiss, and left her standing inside the kitchen doorway, lock engaged, before he left for home.

Chapter Two

MARIE CLAIRE was fifteen when she went to live with the Kingmans. They did for her as they did for their own children. She felt loved. She felt safe. The home appeared happy and healthy. A big fight never went on in the family, ever. What more could a kid want? Marie Claire felt very happy and blessed with her new family. They got her involved in tending their half-acre garden, milking the cow, feeding the chickens, and gathering eggs. Anne Kingman even taught her how to churn butter. Sewing wasn't much fun for Marie Claire. She thought it too feminine for her liking, but she did learn. Anne, who taught her and Cathy side-by-side, made them each learn to make some of their own garments. They made two skirts and a blouse each just last month. Marie Claire also learned chores and housekeeping. In return, she was given the greatest gifts of all - a nice home and horses and the means of training them.

She lived with the Kingman's for about six months before being asked to help her dad clean the bank one night. That was the first time that Francis Kingman abused her. She could have said no, should have said no, but she was so attuned to men having their way with her that she couldn't say anything. She cried when she went to bed that night. She didn't know what to do. She loved her new family. Mom Anne was great. She cared about the kids and she did for them what should have been done for Marie Claire and her siblings at her old home. However, *no sense looking back on that*, she thought at the time. *Maybe, as smart as Mom is, she'll see there is a problem and fix it.* At least, she thought that over the next few days.

Marie Claire was buttering a piece of toast one evening, using the fresh baked bread Mom made earlier in the evening, before going to bed to do her homework. She heard Mom call out Dad's name, and the next thing Marie Claire knew he was there, buck naked, standing for her to see his entire body. Embarrassed, the sixteen year old turned away and ignored him.

Many things happened over the next few months. Now a senior in high school, almost graduation time, Marie Claire had to figure out what to do with the rest of her life. Francis and Anne started fighting just weeks ago. She would cry. He would hit her. Things were turning out to be just like before the young girl came here, except for the drinking. No alcohol touched the Kingman home. Marie Claire wanted to leave, but Cathy would say something and Marie Claire would be talked to or yelled at and she wound up in her room having to think about her actions, then an expected apology came. Thankful that Jill Wynnewood again had her every weekend for advanced lessons, Marie Claire tried her best to persevere. Learning the horse training business, Marie Claire felt she was on her way to freedom. Little did she know!

Cathy started sneaking out at night, drinking and staying out with guys from school. Always cajoling, she tried to get Marie Claire involved in her after-hours activities but Marie Claire didn't go for keeping up with what other kids did or thought. She never even kept up with the fashion trends. *I will do what I want and not follow the others,* so Marie Claire kept her own council. *I know Pastor Mark said to us once in a sermon that keeping up with fads, doing what the world does, and ignoring God's Will is a bad thing.* The teenager had a mind of her own and she was keeping it. Dad Kingman always made a comment to that effect – 'Marie Claire has common sense.' Well, Marie Claire wasn't sure he knew what he was talking about.

Several times a week he would corner her and make her do unspeakable things with him and to him. He rarely ever left her alone. He started using foul language when talking to her and he often complained about the clothes she wore and the way she wore her hair. Marie went from being a happy, healthy, teenage girl to being a sad, listless, unhappy young woman.

She begged. She pleaded. She did everything she could to tell him to leave her alone, but to no avail. He would bring gifts to her. Cards were plentiful. Dinners, trips, cajoling, and threats abounded. The circle never ended. Marie Claire was trapped and she knew it.

*　　*　　*　　*

Roy once again asked for her hand in marriage. It was later in the fall and the sun shone brightly over the mountains, and the crisp air smelled of Puget Sound and salty sea. It was a Wednesday and they sat at the theater after watching a matinee. "I wish you would change your mind and marry me now, Marie Claire. I want you with me when I go to the naval academy. You're a beautiful girl." Roy didn't tell Marie Claire he loved her. However, he went with Marie Claire to see her biological mother, after Marie Claire asked, and Cecelia McCory had been thrilled.

"Why, Marie Claire, I'd be happy to see you marry Roy. You'd do good by yourself." Marie Claire smiled her sad smile. She wasn't sure if she really wanted to marry, but she owed her mother at least this much. She didn't tell her mother that she asked Roy to speak with the Kingman's before she gave him her answer. The girl felt dirty, standing there in that smelly living room.

After a minute Cecelia asked, "Why don't you two have a seat, visit a spell. I'll just get you some cola."

Marie Claire and Roy sat in the tattered green couch. Marie Claire's eyes took in the dirty walls, smudges and fingerprints all over the place, the floor looked dirty with sand and paper. The two windows in the living room showed nose and fingerprints, and they were so dusty and dirty no one could see out of them. *At least no windows seem broken*, Marie Claire thought. She did notice the kitchen was not too bad, with the clean floor and scrubbed sink and appliances. Roy sensed sadness in his friend as her gaze strayed to the hallway where her bedroom used to be. He squeezed her hand and held tight to the small but strong fingers. He knew of her background.

Cecelia came back into the room carrying three glasses of fizzy Pepsi, the cold ice cubes leaving damp trails on the exterior. Roy stood while reaching up to take two of them from her hands. He then waited as the woman took a seat opposite them before being seated once again next to Marie Claire.

"How ya been, kid?" Cecelia asked her daughter.

"Fine, mama. You?"

"We're doin' ok. It's hard now that you're gone. But, I hope you're doin' ok. They ain't hurtin' ya are they?"

"No, mama. Life's good. I even have horses to train, and I'm taking lessons in that for the next year so I can train professionally. I went to a horse show a few weeks ago. It was fun. My horse won first place in almost all the events." Marie Claire just sat as she talked.

"Yeah, I seen ya there. I heard from Miles that the two of you were goin' into that show. Your stepdad took me down. I was surprised to hear you'd trained the horse yourself. Paint, ain't he?" Miles was Marie Claire's cousin on her mother's side. They were just a few months different in age.

"Yes, mama. He's out of a nice stallion called Better Be Quick. Our Ferrier owned him. The colt I took in the halter classes is out of the stallion too. His name is Token. I'm saddle breaking him now. He's my own horse. I'm planning on going to college to be a veterinarian."

"Hmmm. Good for you." Cecelia wasn't impressed. She didn't even seem too thrilled to be talking to her daughter about her new life, other than the horses of course.

After a few minutes of quiet, Roy said, "Well, I promised my father I'd help him with the sailboat today. We better go."

Cecelia sided with her daughter as they stood there at the top of the steps. Marie Claire couldn't look into her mother's eyes, but she did lay her head on the older woman's shoulder for a second. No hug followed, so Marie Claire straightened up and walked down the front steps, the same ones where she broke her leg not so many years ago. Cecelia followed the young couple, stopping at the porch railing to watch as they made their way to the shiny white BMW, sadness mirrored out of her light blue eyes, unseen by the two young people.

I don't see Marie Claire anymore. Marry her Roy. Take her away. Bring her back to see me sometime. I do love my daughter. Not able to say any of this to the kids, Cecelia's heart broke all over again. Tears fell from her blue eyes as she turned and walked through the front door. She turned and ran into her bedroom before she made a complete fool of herself in front of Jeanette, who stood in the kitchen doorway sucking on a Popsicle. *I wish I had never married Jack McCory, Senior,* Cecelia May thought as she plopped herself on the bed. *Grant Jr. is going to be just like his no good father,* the woman thought, and she didn't want anything to do with him, either. Her heart felt torn apart again, just because of what her husband had done to her daughter a few years earlier.

Roy and Marie Claire drove away. Marie Claire, deep in thought, looked out the window not speaking to Roy, and he sensed she needed some quiet time so the young man drove the ten miles to the Kingman's pondering thoughts of his own.

Mama didn't have a black eye or anything. I wonder if he quit beating her. Marie Claire cared about her mother, but she realized that in the two years she'd been gone, life had changed her for the better, in some ways. In other ways, she thought God should have killed her a long time ago. She was enduring humiliation and abuse of a different kind now.

"Ask my dad for my hand in marriage, Roy, and then come back and ask me again. Give me some time to think. I've never been asked to get married before. This is sure something special."

Roy dropped Marie Claire off at home so he could speak with his mother. "I'll be back tonight, Mare. I will ask your dad for your hand." The girl gave him a nice gentle smile and then opened the car door and disappeared inside.

Marie Claire was excited, nervous, and scared really, to the tips of her toes. Kingman, an angry man often times now, caused Marie Claire some trepidation. She didn't know what this latest was going to do to her and her family.

At eighteen, Roy felt devastated. He didn't want to be alone in the world without someone to write home to, someone to dream about, have a picture of, or long for on cold nights. He would do all he could to get his girl to marry him.

When he got home, he told his mother about the afternoon. He told her Marie Claire was the girl for him. "I asked her to marry me mother. She wants to finish school first. I told her she could finish up through the academy's benefits." Nearly in tears, Roy poured his heart out to his mom. He really loved Marie Claire.

She's had a hard life, son, hasn't she? You told me about that. I know you love her. Is she capable of love in return? Ask her again.

Ask her dad for his daughter's hand. Maybe he can talk to her. She has a keen mind. She is right in wanting to finish school. She needs that to find her way in this world. One needs a diploma to get a decent job anywhere. If you love her, do as I ask. Maybe her father will talk to her for you and make her see the right thing to do." Margarethe Copeland then hugged her son.

That night, the Kingman's heard a knock at the door. Anne sat in her armchair knitting, so Francis answered. Marie Claire ran up the stairs when she heard Roy's voice. Anne met them as Marie Claire closed the stairs door.

"Hello Mr. and Mrs. Kingman." Roy greeted the three and followed them, and Marie Claire, into the living room. "I came to see you both about Marie Claire. May I talk to you? Am I interrupting anything?" Roy asked, knowing it was the proper thing to do.

"No, Roy. Have a seat. Can I get you anything?" Anne asked the boy.

"No. I'm fine, thanks. Um, I asked Marie Claire for her hand in marriage. She wants to finish school. I explained to her that she can finish through the naval academy, but she asked me to talk to you, Mr. Kingman."

Francis looked into Marie Claire's eyes. She looked away from his. "Well, I think she is right. She should finish school first. It's different than what the academy can offer." Roy thought Francis Kingman looked angry, but he didn't say anything.

"I finished school when you were in the Coast Guard, Francis. I did ok," Anne stated in defense of the young couple. She told Roy, "I think it's wonderful. You should ask her again. You have my blessing to marry her. When would you like to have it?"

Francis became angry, angrier than Anne or Marie Claire had ever seen. He looked at his wife. He looked at Roy. "Marie Claire is going to finish high school here. That's the end of it."

"But si…." Roy started to say something.

"No!" Francis Kingman screamed at the couple. "You are not going to marry until you finish high school," Francis pointed his finger at Marie Claire, almost touching her nose.

"But sir, she can finish through the service…." Roy tried to explain.

"I know all about what the service can do, but I'll not have it, I said!"

Roy's face turned red. He had never heard either of his parents yell at he or his sisters like Kingman now yelled at Marie Claire. He was sorry he even stepped into this house. Roy felt mortified, and he wanted to run. Kingman jumped all over Marie Claire. He berated her, called her an idiot, and then he turned on Roy.

"Get out of my house. Don't come here again. Marie Claire is not getting married until I say she can get married. That may be never!" The older man's face turned beet red, and his words cut the others like a knife.

"Sir, I love her with all my heart," Roy pleaded but Kingman would have none of it.

"Get out, now, before I throw you out. Marie Claire doesn't want anything to do with you, so don't come back here," Francis Kingman finally ground out. Roy walked out of the house quickly, after trying once more to obtain the love of his life.

Considering that Kingman thought of Marie Claire as his property, it was understandable the man would be this obsessed and angry. But not knowing why her husband became this upset, Anne thought Francis a lot out of line, but she dare not say anything. She thought she knew the circumstances between her husband and the teenager, but she was too timid, too weak maybe, to help the girl.

Many times when Anne would get angry at Marie Claire, she really was hurting inside. Anne wasn't sure if she should talk to Marie Claire, tell her she really loved her husband, loved her, and ask the girl to get on with her own life. She ached for her husband's attention and love once again. They hadn't been intimate or hardly even friends for over a year now.

Anne walked out with Marie Claire to see Roy off. She saw tears forming in Roy's eyes but he didn't cry. For that, she was grateful. She took Roy's hand in hers and quietly said to him, "Take Marie Claire and go away together. I'll send her stuff. Just take her and go. Get her away from here. I care about her, but she needs to move on." Roy just looked at Marie Claire and then jogged to his car.

Anne and Marie Claire watched Roy hurry to his car, a sadness in his demeanor and eyes when he looked up at them for the final time. He waved as he backed out of the driveway and headed home.

"I'm sorry, Marie Claire. You can elope, you know." Anne told the girl as she watched the tears fall, standing there watching Roy drive away. She hugged Marie Claire tightly and then turned and walked back into the house.

Quietly, Marie Claire said to herself, "I don't want to elope. I really don't want to marry, but I'd be safe with Roy. I do care for him, Mom. I'm sorry I'm such a failure." With a large sigh, Marie Claire walked down to her horses.

*   *   *   *

It was fall again, and very rarely did the sun shine. The sky drizzled the light rain that lasted part of the day. The leaves turned dull yellow, or browning, no longer the lush green they once were. The winds carried the weaker leaves down to the ground below, dead as Marie Claire's heart felt. The northwest didn't get the vibrant fall color changes that the eastern part of America enjoyed. The only truly beautiful fall trees were the vine maples that were planted in a few yards, and in the thick groves found in the forests. The leaves bloomed lush green in spring and summer, changed to lighter green and then red, bright then dull yellow and then brown, before baring their branches in winter.

Marie Claire graduated this last June with a 4.0 average. She lived in a dumpy apartment overlooking the I-5 freeway in the heart of Seattle, having moved from Vashon just three weeks ago. She worked as a receptionist in a luggage factory near the waterfront, just a short fifteen minute walk from her apartment.

One late afternoon, after a big fight, she told Francis Kingman that he either marry her or leave her alone.

"Why do you want me? I'm nobody!" she screamed at him. "I have a right to have friends. I have a right to be me. I get tired of sitting around waiting for you to come and sometimes you don't even show up. You don't always call. I just wish I was dead." She had tears falling from her lovely brown eyes, but it didn't faze the man standing across the room from her.

Marie Claire really wanted him to leave her alone, but he didn't and wouldn't listen. She wasn't allowed to have boyfriends now. The fight started over Francis' showing up with no notice. He just walked into her apartment and gave her visitors a glare that would have killed them all if it could.

There had been a company picnic that Saturday afternoon. It had been held at an outdoor covered pavilion at the Seattle Center. Marie Claire begged off knowing that if she went, sure enough, Kingman would show up at her apartment then be angry at her for not being there. Several of her friends from work decided to surprise her and brought her fruit and vegetable plates and chicken and a burger from the company get-together.

No one said a word except Sheila Marks, the luggage manufacturer's secretary.

"We'll see you Monday, Marie Claire. Enjoy the food. So sorry you couldn't have gone with us. It was a great picnic." En mass, the five friends left quickly.

"What was that all about?" Francis demanded angrily.

"Our president gave a special presentation today at the park for our company. They had a picnic. I didn't go because I thought you'd be here. I knew you wouldn't like it if I was gone, so I stayed home. They were thinking of me and brought food. I didn't know they were coming here."

"Humph," was all Marie Claire heard from him before he grabbed her around the shoulders and pulled her to himself, and then he kissed her breathless. "Come on to the bedroom, Marie Claire. I have something for you."

*   *   *   *

After an hour of lovemaking, Francis told her, "You don't need anybody here but me, understand?"

"Yes, but you know, I'm not a harlot. I am tired of being used like this. Why don't you marry me so I don't have to feel so dirty?" With unshed tears clogging her throat, Marie Claire rushed to the bathroom where she lost the contents in her stomach. After a shower, she came out and found Francis gone.

A sadness that depresses the soul came over Marie Claire. She didn't have contact with the real mother that she knew she loved - Mom Anne. She'd been cut off from her "adoptive" siblings, Michael, Cathy, and Kaye. Life was not the same. She could not see where it would ever be good again. The best part of her life, her family, had been taken away.

A few months later, Francis and Anne Kingman divorced. He

showed up at Marie Claire's door with a ring, wine, and a ticket to Paradise, Hawaii. They were married there. Stationed on the big island for a year in the Air Force, Francis Kingman loved it. So for their honeymoon, Francis and Marie Claire spent a week walking the beaches and strolling hand in hand. A hot Marie Claire sweated in the humidity. Francis wouldn't let her wear anything but a T-shirt and shorts. Tennis shoes adorned her feet. She didn't wear sandals or go barefoot.

After getting back from their honeymoon two weeks later, they left Seattle and went back to Vashon Island. Francis decided to leave again, after selling his house, and they moved to Seattle where the couple found a large home in West Seattle. They bought an acre of land with a home situated on the waterfront. Marie Claire sold her horses and left everything and everyone she knew behind. Francis Kingman allowed her nothing of her own.

Chapter Three

Francis Harlan Kingman came from money. His father was a lawyer. His grandfather had been a lawyer. Francis became a lawyer in the same law firm his great-grandfather started in the 1800s. He cleaned the bank in town part time at night to help out for a year or so, until another full-time employee could be hired. The small island bank couldn't find the right person. The islanders worked off island for the most part, and those that worked here sat in the bars or went to drink at the Eagles Hall after work. They already went through three janitors, all of them pickpockets and drunks, before Francis told them he'd be glad to help out for a while. The bank looked for someone from Seattle, but since Vashon Island is cut off from the mainland by all but ferryboat or small private plane, they had a hard time finding someone who wanted to commute.

Nearly two years ago, Francis asked Marie Claire to help clean the bank, and it was here for the first time that he violated Marie Claire. Since then, Francis, who had once been devoted to his kids and family, was now devoted to the firm and to Marie Claire. Since the divorce, Mom Anne and the children were now out of his hurtful reach. They moved far away and Marie Claire, with no mother or siblings, had to pick up the pieces of her own broken heart. Francis continued commuting to Vashon to clean the bank after work, but he gave his resignation last week and had one more week to go.

*   *   *   *

Marie Claire was a good cook and housekeeper. Her only flaw happened to be, in Francis mind, that she spent too much money on groceries. She also handed over all but a hundred dollars of her wages from the accounting job he insisted she take. Marie Claire never told Francis she made more than she gave him. *I have to work for my keep apparently,* Marie Claire often grumbled to herself. She would often receive beatings when Francis took the receipt from the grocery store. He put his wife in the hospital once with a broken rib and fractured jaw. In truth, Marie Claire purchased what they needed to sustain them for two weeks or so. She rarely ever splurged. As the days and months trudged on, Marie Claire secreted away several thousand dollars. The money was kept in a locked box in her desk drawer. Marie Claire needed new clothes for her job and often needed shoes or underclothes. She remembered as a child not having anything and being teased, tormented, and shunned. She would not let that happen again. Marie Claire dare not spend her savings, however, as Francis would wonder where the money had come from to buy whatever the new item happened to be.

Marie Claire, having quite a bad day at work a few weeks ago, was called into her boss's office. Marcia Madsen wanted to have a talk with her employee. They had become good friends over the last two years.

"Marie Claire. Is something wrong with you? Are you sick or is something happening you need to talk about?"

"I can't seem to get my husband to give me any money for new clothes or anything. We had a big fight Saturday because I spent eighty dollars on groceries. I needed essentials as I bake a lot, and of course stuff I was out of and needed for the next two weeks."

Marcia Madsen couldn't get Marie Claire to open up fully, but she did realize that things were not good for her young employee at home. The woman again saw the bruising under the heavy makeup Marie Claire wore on her beautiful face.

"I suggest you obtain a savings account for yourself. Give your husband some of the wages, but be sure to put some money away for you to use." She told Marie Claire, "You work hard and do a great job. You deserve to pay yourself first. He makes big bucks. He doesn't need his wife supporting him. It should be the other way around."

"What if he gets mad?" Marie Claire looked sadly at her boss.

"Give him the benefit of the doubt. Just," Marcia's hands fluttered in the air a second, "open up to him." Marcia was determined to make her protégé see the light and give a little trust to someone else. She sensed the girl had a hard time trusting people. Sometimes even believing what people told her came hard to Marie Claire. It's as though she needed to see before she believed. She listened well, but oftentimes she would walk away with a smirk on her face, lips curled in a disbelieving sneer. Marcia knew that Marie Claire didn't mean to be hurtful, but she did need to be a little more open to allowing others to share with her and guide her. Not everybody lies after all.

I don't know what goes on with Marie Claire at home, other than beatings, but I'll know it has something to do with that domineering husband of hers. Marcia looked with pity at her employee, her hands rubbing the other woman's shoulders. *Marie Claire will come around someday,* and Marcia hoped it would be sooner rather than later.

Marie Claire went home that night and thought about what Marcia told her. The next day, Marie Claire went to the U.S. Bank and opened up a savings account. No other name was on it, just her own. She talked to Marcia again that afternoon. "I'm afraid of what he'll do when I tell him about this account."

"Let him know. Don't keep this a secret. He may surprise you." Marcia said sardonically. Secretly, she thought the younger woman a doormat and a milksop, but she was a nice woman with a big heart and deserved some help - and a better husband. Marcia noticed some of the bruises Marie Claire tried to hide with the makeup. The woman hadn't approved of Mr. Francis Kingman when she first saw the evidence of an abusive occurrence.

One night a few months later, after two more hours of worrying about it, Marie Claire finally asked Francis, "Sugar, do you mind if we talk for a minute when you have some time?" She wrung her hands, worrying about what Francis would do, say, when he heard about the account. She had just finished cleaning up after breakfast when she began preparing loaves of white bread.

The scared woman read a book while waiting for the bread to rise, stopping periodically to consider her thoughts and actions. Then, she finally got up out of her wingback chair to put the pans of dough in the warmed up oven. The smell of bread baking soothed the woman's shattered nerves.

Francis had been in his den working on bills and listening to the news. Marie Claire took her pans out of the oven when the timer went off, and she inhaled the fresh doughy scent of hot yeast and fresh baked bread. When ready to face the dragon, she asked, "Do you have some time now?"

"Sure, Babe. What's up?" He was surprised because she had never asked this of him before. She was always so restitute. He pushed back his plush leather armchair, closed the top down on his desk, and walked over to the sofa where his wife settled and sat beside her. He manipulated her, touching, fondling, and hurting her in his need to devour everything she had to give. Marie Claire was angry inside, but suffered through her ministrations quietly.

Afterwards, she took a shower, put on a comfortable robe, and sat beside him. "I need underclothes and things periodically. I know you said we don't have money for me to spend. I thought, now that I'm making a little more wages, it would be okay with you if I opened a savings account for myself." Taking the bulk of her paycheck from that afternoon, she handed it to him.

He handed one hundred dollars back to her. "Ok," he said happily. "You keep half your paychecks. Don't ask me for any more money. You're making your own now. Learn to live on that. I'm going to bed."

Relieved, she sat there for another hour in the peace and quiet that she seemed to always have a hard time finding. She settled once again in her pink velvet wingback chair, the floral bowled lamp behind her shedding its soft reading light onto her book. A hot cup of cocoa and some mint cookies sat on the table beside her. The grandfather clock in the hallway ticked the minutes and quietly chimed the Westminster tune at the appropriate times.

Marie Claire sat for another twenty minutes, a fresh cup of cocoa at her side, and she thought of the evening with her husband. *That went very well*, Marie Claire thought. *Of course, now that it's over, I shouldn't have any more worries. I should get myself a checking account and a credit card next.* She would have a thousand dollars a month to herself.

Marie Claire spent some time in prayer before going to bed that night. As she knelt beside her chair, tearing up occasionally, she didn't know what to ask for, what to say to her Lord, but she knew He had been with her yet again. She truly was thankful for His love. No one else, she felt, cared about her anymore, not even the man, her husband, who refused so many times to let her go.

Chapter Four

F RANCIS NOTICED that Marie Claire watched a horse show on television one Sunday afternoon. He stood in the kitchen breezeway and saw the rapt look on his wife's face. He went outside to mow the grass and left her to her program.

A few hours later Francis came in to see when dinner would be ready. Marie Claire stood at the counter fixing salad, and the room smelled of tangy herbs and tomatoes. He knew spaghetti sauce sizzled on the stove. The television showed a horse race that Marie Claire recorded earlier in the day.

"You must miss having the horses, Honey. You are always watching shows, races, and rodeos. Ever since I met you, that has been your passion – horses! I guess that's partly why I fell in love with you. You are so beautiful when you ride. You seem to be happiest on a horse."

Marie Claire turned towards her husband and with a wan smile on her face answered him quietly. "Yes, I do Francis. Thanks for saying what you did. It makes me feel good." She lied, but had learned that men have egos women were expected to feed.

"I'll be in my office. Call me when dinner is ready." Francis left the kitchen, after uncharacteristically setting the table, and went to work on bills.

Wondering why he rarely bothered with her at all, Marie Claire did some more cleaning while the meal cooked. She felt she was there for his benefit alone. He never seemed to care what she wanted or needed. Marie Claire had become one lonely young woman.

While cleaning the kitchen, waiting for dinner to cook, Marie Claire thought back a few years and this remembrance came to mind. She worked in her garden one day. A year after getting married and moving to their beach home in West Seattle, Marie Claire wandered outside one morning to do some gardening in the flowerbed. She heard Francis came home early that afternoon. Marie Claire knew he wanted to spend some time with her. When he found her outside, he asked her to come into the house. She wore some old worn-out sweats that she dug out of an unpacked box in her closet, along with a threadbare T-shirt. She hadn't combed her hair or put shoes on her feet. She had a misshapen toe from having broken it at one time. She remembered her mother, Cecelia McCory had wrapped it up for comfort when Marie Claire was younger and still under her care. She couldn't take her to a doctor. Grant would've had a fit. She did the best she could. Marie Claire's right knee was misshapen from a break when she was four and then when she was eleven, both caused by her stepdad.

Francis didn't like illness or handicaps of any kind. He couldn't stand looking at her feet, even though he knew it wasn't her fault. The deformities sickened him. He laid into her real good when she was in the house and the door closed.

By the time she woke up, two policemen and her next-door neighbors surrounded Marie Claire, but Francis wasn't anywhere around. When he came in shortly after she woke up, he acted concerned then hysterical when he saw her condition. He'd told the officers that he had come home earlier, grabbed a sandwich, and went out for a walk. He said, "I could see Marie Claire was almost done weeding and knew she would then take a shower. I saw someone running down the street a short while after I left. He ran by me going the same direction I went, but I didn't pay him any attention. My wife was fine when I left her," Francis told the men as they loaded her into the ambulance on a stretcher.

When they got to the hospital, Francis filled out paperwork while the doctor checked on Marie Claire. She was in surgery for nearly an hour. Francis waited in the cafeteria and then wandered up to the waiting room. He'd been sitting for about ten minutes when the doctor came in to see him. A young agent from the Seattle Police Department, Detective Marshall Jones, was also there. He needed to see if he could talk to Mrs. Kingman.

"Hello, again, Dr. Elgin," The detective cordially greeted the young doctor.

"Detective Jones." The doctor greeted him in a not too friendly manner. It's well known that doctors don't like to see the police around the hospital unless they have family or friends there. When they were there for a victim or perpetrator, it made for a very uncomfortable situation. Hospitals are not the place to have policemen milling about, asking questions and looking suspicious.

"May I see the patient, please? I won't stay long," Detective Jones assured the man.

"This is Mr. Kingman. The victim is his wife. You might as well wait a minute. I'll tell you both what happened. Mrs. Kingman sustained a broken jaw, two very bloody black and blue eyes, and four fractured ribs. She is battered and bruised on almost all of her body. It's a wonder she's alive. She sustained a mild concussion, but she is cognitive. I believe she suffered no permanent damage and that she will heal over time."

Looking at the husband, Dr. Elgin explained the x-rays. "Your wife has sustained many broken bones and injuries over her lifetime. Do you know how that happened?"

"I know she came from an abusive childhood. That's all I know. I don't know any particulars." Francis lied, but being a lawyer, he could pull it off and he indeed got away with it.

"Yes, well, be that as it may, she could die if someone does this to her again. She has a lot of internal bruising, but no bleeding that we can find on CAT scan. That's an imaging process using dye injected into the patient's bloodstream; it allows the machine to detect where there may be internal organ or vessel damage and subsequent blood loss. "This beating, especially on such a small woman, is extremely serious and I hope whoever did this doesn't come back to finish the job." Dr. Elgin said this for the husband's benefit. He didn't trust the man. Something about him didn't seem quite right.

"Well, doctor, that's why I'm here. I'd like to get my man canvassing the neighborhood and streets now. I have no clue who to look for, what kind of car he was driving, if anyone saw anything. The neighbors who called the precinct told us that they heard a lot of screaming coming from the house." Detective Jones explained how he came to be at the Kingman home with the other policeman. He recalled talking to the neighbors but they hadn't seen anything or anyone.

Looking at Kingman, the detective said, "They saw your car, and that you had come home early, but that's all. Did you lock up after yourself Mr. Kingman?"

"No. My wife was outside gardening. I grabbed a sandwich and called to her that I was going for a walk. That's all. I got home after the police arrived and they placed her on the stretcher. I already talked to the police and gave my statement."

"Well, detective, go on in but don't stay too long." When Marshall Jones walked into the room, Kingman behind him, Marie Claire was on the phone. She told someone that she was hurt and in the hospital, but the poor woman could hardly be understood. Her right jaw was wired shut, and the doctor became very unhappy seeing her on the phone. The detective wanted to help, so he took the initiative.

Detective Jones asked, "Mrs. Kingman, may I speak with the other person, please?" Marie Claire nodded and handed the receiver to the man. He liked the woman and wanted to help her, as she couldn't speak clearly. He had gotten enough information from the surgeon that he knew the healing process would take a few weeks.

"Hello, this is Marshall Jones, a detective with the Seattle PD." He explained to Marie Claire's employer that a break-in had occurred at the Kingman home, and that Mrs. Kingman would be back in three weeks. He explained what the physician and surgeon said about Marie Claire needing that time to recuperate. Francis shared earlier about their vacation, and the detective explained the injuries somewhat and that after the couple got home from their vacation to Canada, he was sure her employee would return to work. Marie Claire nodded her head at the detective as he spoke with Marcia.

"Oh, do tell Marie Claire that we'll see her when she's back. Tell her we hope she gets better, the poor thing. I can hardly understand her. Is she really going to be ok?" Marcia Madsen questioned. "Please reassure her that we're here for her. She does have some sick time left and she's to just get better. We'll see her when she gets back to us."

The detective explained the broken jaw and assured the woman that he would pass her message on to Marie Claire. "She will be fine over time. I need to go. Thank you for your help."

Finally able to get down to business, he said to her, "Hi, Mrs.

Kingman. I'm Detective Marshall Jones. Can you tell me what happened?"

Handing the woman a pad and pen, Marie Claire knew to write down whatever she was told. "Well, I don't know. I was outside gardening. Francis came home early and called to me. Next thing I knew, I woke up in the hospital. I don't know anything. I never saw the man who did this to me." Laying down the writing items, Marie Claire started to weep, mostly from the pain she underwent. She was truthful. She came in and when Francis saw her attire, he lit into her. She never saw it coming.

*I stepped into the house a moment after Francis called to me. I remember walking into the kitchen to wash my hands at the sink before changing clothes. A hand grabbed my hair from behind as I stood at the sink, looking out the window. I remembered falling to the floor after I was kicked in the back of my legs. After being lifted and thrown into the living room, landing on the carpet after hitting my face on the corner of the buffet, I remember seeing Francis lift his right foot and then ...*Her mind blocked the incident out. She didn't share any of her knowledge with anyone. It would be another secret she kept to herself.

The detective left after realizing Marie Claire couldn't tell them any more. He didn't know what to do at this point. He hated to think ill of this attorney. Maybe he really had been out for a walk. It just seemed kind of strange that this happened suddenly after he'd gotten home. The detective's hands were tied if the wife wouldn't or couldn't tell the truth of the crime or didn't see the perpetrator. The doctor had said that some of the breaks were more recent, but most of the damage had been done years earlier when she was a child. They could tell that by the callus formations on the bones. The detective felt sorry for the childhood Marie Claire must have gone through, but now, too, because it seemed to him that she was still going through abuse with no one to help her.

Francis later told her, when she was settled in their bed at home two days later, "You looked horrible and I don't want to come home and see you looking like that again. You can look nice while gardening. You don't have to get dirt all over you if you're careful enough. There's no reason to wear drab clothes that make you look like trash." He wanted his wife looking beautiful at all times. After all, he had his image to think of!

Marie Claire wore the right makeup, fixed her hair to suit her husband, and started wearing nice clothes every day, even when she was gardening. She found ways to keep dirt off her person. Her husband came home early once in a while and she wanted to make sure she looked nice for him. He had thrown her work clothes way. They were damaged beyond repair anyway with all the bloodstains on them. The old clothes she kept in the closet, some having been her favorites when she was younger, had all been thrown in the trash by Kingman.

*   *   *   *

Two years later, after a big fight over something Marie Claire said, Sisters of Mercy again housed Marie Claire. She got out of the hospital just yesterday, and the bruises, cuts, and ribs still hurt. Francis stuck himself in his den with the door closed. Marie Claire busied herself making dinner.

The television was on and turned to an old John Wayne western. John Wayne, playing a nephew of an older couple with a missing granddaughter, sauntered out of their front door to mount his tall sorrel gelding. He and two other guys took off on their horses, galloping and shooting at Indians, finally stopping their horses at a stream. The cacophony of the gunfire no longer sounded off in the quiet home; only John Wayne and a blond young man carrying on an easy conversation, voices soft, their horses' reins held lightly in their hands, filled the silence between the two diners. Holsters and guns sat at their sides, belted at the waist, and the sky was deep blue around them. Blue tinged mountains reigning over the desert that was New Mexico filled the backdrop behind them. Marie Claire daydreamed.

Francis loved cowboy movies and they watched that while they ate. *Marie Claire is always watching something horsey,* Francis thought to himself. *She watches these things continually.* He noticed too that she always seemed so sad. He decided to give her a treat.

"Would you like to take a trip through Canada? We can find a stable up there and go riding," Francis asked Marie Claire. He was due for a long vacation, and Marie Claire was fun to travel with. He always watched her silently as she took in the scenery, marveling at something she found interesting, smiling at any animals that they passed.

"Yes, I'd like that. Can we stop and see Victoria first and travel from there? I'd like to see Laura again." She was as excited as she had ever been in years.

"Sure. I will call and let my sister know we will be up to see them. How does this weekend sound? We'll go for three weeks' vacation." Francis' sister and her family lived in Canada. He'd been born in Ontario. His parents grew up there and then came down to the states to be with family in Seattle. He hadn't seen his sister or brother-in-law, Philip, for a year or so. No one in his family would ever condemn him, but he could sense their displeasure in his life circumstances. He didn't care. He always got what he wanted. He'd wanted Marie Claire from the instant he'd first seen her. He waited until he could have her and then he left everyone else behind.

Marie Claire was someone he could keep on a pedestal and use, as he wanted. Heaven help the man who came between them. Someone had been in her life once. He disappeared nearly three years ago. Marie had been brokenhearted, since Roy asked for her hand in marriage just a day or so before his disappearance. She couldn't understand what ever happened to him. He just up and disappeared one night. His parents were still devastated. To this day, there had been no clue as to his whereabouts.

Marie Claire often thought about Roy. It made her sad to think of his abandoning her after she accepted his proposal, and then Kingman's tirade that caused Roy to leave. She was sure something happened to him, but she didn't know what it could be. She did know they were both very happy. She often thought he would come back and carry her off in his big white car. He wouldn't have left her like that, if he weren't kidnapped, or worse, dead.

She knew that thinking about the past was not good for her, but she had to talk to God about everything or she felt she couldn't be forgiven. Even things that she couldn't help, she prayed about and asked forgiveness of God for her misdeeds. She always felt everything was her fault. She had never had an adult teach her what parents are supposed to do to protect their kids. She just knew that grownups were to be obeyed, no matter how bad something seemed. No wonder she felt like a cast away by almost everyone that mattered to her.

Chapter Five

AFTER A few days, Marie Claire felt the soreness sufficiently abate. She'd only been out of the hospital since Monday, but Francis wanted to leave on the trip tomorrow, which was Saturday, so she kept quiet.

I will try to cover the bruises, but I hope I do a good enough job, Marie Claire thought to herself. After telling Marcia that, "I will be back in six weeks instead of the three we previously arranged with you, Marcia. Do you mind? I'll work extra when I get back!"

Marcia didn't need a reason to give Marie Claire extra time. "Hey, kiddo. You do a great job, and you're hurt. I want you to think about yourself for a change, understand! Have a great time. If you need to take more time off, just let me know."

With Marcia Madsen's blessings, the couple left on their trip Saturday morning. They drove to the waterfront. After boarding the *Princess*, they locked their car and meandered up to the upper deck deli for coffee and doughnuts. Marie Claire, due to stress, lost a lot of weight in the last several weeks. She was skin and bones, with a weight of eighty-five pounds. Her husband used to tell her how fat she was. Now, he complained of all the bones he could see and feel on her. He was never happy, it seemed. She wasn't hungry, but to put on a good front she attempted to eat something. She could only finish half of her apple fritter. She did drink several cups of coffee with sugar and cream.

"I hope you're hungry by lunchtime." Francis groused at her.

"You need to gain a little weight. Just don't get fat." He always liked svelte, well-endowed women. Marie Claire's figure would put many women to shame, but he never seemed to like her weight, skinny or a little heavier. Marie Claire had never been overweight. That was something she could never understand. *What do I have to do to satisfy this man with my looks? He's never happy with me no matter what I do.* Marie Claire often thought about this, never seeing that it was Francis who actually had the problem. Again, she laid the blame on herself.

*   *   *   *

The couple stood at the railing enjoying the view as the boat pulled into the dock. The dark, thick green grass surrounding the Empress Hotel shone with bright yellow daffodils spelling out, "Welcome to Victoria". Roses of multitudinous colors grew beside the ivy-covered walls of the Empress Hotel. A sudden ocean breeze brushed the roses against the dark gray stucco walls, the ivy being a soft cushion for them to lean on. The windows of clean clear glass were shining in the brilliant sunlight

"Hi, brother mine! Marie Claire! How have you two been?" Laura Alyce Kingman Dillard excitedly hugged her brother and sister-in-law. She rubbed her brothers arms with shaky hands and her face bespoke of her love for Francis. She was absolutely happy to see the couple. Her eyes shined with happiness, and the light green color of her cotton pantsuit brought out the green tints in her hazel colored orbs.

The boat disembarked right at noon. The day was sunny and bright, the temperature mild. The slight breeze ruffled the water into long white foamy roils of sea foam, and the sun glistened off the deep blue waters.

"It is so good to see you both!" Phillip Dillard shook Francis hand, and in turn hugged Marie Claire. "We should go in to have lunch now, shall we?" He stated to the couple. He and Laura had been sitting on the bench admiring the daffodils and watching the ship dock. They came over to the exit ramp to greet their family when the boat stopped and dropped the ramp.

They dined in a little antiquated room where a famous author stayed many times. He had left his glasses on the 200-year-old Oak table where the foursome now sat. Etched scars from the poet's hand cut into the glossy wood. The hotel owners named this room, the Hathaway Room, after the poet. A very private cubby, its window overlooked the front lawn, and the visitors enjoyed the view. High tea was just about to start and the two couples looked forward to it. They made small talk and drank the hot tea that the waitress served immediately.

"How have you both been? We haven't seen you in a coon's age!" Phillip asked the couple over a cup of tea.

"Busy, but fine." Francis told a little bit about their house, eventually the rambling carried over to his work. Marie Claire kept fairly quiet, letting her husband carry the conversation.

They all enjoyed the salad, cucumber sandwiches, chicken sandwiches, jam and crumpets, and the various pastry desserts that sat on tiers of bone china that had been made available for their dining pleasure.

"This is delicious!" Marie Claire commented over the salad made of currents, spinach, and bacon with some kind of hot ginger sauce poured over it.

"Yes, isn't it?" Laura asked. "We love coming here. The bone china is lovely, isn't it, Marie Claire?" The men were carrying on their own private conversation. The women were left to their own gossip.

During the three different courses, various flavored teas were served. With a salad, they enjoyed a mild mint flavored tea. For the sandwich course, they had been served a floral tea. For dessert, a nice fruity tea with a hint of rose hips was poured.

Marie Claire couldn't get over the floral smells when the teas were brought in. She enjoyed the cucumber sandwiches especially with the tea flavored with a hint of Rose and Jasmine .

"I think I like the mint tea with the chicken sandwich better." Laura commented to Marie Claire. "The jasmine and rose flavoring do go very well with the cucumbers, though."

"I agree," Marie Claire answered back to her sister-in-law.

The high tea was a bit expensive, but Marie Claire enjoyed it so much that the other's felt it had been worth the exorbitant cost.

"What happened to your eyes, Marie Claire?" Laura asked.

Marie Claire kept herself from gasping, and she felt ill. "I fell and hit my head a few days ago. This is the aftermath of that accident." Marie Claire didn't know what else to say. She tried to use enough makeup to hide her bruising, but apparently, she hadn't done a very good job of it. She hoped Francis wouldn't say anything about this, as she glanced his way. He looked into her eyes, but then he turned away and carried on his conversation with Phillip.

After lunch, the couples took a stroll about the grounds of the Empress. They spoke of the weather, flowers in bloom, trees that were planted in the neighborhood recently, and the Dillard children.

"Can we have a picnic here, or do they not allow it?" Marie Claire asked no one in particular as they passed a park like setting with benches scattered here and there.

"No. This area is set up for concerts on the green and whatnot. There is a picnic area around by the rose garden. We'll pass that in a bit." Phillip answered, a smile lit up his eyes when he looked at Marie Claire.

"Oh, look darling!" Laura exclaimed as they came upon a small pond with ducks and geese swimming in it. "Aren't they cute!" Laura had seen the goslings first and wanted the others to enjoy the birds too.

"Oh, you and your geese." Phillip said to her. "You have geese this and geese that all over our house." They all laughed at Phillip's teasing attitude towards Laura.

"Here's the rose garden," Phillip said as they approached the two-acre area. It was fenced with white pickets, and slate walkways meandered through the colorful garden. Roses of red, pink, white, yellow, orange, and every other color imaginable were planted here. The smell was heady and Marie Claire couldn't stay here long. It wasn't one of her favorite flowers, but she did enjoy the colors. The smell though, made her sneeze. She was allergic.

They quickly walked through the rose garden, Marie Claire holding Kleenex to her drippy nose, and then out the backside to the picnic grounds. Here, large oak trees and maples were planted, and grills and picnic tables were stationed throughout the two-acre park so folks could have barbeques and enjoy the squirrels, birds, and chipmunks that inhabited this bit of Victoria. They all sat under a big oak tree in the middle of the park, enjoying the cooling breezes and the animal chatter. The grass was soft and pungent smelling.

Laura wanted to ask about Kaye and Anne, but she felt she better not say anything. She knew that her brother could be, and probably was, a bit of a bully. The children in her family had to live through their father's tirades when he was distressed, which hadn't been often, but he had a wife who followed his every directive. Because Laura's mother had been such an obedient wife, it was only very seldom that their father would beat her or the children. He shouldn't have been a father. Their wonderful mother would've been better off without him.

Laura felt in her heart that Francis had been the cause of Marie Claire's black eyes. She would have to find the time to talk to the young woman. *Marie Claire didn't deserve to be treated that way, especially since Francis had caused such a rift in his first marriage,* Laura thought as she held Marie Claire's hand. The Dillard's knew what the problem had been, but they were not willing to get involved. They just wished that Francis had been a better man.

They enjoyed their three days together. It was now Sunday and the Kingman's had packed the night before and were heading for Alberta after their breakfast of French toast and Canadian bacon. Francis rented a cabin there for a few days.

The women said their teary goodbyes. "Call me if you need anything, Marie Claire. That goes for you too, Francis!" Laura said, afraid that Marie Claire may be in trouble again. Laura hadn't wanted to cause Marie Claire any more grief than necessary. Marie Claire shared on their walk last night about Francis' temper and what he did to her sometimes. Laura shared a few things with Marie Claire also. She hoped to help the young woman out of a bad situation. Laura loved her brother, but what he had done before, and was now doing to Marie Claire, was wrong. She thought, *this marriage should never have been!*

With the last goodbye, the couple took off for their next destination. Marie Claire felt excitement. They should arrive at the cabin in Alberta either tomorrow or the next day. It depended on whether they saw something they wanted to explore further while on their way there.

The trip was beautiful. Smooth was the highway and well maintained, with wide shoulders. Either side afforded views of large, four-footed, round, rugged-trunked, hundred foot high Ponderosa pine and shorter but no less rounded alpines. These Canadian forests were kept in their aged beauty for travelers and wildlife alike to enjoy.

As they entered Alberta the next day, they could see many elk and deer along the roadside and in the forests. Particularly fascinating were the many waterways, lakes, and streams one could see along the Trans-Canada Highway. Many of the large animals could be seen wading in or walking up to and drinking from the cold waters. Moose were plentiful, and here and there they could be seen swimming and playing with their young in the waters.

Marie Claire got out of the car a couple of times to walk into the wooded areas. She came within touching distance of a few elk. Their horns were so large, she thought it would be great if she could see a set lying somewhere and take them home. She knew that they were too big and wouldn't fit in the car. She could wish, though.

Francis told her that, "When hunting season comes around, that is the best time to find horns from the elk, deer, and moose. They shed their antlers in the late winter or early spring. If one dies from old age, wolf or coyote kill, or an injury, and if the wolves and coyotes don't get to them first, the antlers can be found during hunting season in the fall."

"Do you know why animals lose their horns?" Marie Claire asked her husband. She'd been quietly thinking about how the animals happen to grow horns only to lose them again.

"I used to hunt with my dad. He told me that the growth plate on top of the animal's head allows for the quick formation of the bony growth that we call horns, or antlers. They rut in the fall. The males use the antlers to fight off rivals. Later in the year, winter or early spring, the antlers become loose and fall off. They grow back quickly, and if one were to count the points they can tell how old the animal is."

"My dad had a set of elk antlers over our fireplace. When I was a kid, he picked them up, whole, while out on a hunt one morning. They were a beautiful sight." Francis sounded very gentle as he spoke to Marie Claire about his remembrances. He seldom spoke to her like that. She rather wished he would be that way all of the time. By late afternoon, they reached the chalet. It was not far off the main road, but seemed to be in a fairly private area. The manager handed Francis the key as she explained about the bear that roamed around here in the nighttime hours. She told them to be very cautious of being caught outside after dark.

She had earlier stocked the refrigerator as Francis requested when he made the reservations. There were also two extra pillows and fresh wood piled beside the fireplace. "The stove and refrigerator work fine. There is also a microwave in the kitchen. If you need anything, just ask. If I'm not here, my assistant will be," Mrs. Hindan told the couple. "You can see the trail to the stables right out your front door. You can walk a short distance through the woods and you'll see the horses. It saves having to drive around wasting gas. If you go left out of the drive, you will see a restaurant and a small shopping area about a mile down. Enjoy your stay," she said all she needed to say and then she walked off, leaving them to their privacy.

Marie Claire stood in the middle of the driveway looking all around her. *What a beautiful place,* she thought. *I could stay here forever and never tire of hearing the bird sounds and smell the clean, fresh air. I would love to see some wild animals. Maybe I can sit up and look for bear tonight!* She could hardly wait for tomorrow to come. They would be taking a horse ride for the day and she was eager to go.

"Marie Claire, come in now," Francis called to her from the doorway.

She looked back at him and saw the look on his face and the gleam in his eyes. She didn't want to, but she stepped into the chalet as Francis closed and locked the door behind her.

Chapter Six

BEFORE SHE left the couple, Francis paid Mrs. Hindan fifty dollars to bring them a large sausage, mushroom, black olive, and extra cheese pizza to their door. This, along with some extras, was delivered just before six that evening. He also ordered a salad with French dressing and cinnamon buns for them both. They found bottles of iced tea and other goodies to eat and drink in the refrigerator. He wanted to enjoy the time here with his wife without having to go out.

She promised to make him a good breakfast in the morning before they left for riding. They talked and lay in front of the fire when the evening turned cool enough. When their food arrived, they sat and watched a movie while they ate.

In the morning, Marie Claire got up very early to take a shower. She then went outside while Francis was still asleep. She sat on the bench beside the shore of the lake and did some thinking. She hated what Francis did to her. He called it love making, but she called it torture. She was so sore that she could barely sit.

There is a loneliness when you are with someone that cuts right through your heart. Marie Claire had a love/hate relationship with her husband, about her husband, and she wanted out. Not believing in divorce, however, she felt she was stuck. Suddenly a small breeze blew, and Marie Claire found hot tears running down cold cheeks. The sad woman would get the anger and tension out of her system now, before Francis caught her crying and punish her yet again for the slight against his manhood.

God, my Lord, why bring me through such a marriage as this is? What do you want of me? I know I'm here on earth for a reason, but why is that? Are you teaching me a lesson? If so, haven't I learned it yet?

Marie Claire sat on the bench and looked out over the still lake. Mountains reflected off the cold water, mirroring perfectly on the glassy surface. The morning was quiet save for the birds singing and a slight breeze every so often.

I can't love you like I need to and want to when I have these terrible feelings inside. I want to do your will. I do. I just don't see how I can when my thoughts are not what they should be according to you, and my feelings are not there either. Sometimes I hate Francis, I want him to die, or leave me, but that's not happening. It's wrong to have these thoughts, and call myself a Christian. I love you, Lord Jesus. Please help me! Marie Claire got the anger and sadness out of her system as much as she could. God would have to buoy her up and keep her going. He was the only one who could understand her torn feelings.

Francis awoke at nine that morning. He wanted his wife again. *I know Marie Claire is hurting this morning. I was pretty rough last night, but boy is she good. I love her loving. I better cool it or she won't be able to walk at all.* Francis smiled, thinking to himself, and planning their day after he got up. He was enjoying the quietness of the area. Figuring Marie Claire was outside meditating, he looked out the window to the bench he'd seen beside the lake yesterday. *Yes, there she is. She is a beauty. I love her flowing black hair. Her eyelashes are so long and her eyes so clear and beautiful...*

Francis was turned on, but he turned from the window and went to the bathroom. He showered and put on his riding attire. He saw that Marie Claire was wearing black jeans, black boots, white shirt, and a cowboy hat that she'd had forever. Francis Kingman never wore jeans. Dockers were his favorites and he had a dark brown western hat that he opted to wear for riding today. He did have some brown cowboy boots that he put on, as well as his Stetson.

"Marie Claire, where's breakfast? I'm hungry," he called to her. She turned and he could see she was lost in her own little world. She never paid attention to time like she should, but he would give her today since he knew she was excited to be riding again.

"I'm coming. Sorry. I wasn't watching the time and I thought I would let you sleep this morning. We were up pretty late last night. I loved that pizza." She told him the truth there, not denying that. Pizza had always been her favorite food.

They had bacon, eggs, hash browns, and toast. She was starving, which they both took as a good sign that she was doing better. He couldn't believe how much she ate! She looked better, happier, and she seemed to be filling out a bit too. The past several days seemed to have done her some good. Francis was happy to see that.

After breakfast, they watched a bit of news and then they headed over to the stables. As soon as she spied the wrangler saddling up a horse for a woman in line, Marie Claire asked him if she could saddle her own horse.

"Do you know how to ride?" Kirk, the wrangler, asked.

"My wife probably knows more about horses than you ever will, son." Francis told the young man. "Let her saddle the horse and you watch." Francis had his thumbs in his pockets, rocking back on his heels, and tilting his head this way and that, speaking with a slight drawl.

That's one cocky dude there. I hate those kinds of people. The wrangler thought to himself.

When the time came, Marie was handed a black and white paint gelding. "The tack is over there." Kirk told his client, pointing to a rack with a saddle and bridle hanging from it.

Marie Claire tied the gelding to the rail, came back with the tack in hand, set it over the hitching post and proceeded to groom the horse. Afterwards, she put the saddle on him and gradually cinched up. When she deemed he was all blown out, she tightened the cinch one last time and then pulled one and then the other front leg out and set it down again. She put the bridle on the horse and somehow had it in one hand and the horse unhaltered with the other, and quickly slipped the bridle over the ears and made sure the bit was in the mouth and not too tight or too loose. She started backing the horse but Kirk stopped her.

"Please tell me why you did that with the front legs. How did you do that with the halter and bridle? I could hardly see what you did; you were so good at it." Kirk was surprised and dumbfounded. He'd never seen such a thing in his life. The horse just stood there and within seconds seemed he was tacked up and ready to ride.

"Well, endurance riding is what I used to do. You have just so many minutes lead on the others or else you can lose the race, when you're racing. The horse has to be able to be saddled and bridled quickly. I put the lead over the neck so if the horse bolts or acts out, I just have to pull the rope for the horse to know that it's still tied. I cinch gradually so as not to cause a horse to pull back, thus learning a bad habit. I pulled the legs out like I did because sometimes their skin gets caught in the cinch or the hairs get wrinkled. This keeps the hair smooth and straightens out any wrinkles under the cinch. It is not only a courtesy to the horse, but it is also a deterrent to scald or cinch sores." Marie Claire paused for a moment, and in her quiet voice said, "I trained under one of the best for nearly two years, and even today if I have questions or problems, I can call Jill Wynnewood and she'll help me out." Marie Claire hoped that the wrangler was pleased with her answers. She also hoped that he learned something without her seeming to be a know it all.

Francis had been thinking all along that the wrangler didn't know as much as he should about the horse business. *Marie Claire sure put him in his place,* Francis thought, proud of her. *I hadn't realized how much she really learned or remembered of her training. I'm glad to know that Marie Claire retains as much wisdom as I always thought she had,* Francis thought to himself.

Marie Claire really hadn't put the wrangler in his place at all; that was just Francis' state of mind, seeing what he wanted to see. Marie Claire was a gentle soul, and never had treated others as though she were better than them. She knew she wasn't and never would be.

Kirk turned and was surprised to see all the other riders checking their horse's cinches and pulling out the legs. When everyone was saddled and ready to go, he watched as Francis helped Marie Claire onto her horse. *She looks real good up there,* Kirk the wrangler thought to himself. The men then mounted and Kirk said, "Let's ride."

They all were having a great time. They passed elk, deer, and two black bear back in the trees looking for grubs. Marie Claire looked like she was in seventh Heaven as she enjoyed her ride. They were at the top of a small mountain before they realized they had been climbing. They were coming up a wooded trail that suddenly opened up into a rich view of the river valley before them.

They surveyed all the land around them. They saw two big lakes with clear blue water glistening in the sunlight. The river below them was navy blue with white rapids scattered here and there along its path. They spied a smaller lake off to the North, and of course the surrounding mountains and even the little town of Twin Pines just across the lake from the motel where the Kingman's and many others were staying. The chalets were separated from each other by trees and shrubs. All of them were privately situated. The motel consisted of two fourplexes and six cabins and each one looked out onto the lake. The rest was made into single campsites that were fit for campers or trailers with all the amenities.

They ate a lunch of barbecued chicken and ribs there at that scenic overlook. A muleskinner with his team of mules had come up earlier in the morning to get the lunches ready. He toted plastic containers of coleslaw and potato salad out of the canvas packs that were slung over and hooked to the wooden saddletrees that the mules carried on their well-padded backs, as well as all the cooking equipment and other foodstuffs he would need. There were seventeen riders as well as the wrangler this morning. Three hours into their ride, they were thirsty, and hunger pangs were starting up already. After handing out plates of food, they all ate.

The mule skinner took out more bottled water and little snack packs of pudding while the now fed bunch were sitting near the edge of the cliff enjoying the scenery spread out before them.

After packing up and saddling again, the now weary riders were mounting up after thanking the crew for the food. In turn, the wranglers and guide thanked the riders for their patronage of the camp and motel facilities. They turned toward the trees again and started their trek back down the mountain, following a different trail that would afford them more and different scenery.

Back at the stables three hours later, Kirk again thanked everyone for coming. He explained to his clients that, "We will have the same ride everyday through the first of September. Kids usually go back to school the first Monday of that month, so the tourist business winds down about then."

The Kingman's rode once more before leaving for home a few days later. Marie got to see a bear come near the cabin the last night they stayed there. She heard a grunting noise and peeked out the living room window. There he was, sniffing the porch steps and moseying down to the lake to drink. She was excited and shared her good fortune with Francis. She woke him up from a sound sleep, but he hadn't minded. He looked happy to see her that happy, as she hadn't been for quite a long time. He went to the window to see the bear, which now was wandering along the lakeside.

They decided to drive back to Seattle and not take the *Princess*. There were a few stops along the way that they wanted to see, such as Northern Idaho and the tulip fields in Mount Vernon north of Seattle. They were beautiful and the two travelers were glad they hadn't missed them. They didn't go to Mount Baker, but they passed her and, "she is just about as beautiful as Mt. Rainier," Marie Claire told Francis, as she stared at that snow-covered mountain while they drove by her. Finally, they made it home. Tired from their three weeks away, they both slept very well that night. The next day was Monday and they had to return to work. The vacation was wonderful. It was just what Marie Claire had needed. Francis seemed to have a new lease on life too as he readied for his workday. He had never once hit Marie Claire the whole time they were vacationing. She didn't know how long this would go on, but she vowed to savor the reprieve for as long as it lasted.

Chapter Seven

Two months after their vacation, Francis came home from work to talk to Marie Claire. "I have been doing some thinking the past few weeks. What would you think if I told you to look for a house with land, or just some vacant land. I don't care where it is. We can build a house if we need to. I just would like to get into horses with you. I can work from anywhere since I'm a lawyer. One of my partners will keep this agency going if we move out of state." Francis surprised Marie Claire as never before. She never thought they would ever leave this house because it was all they had ever wanted.

"I want you to find a better paying job, one that's closer to home. Gas prices are going up and I want you to try to save money. That's all I ask. Let me know what you find and we'll talk about it tonight, okay?" Francis touched her cheek and smiled at her. Then he went into his den.

Marie Claire thought about his declaration while she finished up dinner. She remembered the beautiful lake in North Idaho that they had passed on their drive-through there on their way home from Canada. They drove down to Idaho, through the northern towns from Alberta, and then crossed over to Washington on Highway 2. She remembered the lake, river, and miles of green fields they passed while driving through Idaho and Washington.

"Remember how beautiful Priest River looked in the northern part of Idaho? Remember the mountains and lakes? We enjoyed driving through that area. May I look there for a place to call home?"

Marie Claire asked Francis as they ate their dinner of steak and baked potatoes.

"Yes, that was a very nice area, quite beautiful in fact. Why don't you call the Chamber of Commerce and get some information?" Francis sat there, pondering on their trip earlier in the spring. He recalled the fishing and hunting that the area would be good for, and the hiking trails they were bound to enjoy. He had been to Coeur d'Alene once. He had enjoyed golfing and fishing there, and he knew it was just south of Priest River. "That would be a great place to live!" he happily told his wife, smiling and talking about all they could do in that part of the country. He explained about the Coeur d'Alene golf course, and that he had played golf there a few times. "Lake Coeur d'Alene is beautiful and you would really enjoy seeing that area also. Green grass and pine trees abound, with parks and the lake for boating. They are building a super mall in Spokane and I know you would enjoy shopping there." After watching the delight in his wife's eyes for a few minutes, Francis said, "Well, hon. Work tomorrow. We better get to bed."

The next morning, Marie Claire phoned the Chamber of Commerce in Priest River. They would overnight a packet of brochures and information, along with a map of the area and of Idaho in general. They also gave her a website for her to peruse before the information arrived. Mildred Hamilton, the Chamber Secretary, spoke with Marie Claire for a few minutes. She told her, "We have a population of 341 right now. But, more and more people are moving in and building up. It's making this area more of a real city rather than a tourist town as it has always been." Mildred also said the same thing about the mall that her husband mentioned to her last night. "It should be done in early spring next year. Everyone I have spoken with is looking forward to that, and Spokane is just an hour away."

"It's been nice talking to you, Mrs. Hamilton. Thank you so much for the information," Marie Claire politely told her.

"It was nice talking to you too, dear. Have a good day and I am looking forward to meeting you sometime soon!" Mrs. Hamilton replied back.

When Francis returned from work that evening, he told Marie Claire not to hold dinner. "I have to leave again. We have a big meeting tonight and I can't stay home. I'm sorry, Babe. I can't miss this one. It's very important. I don't know what time I'll be home, but just enjoy a good book or something." He kissed her cheek and left again after picking something up from his den.

Marie Claire ate a salad and put the rest of the meal in the refrigerator. She had made spaghetti as she'd been asked to do for tonight. It would be okay for a few days in the refrigerator. She'd heat it up for tomorrow's dinner. She put a movie in the VCR, sat down in her wingback chair, and put her feet up on the ottoman. She would enjoy her time alone.

Francis didn't get home until one in the morning. Marie Claire didn't think anything of it. She figured after the meeting he'd gone out with the guys and did whatever it is guys do together.

After breakfast the next morning, Marie found her brochures in the mail and brought them in the house. It was a Saturday, and Francis suggested they drive to Priest River, Idaho and start looking around for a place to settle down. "If you want to look for some horses next week, go ahead. We can board them somewhere, as I think I saw some stables off of Highway 16. Maybe you can check that out next week. It's just before Midway, and you can't miss it. Take 16 South, and it's right there on your right. It looks to me like it was an old dairy."

Marie Claire had been staring at her husband, admiration and surprise warred with love and excitement. He could see her mind spinning. He smiled at her, took her hand in his, and said, "This is an early birthday present for you. I love you."

"Thanks so much, Francis. I love you too." She got up from the table and sat in his lap. She kissed him as if she would never see him again.

He handed her off his lap and stood up. He hugged Marie Claire and told her, "Get ready to leave. It's a long drive." After walking up to the car, he helped her into the front passenger seat of their new Cadillac. He bought it last night, turning in his other one. She hadn't even noticed it much. She never was consulted on anything Francis did or thought of doing. She felt she was worthless to him for the most part. She did enjoy riding in the new Caddy, but she kept quiet except to say that, "This is a very pretty car. I like the maroon leather seats, but it sure has lots of gadgets," as she looked at the dash. Marie Claire didn't care anymore what Francis did.

It was a six-hour drive from their home in West Seattle to the northern city in Idaho. Marie Claire set the packet from Priest River

on her lap and she was going to be perusing the note and information
on the long drive. In a few moments she knew just what she wanted
to look at from a real estate brochure that was enclosed with the other
information.

Chapter Eight

THEY ARRIVED in town at four that afternoon. The real estate office was open, along with a few antique shops, grocery, and feed stores. They ate a burger at the Brown Bear restaurant and then meandered over to the realty office. Jack Morgan, a real estate agent in the city of Priest River, said he could be available to show the property that Marie Claire had seen on the real estate brochure. The forty acres was still available. They spoke with him about the area as they rode in his car down the narrow two-lane road that ran adjacent to the Priest River, which ran beside the town of the same name.

Sharing some history of the area, Jack told them, "A priest founded this area when walking out of the northern woods. He had been living with some Indians, teaching them to grow their own food, and teaching them about Christ. He built a monastery across the river there, and you can see the pilings from the pier that he had built." They could see old relics pushing up out of the water. They saw something that resembled an old raft with posts sticking up at the front. "Those pilings are what are left of an old bridge that used to be here."

When they reached the property address, the couple couldn't help but walk around and enjoy the view. "There are one hundred twenty acres for sale here. These forty acres comprise five acres of woods. The tree line on the far eastern border is where the forest lands starts. There are miles and miles of riding trails. The couple who own the blue house to our left belongs to the Bascolms. They closed on it last week, and they will be moving in shortly."

The property was okay for mobile or stick built housing. The Kingman's drove around for the remaining hour of the afternoon and into the evening, taking in the beautiful sights of Sandpoint, Coeur d'Alene, and Priest River. Marie Claire enjoyed perusing through the antique shops in the little town. The couple stayed in the hotel overnight, and the next morning they went to the property to see what was entailed to build here, measure, and set up stakes where they wanted the house and well placements.

"I think I would like you to look at a modular home and pick out what you think we'd like. Let me know the dimensions and layout, and then we'll go from there. I'm going to let you stay here for a few days," Francis told his wife. "I will rent you a car, and I'll check with the office and be back here on Wednesday if there is no pressing business."

Marie Claire was flabbergasted. "Ok," she said, a bit tentatively, "but wouldn't you like to stop at the mobile home dealer in Spokane? We can do that on the way home this afternoon? What about my job? Marcia will be expecting me. I.." throwing up her hands, Marie Claire really wasn't too thrilled to be looking for such a big purchase on her own, and her face showed it.

"I'll talk to your boss. Don't worry about it. Let's meet with the realtor and get that paperwork out of the way. The land is cheap enough so I'll pay cash for it today. We'll stop at the first modular home dealer that we see," Francis interrupted Marie Claire.

They returned to the crest of the property and walked around a small wooded piece that would work fine for the backyard of the house. There was about a quarter acre between the woods and a knoll that would be perfect for the house site. Francis started walking toward the car but then he stopped. Marie Claire could see that he had something on his mind.

"Give your notice. We'll go home tonight. Meet with an architect this week and figure out what you want for a barn. It may work okay catty cornered from that end of the house. I'll have a well drilled at this corner," he said, gesturing toward a spot behind the car.

Marie Claire's mind was so full of directives and ideas that she wasn't watching where she was walking. She tripped over a rock. Francis helped her up, saw that she wasn't hurt, and then they got into the car and proceeded to drive toward town. Francis called the realtor from his car phone. Jack and the sellers would meet them at the office in twenty minutes.

Paperwork signed, the land formally belonging to the Kingman's, they drove to the Coeur d'Alene Resort for an early celebratory dinner. They stopped at Jasper homes where they chose a floor plan that they liked. They ordered their colors and flooring, then, all the necessary things done for the day, they drove home.

Monday, Marie Claire talked to Marcia Madsen. "We went to Priest River, Idaho over the weekend. Francis bought acreage there. I will give my notice when I know my last day."

"Marie Claire. I want you to be happy. If you need to come back for any reason, your job will be here. I will look for a replacement, but I bet I won't find someone as nice as you to fill your shoes. You've done a great job. I will miss you." Marcia worried about this young woman, but she would pray that Marie Claire would be kept well.

After work, Marie Claire drove to the stables to see if they had any space for two horses. They had room for more than that, but they didn't have any horses for sale. Marie Claire called a breeder in the southeastern part of Seattle. She went there next to look at some animals the breeder had for sale. Marie Claire wanted to train her own so she looked for youngsters under three years old. She found a sorrel and white paint filly and ended up purchasing her. The filly just recently turned two and was just right for training. The filly's name, the breeder told Marie Claire, was Scribb's Silhouette, out of the great paint stallion, Scribbles. Marie Claire loved Indian names, and she knew the word Tanukar meant to write, so she nicknamed the filly, Tanny, to shorten the longer name.

Marie Claire telephoned the stable manager and let her know to expect the young horse in the morning. Feed would be brought in with her, and Marie Claire stated, "I will be there after work tomorrow to take care of Tanny, the filly, and make sure she has everything she needs." Somehow, God had been listening to Marie Claire's prayers. So busy with horse business, she didn't pay attention to the time. Dinner needed to be started before Francis showed up from work, and with her luck, she was going to be home twenty minutes after Francis. He called her just as she was getting ready to leave the stable on Tuesday evening.

"Don't hold dinner, Marie Claire. I'm going to be late again to-night. Love you." And then he hung up.

Marie Claire breathed a sigh of relief. She would spend some more time with her 'big kid' and then she'd buy herself dinner out. She kept a book with her at all times and she had no problem eating alone. She rarely could get by herself long enough to do that, and she was looking forward to her quiet time.

Francis sure spends more and more time away from home. Ever since he beat me that last time, he's been coming in later and later. He hasn't been on my case at all, and we've had no arguments for a while. Marie Claire was thinking about the change from normal. She wondered if maybe someone else took her place. It didn't matter to her, but what was to happen to her if they were no longer married?

She called her friend, Lee, to talk to her and Clint about her feelings. "Lee, I have some questions. Is Clint there?"

"No, Marie Claire, he's still at work. Can I help?" Lee asked her.

"Well, I think a man would better understand another man, but I have a funny feeling my husband is seeing someone else." Marie Claire didn't cry, but she voiced concern.

"I can tell you all you need to know. I have been married to Clint for ten years, after all. You don't need to speak to him!" Lee sounded self-righteous, but Marie Claire hoped she could help. Marie Claire wasn't happy, feeling instead that a man could better help her. She also hadn't spoken to Lee in a while and though good friends, Lee didn't seem herself either.

"Well –" and Marie Claire told her what was on her heart and mind regarding her marriage. She never told Lee about the beatings at all. She felt that was a private thing and was too embarrassed even to tell her friend.

"I'm married to Clint, but you know, he isn't the best husband. He needs to quit yelling at the boys so much and just let them be themselves. He needs to lighten up on me, too." When they finished talking, Marie Claire felt sure that Lee didn't know what she was talking about. Clint, Marie Claire knew, was a nice man, but Lee didn't have good things to say about him. She didn't want to cause grief for her friends, so she decided to just wait it out and see what the future held.

Chapter Nine

MARIE CLAIRE quit her job and was in the process of moving to North Idaho a little over two months later. She found a position in Sandpoint as a medical assistant and she would start in two weeks. Francis hired a moving company to pack up and deliver their belongings for them. Marie Claire supervised them for a short time and then she took the truck and horse trailer they purchased a week ago and went to pick Tanny up.

She got back a little over two hours later. Francis purchased a brand-new Jaguar for himself a month earlier, but he left it with a friend as he drove ahead in the Cadillac, so Marie Claire would have that car at the ranch, as well as the truck. *The Cadillac has 30,000 miles on it now, but Marie Claire will get enough use out of it for a few more years*, he thought to himself. He'd promised her yesterday, "I'll send some money every month, but you'll have to learn to live on what you make for the most part. You can use the truck for work, if you have to do so." It took more gas but he hadn't cared about that.

Francis Kingman made it to their property two hours before Marie Claire arrived. He could see that the barn building was nearly done, and the hired locals he'd found put up the horse fencing he requested around the acreage. A blacktop driveway had been installed and, *the house should now be livable*, Francis thought.

He signed the paperwork off as soon as he inspected the house for the contractor. This has to be done before contractors were ever allowed to let homeowners take possession of their new properties. They did a beautiful job and Francis felt sure that Marie Claire would really enjoy her new home.

The well and the septic were indeed placed where Francis had stipulated them to be. As a surprise, he ordered a small guesthouse be built ten feet from the South end of the big house. That looked ready for habitation, too. Francis, unbeknownst to his wife, had been working on something that might help her, and in the process, himself. His research was ending any week now, and he abhorred the thought of Marie Claire being alone here, while he remained working in the big city.

Francis Kingman, husband, attorney, big shot, knew he didn't have any plans of ever moving here, but Marie Claire did not know that. His wife thought he was coming to Idaho as soon as he could find an office to open up in this part of the state. Things were too good for him in the city for him to want to leave. He just wanted the prestige that having a dutiful wife and a horse ranch could afford, while having his freedom to carry on his own extracurricular activities that Marie Claire wouldn't have to know about. He didn't want a divorce, so he kept secrets!

*   *   *   *

Marie Claire arrived in Priest River in the late afternoon. She didn't drive as fast as most because of the precious cargo behind her. The moving truck arrived a half hour earlier than herself, and Francis watched her come down the mile-long driveway. He oversaw things as she parked the truck and unloaded the horse from the three-horse slant-load trailer. He then came out to show her the beautiful stalls that were waiting to be filled with steeds. All that the men had left to do in the barn was to finish the lighting in the one hundred by one hundred foot covered arena that adjoined the stall area.

Francis explained the tack room and the barn essentials he told the contractor to install. He opened the gate for her and led the filly through the twelve-foot doorway built for convenience. They could walk right into the stall area instead of having to go around to the end of the arena and walk the length of that to enter the stall section. He didn't want horses walking past the hay storage or near the autos that were parked in the garage and the front. The tack building was attached to the west of the garage. Marie Claire would have easy accessibility to everything she needed to do. She even had a one hundred gallon heated water tank for winter use, and freeze faucets so she would never have to worry about freezing water in the winter. Francis made sure a water heater was installed for her in the tack room for washing her horses in a comfortable temperature.

Marie Claire saw everything as she walked the horse to her new home. She could see that Francis thought of everything. Later, she would install nameplates for each horse she obtained. There were twelve stalls. *He must've been paying attention to some of those programs I watch all the time*, Marie Claire thought. Pleased with her husband's thoughtfulness, Marie Claire's smile touched her eyes. Tongue and groove cedar made up dividing walls of the stalls, and horizontal bars above that would keep the horses from nipping or biting each other over the walls. They could see without hurting each other. There was plenty of light, and the newness added a warming touch to Marie Claire's soul.

"This is beautiful, Francis. I love it!" She reached up and drew him to her. She kissed him sweetly on the lips. "Thank you for everything," she happily and sincerely told him.

"You're welcome. Now, when you get the horse fed and watered, will you take me to the airport? I have to get back to the city." He hugged her. He had seen the stricken look in her eyes. "I'm sorry, honey, but I have to work tomorrow. Another big case just came up. I won't be here very much."

Marie Claire drove Francis to the Spokane airport. It took a little over an hour to get there. His plane left in just under two hours, but travelers had to be at the airport an hour early to departure. Marie Claire cried very little on the way back to the ranch. Late afternoon in mid-summer, alone, and though this would be a lonely time for her, Marie Claire looked forward to the peace and quiet she would find here in her new home. She parked the Cadillac in the garage and checked on Tanny before going into the house. Marie Claire, unable to ever have children, would find sweet comfort in her horses. She would end up calling them 'big kids' with joy and pride.

Marie Claire was coming out of the barn and planned on walking around the outside of the house to get a feel for the landscaping she would like to have, when she noticed a man and woman walking around the arena and coming toward her. She met them at the paddock gate.

"Hi. I'm Sam. This is my wife, Julia. We noticed you leaving with your husband, and that you returned alone. We decided that maybe you were left here to fend for yourself."

"Yes, that's right. My husband, Francis, is an attorney in Seattle and he just received a big case to work on. We lived in West Seattle, but he's going to rent an apartment there until he can move over here." Remembering her manners, she belatedly introduced herself. "Hi! I'm Marie Claire Kingman. We closed on this place two months ago. The house is now livable so here I am," she told them as they shook hands.

"Yes, our realtor, Jack, told us when we moved in that you two bought this property. Looks like a nice house. May we see it?" Julia asked, smiling and hugging Marie Claire. They walked through the back door into a small laundry room with a half bath on the left. This is where Marie Claire, or anyone, could wash up before going into the main house after being around the animals. They then walked into an entry with the living room on the right, an exercise room on the left, and the gourmet kitchen and dining room beside it straight ahead. The white walls filled the house, but the kitchen was painted a pale green with ivy motifs, with complimentary deeper green slate flooring. A deep gray carpet covered the floors throughout the rest of the house. They turned right and she showed them the master bedroom on the left, painted in orchid, and the bath afforded a large sunken tub with a separate shower, many storage cabinets, and Marie Claire painted it in cream with seaside borders at the top of the walls. Back to the living room on the opposite side of the master suite were two smaller rooms, which one was a guest room and the corner room became Marie Claire's office. A full bath filled the space between those two rooms. Marie Claire had a fireplace on one wall in the living room, which housed a deep cushioned sofa and armchairs. It was a very lovely home.

"Sam and I will look out for you! If you need anything, please ask. Will you go to church with us next Sunday? The church down the way is very good. We have a nice new pastor and his name is Dirk Dixon. He preaches from the Bible, the truth of Christ. We sing all the old hymns also. It's hard to find a church that does that anymore. Most of them have lyrics no one ever heard of and they're always projected on the wall."

"What kind of church, is it, Julia? Community, Presbyterian?"

Marie Claire asked the woman, interested now that she knew it was near home.

"It's Mountain Community Church, sort of like Baptist. It's not even a mile from here. Turn left out of your driveway and it's on the right. Go with us next week! We'd love to have you. We'll take you out to lunch afterwards." Julia explained to Marie Claire. She also shared where she works.

"Oh, how funny. I start work at the clinic the week after next. I didn't see you when I went in to interview with them! I'm so glad to have a friend. I wasn't looking forward to living here all alone. I have no family close to me except my cousin, Charlene, and her young daughter, Lisa Marie. Lisa is really my second cousin, but I call her my niece. They live in Seattle also." And so began a wonderful new friendship that would last for all time. The Bascolms were twenty years older than Marie Claire. She was now thirty-two. They didn't know it, but the Bascolms would be Marie Claire's guardian angels.

Chapter Ten

SIX MONTHS later, Marie Claire went to the southern end of Seattle to buy another horse. The two-year-old stallion, Excel's Pride, was beautiful and she called him Pride.

After a night on the town with Francis, he and Marie Claire stayed at the Hilton in Tacoma and enjoyed a late night glass of wine before retiring.

Marie Claire took Pride home the next day and set him up in his own stall. He was two years old and a real beauty with flowing black mane and tail, a white star on his forehead, and four black stockings. His dappled coat was pale cream. He was aptly named, for he was her pride and joy. He had to be the most beautiful buckskin she had ever seen. Marie Claire put nameplates on each of the two stalls that next day.

Marie Claire kept herself busy every day after work and on the weekends putting in her landscaping, and also relaxing by stalling the two horses, feeding them more hay, and as they munched she combed their manes, tails, and bodies until they shone.

Because of gophers and moles, she put battery-operated Gopher-Gone posts here and there to keep the critters away. Marie Claire planted low growing plants that would endure the extreme cold and short growing season. She planted locust and tulip bulbs, as well as a few roses and other colorful plants. After one grueling weekend of digging and moving dirt, she installed a fishpond. Over the next few days, she built herself a waterfall made of midsized boulders with a tube running up the center into a bowl at the top allowing the water to cascade downwards to the pool below via a channel that she made of grooved cement.

Julia and Sam came over when they spied her sitting on her stoop in the back yard, trying to relax after her hard work. They took her to Sandpoint where they ordered pizza at a small restaurant, called the Hydrangea, for lunch. It was a nice little restaurant and Marie Claire had never seen anything like it before. There were handmade papier-mâché animals hanging from the ceiling, and next to a fireplace there was a small room that was very private. The pizza came stacked nearly six inches high with sausage, black olives, onions, mushrooms, and extra cheese. The crust was very thin, and it was the most filling thing to ever come into Marie Claire's life! The Bascolms didn't know it, but pizza happened to be Marie Claire's favorite food.

"I love pizza! I didn't know they made it like this anywhere. It's so good, too. Thanks guys, for bringing me here. I love it! This little room, too, isn't it just cool! The fireplace in that big room," Marie Claire pointed, "makes it so homey. It gives the place ambience." She talked a mile a minute with Julia. She finally wound down and then, before his wife could open her mouth again, Sam spoke for the first time since they'd arrived.

"What brought you to North Idaho, Marie Claire?"

"Well, we took a trip through Canada in the spring. I fell in love with this place, and when we got back from our trip, coming home via Highway 2 and going through Priest River, I kept talking about how beautiful it is up here. The next thing I knew, Francis asked me to look into the area for property and a house, and I found this acreage for sale. It was dirt cheap, so we bought it. We found a modular home in Spokane. We just happened to drive by a place that had modulars for sale, and they looked really nice so we thought we'd stop and check it out. Francis is going to finish his case and then he'll open an office here somewhere."

Feeling the Bascolms would understand, Marie Claire shared her life story with them. Some things were just plain private, but Marie Claire had to share some of the bad times with them, hoping her new-found friends would be able to help her should she need them down the road. Getting ready for her life here, she just didn't know how much she would depend on this wonderful couple. They were a gift straight from Heaven, and she told them so.

"Francis doesn't like me talking about our lives, but you need to know that he isn't as nice as he seems. I think God in His mercy brought me here so I can have you two as neighbors. I feel very close to you already, and we haven't known each other very long."

"Well, we like you, also, Marie Claire. It's a pleasure to have a nice young lady nearby. Julia will be able to pamper you since you're all alone." Sam enjoyed the camaraderie that he and Julia found with Marie Claire. They enjoyed having some nice neighbors, but Julia had taken a strong liking to Marie Claire. They didn't know Francis, so they would hold judgment on what she'd said until later.

Sam commented on the hard work, and wonderful pond she built. "I can't believe that a little thing like you could work so hard and make such wonderful landscaping. You be careful, Marie Claire. You can get hurt. Can't you hire someone to do the heavy work for you?"

Marie Claire didn't answer, knowing they wouldn't like to hear what she would say.

They took her home and Marie Claire fed the horses. She went in and walked the dark green-carpeted rooms of her new home. She noticed she had a call while she was away, so she checked her caller ID and found that Francis had left four messages. She decided she better call him back. He answered on the first ring.

"Where have you been? Do you know how worried I was when I couldn't get in touch with you?" Francis was screaming at her. When he ended his tirade, she quietly answered his accusations.

"Julia and Sam, our neighbors, asked if I would like to go to lunch with them. I was exhausted from working in the yard, and I guess they wanted company, so I went with them. They are very friendly and neighborly people. I can hardly wait for you to meet them," Marie Claire told him. While trying to get him to calm down, she quietly spoke of the work she had accomplished by that afternoon. She had no intention of letting her husband ruin the wonderful day she'd had. She felt sad, but knew she had done nothing wrong.

"Well, at least you accomplished something. Take care. Call me once in a while." He hung up without even asking how Marie Claire was doing otherwise.

Marie Claire didn't know what to do, what to think. She kept her trepidations inside for a long time.

Marie Claire carried on every day as she needed to through the next several weeks. She called Julia one afternoon two months later. It took Marie Claire a long time to think about things before baring her soul to anyone else.

"Marie Claire, I think you need to stop and think about your life circumstances. Your husband, I'm sorry to say, has a controlling personality. We haven't met him, but we don't think we like him much. You need to learn how to keep him from hitting you. Maybe he has a heavy workload, or maybe he is seeing someone. Something has to be setting him off." They saw Marie Claire one Sunday night when she'd missed church that morning, and Francis left for Seattle. They saw the bruises she'd tried to hide with heavy makeup.

Julia explained to her, "Sam and I tell each other everything. We keep nothing to ourselves. We share. You and Francis don't do that. It seems he is the one who hides things from you, and I'm not being nosy, just motherly. Take my advice or not, but you are a precious friend, and we care for you very much. We haven't known you very long, but we think you're a very nice young lady. We just want to help."

Julia was discreetly trying to get Marie Claire to wake up and see what her life is like. "Hopefully, she'll get a clue and try to remedy her situation," Julia told Sam.

Julia called the next morning to check on Marie Claire. Sam spoke with Marie Claire for a moment after Julia handed the phone to him. He wasn't being nosy, but he wanted to help her. He asked, "Marie Claire, you've been sharing a lot of things with us the past few months. Would you mind sharing your financial situation with me?"

Marie Claire explained about her savings account and what Francis expected of her financially. "I am supposed to live on my income, which I could do, but I can't make the house payment without help. I don't earn that much. I'm not sure what I'm expected to do as far as Francis is concerned. He's getting cruel again, and I don't know if I can trust him." Marie Claire thought, *the Bascolms are wonderful, and I'm glad that they are willing to help me grow.*

After getting the confirmation he was hoping for, they set a date for the following Sunday, with Marie Claire promising to bring all of her financial records to their house after church.

Chapter Eleven

M<small>ARIE</small> C<small>LAIRE</small> didn't get a chance to go to church with the Bascolms. Francis showed up unannounced on Saturday evening, and Julia and Sam were outside enjoying the warm evening in lawn chairs on their newly mown front yard. They heard screaming coming from the Kingman home and they called the police when it happened three times.

Sam ran over to the house and pounded on the back door. When he didn't get an answer, he ran around to the front door and what he saw made his stomach turn over. *Francis has killed Marie Claire* Sam thought at first, even though he hadn't seen the attacker at all. Her face was beaten to a pulp. She was lying on the living room floor. He heard a car start up and saw the taillights speeding out of the driveway. It looked like a silver Jaguar, but Sam couldn't really tell. The police arrived within minutes of Sam's phone call. They got in by way of the now unlocked back door. The deputy called for an ambulance. Sam yelled at them all, "An ambulance should have been called right away when I told you I heard screaming." He was as angry as he'd ever been.

"The screams, since you didn't see anything, could have been a TV, or they could have been making love. You know how some women are," the older deputy, having not taken a good look yet, smirked as he stated this to the outraged man.

"This is not a laughing matter, Sheriff. I should have shared her story with the man on the phone. Maybe then you would've done the right thing." A livid Sam knelt beside the woman, hoping she wouldn't die. He then went and called from Marie Claire's kitchen phone. "Jules,

Marie Claire is hurt. Meet us at the Holy Family hospital. The deputy, when the ambulance arrived, told Sam where she would be taken. He rode in the ambulance with her so that if she woke up, she would see a friend before she saw anyone else.

They were almost to the hospital when Marie Claire opened her eyes and asked what had happened. Then she remembered. "Where's Francis? Where is he?" Marie Claire became hysterical and Sam had to put his arm across her chest, which made her cry out.

"Marie Claire. Your husband left. Julia is meeting us at the hospital. We'll talk later. Just rest for now, okay? You're with me. I won't let anyone hurt you." Sam quietly comforted her, speaking very softly and calmly. It helped Marie Claire to calm and she lay back down.

"I'm so sorry this happened. He was mad because I wasn't home when he called last Sunday. I told him I went out with you two but apparently he didn't like it. He is very jealous and wants his own way. I want out of this marriage, but I don't believe in divorce. I try to keep my word in all things. I'm sorry you have to be involved." Marie wasn't speaking very well, it sounded as though she had a mouthful of cotton. Her nose started to bleed and Sam was coping with that while the attendant checked her blood pressure before taking over for the other man.

Sam told the attendant, "I think Marie Claire has some broken ribs. She yelled when I touched her across the chest to get her calmed down."

The attendant concurred. They checked her over when they got to the house and before they loaded her on the stretcher. He was sure she had internal injuries. Her jaw had been broken at one time, and could be this time also. He saw the scars and told Sam about them. "They'll take full body x-rays at the hospital," the attendant explained.

"I'll make sure you and Julia are listed as next of kin, is that okay with you, Sam?" Marie Claire had spoken out after realizing she really was all alone. No one seemed to care about her but these two people she just met recently. It didn't seem fair to them, to be caught in this situation, but she had no one else.

"We'll get through this together, sweetie; all three of us. Don't worry. I'll let Pastor Dixon know what happened. You'll have a lot of prayer warriors on your side," Sam smiled at her and squeezed her hand, and that made Marie Claire wince but not cry out. *She is hurt just about everywhere,* he thought to himself.

Julia was waiting in the lobby of the ER when Sam and Marie Claire arrived. She watched them rush the woman into a back room. Julia told Sam, "I didn't know what to do about the paperwork, so I waited until you got here, Honey."

"Marie Claire and I made a pact. You and I, and Marie Claire, will take care of business. The three of us will work together. She told me she wanted us to be next of kin, and I know she feels all alone, so let's do as she needs us to do. We will pray and God will supply." They called Pastor Dixon and they all prayed together on the phone. Sam turned on the loudspeaker of his cell so that Julia could be part of the conversation, and they stayed in an out of the way corner so as not to disturb other patients or their family members.

"I'll call the head of the prayer chain and we'll get the prayers going," Pastor Dixon shared with his church elder. "Let her know her church family is behind her all the way." Pastor Dixon had not met Francis yet, but that man didn't leave a good impression. "Would you like me to come down there? I don't mind sitting with you and Julia."

"No, Pastor, that's fine. I'll call when I know more about Marie Claire. She is very embarrassed. She's not been here very long and she knows no one very well. To have this happen, and Julia and I are essentially still strangers to her yet, it's sad. We took her out after church last week, but that's all we've seen of her for the past few days. She cried because we felt we needed to get involved, but she needs help." After Sam shared their discussion in the ambulance, with the pastor, they prayed some more.

"Keep me posted, Sam. Thanks for calling me. I'll get the prayers going right now." Sam took Julia in his arms after saying goodbye to Pastor Dixon. She cried for Marie Claire, and they were still hugging when the doctor walked into the room.

"Hi, folks, I'm Dr. Silverman. Your daughter is very beaten up. She has three fractured ribs, a battered face, and is bruised everywhere. Her jaw was dislocated but not actually broken, as it has been in the past as we can see from x-rays. Her hands are bruised from trying to protect herself, and whoever did this almost killed her."

"She told us it was her husband, Francis Kingman. I saw a man leaning over her but I didn't see anything else. I saw his car leave the drive as I ran inside to attend to Marie Claire." The police detective,

Paul Traylor, was sitting across from Sam and taking notes from that man. He was waiting, with the couple, for the doctor to come out and give them the woman's condition.

Dr. Silverman, with x-rays in hand, asked the trio to come into the room and he would share the films with them. He placed the first x-ray to the light. "These here," he said, pointing to the x-ray, "are her fractured ribs, the lower three. Her bruising suggests a major kick to her chest; probably when she was down on the floor, not falling or getting up." He placed two more x-rays up to the light. "Sometime in the past, though not too long ago, she did have her jaw broken and you can see the healed calcium deposits here and here," he said as he pointed to the objects mentioned. "As I said before, her jaw was only dislocated this time. What you see here, here, and here are past fractures that have healed. See the difference in texture? That means that this one is fairly new. The others are solid and dark colored. They are older." He had exchanged tonight's x-rays for the old ones, all depicting old healed fractures.

Julia cried for the lovely young woman they'd spent the day with a week ago. To know this much about her past brought unbearable heartache, but also admiration for someone like her to have such a love for Jesus. They would have to ask her how she could be so strong in her faith while having to endure all the torture they could see she had gone through. Maybe she would share more of her life with them and not just the obvious abusive times.

Julia called their boss, Dr. Snow, at home and explained why she was in the hospital with their new employee. "Tell Marie Claire we will see her when she's better. Will she let us have a doctor's report? If so, have her physician fax or mail one to us. Her job is safe. Assure her of that, would you please Julia?"

"Yes, I will. Thank you, doctor." Julie and Dr. Snow ended their conversation.

Marie Claire stayed overnight in the hospital. The detective had gone to the Kingman home to check and make sure no one was there. He doubted Francis Kingman would show his face right now, but who knows what a man would do in this type of situation. He had found out that Francis Kingman was a celebrated prosecuting attorney in Seattle. Since no one actually witnessed him beating his wife, the law enforcement in Idaho had their hands tied.

Chapter Twelve

MARIE CLAIRE couldn't believe her job was still waiting for her two weeks later. Francis hadn't shown his face since that Saturday he beat her up. She'd been visited once by the police, but, the sheriff only told her, 'We can't do anything about your husband'.

Francis called nearly every day, apologetic and supposedly remorseful about his actions against her. "You know it was your fault, don't you, Marie Claire? If you were there for me I wouldn't have been so angry. I'm sorry I did that to you. I won't do it again. I promise." Well Marie Claire had heard that before and it was always the same. If she displeased him she got beaten up. She heard him, but she didn't believe a word he said. He'd sent her a dozen red roses a few days ago and they went in the garbage.

Julia came over every day to minister to Marie Claire. She helped with the housework and she fixed lunches for her friend. They sat and talked, and Sam would sit with her and go over finances and how he would like to see her take care of her money. Marie Claire learned well, knowing one day she would be left with no more financial help from Francis. She felt this in her heart. She knew she could pay her smaller bills, but the house payment was another story. This caused her a large amount of grief, but she felt sure that God would see her through.

One weekend two months later, Francis showed up with Cecelia McCory, her biological mother. The woman looked battered herself, but Marie Claire knew that her husband had died of lung cancer years ago. She never knew what had happened to her mother after that, and she hadn't really cared.

"Your mom has been living on the streets. I finally found her. I have spent months looking for her and I only had that one picture of her that you kept in your bureau. I thought it would be better for you to have company here. She can live in the guest house." Francis said, again dictating what was to happen in her life. Francis, who now made sure someone lived here to keep an eye on his wife. Francis, who constantly expected her to make ends meet on her good, but inadequate salary.

Cecelia stared at her daughter, her beautiful daughter, with admiration. When she got the chance, she walked up to Marie Claire and hugged her, and she received a hug in return. When Marie Claire heard the words her mother had to say, she felt tears come to her eyes.

"I am so sorry for your life, Marie Claire. You're a good girl, and always have been. He wanted to move on and I allowed it," Cecelia said, speaking of her late husband. "Everyone goes through abuse, but we just gotta to learn to live with it. We gotta to do the best we can and go on from there." Cecelia McCory looked into Marie Claire's eyes, and there was a sad look there, undecipherable, which, Marie Claire figured she needed to forgive her mother for the hurting years she herself had had to endure. She got her mother settled in the guesthouse and when Francis left on Sunday, she took her mother shopping for some groceries. When getting home again, Marie Claire called her cousin, Charlene.

Lisa Marie Busche came to visit quite often these days. She just turned twelve years old today, Friday, October 3, and Marie Claire sent for her niece as a birthday present. Lisa came down by way of Southwest Air, and Marie Claire planned to take her to Coeur d'Alene to see the lake and to visit the zoo and various other fun places kids enjoyed in the area. Lisa's mother, Charlene Busche, had to work all weekend and through the next ten days, so she was happy her daughter had something to do, and someone who loved her to do it with. It meant that she wouldn't have to worry about a sitter, or what to do when her daughter got bored. Charlene and Marie Claire remained very close, as close as two people could get.

Charlene, up until two years ago, had been in an abusive marriage herself, but her husband was killed in a drug deal gone badly. She and Marie Claire talked quite often about Marie Claire's trials. "I don't know how you can stand this creep for all these years, Marie Claire. You need to leave Francis!" Charlene talked to Marie Claire numerous times over the years, but her cousin was a softhearted person and wouldn't listen to anyone. Marie Claire just thought 'Francis would hurt himself, or be too devastated' if she left. Besides, 'what will I do without him?' Marie Claire often asked.

Lisa was on the two o'clock flight into Spokane that afternoon. Marie Claire, Julia, and Sam were all there to greet her. Cecelia opted to stay home. "You guys don't need me hangin' 'round. Just go enjoy yourselves. I'll stay with the animals." Marie Claire wished her mother wasn't such a homebody, but that was fine, not so much trouble that way. Her mother always complained about something or someone. Marie Claire was glad for the reprieve. She knew Francis wouldn't be back for another week or more, and this would be a good time to really enjoy herself with Lisa and the Bascolms.

The three took off for a week and had a wonderful time. Sam paid for the whole week of the trip. He said, "We don't have anything else to do, and your mom said she'd cover the place while we're away. Why not take advantage of it!"

The trio not only toured Idaho, they also went to Montana and enjoyed the sights around Glacier, Whitehorse, and Billings. Marie Claire trained horses for three hundred fifty dollars a head. She also worked with riding lesson clients by this time and she was having a wonderful time, but she needed a break. Everyone paying their dues understood and it gave them a reprieve from the twice-weekly lessons. Besides, Dr. Snow told her that off time was due her, and asked her to take her vacation. He took his also, and the office closed for a week.

*   *   *   *

Marie Claire took her mother to the Social Security office to sign up, a few days after the three of them got back from their trip. They saw Lisa Marie off at the airport and watched as her airplane carried the little girl home to Seattle. Cecelia obtained her Medicare and Medicaid benefits as well as, she found out, being entitled to her husband's pension which would be received monthly as a credit to the checking account she'd had to open at the Bank and Trust in Sandpoint. Afterwards, they went to the Hydrangea for lunch.

*   *   *   *

It was spring once again and Marie Claire was strictly living on credit cards by this time. On her meager pension, Cecelia McCory spent more money than she had coming in. Marie Claire paid all her own bills, and made minimum payments on the seven cards she had. The credit cards all had 18% to 20% interest on them, and there was no way to pay them off with minimum payments; but, she was also trying her best to keep her mother from wringing her dry as she tried to help keep up with those bills too, but to no avail. Cecelia had her own electric setup that she said she'd pay the bill on, plus credit cards of her own. Marie Claire forced her mother to file bankruptcy two years into their life together.

"We're having a little trouble with the finances here in the office, Marie Claire. I can send what I can, when I can, but you'll have to get a second job or do something! I don't want to sell the ranch, but we may have to do that if we can't find a way to pay the mortgage."

Right out of the blue Marie Claire was again hit, but this time, it was verbally. *I knew this day would come, I just knew it, but with the training I'm doing for people, and the lessons I'm giving, I should do ok. I'm still at the clinic so, God, I just ask that you continue to sustain me. Lead me where I should go and direct my finances.* Marie Claire kept her faith, and now all she could do is rely on God. He had never let her down.

Francis again decided to come to the ranch about once a month, either to make love all weekend, or to take his frustrations out on his innocent wife. Marie Claire persevered, and she kept praying. She was getting closer to asking for a divorce, but she couldn't see her way yet. She knew that God hated divorce, and she didn't want to go against His wishes.

Three years into their life in Idaho, Marie Claire decided to again speak with Sam about what to do. She wasn't getting any younger, nearing forty-two, but she felt like an old woman. Life had not been good to Marie Claire, but somehow she stayed the same sweet woman she had always been.

*   *   *   *

Clint Bellham called Marie Claire one night shortly after her last discussion with Sam about her finances. Marie Claire hadn't seen him in quite a while, actually since she moved to Priest River. She shared her concerns with Clint.

"Hi, Sunshine," Clint greeted her with a smile in his voice one night shortly after her weekend with Lisa Marie. "How are you two doing?"

"Mom and I are fine. How are you?" Marie Claire thought highly of Clint. She had been wondering about that family since Lee hadn't called in a long time, and she herself had gotten so busy working at the office and home, and there had been no time hardly to relax.

"I called to let you know that Lee left us." Clint gave this some time to sink in.

"What!" Marie Claire was appalled. She thought Lee loved her family. "When did this happen?" She managed to squeeze out the question.

"Three days ago. I caught her at a motel with her lover, and a friend of ours, the boy's scout master." Clint had tears in his voice. "I don't know what to do."

"Why don't you and the boys come over for a few days?" Marie Claire asked her friend. Clint, Lee, and Marie Claire had been good friends for so long that they knew each other very well, and the boys had always loved Marie Claire. She adored them too, and never forgot their birthdays or Christmas. She'd "borrowed" them whenever she got a chance when she was still living in Seattle, and they would go to the fair, the movies, zoos, parks, or just for day trips. Sometimes she would keep the boys for the weekend or overnight if Clint and Lee had someplace they wanted to go alone. Francis hadn't like it, but he was friends with Clint too and didn't want to hurt feelings. Marie Claire often wondered why Lee stopped calling at least once a week, and why she'd heard nothing from her about taking trips over to Idaho, as she was prone to do periodically. They met when they attended the same church in Seattle years before.

"I may do that Marie Claire. I'll take Friday off, since we're not too busy, and plan on a week. Would that work? Would it be ok with Francis? How is he, by the way? He never calls me anymore, and I have not had an answer to my phone calls and messages I've left." Clint had tried to talk Marie Claire out of moving to North Idaho.

He knew what Francis planned for his time away from her, but didn't want his young wife knowing his business. Clint already knew he was abusive to Marie Claire, and he hadn't liked it, but he felt it wasn't his business. After having gotten a call from Julia after one bad beating Francis had given Marie Claire, he decided to keep in better contact with her. Julia shared a lot over that one phone call, and Clint feared for Marie Claire's life.

Over the next year, during and after Clint's divorce, Marie Claire introduced him to all her single women friends and acquaintances in the church. Clint didn't want to be associated with a non-Christian. No lasting relationship had ever come about for Clint. He made friends with the women, but he was such an honorable man that most of them didn't know how to take him, and men liked him but only the most honorable among his peers kept a deep friendship with him.

"What's wrong with me?" Clint often asked Marie Claire. Why don't women like me? He told her which women he dated that he would like a deeper friendship with.

Marie Claire told him, "You are so different from most people, that no one knows how to take you or appreciate you for who you are, that's what Susan, one of your dates, told me. I was complaining to her that none of the women dated you more than once, and I told her what a nice guy you really are. She said she 'just wasn't ready for romance." Marie Claire felt for her friend. It had been six months, and Clint really wanted a relationship so he could have a mother for his boys.

"Thanks for sticking up for me, Sunshine. I'll just wait a while to date again." Clint decided that he'd just keep in touch with Marie Claire and her mother. I don't need a woman, I guess. Clint spent an hour in prayer with Christ. By the time he was finished, his heart felt lighter. Clint told God that he would just let Him lead, and he himself would follow. If marriage or friendship with a woman was in the future, God would supply.

Clint and the boys came over that next weekend. Sam and Julia walked over to Marie Claire's, and Clint put on a big barbeque of chicken and ribs. Cecelia made baked potatoes and Marie Claire made corn on the cob and a large green salad. Julia brought homemade baked beans and an apple, cherry, and lemon pie. They enjoyed the meal and the conversation that followed. Francis called to let Marie Claire know that he would be over the following weekend. She never told him Clint was there. She was wary of her husband, and even though they were all friends, she wasn't sure what Francis would do since he seemed so jealous and watchful of how she spent her time.

The Bascolms had seen Clint and the boys over to Marie Claire's on other occasions. The first time they saw a strange man over at the ranch, they came over to meet him, and the boys were there too. They weren't nosy, just watching out for trouble should it raise its head. They approved of the foursome's friendship.

Sam told Clint, "Marie Claire needs someone to watch out for her. She is knowledgeable, wise in her way, but a little naïve. Julia and I approve of your friendship, just keep your noses clean. We would hate to see her hurt because of a misguided trust on her part." This was last year when Marie Claire had gone into the hospital for the third time and Julia called Clint, knowing he was a friend. Clint came to surprise Marie Claire, not even telling Julia he would come. The Bascolms had been impressed. The boys didn't come with him, as Clint knew that Marie Claire wouldn't want them seeing her like that. She was pretty hurt, her face being battered and her left arm broken.

This weekend, they were glad to see the boys and Clint again. It had been quiet for the past few weeks, and Marie Claire, though seemingly lonely, exuded happy nevertheless. She and Julia spent some time shopping with Cecelia this week, and they could see how Marie Claire's spirits lifted upon knowing she would be seeing the boys again, and Clint.

When the Bascolms went home after dinner and a couple of hours of conversation, Cecelia left for the guesthouse and the other two went in to watch the news. The boys were tired so they went to bed after hugging and kissing Marie Claire goodnight. Clint took an easy chair beside the wingback that Marie Claire always sat in. They watched an hour of news, made small talk, and said their goodnights to each other. Clint hugged Marie Claire. She felt strange, but she gave him a small hug in return. Clint and Martin slept in the guest room, and Jon was in the office in a sleeping bag Marie Claire kept in the back of a closet.

The next morning, Marie Claire made lattés for the adults, Cecelia, Julia, and Sam were included as they had come over for breakfast. Then they headed for church. Clint knew everyone, having gone to services many times with them when he'd come over in the past. Clint felt not the least bit strange seeing any and all of his dates again. It was their loss after all, not his. The women shared some of Marie Claire's trials with him on their dates. He was thankful for that much from them.

The Bascolm's enjoyed going to church and visiting with Marie Claire and Clint afterward before going home. He always told Marie Claire that he would be very happy to help her in any way he could. When Lee left, leaving three broken hearts behind, Clint had no recourse but to seek a divorce. Now almost one year later, and a single dad, he sought solace in his friendship with Marie Claire. She was a good friend, his best friend, and there was nothing else to it.

Chapter Thirteen

Marie Claire had spoken several times with Patsy Jenks, one of her coworkers and a sister churchgoer. She explained to Patsy several times in the past year that her mother expected her to buy trivialities for her, take her shopping, and buy her groceries. She told Patsy that she hadn't wanted her biological mother living with her, but since she was, Marie was doing what she thought God wanted of her.

Marie Claire explained to Cecelia until she was blue in the face that they both needed to stick to some kind of budget. Patsy, unbeknownst to Marie Claire, gossiped terribly and word got back to Cecelia that Marie Claire would rather she not be around. When her mother told her not to talk to Patsy, Marie Claire never asked why. She told her daughter, "Patsy Jenks gossips too much. You shouldn't be talking to her."

Marie Claire didn't know the damage that woman had caused. She would never knowingly hurt her mother, but by talking to Patsy, that is just what she'd done. Cecelia's heart was broken. She called her daughter, Jeanette, who assured her she would be over to get her the next weekend. Jeanette never once called Marie Claire to find out what was going on.

*   *   *   *

It was early Saturday morning, and her mother was gone. Marie Claire called to ask her to come over for coffee, but Cecelia let her know that

Jeanette, Cecelia's youngest daughter, and Marie Claire's half sister, came over the night before, from Seattle. Marie Claire and Jeanette had been estranged for almost twenty-five years. "I'm leaving here. I want to live in Seattle. Besides, Patsy told me you don't want me here." Unbeknownst to Marie Claire, Jeanette helped pack up her mother's belongings the night before. The two of them left early this morning. Marie Claire saw their trailer lights as she flew out her door to see what was going on, and try to talk Cecelia into staying.

Marie Claire cared for her mother as best she could; but the financial deficit took its toll on both their lives and the tentative relationship. Cecelia "wanted to live in Washington" apparently, and Marie Claire didn't want to move. Cecelia never would listen to Marie Claire's pleadings.

Feeling like a failure, dejected and alone, Marie Claire spent the morning cleaning out Cecelia's home, vacuuming and cleaning. Her heart heavy and her feelings and mind and heart churning with emotion, depression settled in well. Marie Claire waited out the rest of the morning, hoping Francis would get here, and then she thought, *I'd like to be free of my husband, too. I don't know what he'll do when he finds out my mother left me.*

A few hours later, in her own home once again, Marie Claire walked outside to see if Francis had shown up yet. He called and told her last week that he would be home today. Marie Claire sat on her steps and cried as she thought about all that had gone on, up until today, and knowing that she would never see her mother again with no way to make restitution. Sam saw and hated the proceedings that happened earlier; he felt guilty. He knew from the way Marie Claire now sat looking like she'd lost her best friend that Cecelia had not told her daughter she was leaving. Julia shared that little tidbit with him just a few minutes earlier. Cecelia walked over to say goodbye to them, but Julia was outside so Cecelia just told her she was leaving, why, and that she hadn't told Marie Claire. "I'm worried about Marie Claire 'cause I didn't tell her I was leavin'," Cecelia had said, then with a wave of her hand, she met Jeanette by the barn and together they took off in the truck, towing a small trailer. Sam heard from Cecelia herself that she was leaving, but the woman avoided the truth. Sam and Julia thought Marie Claire knew and wished not to say anything. Sam watched now as their dear friend sat crying brokenheartedly. Julia was busy in the kitchen but interrupted her work to herd Sam out the back door when she saw the anger and hurt in her husband's eyes. Sam came over to help. He sat with Marie Claire while she cried on his shoulder. At that inopportune moment, Francis drove up.

"Hello Francis," Sam sadly stated, shaking the man's hand.

"Hi, Sam. I need to talk to my wife." Sam could see the anger in the other man's eyes, hear it in his voice. Slowly, ever so slowly, Sam walked home, anger in his heart towards Marie Claire's husband and mother, and a fear for the young woman's safety. Sam prayed as he walked. He interpreted Francis' nod and saw the hatred in the man's eyes.

Not seeing for himself what occurred before Cecelia left, and not wanting to listen to Sam explain what happened and hear that he was only consoling Marie Claire, Francis sat beside his wife while she tried to get herself together. Francis could not know the extent of heartache Marie Claire endured this morning.

"What happened here, Marie Claire?" Francis ground out, but tried to sustain himself from becoming angrier than he felt. He listened while she explained what occurred earlier, that her mother was out of their lives. He never knew his wife to talk about her life to others and became livid about that. Anger seethed in his heart and his face turned red. Marie Claire didn't notice. Francis thought back to the day he talked to Marie Claire about privacy. He told her years ago to keep their affairs private, and he meant it. He didn't care that Marie Claire only tried to find some help from the only real friends she'd made. She did not know what else to do and wanted only to better her circumstances. This is what Sam and Julia were trying to instill in her. To stand on her own feet, and they were giving her the help she needed to do that. They just didn't realize, but maybe should have, that Francis' jealousy problem went deeper than they thought.

"What are you? Nuts? I've told you to keep your mouth shut. Our lives are private and not to be discussed. I've told you over and over again to keep our affairs private. Talk to me if you have questions or problems." Francis stood in front of Marie Claire, waving his arms, yelling, pointing his finger at her, and in his anger he slapped her once then walked into the house.

Still early afternoon, Francis called Pastor Dixon and asked if he could see him. The pastor and Francis had become friends and they'd spoken together on several occasions. Francis couldn't rid his mind of the picture of another man holding his wife. The remembrance stuck in Francis' head and he remained angry, just as earlier. His face turned beet red with each remembrance of Marie Claire's disregard for his feelings, his eyes glinted shiny with hatred. Francis' hands were clenched into fists and his heart pounded in covetousness. Nothing else mattered to him. Marie Claire belonged to him and no other man was going to touch her.

*   *   *   *

Francis entered the pastor's home. Mrs. Dixon served coffee while the man tearfully spoke about catching his wife with another man. The stories he told about his wife's indiscretions were horrible - and lies.

"I drove up and there was Marie Claire, in the arms of another man. He was kissing her senseless and she seemed to be happy to be in his arms." Actually, what happened was that Sam was holding Marie Claire and he kissed to top of her head as she slumped on the stoop crying.

The clergyman was angry at Marie Claire. He would call tonight and talk to his elders and deacons about this. Marie Claire would not be allowed in the church until such time she could seek forgiveness from God and then she would need to ask the congregation for their forgiveness. Seeing Marie Claire every Sunday, he would not have guessed that she was that kind of woman. He did mention to Francis the many times that Clint came to visit her with his two boys, the most recent being just last weekend. He hadn't thought much about it, and the boys seemed to love the woman. Together, the couple shared all the times Clint had come to church with Marie Claire. What he didn't mention was that they were always with the Bascolms.

"I imagine their father is in love with her. Why else would a man come over to see a married woman? Can you tell me that?" Francis broke down crying. The pastor and his wife were trying their best to comfort the inconsolable man.

Several hours later, Francis made it back to the house. By this time, the anger he felt toward Marie Claire erupted as never before. His wife, in the middle of cleaning, stood at the kitchen sink when he walked in the door. He didn't closed it behind himself when he saw her. In his anger, he tromped over to her and proceeded to lay into her with all his might.

She screamed long and loud. The screams erupted involuntarily, several times. She tried to stem the tirade, but she had no way to fight back. Very tired and weak, Francis kept at her. Marie Claire could see no way to keep her husband off her. Francis raped his wife, beat her unmercifully, and he finally took hold of the olive oil bottle that was within reach on the counter. Raising his arm, Marie Claire could see it coming, and she blocked the blow with hers, not realizing that he broke the bottle nearly in half as he hit the counter edge with it. The broken shard that had once been solid glass, sliced into Marie Claire's left limb. Francis saw the blood and hoping she was dying, he kicked her in the head. Sam made it inside just in time to avoid the second kick to Marie Claire.

Sam manhandled Francis and pulled him outside. Sam, extremely angry, felt the adrenaline flowing through his blood. The older man left Francis sitting in the river rock that Marie Claire used to form some of her landscaping.

Sam yelled at Francis, "Leave before I call the police. What's wrong with you? Are you crazy? Not man enough to act like one? You sure like beating up defenseless women! Get out, now!" Sam stalked off to the kitchen and leaned down to Marie Claire.

Puzzled about how he got on the rocks Francis pushed himself up, and with one last grizzly look at Sam's retreating back, he got in his Jaguar and left the premises, tires skidding and throwing gravel every which away.

Julia watched Sam throw Francis into the rock pile. She called 911 and asked for an ambulance, and then she waited as Francis got up and took off in his car. The couple, quite used to this, knew what to do. Julia showed up just in time to help her husband stem the flow of blood spurting out of Marie Claire's left forearm. She grabbed two dishtowels and made a tourniquet out of them. The bleeding stopped by the time the ambulance arrived.

The paramedics took over for the couple. Julia rode in the ambulance with Marie Claire as Sam ran home to get his car. He would see them at the hospital. He stopped to ask a neighbor to go over and feed the many horses at Marie Claire's ranch. The neighbors were big into 4H with their kids, who were taking lessons from Marie Claire.

Because of the children and horses, and because the horses were very important to the children and to her, Marie Claire named her holdings the Rocking Horse Ranch. The group leader, Jennifer Zimmerman, assured Sam that the horses would be taken care of by the 4H group. She also said, "Sam, we all in the club love Marie Claire. We'll be thinking of her, and please, give her our best." Sam needn't have worried. The whole group came, parents and all, and fed and curried the horses that night and the next morning.

When Sam reached the hospital, Julia was sitting there and crying. They had fallen in love with Marie Claire and hated to see her this bad off. Sam explained to Julia what he'd seen when he arrived in Marie Claire's kitchen, some of it Julia surmised for herself. Her heart broke for this young woman she thought of as a daughter.

Chapter Fourteen

S AM AND Julia sat in the waiting room, talking about Marie Claire and Francis. The Kingman's were in trouble, and Julia wanted to see him sent to prison for what he'd done to his wife and their best friend.

Marie Claire spent several years after moving here, teaching riding lessons, entering and leading endurance rides, and training horses for others. She had several children, young people, and adults under her tutelage for horseback riding lessons. She was a gentle, caring, thoughtful trainer and rider. She always treated her horse's comfort as first priority. The students who came to her for lessons loved her gentle guidance and thorough teaching.

The ranch was not bringing in enough funds, however. Sam counseled Marie Claire often about raising her fees, cutting back on spending, and asking for a raise at her job. The raise happened, but she didn't know how to go about cutting back on spending. Her mother had drained her spiritually as well as financially when she was living with her. Marie Claire didn't think she would ever pay back what she owed to take care of the two of them.

Marie Claire struggled. She couldn't pay all of her bills. She had done the best she could, but earlier in the year she went to the bank and took out another loan, and now, in dire straits, she couldn't seem to make ends meet. Sam told her many times to charge more for her lessons and training, but Marie Claire felt adverse to do that. She didn't want to feel like she was robbing her clients. She wouldn't listen to Sam's advice, much as she needed to do so. Her friends knew that bankruptcy loomed on the horizon, and though they could help her out, she needed to learn a lesson. Marie Claire would be okay. First, she needed to get rid of her husband. They would be more than willing to help her with that. She needed to get through this latest ordeal, and then they would talk with her.

"Jules, I want to leave our holdings to Marie Claire in case anything happens to us someday." Sam explained more of his thoughts to his wife. "I want to help her out. She has a good business going, but she won't raise her prices. She's a stubborn girl."

"That she is, Sam. We need to let her come to terms with her finances on her own. We can't help her out and risk her dependency. I'd like to see what she does if she loses everything. I bet she'll come out on top of things. She may lose all, but why don't we wait and see, hmm?" Julia sat holding her husband's hand, thinking about his present to Marie Claire. "What a treasure you are! I think having Marie Claire as our beneficiary is a wonderful idea. I hope she lives through this ordeal." Julia said to Sam, just as they watched the ER doctor go into ICU.

Dr. Snow, too, waited with them to hear the outcome on Marie Claire. He made his rounds at the hospital and then checked on Marie Claire, though his employee and not his patient, seemed to be coming out of her coma. It had been six hours since the attack. Seeing Dr. Vandergarden, the ER physician, come into the room, Dr. Snow greeted his colleague and then strolled into the waiting room. He just finished rounds and was on hand to hear what the ER physician's prognosis would be. He'd gotten a call from Julia to come to see them after his patients were all checked. He talked to the physician about Marie Claire, but he would defer the latest news for the other doctor to share.

"Marie Claire needs to divorce her husband. I don't believe in divorce, but God does not expect us to live like this. He expects men to love and respect their wives, not attempt to kill them. How many times is this now that you've been here for her? Too many to count isn't it? Have you tried to talk to her some more?" Dr. Snow finished questioning Julia on this matter. He didn't know what more to do for his assistant. Julia didn't know what to say, so she didn't say anything, she just let her boss rant.

Marie Claire worked hard and thoroughly. She had always been dependable and willing to take on any new chore that Dr. Snow handed her. She worked well with the patients and his office staff, and they all loved her. *If she makes it through this,* he thought, *I will make sure to keep her safe, even if it means her having a security guard on hand 24 hours a day seven days a week.*

*   *   *   *

Dr. Vandergarden came out to see them after an hour. He greeted Dr. Snow and the Sheriff, Stanley Wright, who arrived a few minutes ago, before asking the four of them to come into his office.

"Mrs. Kingman sustained a cracked skull. Her jaw is broken and she sustained four fractured ribs, and her brachial artery was nearly severed. She will have an ugly scar on her arm, which we may be able to have a plastic surgeon work on, but otherwise we were able to affix the cut artery and suture her muscles back together. When she wakes up we'll see if she retains full use or not of her left arm. Her right wrist is sprained, and her nose is broken. She looks pretty bad, but she is stable now. You may see her when she goes into recovery. She is still slightly sedated and will be awake, hopefully, in a little bit. We worked on her arm and face wondering if she would even live, but we couldn't wait. It was hard to work on her jaw, as it was broken before. We managed to clean out some of the old calcium deposits so we could affix the jaw properly. She should have full movement and use of her mouth with no trouble. She did come out of her coma though. We'll see how her brain function is when she feels a bit better. We'll do a scan in a couple of days."

He showed them the x-rays and the past and present breaks she'd endured. "If she has one more beating like this one," he severely told them, "she could die. She may have this time, but apparently she had a slight concussion and no other major damage to the brain. There is some internal bleeding, but it was almost stopped before I spoke with you. She is still under watch until the bleeding is totally abated. We want to make sure we don't have to go in and repair any internal organs. We did repair a tear in her left kidney, but that's okay now. We saw some enlargement of her liver and spleen, but no patent blood was present. Will she be staying with you, Mr. and Mrs. Bascolm?"

"Yes, she'll stay with us. We'll hire someone to feed and care for the horses until she's better. She stayed with us before, but she was never hurt this badly before either," Sam told the doctor.

"Good. She'll need to stay quiet for a week or two anyway, won't she Dr. Vandergarden?" Dr. Snow knowledgeably questioned, and then he deferred to the ER doctor.

"That's right. She will need at least that long, after she gets home, to recuperate. She works for you, doesn't she, Dr. Snow?"

"Yes, she does. She's been one of my best assistants and she'll have her job waiting for her. I'll hire a temp in the meantime, because I don't want her worrying about her job while recuperating from this episode on top of it." Julia was tearing up, thankful for such a wonderful boss. Everyone one his staff loved him. Dr. Snow treated everyone kindly, but with a deep concern about their welfare. He didn't mince words when his patients told him their vices. Smoking, drugs, and alcohol - they were all bad for the health and welfare of everyone concerned.

"With the contusions, we need to monitor her for blood clots. She is catheterized so we can monitor the hematuria - blood in her urine." He reiterated for the Bascolm's benefit. "When that goes away and if she is feeling better, she can go home in a few days." Dr. Vandergarden told them all he could for now. They were just happy that she would live.

Julia would make sure Marie Claire signed a restraining order on Francis this time around, and that she would be getting a divorce from her husband. They couldn't take anymore of this and they were not going to allow Francis Kingman to maybe kill her next time. He wouldn't acknowledge that they needed counseling. He was angry at Marie Claire any time she brought the subject up. So, no one close to Marie Claire could see any other way for her to get the safety and comfort that she needed.

Dr. Vandergarden returned to the ICU, where Marie Claire was still ensconced. His assistant needed him and called him in to Marie's room. After checking the machines and making sure every vital sign read normal, he told his assistant to let her go to the private room that awaited their patient. All the bleeding stopped by this time, and there was no longer blood in her urine.

Marie Claire woke up an hour later, but she soon fell asleep again. A few hours later, still a bit out of it, but with her head taped in one place to keep it still and the good care she received at the hands of her friends and the physicians, she was doing medically better and the anesthetic, finally, wore off.

"Marie Claire, dear, it's me, Julia. Wake up, sweetie. Please, wake up." Julia cajoled quietly, bending over the patient.

Marie Claire heard Julia's voice and when, alas, she was fully awake and cognizant, she saw that Julia was standing beside Dr. Snow looking at the 'poor girl's' injuries. Sam sat in a chair by the window opposite Marie Claire's bed. His head rested in his hands, and the man looked thoughtful and a little sad. Tears of relief ran from Julia's lovely green eyes, because they were assured that Marie Claire would be fine.

"Oh, how am I?" Marie Claire asked quietly. "Where am I? Did I die?" All were inane questions, but ones most often asked in such circumstances.

Sam jumped up and ran to Marie Claire's bedside next to his wife. He leaned over and kissed her forehead. Chuckling, he looked into Marie Claire's battered and bruised brown eyes, "No, Marie Claire. You didn't die, but we almost lost you. How do you feel?"

Marie Claire couldn't open her eyes fully, but she did see minimal movement out of the slits. Her eyes were swollen, red and bruised, with cuts around the cheekbones and forehead.

What's wrong with that man, Francis Kingman, that he could do something like this to such a gentle, kind soul. Marie Claire is not only beautiful outside, she is beautiful inside. We love you, Marie Claire. Julia thought about the young woman's situation all the while she held Marie Claire's hand in hers, rubbing the wrapped wrist.

"Mrs. Kingman? Can you talk to me? I want to take some notes," the Sheriff asked Marie Claire.

"Yes, but I don't know what to tell you. Every time I talk to the police nothing gets done. Francis is a big shot prosecuting attorney in Seattle, and no one will touch him. I want out! Now, I want out. Why did I wait so long?" Tears flowed from Marie Claire's eyes, but it only cost her more pain so she tried to stop. She struggled with her feelings, hurting, and Sam sighed and held her hand tighter and prayed audibly for her. Julia, Dr. Snow, and Sheriff Stan Wright joined in.

Marie Claire thought it a miracle that the Sheriff, she was told, was also a Christian. She felt relief, happiness, and she hoped that he would want to help her. Marie Claire, still a bit woozy yet, would be fine; and she tried again to open her eyes fully but could only open them to slits. She saw a handsome man and that he wore a wedding ring. He appeared middle-aged and she hoped that he loved his family and never hurt them.

After praying, Julia noticed Marie Claire's eyes, some type of questioning look in them. "Can you see okay, Marie Claire? I'm so sorry you're hurt. I want you to do me a favor, okay? Can you do that for me?"

"Anything for you, Julia. What? Do you want me to dance a jig? I can't right now. I hurt too much!" She smiled, trying to cheer herself and her best friends up. She didn't want to cause any more grief to the Bascolms.

The trio laughed with her, happy that she could tease, though none in her sphere had ever heard the woman kid anyone before. Sheriff Wright handed Julia a paper and the woman sat beside Marie Claire on the bed. "I want you to tell the Sheriff all you can. Will you do for that for me? I also want you to sign this restraining order. We do not want you killed, and your husband may come and do that to you next time. Can you understand? Do you understand?"

Marie Claire thought about it for a moment, and then she asked for a pen. "Will you hold my hand, Sam? I can't see very well and I want to do this thing right." With Sam holding her right hand steady, Marie Claire signed the restraining order keeping Francis away from her property and her person for a period of six months. The judge wouldn't restrain the husband longer than that. Marie Claire did this just for Julia, and she promised, because she didn't like seeing her friend cry. She also understood the pleading tone in Julia's voice. Marie Claire pleaded enough herself over the years, but God hadn't brought help until now.

"Now, Marie Claire," Sam said, handing the signed paper to Sheriff Wright. "I want you to tell this officer what occurred. Tell him all he needs to know. You need to do that in order for him to proceed to keep you safe, okay? Do that for us, please?" Sam sounded very concerned and she could hear the tears in his voice.

"Okay." She told the Sheriff what set Francis off this time.

Sam, thinking he was the cause of Marie Claire being beaten up again, became quite upset. He berated himself, *Why did I comfort Marie Claire? I know I did it because we love her, Julia and I. Why couldn't I see that I was hurting Marie Claire in the process? God, please, you should have punished me instead. I caused this.*

Julia took her husband's hand and led him out of the room while Marie Claire talked to Stan Wright. "Sam, this was not your fault. So much happened today that anything and everything may have set him off. Who knows? Maybe he just came home to start a fight like he always does. Nothing Marie Claire can do makes him happy. I have a feeling he's mad because she has a wonderful life among her horses and the people that she teaches. He's probably jealous about that." Julia didn't know it, but she'd hit the nail on the head so to speak. The heart of the problem - Marie Claire's independence. She learned to live on her own, and Francis was livid with jealousy, and in need of the control he once held over his wife.

If Marcia Madison could see her out at the ranch, she would be very proud of her former employee. Marie Claire, finally growing up, knew that she needed to make her own choices, good or bad, just like everyone else. Sam, Julia, Marcia, and others - they had all helped Marie Claire to see that she needed to find her own mind, and her own way in the world. The marriage to Francis Kingman, and the culmination of years of terror in her life, came to fruition on this day – eighteen years later, and the young woman's eyes were finally opened.

Chapter Fifteen

Marie Claire came home three days later. She went to stay at the Bascolm's. She received a visit from Candace, the oldest neighbor girl, the day after she arrived home from the hospital.

"Mrs. Bascolm, may I see Mrs. Kingman? I have something terrible to tell her." Candace, crying hysterically, fairly screamed out.

"Candace, I can't understand you. What is the trouble?" Julia held the girl's shoulders in her capable hands, then hugged her.

Candace, leaning back and away from Julia, wiped her face with a hanky and blew her nose. Still upset, she retold Julia what happened this morning. "I went to feed this morning and I saw Pride lying in the arena. He wouldn't get up. I called my mom to check on him and he's dead. I don't know what to do!" The girl knew how much that horse meant to her teacher.

Sam, overhearing the conversation, almost vomited. He felt sick knowing the torture Marie Claire would go through. He quietly left the house and went to Marie's arena. He found the buckskin lying there, dried sweat covering his hide from head to foot.

He called Julia from his cell phone, "Jules, it looks as if colic killed the gelding. I checked the feed bin first but found nothing there." The feed looked good with no added powder or pellets to cause the death of Marie's beloved endurance and performance horse. The hay looked good and free from mold. "I've called Dr. Sheridan to come out. He'll be here in a few minutes."

The vet, after putting on a sleeve that covered his hand and arm up to the shoulder, did a colon check and found that, indeed, colic killed the horse. "There would've been nothing to do but to put Pride down, even if we found the problem earlier. Someone had to have poisoned this horse since he was fine last night and dead this morning. He's been dead most of the night. Only a poison of some type would do this," Dr. Sheridan shared with Sam.

Sam paid the vet and then headed home to get his backhoe. He would bury Pride in the enclosure Marie Claire had made for them when the day came to bury her beloved pets. She even placed name placards on the fence marking the burial site of Tanny and Pride. Sam changed out the signs. Pride would have to be buried first so he would be at the end of the enclosure. The mare's name plaque would be closer to the middle of the enclosure. Tanukar was at the breeder's and would be home in the next few days. He hoped she would be okay for the rest of her life. Marie Claire would be more than devastated if she lost them both close together.

When Sam got home, he put the backhoe away. He went upstairs where he heard Julia talking to Marie Claire. Apparently, she already told the young woman what had happened.

"I told Dr. Sheridan to check the horse. He did indeed die of colic. It happened too fast to be an accident. I checked the feed, ran my hands through it, smelled it and the hay, and it was all okay. I saw no sign of tampering. The grain smelled normal. Someone had to have given the horse some poison for it to happen this quickly." Sam explained to them what the vet had told him. "I am going to have an electric gate installed so no one can enter the ranch that doesn't have a code. The fence company people are on their way now. I called the Sheriff, but nothing can be done because no one saw anything."

Marie Claire sat there on her bed, propped against her pillows, wallowing in self-pity. She did not say a word. *I know deep in my heart that Francis did this out of spite*, Marie Claire thought, *but I can't prove it. I'm grateful that Jules and Sam came to see us in the shows, and that they loved him almost as much as I did.* She was proud of the horse for all the trophies they won through the years and some of them hung on the large wall in her study. The others hung downstairs in Sam and Julia's entertainment room. Marie Claire loved the horse and would never forget him.

"I buried him, Marie Claire. His plaque is on the fence right where it should be. I switched Tanny's over to the gate end, to make it easier to bury Pride. I moved Pride's name plaque down where the mare's was. We'll have a little service when you're able to get out. Okay?" Sam sat on the bed beside her, holding her hand, kneading it, and trying his best not to cry for her, with her. She didn't deserve this, but the deed was done. He just hoped Francis Kingman would get his just rewards sooner rather than later, when only God could do the punishing.

A week later, Tanny came home from the breeders. Last year's filly met her at the gate when she arrived back at the ranch, but Pride didn't sound his happy whinny, and Tanny smelled death somewhere on the wind. Marie Claire's beloved mare looked all over for him, whinnying and worrying. Marie Claire saw the torment in her horse's eyes, the brokenness of not having her lifelong pal by her side. The mare went down two days later.

The vet again came out to the ranch. He diagnosed her with stress colic and was forced to put her down. The mare, terribly sick, was found too late to save her. Another hard blow hit Marie Claire, but this time it hit her in the soul. Inconsolable for a week, Marie Claire cried, screamed, and cursed Francis Kingman every chance she got. She hated the man, and she asked Sam and Julia to take her to a lawyer. Through many hours of struggling with her decision, thinking of so many years of abuse, knowing God hates divorce yet knowing that Francis had taken her childhood away from her, and everything and everyone else she had ever loved, her mind won out. She filed for divorce.

*   *   *   *

A few weeks later Marie Claire asked the boarders to take their horses home. She told them she would be selling the ranch and moving on. She didn't tell them that she filed for bankruptcy. Getting out of the area and away from the memories, Marie Claire knew she would never get over the loss of her two beloved horses, but she would devote her time to healing and getting on with what she hoped would be a better life. She knew that with God's help she would start a new life somewhere else. Julia and Sam had helped her so much through her years here, and they all loved each other deeply. She felt their love and their compassion for her. God doesn't allow anyone to see the future, so without foreknowledge, Marie Claire didn't know she would be losing them soon, also.

Chapter Sixteen

Sometimes it takes a tremendous heartbreak to get someone who believes in God to realize that they never really let Him lead their lives. People think that they can ask Jesus into their hearts, accept Him as their Savior, and try to live the life Jesus expects, but never really let Him be Lord.

Marie Claire was no different. Oh, she definitely believed in Christ, no doubt about that, but there was that important piece missing. She did not realize until the day her divorce became final that she never really let Jesus be her personal Lord as well as her Savior.

Her divorce papers were to be picked up one afternoon after work. Her lawyer called her late in the morning.

"Marie Claire. This is Diane Hackett. You are officially a single woman and I need you to pick up the papers after you get off work tonight."

"Really? Is that all? What do I do now? I've never been divorced before." Marie Claire felt a sick kind of sadness in her soul and depression set in all the rest of the day. No one could get her to smile. As she walked out the office door into the parking lot, Marie Claire fell to her knees. The burden she felt on her shoulders, in her chest, and in her heart felt like a weight she knew she couldn't carry alone. It was a pain and remorse heavier than she ever felt before. She fell to her knees on the hard cement of the parking lot, the tender skin of her knee caps cracked, but no pain registered in her brain.

"God," she cried, looking up into the cloud filled blue sky, "I am so sorry. I never should have lived like I did. I accepted you and your love, so many years ago, yet I lived in sin all my days. I couldn't really be yours all the while I lived with my hateful thoughts and actions towards Francis all these years. I tried to get him to attend counseling with me, but he refused. I don't know what else to do. I am so sorry, my Lord. Please forgive me." Tears pouring from her brown eyes, pulling her hair, and then railing with her arms raised toward the sky, no one came around the demented woman. It seemed as though God gave her this time to speak to Him with no interruptions. Marie Claire cried inconsolably, her loud voice carried to Heaven and back. She bent, doubled over in grief, her head nearly touching the concrete of the parking lot, and she knew in her heart of hearts that God's ear bent toward her mouth. She quieted, speaking to God with her mind, her heart, her soul.

Marie Claire knelt there on her knees for about ten minutes. She poured her heart out to the God she loved. She asked for forgiveness, promised to let Him guide her heart and lead her steps, and asked Him once again to come into her heart, her soul, her life and be her shepherd.

Eventually, she arose and walked to her car. As she started it up, her coworkers came out of the medical clinic with no one seeming the wiser to Marie Claire's breakdown. *Everyone is acting normal. Maybe God kept me invisible to them. I sure hope that is the case,* Marie Claire thought to herself as she waved goodbye to each one who waved to her.

All the way home Marie Claire talked to God. She vowed always to read His word, and listen for His voice to tell her what to do. She knew she should always go to a pastor if she was ever in need or in trouble. She promised, if He would tell her what to do, that she would always try to be a light that shines for Christ.

It would take several weeks for Marie Claire to get over the hurt she caused Francis. It would take years to realize, even through two years of counseling, that men who do what Francis did to her as a teenager, are pedophiles and predators.

Marie Claire seemed always to have a forgiveness for any little slight against her. She did not forgive in her own power, but something, maybe the faith that kept her believing in Christ, allowed her to forgive on the spot, unconditionally. Several years later, Marie Claire would

pick up on that, but in the meantime she would keep seeking and clinging to God even more.

God in His infinite wisdom and mercy, provided Marie Claire
with a big heart, and someday she would come to realize that God never
left her, as He promised that whomsoever accepts His sacrifice for sins,
in no way will He let them go away from His care. He just allowed her
to go through something that, in the end, would only draw her closer
to the Jesus she loved with all her heart.

Chapter Seventeen

S AM BASCOLM called Clint Bellham a week later. He explained what had happened in the last two weeks since the divorce became final. Sam and Clint set up a time for the following Saturday. The three of them, along with Marie Claire, would be searching for a new apartment for Marie. Julia and Marie Claire were talking about this earlier, and the younger woman thought that the best thing would be for her to settle down in Seattle for right now, get her thoughts together, and decide what she wanted to do with the rest of her life. First off, she would have to find a job, but she thought that Marcia would be willing to have her back.

She received her first alimony check early that afternoon from Francis Kingman. A note was attached. It read, 'I think you're foolish, Marie Claire. To me, you will always be my wife. You won't get away from me that easily.' She kept the note and her thoughts to herself. But, she vowed to have a good time with her friends and not worry about anything.

Clint, Martin, and Jon arrived at Marie Claire's ranch late Friday evening. They took her to a movie, to a late dinner, and a nice drive around Sandpoint and Lake Coeur d'Alene . Marie Claire, being quiet, enjoyed the efforts the men performed for her this evening. She knew she was blessed to have these loved ones in her life, and for their sakes she kept a smile on her face.

At midnight, they stopped at an all-night café and Marie Claire bought them milk shakes. They arrived back home at one in the morning. After hugs goodnight, they all retired.

The next morning, everyone awoke to a light drizzle. Clint took them out, with Sam and Julia, for breakfast. Upon arriving back at the house, they noticed the Atlas moving van just backing up to the front door. Marie Claire's belongings would be taken to the Sunrise Storage facility in Spokane. It was reasonably priced, and in the circumstances, Marie Claire wanted her things kept on this side of the mountains. She liked the weather and terrain here and thought maybe she'd be back.

It took three hours for the truck to be loaded with all of her belongings, except for two bags of clothes and another bag of odds and ends that she wanted to keep on hand. Clint stuffed these in his trunk. Not having quite enough room, he put more items in Marie Claire's trunk, and some bags in the back seat. It was a tearful goodbye to the Bascolms, but as they walked home, Marie Claire wandered one last time around her property. Wanting to give Marie Claire a little bit of time to herself, Clint checked the barn and tack room to make sure nothing was missed. He made one last walk through of the house, and found that nothing was left behind. He then sat in the car waiting for Marie Claire.

The Koi that swam in her pond, Marie Claire gave to Candace's brother, Keith. Marie Claire made one last walk-through around the inside and the outside of her house. As she stood looking at her large gourmet kitchen, she knew she was really going to miss it here. *"Lord Jesus, I ask you to guide me, direct me, and lead me where you would want me to go. I don't ask for this to be given back to me, but teach me what you want me to learn and keep me in your care."* Marie Claire spoke aloud, feeling that God in His infinite love was there with her in heart and soul. After this prayer, Marie Claire went to the car. She never did visit her horse's graves. She felt she would die if she did that. She just said goodbye to them in her heart, and quietly asked, "God, please, let me have them back when I get to Heaven. They were my family, and I loved them so very much. Take care of them, Father." Moreover, she believed with all her heart that God heard and her prayer would be answered.

Sam would be storing her truck and horse trailer at their place until such time she made a decision to sell. She stood by her car and waved one last time toward the Bascolm home. Marie Claire though she saw them waving from their window. Entering her automobile, fastening the seat belt, and turning on the radio to an old western station, she then followed Clint and the boys down Interstate 90 to whatever awaited her in Seattle. Sam and Julia were flying over, and they would meet the couple at SeaTac Airport later this evening.

Half way to Seattle, Clint pulled over to the side of the road. He checked to make sure the cars were far enough off the road so he could talk to Marie Claire.

Rolling down her window, Marie Claire looked out at Clint who just sidled up to her door, leaned down to look at her, and then he said, "I'd like to stop in and have dinner in Moses Lake. There's a nice steak house there. Are you game?"

"Sure," Marie Claire told him, smiling a demure smile. She then tweaked his cheek. She loved to tease Clint and it showed, all the time! It seemed to Clint that she was finding her way to happiness, one day at a time. Marie Claire was coming out of her shell and he couldn't wait to see the final product. In the meantime, he promised himself to keep on praying for his Sunshine.

Chapter Eighteen

NEARLY SEVEN hours later, Clint and Marie Claire picked the Bascolms up from the airport. Clint's boys went to stay with their aunt and uncle. The Danforths, Clint's sister and brother-in-law, lived in Tacoma, but Clint's sister would stay at her brother's house. She would see that the boys got to school every day. They had one week left then the summer vacation started. The Danforths would keep the Bellham boys for as long as needed.

Dusk was on the horizon, and the clock read six thirty, but the four of them were going to look at an apartment on the waterfront in Midway. Marie Claire picked an apartment on the third floor, which had a beautiful view of Puget Sound and the Olympic Peninsula far to the west. From the hallway, stepping into her new apartment, the living room loomed large, and straight ahead was her dining area. To the right of this sat her kitchen, which seemed rather large, and the whole main area of the apartment breathed comfort because of the open floor plan. This reminded Clint of Marie Claire's home. The rooms were very similar in size to her home, and, he thought, *would help her to better adjust.* The bathroom off the kitchen was nice sized and beside that, Marie Claire enjoyed a large bedroom.

"Oh, Marie Claire, this is beautiful," Julia commented as she stepped through the sliding glass doors from the dining room and onto a wide veranda. She marveled at the view. She saw Mt. Rainier off in the southeastern distance. The Tacoma tide flats sat due South, and Puget Sound and the western Olympic Peninsula sat due West. There wasn't much to see North except the city buildings and the freeway, but it held its own kind of beauty. The air smelled like fresh seawater, and seagulls flew overhead. They weren't far from the beach and the marina here. "Sam! Sam come out here and look at this! Isn't this gorgeous?"

Sam walked out and stood beside his wife. He scanned the entire scenic beauty for a good five minutes. "This is beautiful, Julia, but get that thought right out of your head. We are not moving," he stated in a matter of fact tone.

"Why, Sam. I'm not thinking of moving, just maybe having a little vacation spot here! Wouldn't that be wonderful? What do you think about my idea?" Julia lovingly smiled at her husband with just a glint of mischief in her eyes.

"Humph," Sam grunted at her, "Jules, I know you. You've got your little chick here and you want to be with her." Looking deep into Julia's eyes, and thinking, Sam said, "If you'd like, let's stay here a couple of weeks. We can afford it, and Marie Claire probably really needs us right now. How about I run down, check with the manager, and see if we can work something out? Would that make you happy?" Sam asked his wife.

"Oh, Sam, I would love that. Thank you so much. I'll let Marie Claire know what's happening and you go on down." Julia smiled at her husband, patting his right cheek with her left hand. Sam left the apartment and Julia went back inside and gave hugs to Marie Claire and Clint both.

"Where did Sam go, Julia?" Marie Claire asked.

"Oh, I'll tell you later," Julia quipped, a glint of laughter in her eyes.

Clint stated, "Sam and I will be making a run to Spokane for some of your furniture, Marie Claire. Would you mind making a list for us? We'll leave early in the morning and be back sometime tomorrow night."

Marie Claire stood at the kitchen counter, and while looking at each wall in her new surroundings, she notated each box and each piece of furniture that she would need. She handed the note to Clint, and starting from the fireplace on the far wall, she strode through her new home, taking in the silver gray carpet on the floor, the white acoustic ceiling above, the deep gray slate floor in her kitchen, and the very pale yellow walls throughout.

To most folks, the most important room in any house is the kitchen, and Marie Claire seemed very pleased with this one. The oak cabinets were light-colored. The stove glistened shiny red with white knobs and a clock and push buttons on the black panel. Above that, there hung a shiny red fronted microwave oven and an inset double oven to the left of that. A countertop made of Montana marble, of an off-white color with dark pink and gray veins throughout, went around either side of the stove. At the end stood a double-door shiny red refrigerator with a large freezer at the bottom. Overall, it emanated every gourmet cook's dream. Lots of counter space, a beautiful Montana marble sink with gold faucet and handles that sat across from the stove with a red fronted dishwasher beside that, and windows throughout the front and one side of the apartment made everything around Marie Claire bright and cheerful.

"Is there anything else you need to add to this list, Sunshine?" Clint asked his friend.

"No, Clint. I think I have everything down. If I missed something, I can always go shopping. I did mark the boxes so you can just pick out the master bedding and the kitchen appliances. I wrote down all of the furniture I'd like, but if you think I missed something pick it up too."

With that all done, Sam walked back into the apartment. "Julia, dear, we're all taken care of."

Marie Claire looked at her two friends, puzzlement in her eyes. "Okay guys, what's going on?" She asked. She could see the conspiratorial looks between the older couple.

Sam smiled at her, and then at Clint. With a twinkle in his eye, he motioned to Clint, with a tip of his head, and the two men walked out on the veranda.

Julia sat on the hearth, pulling Marie Claire down beside her. "Something must be going on," Julia said. "Sam went to see the manager about our staying here for a couple of weeks, but I sense something more than that."

The two men walked back into the dining room and smiled at the two women. "If you two are ready to go we're going to take you out for dinner at the Snoqualmie Falls Lodge."

Squealing, Marie Claire jumped up and gave the two men big hugs. "Oh, that's my favorite restaurant. Jules, you're just going to love it." she squealed again and danced a little jug. The others marveled at the happy woman before them. None of them had ever seen her this happy.

It was springtime in the northwest, crocus disappeared and tulips now took their place. Lilacs and irises budded, just about to bloom. Within the hour, they reached their destination. Here, the lilacs were in the blossoming stage, and the air smelled pungent with their sweet scent. Washington State endured a rather rainy winter so the falls were the fullest they'd been in years and roared as never heard in a long time. The jagged, rough walls of the canyon shined of wetness from top to bottom, and moss grew long from the trees clinging to the craggy edges. Long ago, a large tree died and fell across the chasm, and it hung in space with moss growing all over and hanging down from its aged dead trunk. This was the first time that Julia and Sam had ever come here, and the spotlights that illumine this area at night gave them a fantastic view that otherwise is seen only in the daytime.

The foursome entered the restaurant and took a table near the window overlooking the falls. They dined on steamed clams, and for the main course, since everyone liked it, they ordered prime rib and lobster and made small talk. The meal was very filling, so they by-passed dessert.

Over an after-dinner drink, Marie Claire having a strawberry daiquiri and the others margaritas, Sam told them, "Julia, we will have the apartment next to Marie Claire for a month. Marie Claire, I have leased the apartment for you for a year. I paid everything in advance, and you don't have to worry about anything. This is our treat to you, so that if you want to get a job you can, or if you want to wait and get your thoughts together about starting your new life, what to do, you'll have no worries."

Clint looked at Marie with tears in his eyes. *I can't believe these people are so wonderful to her,* he thought. *I'm so happy for this woman in my life, my dearest friend. Thank you, God, for watching out for my Sunshine, the woman that I love.*

Marie Claire, tears standing ready in her eyes, felt so thankful and surprised that she didn't know what to say. She sipped her daiquiri then turned her attention to the Bascolms. "Sam, I don't know what to say. Thank you seems so small, but my heart fills with gratefulness to you both. You really need to take care of yourselves - take a big vacation around the world or something, and not worry about me. But, I thank you so much for your love and care."

"We love you, Marie Claire," Julia said. "You've been the daughter we were never able to have. We are very wealthy and we're happy to be able to help you out. We've been around the world, twice in fact. We're happy where we are. We're giving you this year to prove to us that you can take care of money responsibly. So far you have surpassed our expectations. That savings account that we didn't know you had surprised us. We are so glad you kept money aside, even though you needed to pay bills. That really surprised us." Julia smiled lovingly at the young woman. The savings didn't amount to much, but the couple knew that Marie Claire could use it for the next month to eat on and buy whatever she needed for the apartment.

"We hope you don't mind our butting into your life, dear one, but we know your story and we do not judge you. We are glad that you're free and have a happy life to look forward to." Sam, too, smiled at Marie Claire.

Clint wiped his eyes, keeping his head down. They all knew him to be a decent, kind, affectionate, and softhearted man. Eventually, Clint looked up and said, "Thank you both for taking such good care of my friend. I appreciate what you've done. We do need to leave because we have to get up early. Since we have no bedding, how 'bout we stay at the motel down the road? My treat! It's very nice. You and I can leave from there Sam, and Marie Claire and Julia can spend the day," with a wink at Marie Claire and putting some bills in her hand, "window shopping."

Marie Claire appeared dumbstruck. No man ever freely handed this much money to her before. The unsaid 'thank you' gleamed from her eyes to Clint's. A chaste kiss on the cheek is what Marie Claire paid to her friend.

After the men paid the dinner bill, arm in arm, the four walked to their car, happy to help Marie Claire start a new life.

*   *   *   *

Clint and Sam left at eight that next morning. Clint had been able to take the week off work, so he spent quite a bit of time helping Marie Claire arrange and rearrange her apartment when they got back from

Spokane at six thirty that next evening. The Bascolms prepared their new apartment. Afterwards, when the four gathered at Marie Claire's, she took the three on a tour of her new place.

No one had really noticed the covers on her electrical outlets. In the bedroom, she put up cream-colored blinds on her two small windows that overlooked the nightstands. The queen sized bed sat between, and Marie Claire adorned it with a quilt depicting horses, all over it and of every color, on a background of green fields. The pillow shams, curtains, and outlet covers matched.

What store has all this stuff in it? I can't believe what Marie Claire has done to this room. I'm pleased that she found something she loves, and that will help her cope with her horse losses. Clint didn't say anything about anything. He processed his feelings for his 'Sunshine'.

"Marie Claire, how did you ever find all this horsey stuff?" Sam asked.

"I found a western wear store downtown that also had the bedding. Look at my sheets!" Marie Claire said as she pulled back a corner of the bedspread. "They match the bedspread! Isn't this cool?" They all laughed. The music of Marie Claire's laughter surprised them all. Clint, after he came into her life but before becoming a good friend to her, had never seen her smile, let alone laugh. Julia and Sam knew her to smile with them a lot, but only tentatively at first. This was the first real jovial sound they ever heard from her. Even with her students in North Idaho, she remained attentive and demonstrative, smiling minimally, but mostly stoic.

"They took me to their basement and that's where I found the curtains and shams. The outlet covers were almost gone upstairs, but there were more downstairs. I bought them all." Marie Claire actually giggled and her eyes sparkled. Sam, Julia, and Clint, all three were amazed at what a transformation overcame Marie Claire's beautiful face when truly happy. She became even more beautiful.

She led them over to the bathroom and horse borders adorned the upper part of her walls. She'd somehow found a shower curtain that nearly matched the outlet covers throughout her apartment. *Nothing feminine for this lady,* Sam thought to himself.

Sam would kill me if I had flowers everywhere like Marie Claire has horses! I'm just glad that she's found something that makes her happy. I wish she'd listened to us years ago, but she's going to be fine, now. What a surprise Sam has for her. I can hardly wait until she sees our lawyer someday. Julia kept quiet as she pondered lots of thoughts of her own. Marie Claire would be flabbergasted when the Bascolm's wishes were finally shown to her.

Clint thought his thoughts also, and he'd been thinking them for the past month. He came prepared today to share some of those thoughts with his Sunshine.

Marie Claire made pizza for dinner for the four of them. Clint called his sister while the pizza baked. "Hi, Joan," Clint smiled while greeting his sister. "How are the boys doing?"

"Hi, brother. They're doing fine. Jon fell off his skateboard and cut his forehead, but he's so hardheaded anyway that the doctor said he'll be fine. He just suffered a slight cut, no stitches needed. That's the worst of it so I didn't bother to call you." Joan went on to tell Clint about more personal information.

Clint told his sister what he planned for the morning. "Will you be able to stay with the boys for another week or so?"

"When do I get to meet this paragon of virtue?" Joan kidded.

"Why don't you bring the boys down for breakfast in the morning? You can meet her then, and the boys can see her for a couple of hours. She loves them a lot." Clint kidded back.

"How about we get there about eight? Do you want me to keep them home from school then?" Joan queried.

"Sure, they can miss one day. It won't hurt anything." Clint could hear the boys whooping it up after Joan told them they would have the day off school tomorrow.

"Will we get to see Marie Claire?" Martin asked. "Shall we bring her some flowers?" He grabbed the phone from his aunt and talked, excitedly, to his dad.

"I think she would like that. Yes, roses, red ones." Clint whispered to his youngest son. "Ask Aunt Joan for the favor of taking you shopping, and I will pay her when I see her tomorrow."

"Ok. Thanks, dad. We'll see you tomorrow." Martin asked his aunt a question and then to his dad, he said, "Aunt Joan said that would be fine."

"Son, thank you. Can I talk to your brother, please?"

When Jon took the phone Clint said, "I'll see you both tomorrow." He told Jon what he'd planned for Marie Claire. An excited Jon promised, "I won't say anything to anyone, dad. I think that's great. You know she loves us, and we love her. I hope all goes well."

"I didn't ask Martin, but I'm sure he feels as you do. What do you think?" Clint asked his oldest.

"Dad, you know he'll be just as happy as I am. Gee, dad, I hope she doesn't hurt your feelings!" Jon remembered how the other women rebuffed their father. The women lost a lot not caring for them. "*Oh well*, Jon thought, "*their loss, Marie Claire's and our gain!*"

"She won't! Don't worry. We'll see you in the morning. I'm going to make pancakes, scrambled eggs, and cut up cantaloupe. We'll have sausage, bacon, and ham also. Come hungry!" They signed off and Marie Claire called Clint in to dinner.

*   *   *   *

The next morning just before eight, Joan, Ted, and the boys stepped into a beautifully appointed apartment. All over the right wall as they stepped into the suite, horse paintings, pictures from rodeos, horse shows, and various mountain rides were plastered such that not a speck of paint could be seen. The boys and Clint, after he greeted his sister and brother-in-law, went to the kitchen to gab with Marie Claire about their school and friends. Clint finished making breakfast, not allowing anyone else to help. Julia kept busy setting the table and asking the boys about their friends. It was a jolly crowd that finally sat down, twenty minutes later, at the large dining table to partake of 'the best breakfast they'd had in a long time', according to the boys.

The Danforths, after meeting Marie Claire, expressed pleasure with Clint's new love; and upon helping her brother clean up afterwards, Joan expostulated, "She sure is different from your ex-wife. You can be proud of the home you own and the company you keep with that one. Congratulations, or is this too soon?"

"I haven't asked her yet, Sis, but I will tonight. I'll let you know tomorrow." Clint smiled at Joan and they finished their ministrations to the kitchen and went in to join the others in the living room, where Marie Claire stood at the wall, explaining to the boys and Ted what each of the pictures portrayed. Afterwards, they all took off to visit the zoo and take a drive to the mountains.

*   *   *   *

Back at the apartment, several hours later, Clint asked Marie Claire, "Would you like to take a drive with me, Sunshine? We won't be long."

It was nine o'clock and Ted, Joan, Julia, and Sam said goodnight and promised to see the couple in the morning. They waited as Clint said, "Sis, boys, I'll be home after I drop Marie Claire off here later."

"Why don't you just stay here tonight, dad." Martin said.

"Martin, you know what dad says! He can't stay here. He'd be going against his own beliefs." Jon lectured his younger brother.

"Oh, yeah. Sorry." Martin seemed truly remorseful; not wanting to hurt his dad, but Marie Claire hugged him and told him everything would be all right. Pleased to have a place in the boys' hearts, Marie Claire hugged them tightly and kissed them goodnight.

"Your aunt and uncle will bring you over here tomorrow. We'll have lunch together. How's that?" Pride of his two sons shown in Clint's eyes and smile.

"Um, no. We have school tomorrow. Maybe the weekend?" Martin could be hopeful, but he also knew that his dad didn't tolerate school skipping.

"No, I'll be glad to bring the boys again next Saturday. Would that work?" Joan asked.

"See you guys next weekend. Be good. I love you." Marie Claire told them as Clint guided her to the door to take that drive he promised her.

She did give the Danforths, Bascolms, and the boy's hugs before she left. *Clint is sure getting impatient,* she thought. *I better leave.* With a last goodbye, Clint shut the door behind them.

Chapter Nineteen

CLINT TOOK Marie Claire down to the Seattle waterfront. They walked the beaches, as the tide hadn't started to flow back toward the mainland yet. An hour later, they turned and came back to where they started, at the aquarium. Of course, the 'Closed' sign hung on the door, as was just about everything but a coffee shop, Seattle's Finest, and here they found a seat in a far corner near a small window overlooking the hotel across the street.

"What can I get you, Sunshine? Do you still like hazelnut flavored coffee?" Clint smiled into her eyes. Surprised at the vehemence of her answer, Clint remembered that Francis' liked Hazelnut, seemed to be his favorite flavor actually, and he made sure that Marie Claire drank the same thing.

"No, I don't. I hate it." Marie Claire retreated in her seat, no longer the happy woman that had walked through the coffee shop door ten minutes earlier.

"Hey," Clint whispered. "You're with me now. No more stress, ok? I want to see your smiling face, not a frown. You've got to be careful! Cooties and gazorkeses will get you!" Marie Claire looked up at Clint, and seeing the laughter in his eyes, she chuckled and was smiling once again. Tears stood at the ready in his friend's eyes, but Clint knew it would be all right. Always being able to cheer Marie Claire up, Clint was glad to see her beautiful smile come back. "What flavor do you think you'd like?"

Marie Claire sat thinking for a little while. On her shopping spree, with the five hundred dollars Clint handed her to "window shop," Clint enabled her to buy more at one time than she'd ever been able to do. She tried on different perfumes yesterday, and she found a vanilla scent that smelled Heavenly. She bought a bath/shower set, and two bottles of Elizabeth Maxim's Vanilla Flower. She wore it now. She planned to buy some vanilla room spray as soon as she could.

"I want a French Vanilla latte. I want it to be the vanilliest, biggest, and best one they can make, and I want chocolate dribbled over whipped cream on the top." She smiled at Clint.

When their waitress arrived at their table, Clint ordered two extra large, triple shot vanilla lattes. "My girl wants the biggest, vanilliest coffee you can make!" He tipped the waitress five dollars, and then as she turned to walk away, he took Marie Claire's hands in his. "I am going to try that myself," he said, rubbing Marie Claire's hands and smiling once more into her eyes.

"Marie Claire, I have something I want to ask you." He, unforeseen by Marie Claire, took a small box out of his pants pocket.

"What? Do you want to stay overnight?" Marie Claire quipped happily, with a smile in her eyes.

Getting down on his knees beside Marie Claire, still holding her left hand, he asked, "Marie Claire, would you do me the honor of being my bride? I'll make you as happy as I can. I'm not wealthy, and not the best looking, but I love you, have loved you ever since the first time you hooked me up with that first woman friend of yours. The boys love you and you love them. I can't ask for anything more. What do you say?"

"Oh, Clint. I really don't think I want to be married again." Marie Claire swallowed the lump stuck in her throat. She saw hurt, and then something indecipherable in his eyes.

"Well, you either marry me or live with me. I will not live without you!" Clint said this, dead seriousness in his tone. He sat back in his seat, sipping the coffee that the waitress brought over, staring at Marie Claire.

Marie Claire sat still, looking at her friend for the first time in a long time, really seeing the man. Clint's eyes were hazel, hair dark brown, dimples when he smiled, and perfect, even teeth. His chest was large, his shoulders broad, his hips were skinny with a small tight derriere, and his legs were long and lean. Clint stood six feet tall. With the white jeans and black western style shirt he now wore, he looked like a cowboy. He resembled Robin Williams, actually. Marie Claire knew his heart and loved his soul. She never had heard him say, or see him do anything to hurt another human being. He went to church every Sunday. He really cared for his friends, her in particular.

"Yes, Handsome, I will marry you," She finally made up her mind that she needed to take another chance at love. She couldn't see living single the rest of her life. She needed to be needed, and Clint and the boys needed her. Most of all, they loved her.

"I've only been divorced for a little over a few weeks. Is that ok?" Marie Claire didn't want to be in any trouble. She didn't know how divorce worked, what was or wasn't allowed, and whether, being in Seattle, she would run into Francis Kingman.

"It is proper to wait a year, but I can't wait that long, Sunshine. We've done nothing wrong, and we love each other, don't we?" Clint questioned.

"Yes, I guess we do!" She picked her coffee cup up and saluted her fiancé.

"Well," Clint breathed, "I guess it's time for this, now." He knelt beside her chair once again. He didn't know the waitress had been watching them the whole time or he would have been embarrassed.

Out of the box sitting on his chair, Clint took a one-carat solitaire diamond ring. Surrounding the solitaire was a two-piece engagement ring filled with diamonds and rubies. The wedding ring would eventually be welded between the two. Flabbergasted, Marie Claire gasped. She wore a simple solitaire ring the first time. This one was nice enough to belong to a queen.

"I love it!" Marie Claire squealed.

"Well, I'm glad. Now, how about next weekend we go to Las Vegas and get married at the Excalibur. There is a real pastor there; no trashy, new age stuff. I'll contact him and let him know we want to have a service pertaining to friendship, honor, and lasting love. No obeisance stuff, ok? I feel you've had enough and shouldn't be asked to act, look like, or do everything I say. We'll be equals, buddies, best friends, and I would never do anything to hurt you."

Marie Claire appreciated Clint's thoughts. She knew she would have nothing serious to worry about with him around. She vowed to honor and obey him, but it was nice knowing he wouldn't be like

Francis. Marie Claire knew she didn't want to wear the pants in the family, even if she did like horses and wore jeans a lot, but this was different. She wanted, looked forward to, a real man leading his family and Clint seemed the perfect one for her. She would *take good care of this guy*, she vowed in her head and heart.

The waitress overheard most of their conversation, in between late night customers, and tears now streamed from her eyes. She went to the back to clean her face. Happy for the couple, she thought, *I hope I can find a man like that someday.*

*   *   *   *

Clint dropped Marie Claire off at her apartment. It was nearing midnight, and they were both tired. Marie Claire lay in her bed admiring her engagement ring. She woke up the next morning with the light still on. She turned it off and lay there a little while longer, thinking about the prior evening. She thought about Clint's job and, thankful that his boss let him go for the week, she would have to ask exactly what he did at the plane factory.

An hour later, after a shower and dressing in a lavender pantsuit, Marie Claire went out to answer the door. She planned on some more shopping today, as she wanted to get a door chime and a floor lamp.

Before Clint got there, Marie Claire tried to call her grandparent's house. An automated voice told her that the number was no longer in service. She didn't know what else to do. She took out her mother's address book that she kept in her box of important papers, hoping to update it for her mother, but Cecelia had left before Marie Claire could get that deed finished.

Going through it, page by page, she finally came across Jeanette's number. Marie Claire hadn't seen Jeanette since leaving home the last time, and she felt trepidation at having to talk to her sister now. The need to find out what happened to her grandparents was important to Marie Claire, so she felt she needed to make a call to her sister. She couldn't imagine them moving, but maybe the farm got to be too much for them.

Marie Claire let the phone ring forever before her sister's answering machine finally picked up.

"You have reached the home of Jeanette McCory. I am not able to answer the phone at this time. Please leave a message," Marie Claire heard in Jeanette's happy sounding voice.

"Jeanette, please give me a call. This is Marie Claire."

She left her number and hung up, hoping her sister would call her back tonight.

*   *   *   *

"Good morning, Sunshine," Clint smilingly greeted her. "Did you sleep well? You look very nice." He wrapped her in his arms and kissed her deeply. For the rest of the day, Marie Claire would not remember trying her grandparent's number, and leaving a message for Jeanette. Her thoughts were solely on Clint. She wanted him, needed him, but she would wait until they were married to have more than a good friendship with him. She felt her body was God's temple, and she vowed not to defile herself in that way until she became one with her husband.

Giggling, Marie Claire wrapped Clint in a bear hug. Taking a step back, she said, "I am extremely fine today. I need to go do a little shopping. Would you like to go with me?"

"Sure," Clint answered, "I'll go with you."

At that moment Julia and Sam appeared. "You two look very happy this morning," Julia laughingly replied. "What happened last night? Do you care to share?" At that moment, she saw the ring on Marie Claire's left hand. "Oh, congratulations! Sam, look, they're engaged!" Julia cried with happiness.

"Well," Marie Claire answered, hugging Julia, "do you want to go out to breakfast with us and we'll tell you the news."

"Sure we'll go with you," Sam replied, hugging the younger couple. "We have a little shopping to do. Would you like to go with us?"

"Marie Claire has a couple things she wants to pick up," Clint replied.

"Julia wants to pick up a lamp," Sam said. "Do you mind going to a furniture store with us?"

"Just what we need!" Marie Claire laughed. "Who is driving?"

So began the day. The sky shone bright blue, with a few wisps of clouds. The temperature hung in the low sixties, and it was with easy camaraderie that the two couples spent the day shopping, going to the aquarium and waterfront, and out to dinner that evening.

*   *   *   *

After getting back from their busy day, the couples dropped their items off in their rooms at the apartment complex. They then walked the full block to the seafood restaurant that overlooked Puget Sound, the tide flats of Tacoma, Vashon Island, and the Olympic Peninsula beyond. After the waiter seated them at the large picture window, Sam ordered them each a margarita and steamed clams for the appetizer.

They sat there for a short while just talking. Sam, not knowing Clint as well as Julia did, asked him about himself. "What brought you to Seattle, Clint?" Sam queried.

"Well, my dad's name was Jonathan and mom's name was Hannah. They were immigrants. Dad came from Bjorn, Germany, and mom came from Worms, Russia. They homesteaded in North Dakota, farmed some land, and raised my sister Joan, brother Mike, and myself." Clint took a sip of his drink. "Seattle is a far cry from North Dakota," Clint told them. "It gets forty below in winter and it's hot and muggy in the summer."

"Do you think you'll ever go back, Clint?" Julia asked.

"No way!" The answer came out curter than Clint intended. "I can't take the cold and heat there. I graduated high school in 1965, turned around and joined the air force, and four years later I got out of the service and married my ex-wife, Lee, on the rebound from another relationship that didn't work out. I hope my boys are smarter than I was back then! I knew within the first week that I'd made a mistake. She couldn't cook, wouldn't clean house, and read books or shopped all day long."

"Sorry about your experiences that way. My Aunt Lois lived her life similar to that, and she ended up alone. My uncle couldn't take it anymore and walked out." To change the subject, Sam asked, "How's work going for you, Clint? Who do you work for?"

"I worked for Boeing for a few years after I left the air force, and then I met Joseph Kirkpatrick. He was a designer at Boeing, but quit to start his own business, Aerdinae Aircraft Company. He inherited it from an uncle, thus the name. Patrick didn't want the hassle of the nomenclature and paperwork change so he kept it. I've been working with him for nearly twenty years. He's a good guy and we keep pretty busy." Clint answered. "I'm a tool designer and aircraft parts repairman. I'm also a toolmaker and Jack-Of-All-Trades. I learned a lot at Boeing, but Patrick really took me in as an apprentice. He taught me everything he knew, knows, and we have a good partnership. You'll get to meet him. He and his wife, Maggie, will be at the wedding, too."

So the night went on, casual conversation, laughter, smiles, and each one knowing that they were a part of a much bigger picture. Marie Claire stayed quiet, not speaking much, but she had enjoyed the whole day just soaking up the casual conversation. It was now eleven, the moon shone bright and full, and Clint and the Bascolms bid her good-night at her door. Marie Claire lay in bed for another hour and she finally picked up the phone.

Ring, ring, ring.... "Hello," a surprised Clint spoke into the receiver.

Marie Claire said hello, rather demurely, hoping Clint wouldn't mind such a late call. She laughed at Clint's guffaw at the other end.

"Sunshine! Didn't I just drop you off? We did just spend the whole day and half the night together!"

"Yes, I did just spend a wonderful day with you, but I thought you were missing me so I called." Marie Claire felt lightness of heart each time she teased with Clint. Teasing coming from her was new, and she hoped no one minded.

"I think you're a nut, but I love ya anyway!" Clint laughingly told her.

"I just wanted to say goodnight again, and tell you I'm excited! Just two more days and I'll be yours!" Marie Claire sounded happy as never before, and Clint said a silent prayer of thanksgiving because he could hear that happiness in her voice.

"Oh, Sunshine, I know what you mean, but you belong to God - and always will – not to me." Clint kept his mind God centered, and he wanted Marie Claire to know that she needed to keep Him in first place, not anyone else, including himself.

"I know. Thanks for the reminder. I just meant that I can hardly wait to marry you! I never thought there was anyone as nice as you left in the world."

They said their final goodnights and Clint and Marie Claire, thoughts of each other on their minds, drifted into an easy, restful sleep.

Chapter Twenty

IT WAS Monday, and Marie Claire, with a lot to think about the rest of the week, kept herself busy as Clint worked and she had a lot of time on her hands. Sam and Julia attended to personal things today, and that left Marie Claire with a whole day to herself to think.

She sat for a couple of hours pondering Clint's proposal. Knowing Clint to be a good man, she still worried about what God thought of her right now. Marie Claire got up from her chair and meandered to the coffee maker. She filled her cup for the third time, and then wandered around the apartment.

I know Clint is a Godly man, but Francis supposedly was too. I can't ever forget what he did to me. I should be shot for letting him control me as he did. Marie Claire tormented herself over the life she led before, and she remained in counseling. She started two weeks ago, with sessions twice weekly. She tried to remember what her counselor, Tami, told her about men like Francis Kingman.

Marie Claire sat down and called Clint's pastor and two of his good friends that she met so long ago. "Hi, Pastor Frank. This is Marie Claire. Clint asked me to marry him and I said yes. I'm calling because I have some questions."

"Congratulations, Marie Claire. I'm so glad you took Clint up on his proposal. He's a very good man. What can I help you with?"

"Well, Clint called one night to check on Mom and me, and he was having a beer with the boys. He said he let them have just a little bit for taste. I want to know if he's an alcoholic. I grew up in that atmosphere and want nothing to do with alcohol."

Pastor Frank Star laughed. "I'm sorry, Marie Claire. Clint is not an alcoholic. Sometimes the men's group gets together to watch a game or something, and they drink beer. There is nothing wrong with that. Jesus said, *do not be gluttons and drunkards.* You don't have to worry about Clint. He's not like that at all."

Marie Claire giggled herself. "I didn't think so, but I wanted to be sure. Thanks for your help."

"Do I have to wait to be asked to officiate a marriage?" The pastor had a smile in his voice. Marie Claire could hear it.

"No. Clint wants to go to Vegas to be married. He said he'd had one huge wedding when he married Lee. He didn't want another one. Don't worry. He said he found a real minister there, not some new age person. It will be on Saturday next weekend. Can you and your wife come?"

"Oh, no we can't. I'm sorry but we have a wedding to officiate that day here at the church. Clint knows the couple, Jim Saunders and Grace Frieze."

"I'll let him know," Marie Claire told the pastor. "I just wanted to be sure to give you an invitation."

Marie Claire and Pastor Frank hung up. Marie Claire called Clint's two friends and after being reassured she wasn't marrying a drunkard or a wife and child beater, she relaxed and baked cookies and bread the rest of the day.

At five o'clock, Clint called.

"Hi, Sunshine. How did your day go?"

"It was great. Are you off work? Do you want to come over for dinner? I'm making steak and I baked bread and cookies today."

"Yes, and I will be there in fifteen minutes. See you soon!" Clint hung up.

That is one thing that puzzles me, Marie Claire thought to herself. *Clint is a man of few words. He says what he wants and then he hangs up.* Thinking about her fiancée, Marie Claire giggled to herself. *Life is going to be interesting from now on! I really do love that man. I can't understand my friends giving up on him after the first and second dates. Oh well, their loss!*

*   *   *   *

Marie Claire and Clint sat down to dinner at six that night. Marie Claire had a lot on her chest that she needed to get out. The first regarded her phone calls. After praying over their meal, Marie Claire started talking to Clint.

"I don't want any secrets between us, Clint. I have to confess that I called your pastor and Mark and Steven. I wanted to make sure I was marrying the right guy. Remember when you called in north Idaho to check on Mom and me, and you were having a beer with the boys? Well, I felt that kids shouldn't be drinking alcohol, and I got worried. So, you passed my questions with flying colors. I found out you're not an alcoholic and that Lee left you because she found someone of her own size and mentality. I know you don't beat your boys. You yell a lot at them when they've done something stupid, but then you spoil them, but you love them and they love you. So, I'm happy being your wife."

Listening quietly while Marie Claire quickly told him her spiel, Clint had a slight smile on his face.

"I'm glad you checked me out. You didn't need to do that, but I understand your concern." Clint then bowed his head and looked back up. An understanding smile had replaced the earlier one, and Marie Claire knew Clint needed to tell her something bad, as his face took on a bitter look.

"My dad was an alcoholic. That's what killed him when I was twelve. Mom had a rough life. She sold eggs and milk to feed us. I often had to wait in the car while my dad drank in the bar with his buddies. Mom cooked three meals a day for us, after having to plow the fields and do my dad's bidding all day long. He was lazy. My two brothers and sister had to work hard too. I know why you worry about marrying me. I thought, after hearing of your life when you were a kid, that you'd have questions. I don't like to talk about my life, but I know you understand."

Clint didn't look sad or mad, but he sat there letting everything out that he'd been holding inside for so long. "I could never talk to Lee like I can talk to you. She always acted like a child, was childish, and she never cared about my day at work or understood what I do so I could bring a paycheck in every week. She just acted prissy, getting her nails and hair done continually, and let the boys run wild or left them with her parents. Her folks pretty much raised the boys when I was at work. They didn't mind, but Lee and I sure fought over it all the time. She eventually fell in love with Martin's scoutmaster and left us high and dry. I nearly died when she left, not knowing what to do, how to care for the boys and work too. I went into the hospital. I thought I was having a heart attack. Why didn't you come see me?" Clint had a teary look to his eyes.

"I cared for you, maybe too much, and I knew Francis wouldn't have liked it. I asked him once if we shouldn't go to see you. He told me he'd go, but that it wasn't good for me to go too. So, I stayed home."

Marie Claire reached across the table, squeezed Clint's hand, and then stood to get him a refill of coffee after snagging his near empty cup from his hand. Clint watched her walk across the kitchen to the coffee maker. He admired her beauty, her grace, and the sway of her hips. She had the longest legs of any female he'd come across. She turned and he caught the gleam of love and compassion in her brown eyes. Clint felt lost, so infatuated and in love with Marie Claire, and he held her gaze as she walked back to the table and sat down.

Picking his story up from there, Clint started his recitation again. "After Dad died, Mom and I moved to Jamestown, North Dakota. We lived in a smaller house there, right in the city, close to her work and my school. "

Marie Claire handed Clint his refilled cup. "Why did you guys leave the farm?"

"Well, Joan left when she was sixteen to get married. She married a very nice man and gave birth to one son. She's ten years older than I am. My brother, Mike, six years older than I am, left when he turned seventeen to join the army. Gus, two years older than I, still lives in North Dakota with his wife, Patty. Mom couldn't handle the farm herself. We owned over one hundred acres. She sold the cows and livestock, chickens, and the horses and mules. We moved to town."

"Was your dad mean to your mom?" Marie Claire asked tentatively. Unsure if she should have asked that, but she wondered if Clint grew up abused as she had been.

"Not that us kids saw. He may have been behind closed doors, but if so, us kids never heard or saw anything."

Marie Claire, glad of that mercy, just sat there, listening, and periodically glanced up at Clint with an understanding nod of her head.

"What happened to Mike? Is he the brother whose funeral you went to a few a few years ago in North Dakota?" Marie Claire remembered Francis saying something about a funeral Clint went to when they first moved to Idaho.

"Yes. He was an alcoholic like our dad. He had a bunch of kids. I've never met any of them, though. That's why I never wanted to drink. I didn't want to be like my dad. I've warned the boys not to become alcoholics either. It would be so easy for them to get caught up in that lifestyle."

Marie Claire had some more to talk about and they moved to the living room. Marie Claire sat in her rocker while Clint took a seat in the recliner.

"Our lives are so similar. Do you think that's why we are so attuned to each other?" Marie Claire looked into Clint's eyes.

"Probably," was all Clint said as he nodded his head, taking a sip of his still hot coffee.

"Clint," Marie Claire placed her coffee cup on the end table then leaned forward, placing her elbows on her knees, cupping her face in her hands as she looked up at Clint. "I believe Jesus is the Christ, the Son of the Only Living God, and I have accepted, and do accept Him, as my personal Lord and Savior. Do you feel the same? I have never been perfect, but I know that I am forgiven. I have to know your thoughts, too. It's important to me that we're on the same page. Francis told me that he became a Christian when his dad was still alive, but he didn't live the life he should have. How did you come to know the Lord?" Marie Claire had, months earlier, shared her story with Clint of when she stole some socks and ended up accepting Christ's redeeming love.

"I didn't grow up in church, but Mom took me to the Lutheran church she attended periodically. I was baptized there, but I didn't know the Lord until I went to services with Lee and her folks. Pastor Star brought me the Word, and I accepted Christ in that church. I became an elder for many years, and I never lost that position, even after Lee left me. Pastor and the other elders knew me and knew that wasn't my fault. I, too, believe as you do. Remember me asking you a few times, where's your faith?"

Marie Claire teared up at the remembrances of those hard times when she felt God deserted her. She remembered calling Clint and Lee and asking what was wrong with her because of the financial troubles that plagued her. It happened after Francis left her with her mother.

With a nod of her head, Marie Claire assented that she did indeed remember. She knew at that moment just how much she needed this wonderful man in her life. No one, ever, aside from her grandfather, talked to her calmly and lovingly like Clint did to her. She would be all his from now on. They sat there a moment looking across the chasm into each other's eyes.

Saying about all they could for the time being, Clint put hands on his knees and stood up, as he said to Marie Claire, "I better get going. I have to be up early in the morning for work. I promised Joseph I'd work longer hours to make up for the time missed while we go on a honeymoon. We'll talk about that later!" Clint smiled at Marie Claire as he stood, stretched, and reached out to hold his fiancé to himself.

He kissed her lingeringly before she pushed him away. There were feelings she had no right to feel. She knew that in a few more days it wouldn't matter, but for now, she needed to let him go home.

"Before you leave, Handsome, I do apologize for checking you out with your friends and pastor. I just needed to be sure, you know?" Very honest in her amends, Marie Claire looked a little sad.

Clint tipped her chin up with his fingers. "Hey, that's fine. I do understand. Better to be safe than sorry, in any situation. No offense taken, ok?" Clint again kissed her. "No one is perfect, except Christ Jesus, but as Christians, we are forgiven. Isn't that something? God's Grace is wonderfully awesome." He then turned on his heel and walked out the door.

"Yes, It is," Marie Claire answered. She smiled as Clint took his leave. *Thank you, Father God, for bringing Clint into my life. Please, please be with us, with me.*

Chapter Twenty-One

THE NEXT morning dawned overcast. The weatherman predicted drizzle for the afternoon and all through the weekend, but the newly engaged couple couldn't care less. Clint called his sister earlier in the morning to give her the news, and then he told the boys that Marie Claire accepted his proposal.

"Hey, dad, that's great!" Martin and Jon, both ecstatic, congratulated Clint. Marie Claire loved them, they knew that, and their pleasure knew no bounds.

"Let me talk to your aunt again," he said, after speaking with Jon for ten minutes.

That young man had plans of his own now that he turned eighteen. He told his father that he wanted to work at a construction company where some friends of his got employment. He thought it would be great to have his brother stay with him. "I'll make sure he gets off to school every morning, Dad. He'll graduate next year, and then he can get on board with me at the company. Victoria, the boss, and her husband are growing their construction business. They'll need another person by the time Martin graduates. Would you mind, Dad?" Knowing how truthful and dependable Jon was, Clint acquiesced.

Clint didn't see a problem with that. Jon was a good son, they both were, and he knew he could trust that Martin would finish school. He'd tell Ted to take Jon car shopping this week. The boy deserved it now that he was going to be working.

Clint later talked it over with his sister, Joan, and she thought it a good opportunity for Jon to have some responsibility 'for when he has kids of his own'. Clint chuckled at that, knowing his sister and brother-in-law, as close as they felt to them, would be checking in with the boys, as would he and Marie Claire. She also told Clint that Jon wanted a Ford Mustang. "Come get the money from me, Joan."

"Okay, rich brother of mine!" Joan laughed with Clint.

*   *   *   *

Saturday arrived, the light breakfast quickly finished, and an hour later, the wedding party was seated on the plane and soon in the air. Two hours later Clint and Marie Claire were ensconced in an elaborate medieval room resembling a castle. They were met at the door by a matron who showed them to their hotel room. A concierge led Clint to a room off the church office, where his clothes were laid out for him on a velvet-covered divan. Ted and Sam waited there in the room to help him.

They were dressing for their marriage service. The matron helped Marie Claire as she donned an off white, puff-sleeved, mid calf length dress. Tiny red roses and green leaves adorned around the neckline and hemline. The front sported a heart shaped design that showed just a touch of cleavage. Julia, a long ago stylist, had fashioned Marie Claire's silky black hair in a chignon, with a spray of gardenia above the right ear. Julia placed the veil, made of white lace and edged in the same red roses, on Marie Claire's coif. Marie Claire's short heels matched the color of her dress.

Clint wore black dress pants that fit tightly and flared somewhat at the lower legs. He wore a white western cut dress shirt with an eagle bolo tie made of gold and black leather. He wore no hat, but his feet were adorned with shiny black leather boots made of alligator skin. They were a handsome pair in their simple yet stunning attire.

Julia and Marie Claire's cousins, Charlene and her daughter Lisa Marie, escorted Marie Claire downstairs, and at the door to the chapel the boys greeted them, as well as the Danforths and another couple, who were Joseph and Maggie Kirkpatrick. They knew who Marie Claire was right away, and the boys introduced them. Afterwards, they left Marie Claire standing at the door of the sanctuary as everyone took their seats. A smiling Marie Claire knew why

Clint admired his boss so much. She felt cared for by them, and she only just met them!

Breath abated as the organist played the wedding song and everyone stared admiringly at the beautiful young woman who sauntered down the aisle in her wedding finery. Marie Claire's eyes shone with love as she stared into Clint's eyes while she strolled down the aisle. Only once did her gaze falter to look at Julia and Sam. She winked at them, then again locked her gaze with her soon to be husband. She stepped up to the dais and turned slightly toward Clint.

I have never seen anyone as lovely or as poised as Marie Claire. Father God, keep her safe, always. Let me love her forever and ever. Thank you that she loves the boys and me so much.

The music stopped and Chaplain Bishop took his stance between the couple. He read from the Bible how two people become one, and then the vows exchanged, a kiss ensued, and finally the chaplain introduced the couple as Mr. and Mrs. Clint Anthony Bellham. Everyone cheered. Julia and Joan cried while their husband's enfolded them in their arms. Charlene, Lisa, and the Kirkpatrick's smiled and Joseph handed something to Clint before shaking his hand then hugging his shoulders. He came to Marie Claire and asked for a kiss. She obliged. Clint, proud of his beautiful new bride, told Sam and Ted, "I will take very good care of Marie Claire. She's beautiful inside and out and God blessed her with such a big heart. I love her deeply."

Jon and Martin hugged both Marie Claire and Clint. Jon handed a package to Marie Claire. She opened it, and inside was an antiqued silver frame holding a tinted mirror with a poem on it. Essentially it said that Jon loved her since he met her, loved her now, and would love her always.

Martin too gave a package to Marie Claire. She opened it and she held an antiqued gold frame holding a brown tinted mirror. A poem about friendship was written there on the glass. Tears of joy came to the bride's eyes, and she enfolded each young man in her arms and gave him a bear hug and a kiss.

Three pairs of eyes, staring into each other, glistened with tears of happiness and love. Clint's heart swelled with pride. "What a beautiful family I have," he spoke quietly. The people standing around him smiled their pleasure and agreement.

The church quieted and Marie Claire threw her bouquet and Lisa caught it! Charlene smiled at her daughter and said something in Lisa's ear. Lisa Marie laughed her tinkling laugh and then she and her mother came over to wish the newly married couple well. "I love you, Marie Claire," Charlene told her cousin. "Is it ok if I let Jeanette know you got married? She keeps up with you through me and my dad, you know."

"Sure, that's fine. Tell her I wish her well." Marie Claire told her cousin.

Back at their hotel room, Clint took Marie Claire's veil off her head. He kissed her deeply and lovingly. "Shall we see what's in this envelope Joseph gave me?" Undoing the seal, Clint handed Marie Claire tickets while he read the brief note. Marie Claire looked at Clint, and he looked flummoxed, for in their hands they held a month's honeymoon for everywhere in the world.

The handwritten note read,

Our dear Clint,

You have yourself a prize there, son. Take good care of your new bride. Here's permission for a month off and two tickets that will take you to Hawaii, Rome, Italy, Paris, and Switzerland. Have a great time, and don't forget to send us postcards!

Joe and Maggie.

PS: Just kidding. Forget us for a while! Congratulations. We love you!

They all ate lunch together, and then the Danforths gathered the boys as they were going back to Seattle. Ted started work again on Monday and the boys had school. The Bascolms planned to stay in Vegas for a few more days. Joseph and Maggie were flying to San Francisco for a week, and Marie Claire gave Charlene and Lisa a few hundred to spend a few days and stay in their hotel room, which Clint took care of the cost.

The hotel concierge told them where they could buy luggage because, of course, they wanted to leave immediately and the flight was at six in the morning. Clint and Marie Claire walked a block to the

Everything Travel shop and bought two large bags and two smaller bags. Of course, Marie Claire needed a satchel for her carry-ons. Clint teased her about that.

"Don't you think we have enough luggage now? I suppose we'll be buying out all the stores we visit! We'll have to rent a 767 to get all the stuff home with us!" He watched as Marie Claire stuck her tongue out at him and then giggled. He loved the merriment in her eyes.

Back at their hotel later that afternoon, the couple packed the needed items and then they left the rest of their things for the Bascolms to take back with them. Clint then took Marie Claire down to the casino. She'd never been to one before. She carried ten dollars that she allotted for her gambling foray! Clint got her started and then he went to a different gaming machine than his wife's. He didn't like her chosen game. The hour was late and Clint came back to get Marie Claire. She played at the same slot machine.

"Do you have a nickel? I want to try once more. I haven't won anything," she groused at him teasingly.

"Sure. Here." he handed her the nickel. "That's the way it is most of the time. You lose and the establishment wins." He smiled at her, but it was near dinner time and his stomach told him it was getting hungry. He saw Joe and Maggie across the room and started their way. Suddenly, after taking about ten steps, he heard a loud calamity behind him. He turned and Marie Claire's machine flashed changing colors, clanging bells, and dropping coin sounds clashed loudly. He quickly went back to Marie Claire's machine as the ticker tape slid out of the contraption.

"What does this mean?" Marie Claire asked Clint, Joseph and Maggie now standing beside him.

"It means you won some money." Clint told her. He took her hand and led her over to the cage that held the cashier's office, Maggie and Joseph trailing behind, juice drinks in hand.

"My husband said I won something," Marie Claire tentatively said, handing the paper over to the cashier.

"You sure did, my dear. You have won $1,323.00 to be exact!" The cashier smiled at the young woman, noticing her still donned wedding dress but minus the veil and heels. He handed the cash to Marie Claire in multiple denominations. "Enjoy spending it, and congratulations," he said, his gaze sliding from Clint to Marie Claire.

"I will! We're going on a trip around the world," Marie Claire excitedly told the man, squealing her excitement.

The next morning, Clint and Marie Claire thanked the Kirkpatrick's for their generosity. They then said goodbye to everyone, excitement on the wind, and blowing kisses and with one last wave they entered the plane and finally flew into the sunrise.

Clint never did get his nickel back.

Chapter Twenty-Two

CLINT AND Marie Claire enjoyed every day of their honeymoon. Now back in Seattle, tired and needing a rest, they slept late into the next morning. They had gotten back yesterday, but still exhausted, they opted to skip church this morning. They decided to spend the day visiting with the Bascolms and the Danforths. They bought T-shirts and books for the boys from all the places they visited, and travel books for everyone else. Marie Claire was just about to call the Bascolms when her phone rang at eleven that morning.

"Good morning," Marie Claire cheerfully greeted her caller.

"Marie Claire," the caller said.

"Yes, who is this, please?"

"This is Jeanette, your sister."

Marie Claire had forgotten all about Jeanette. Dumbfounded to hear her half sister on the other end of the line, her insides churned, and her heart seemed to harden suddenly. "What are you calling for? What do you want?" Marie Claire sounded hard, angry wasn't quite the word, but her voice came out of her mouth in anything but the usual calm, soft voice others heard.

"Charlene called the night of your wedding. She told me you got married to a wonderful man. She gave me your number, but you'd also left me a message to call you. Don't you remember?" Jeanette sounded as though sorry she'd called, but she went on. "It's been years, really, and I want to say how sorry I am about how the family treated you. I don't know if you will ever forgive me, us, but, please, I need you. I need my sister." She sounded very sorry, and suddenly Marie Claire heard Jeanette crying.

Not hearing anything for what seemed like minutes, "Marie Claire, are you there? Please, talk to me!" Jeanette, still crying, realized that maybe her sister was just displeased. "Well, I just wanted to tell you how sorry I am. I guess I better hang up." Jeanette sounded calmer, still sad, but resigned to the circumstances.

"No, wait, it's ok. I just, I didn't know what to say. I'm surprised you called me. Yes, I had forgotten I'd left you a message." Marie Claire told her sister.

Marie Claire recalled Jeanette's bright blue eyes, just like their mother's. Her perfectly set and very white teeth came to Marie Claire's mind, at least this is how she remembered her sister from so long ago, nearly thirty years in fact since Marie Claire last saw her sister. Jeanette's hair had once been dark brown, almost black like Marie Claire's own, but where Marie Claire's hair was thick and straight, Jeanette's came out naturally curly, again just like their mother's. Jeanette stood five foot five and her physique resembled her dad's, very skinny.

Realizing Jeanette just said something important, she asked her sister to repeat herself. "I didn't understand that, Jeanette. Would you repeat it, please?"

"I said I'm sorry about what happened to the Bascolms. There was a plane crash a few weeks ago over California. Charlene called me and said that that the plane that carried everyone flying back home from your wedding collided with another plane; a Cessna that took off and did not fly the right way. They crashed in the northern mountains of California. No one survived." Jeanette let this sink in, but there was more to be said.

Clint took over the phone. He heard the strangled gasp Marie Claire emitted. He could see how distraught his wife became, and he tried to send her to their room, but she just clung to him. "This is Marie Claire's husband, Clint. Can I help you?" Clint asked Jeanette, while at the same time hugging a catatonic Marie Claire to his bosom.

Jeanette recalled the account of the plane crash again for Clint's benefit, and then she told him, "I don't know what happened, but Charlene was in the hotel room when someone killed her and apparently took off with Lisa Marie. It must have happened just after she spoke with me on the phone."

"How did you find this out?" Clint asked her.

They found my phone number by Charlene's bed table, and being the last one she called, according to the phone system, they called me and when they found out I was Charlene's cousin, they told me at the hotel that you'd let Charlene and Lisa have your room. They found her that Monday morning when the crew went in to clean. They knew her daughter was staying there, too, but they didn't find her. They didn't know what to do about Lisa and Charlene's belongings so I asked them to let the police handle it. The police called me later and they're sending the bags to you. I didn't have your number, and didn't want to bother you on your honeymoon anyway, so I waited. I did the best I could." Jeanette sounded worried, and tried to staunch her crying spells, but she'd loved Charlene too.

"I have to ask you to call back this evening. Let me talk to Marie Claire. She's pretty upset. The Bascolms were her family and they were close, very close. Is that ok with you?" Clint sounded sick to his stomach, deeply saddened by the circumstances and that his lovely wife had to go through more heartache.

"Sure, um, I forgot your name." Jeanette squeaked out.

"I'm Clint Bellham. Call around five or six, ok?" Clint hung up as his wife fainted in his arms.

*   *   *   *

Clint picked Marie Claire up and laid her lithe body on the sofa. He ran to get a cool washcloth and he put this on her forehead. In a short time, she came to.

"What happened? Are they really gone?" Marie Claire again bawled her eyes out.

"Honey," Clint started, "there's more to it."

Marie Claire looked into her husband's tormented eyes. She knew worse news was to come. She just drew on some inner strength and sat there as Clint told her the rest of it.

"We've got to find Lisa. We have to search for her, Clint. She's only twelve! How could she be missing?" Heartbroken Marie Claire with so much, too much to think of, to do, felt overwhelmed.

She and Clint talked and devised a plan on what to do next. "Sunshine, let me take care of some business, ok. You go take a rest for as long as you can. I am so very sorry for the losses, Sweetheart.

So sorry." With a kiss on the top of her head and a push towards the bedroom, Clint finally sent Marie Claire to their room.

He called the airlines to check on the status of the dead passengers. Most had been buried already, but those like the Bascolms, waiting for family to claim them, waited at the morgue. Clint, knowing of a very nice funeral home on the shores of Lake Washington, called them and made funeral arrangements. He called Troy Waldon, the Bascolm's lawyer, and talked to him. He called the Seattle Police Department next.

"We are directing all calls to Dean Manning who is with the Washington FBI. He's collaborating with Robert Zwieback, the Seattle prosecutor. They will work directly with the FAA on this case."

Clint called and spoke with Dean. The FBI, Marie Claire, and Clint would meet at the prosecutor's office the next morning. Two hours later, Clint woke Marie Claire up to speak with Jeanette on the phone.

"Hi, Jeanette." Marie Claire sadly stated.

"Hi, sis. How are you doing? Can I do anything to help?"

Marie Claire, still deeply upset by everything, took a deep breath before speaking, but it didn't assuage the guilt, the pain, the anger that thinking of Jeanette invoked. She took it out on Jeanette. "I put up with a lot in that house growing up. I married someone I never wanted to marry, should never have married, but now here I am. He and I are divorced, you probably know that. I couldn't take the beatings and heartache anymore. But you people never did come to Idaho to see what was going on. You never saw the home I gave your mother. How I took her off the streets and gave her a nice, safe place to live. Your father never saved money. I partially blamed her. She needed a place to live and money in her pocket after he died, but she never looked ahead either." On a roll, Marie Claire just kept venting.

"You just judged me and let Mom leave me to end up begging again. It wasn't that she left; it was the way she took off. She let you know she wanted to leave me, and you helped her. I never knew why she needed to go like that. Well, it's done. I want to forget it." Standing rigid, Marie Claire, in an adamant voice, let her sister know that this conversation just ended.

"I am meeting with the prosecutor tomorrow morning. You can

come or not, it's up to you. Charlene was your cousin, too." Marie
Claire stated, not unkindly.

"Marie Claire, Charlene was more of a sister to you than I ever
was. I'm sorry. I judged you and never did anything to help you. Grant
Junior never helped you either. I understand why you never wanted
anything to do with us. You disowned us for a reason, and I am just
so sorry it had to be that way. You need to know that mom died a few
months ago of cancer. There wasn't anything anyone could do for her.
They found it too late." Jeanette, crying again, gave pause to Marie
Claire who knew that her sister hurt also. Reasoning it out for a moment,
Marie Claire felt her heart quicken to forgive – not through anything
Marie Claire could have done, but through her faith in Christ that let it
be so. She also knew that Jeanette was indeed sincere in her apology.
Marie Claire didn't feel remorse for their mother. Life was what you
made it, and she'd made her peace with God regarding Cecelia McCory.
There wasn't anything else to do but pray about that situation, and
Marie Claire had done a lot of that. The living is what mattered now.
God, I do hope that Lisa Marie is found alive.

Marie Claire finally asked Jeanette, "Does anyone know who
killed Charlene? Is there anything on Lisa Marie?"

"No, nothing that I know of. I haven't really spoken to anyone,
though. I thought since you and Charlene were so close that you'd
want to handle it. I'm working and don't really have time or know
what to do."

"Do you know whatever happened to Leroy, Jeanette?" Marie
Claire asked her sister.

"No, I don't. Leroy's truck was still there at grandma and grandpa's house. He left and never did come back. It was strange!" Jeanette
answered. "Did you know he raped Charlene and messed with me,
too?" Jeanette asked.

"Well, yes and no, but I'm sorry that happened to you." Marie
Claire said, "It's all for the better. I never wanted to see him again
anyway. I knew about Charlene. She shared with me at school a few
days after the incident about what happened. I never did know about
you, but I'm not surprised at all."

"Do you think mom knew?" Again Jeanette queried.

"She said something to me once, but then just said we would live through it. 'Everyone does.' I think he hurt her too." Marie Claire shared the information quietly.

"Why didn't she do something? She was our mother! Shouldn't she have protected you?" Jeanette sounded upset, loudly protesting the injustice of it all.

"Jeanette, I think she was so beaten down by her own stupidity on top of what your dad did to her, that I don't think she cared anymore. I don't want to talk about this anymore. It's in the past. We can't forget, but we have to forgive. Let it rest." An adamant Marie Claire made it clear that she didn't want to talk about the past anymore.

"Grandma and Grandpa are dead now. They were in a car accident a few weeks ago. Apparently, they left everything to you." Jeanette felt sad, sounded sad, Marie Claire could hear it in her voice, and Marie Claire felt her own heart would break all over again for the heart wrenching losses in her life.

"I'm so sorry to hear about them, Jeanette. How do you know they left anything at all to me? I have all but abandoned them through the years. They don't owe me anything. I owe them my life." She started to cry quietly, the kind of heart-rending hurt that said it couldn't hold any more pain lest it break in two.

"Mr. Schultz, the island lawyer, looked me up. He wanted to know how to find you. I told him where you were, in Priest River. I didn't know if you moved or what. He called and left a message yesterday. I've been on vacation for a few weeks and not home, so I got everybody's messages when I got in last night."

At that moment, Marie Claire heard her door chime. "I have to go, Jeanette. Someone's at the door. Talk to you later." Marie Claire hurriedly explained.

"Yes, later. Marie Claire, baby steps, that's what it will take. Just baby steps."

Marie Claire understood her sister's sentiments. She felt a burden lift from her shoulders, and she realized the capability to forgive everything then. She realized that this is what God expected, needed, her to do. He could then finish His work in her. He'd already stilled her mouth to listen to Jeanette when all Marie Claire wanted to do is rail. Progress would be made, and Marie Claire felt better off for it.

They hung up and Marie Claire turned to see a gray suited man standing beside her husband.

"Marie Claire, this is prosecutor Robert Zwieback. My wife," Clint said, pointing towards Marie Claire.

"Hello, Mrs. Bellham. How are you today?" The prosecutor asked congenially. "I'm sorry to have to bother you, but I need to talk to you about your cousin, Charlene Busche."

"It's all right," Marie Claire told prosecutor. "We've got to try to find Lisa. Do you know anything yet?"

"All I can tell you is that Charlene is being sent home so you can lay her to rest. Other than that we have two leads but that's all. There is nothing set in concrete."

The men watched the worried look come over Marie Claire's face but, as she asked Clint and Mr. Zwieback to have a seat, she remained calm.

The prosecutor went on to inform them, "It looks to be a child napping made out to look like a burglary. The money in Charlene's purse was gone, but we found a couple of hundred in her dresser drawer." Marie Claire knew it was some of the money she'd given to her cousin.

Clint had a question. "If Lisa was taken, how come nobody in the hotel saw anything - or did they see something and not realize it?"

"The concierge of the hotel remembered your wedding, and the minister recognized everyone who had been there. The concierge had seen Charlene and Lisa several times that day, once on Sunday, but nothing after that. The time of death happened around five Monday morning. We have a possible truck description, but that's all."

Getting up to take his leave, Robert Zwieback thanked the couple for their time and asked, "Would you meet me in the office at nine to-morrow morning?" He handed Clint a business card.

"We'll be there, detective." Clint saw the man out and went back over to the sofa to sit with his wife.

Chapter Twenty-Three

THE NEXT morning, Jeanette met with Clint and Marie Claire at the King County Prosecutor's Office on Fourth and Vine. Coffee and donuts awaited Robert Zwieback's visitors. Jeanette smiled and hugged Marie Claire. Marie Claire came across cold, despite sensing a fondness coming from Jeanette, who felt that her sister was keeping herself aloof because she disliked Jeanette. That wasn't the case, but it would be worked out later. Marie Claire felt sorry for her cold greeting, but she hurt right now.

"Good morning," Robert greeted them. "This is Detective Dean Manning and his partners, Jeffrey "Jeff" Farthingworth and the head of the Washington FBI, Ben Jackson."

"Nice to meet you," Clint said. "Marie Claire," he stated, but stopped as he saw the look on his wife's face. After a moment, he finally managed to ask, "Do you two know each other?" He'd seen the surprised glow in Marie Claire's eyes and the incredulous look on her face.

"Marie Claire. I always wondered where you disappeared to after college." Jeff said to his onetime friend. "Remember that calf you pulled out of the cow's womb, and how you cried when you saw his little white face and the mother's wonderment at her new little one?" Looking at the others, Jeff continued, "Marie Claire was Dr. Payne's assistant. He was not a nice vet. He was cruel to dogs. He blackened the eye of one when he tried to give it a shot and it balked. He hit it hard in the face. Marie Claire didn't stay with him long." Jeff addressed the rest of the room.

"I remember. I often wondered about you, too, Jeff. It's so good to see you again. How did you go from being Mr. Brown's assistant to being an FBI agent?" Marie Claire spoke, shaking Jeff's hand while holding it a little too long. She saw something akin to pain in her friend's eyes.

"Let's all meet later for coffee or something, shall we? We can play catch-up then!" Jeff commented quietly to Marie Claire.

With a nod of her head, Marie Claire said, "I need to find out what happened to Charlene. Do you have any information yet? I need to find out what happened to Lisa - I don't know anything." Marie Claire started to cry, and Jeanette helped her sit in a chair that the detective had pulled out for her. "Do you have a file I can see? I would like to know what this animal did to my cousin," she demanded in an angry voice, stifling the tears. Marie Claire put her elbows on the table and held her downturned head in her hands.

"Let's discuss some things first and then I can let you see the file," Detective Manning said. "It won't be pretty. She was beaten very badly and yes, she was indeed in the hotel room. It looked like she and Lisa were getting ready to go somewhere or do something early Monday morning. The lock showed evidence of tampering, and yet it also seemed like a key card was used, possibly someone on the hotel staff came to let the person or persons in. The people down there in Vegas are researching everyone who came in contact with the room. The coroner estimated time of death to be around five o'clock Monday morning. The cleaning crew came in late that afternoon, and that's when she was found. The crew leader contacted the hotel manager and told him what she'd seen upstairs. The concierge knew that there should be a 12-year-old with her mother. They searched the entire hotel but could not find Lisa. A few of the employees thought that they saw a white colored truck, possibly a Ford, and we're trying to track down any possible leads." Dean Manning answered Marie Claire in a matter-of-fact manner tempered with compassion.

"Upon the arrival of Sergeant Rodney Pierce of the Navajo County police, evidence proved the lock to be forced, but not enough damage to allow the intruder to get inside the room. Thus, it's believed someone opened the door with a key card and that's when the attack took place. In the proper procedure, Sergeant Pierce walked into the hotel room of Charlene Busche and found her unclothed, lying on her bed.

Underwear, a slip, and a flowered cotton sleeveless dress were found strewn around the floor - all of them torn. There was cutting and bruising of her torso, and they found a red ribbon wrapped around her neck. The tentative verdict is that she died of asphyxiation. Her body is in the Las Vegas morgue where she is being examined for exact cause of death. She was, by the way, raped, and stab wounds were found around her vaginal and anal areas." Detective Manning gave the MO found at the scene.

The file contained crime scene pictures. Marie Claire knew she needed to look or she'd never understand what happened. The pictures, though gruesome, made Marie Claire angry enough at the attacker to kill someone, but she kept her temper abated. She swallowed continually, the lumps that formed in her throat, and her eyes glinted hatred, unseen by the others because of her down bent head. Jeanette cried on Clint's shoulder. Charlene apparently put up quite a fight. Her face took a terrible beating, and her eyes were swollen shut. Her hands showed numerous scratches and cuts, with bruises encircling her wrists. The heart and lungs showed the worst, and Marie Claire sickened at the scene, for there were many knife wounds. She looked like she'd been kicked, stabbed, and beaten for a long time. The last picture showed the ribbon around Charlene's swollen neck, which turned black from dried blood.

Jeff took the pictures from Marie's cold hands and stacked them neatly back into the folder. He set the folder at the end of the table away from the women. *I just cannot understand how anyone can treat a female this way,* he thought. *I hope whoever did this work will be executed. Marie Claire and her sister must be devastated.*

Jeff left the room for a moment, and his secretary went to the refrigerator and handed him four plastic bottles of cold water. She also gave him a pack of soda crackers for them to munch on. Reentering the office, Jeff noticed that the detective and prosecutor spoke quietly together about what comes next. The crime happened in Las Vegas, but the woman and daughter resided in Washington State. They had a lot of territory to cover.

After another twenty minutes, Dean Manning thanked everyone for coming in, and he assured Marie Claire that they would get right on the investigation. She would be kept apprised of anything pertaining to the case.

"Detective Manning, what will happen to Lisa Marie when she is found? Will I be able to adopt her?" Marie Claire hurt inside and couldn't voice her feelings any further. Dean saw the love in the woman's eyes for her cousin, and he knew just how much her heart broke over these developments.

"Detectives, Jeff, Sam and Julia's funeral is next Monday. I would be honored if you would be there with us. They were my best friends, almost like parents, and I loved them very, very much."

"We will be there Marie Claire. Thank you for allowing us the privilege to be your friends also. In answer to your question, I don't see why you can't adopt, if there is no other family to take her in." Dean Manning told the woman, as he reached out to hold both of hers, giving a gentle squeeze of understanding.

"Thank you," was all Marie Claire could say. Tears clogged her throat. Pain showed in her eyes as she turned to leave.

Clint, Marie Claire, and Jeanette walked out of the agency together. The sky reflected a gray overcast, and a light drizzle fell, mirroring the women's pain.

"Clint, can we walk a few blocks and I'll buy you both some coffee?" Though hurting herself, Jeanette knew that she needed to be here for her sister. Charlene and Marie Claire were as close as two people could get without being married, and Jeanette remembered the times when the two used to hang around together. Those times, the only ones that Jeanette remembered ever having seen Marie Claire smile.

They spent the rest of the afternoon walking the streets of Seattle, talking quietly, and only coming in out of the rain when the women became too tired to walk or talk anymore and their bodies and souls seemed ready for rest.

Clint called his boys and otherwise kept busy long into the night. Jeanette went home and Marie Claire slept deeply in their comfortable bed. Clint finally sat and rehearsed in his mind everything he'd heard the women talking about. What a childhood they'd lived through. *At least they were alive*, Clint thought, *when so many children don't live through half of what these kids had to bear. Marie Claire's heart must be saturated with love. Jeanette apologized for their mistreatment of her, and my wife acted ever so gracious.* Clint thought back to this particular conversation. Marie Claire's sister shared a lot today about the abuse she herself, and Charlene and her brother Niles endured. *Only*

God knew how many others had undergone mistreatment at Leroy's hands after Marie Claire left home. Clint felt sick to his stomach at the recitation.

"Jeanette," Marie Claire said to her sister, "it's God that gives us the grace to forgive. I can't forget, anything, but there is nothing we can do to change our life circumstances. We need to each find our own way in this life. I tried to teach you and Grant about Jesus, about love, that He's the only way to salvation. It's through Him that I can get through the messes of my life. I've had counseling and have been able to put most of the past behind me. Without my church and my wonderful friends Charlene, Sam, Julia, and Clint, I wouldn't be here today."

She wanted to help her half sister, so she talked to Jeanette with her heart, lovingly. "You are different. You tend to hold grudges and you don't know our Lord and Savior Jesus Christ. You need to get into counseling like I did. The past will just be a far memory, and you will be happier for it. You need to know that if you believe in something, believe so much that you find release for what bothers your soul. That's what my faith in Christ has done for me. We're not bad people; we've just had no one to bring us up properly. We need to share our thoughts and purge the anger from our systems, and you, Jeanette, need to find peace. Look up," Marie Claire said, tears in her voice, "See what a beautiful day this is. Let's glean some happiness from it, and remember Charlene with love and laughter. She would want that." Thinking for a second, Marie Claire ended with, "we need to pray that we find Lisa Marie soon!"

Clint, with heavy heart and tears in his eyes, prayed for them all as he sat there on the sofa four hours later, loving his wife as never before and appreciating the qualities and fineness that was his Sunshine, Marie Claire.

Chapter Twenty-Four

Today, Tuesday, Marie Claire felt a loss, but she knew she needed to remember the love and laughter, the good memories of her two best friends, friends that should have been her parents. Sam and Julia now lay in the ground beside Lake Washington. The services commenced yesterday morning, and by late afternoon, the visitors and attendees, after bringing food to Marie Claire's apartment, left to carry on their own life among the living. Jeff, Dean Manning, and the Bascolm's lawyer, who had been their best friend for years, attended the service. Jeanette came, of course, with her sister and brother-in-law. Marie Claire held the support she'd needed in the loved ones still around her, but it hit her, hard, knowing she would no longer have Julia and Sam beside her.

The apartment manager refunded Sam's deposit to Marie Claire when he found her in the Bascolm's apartment. "I'm so sorry for your loss, dear. I know they loved you very much." Marie Claire thanked Mr. Zimmerman for his thoughtfulness.

After spending the rest of the day cleaning out their belongings, Marie Claire sat and pondered the past twenty years of her life, the recent events, and where she should go from here. She'd not spoken with her other good friends, Rand and Kara Mallory, in several years. Francis hadn't cared for the couple, though Marie Claire couldn't see what fault he could find in such a warm and loving couple.

They loved her and treated her just as well as Sam and Julia had, and she did pay off a loan they'd cosigned for her sooner than she had been expected to pay back. That was a good thing for her, because she and Kara spent quite a bit of time together when Marie Claire first left the island. Rand knew he could trust Marie Claire and it drew him closer to her and to his own children, knowing there was hope for them, too. At first, she'd babysat their three kids, and later, they'd been there to give her advice when she needed it. She'd depended on Kara to be her surrogate mother and the relationship just grew. She wished then that the Mallorys had been her parents, and not the Kingman's. She thought about Rand and Kara and the comfort they would be. She made a vow to give them a call in the next few days.

Clint went back to work Tuesday morning, after making sure Marie Claire would be ok now that her friend's funeral was over. Aerdinae's new contract assured their building another new airplane, and Clint had to be there to make the tooling. Joseph gave him a directive to hire more people. They had just received several orders for their new concept jet, and they would need more employees to manufacture the parts and assemble the airplane.

I'm going to need at least four more toolmakers and possibly start out with six layup people. In a few weeks I'll figure out where we are and hire the right amount of assemblers, Clint thought to himself while he built the first tool. This plane would be a four-passenger commuter jet. Due to gas prices, the economy, and traffic jams throughout the country, a plumber by the name of Kenneth Hirsh came up with the idea of a jet taxi service. This was to be stationed in San Francisco, California, the first one ever created.

Joseph needed to be in England for the next week or so, speaking with the prime minister of commerce on how many planes they will need to order. Someone on the prime minister's staff saw the write up in Airline America Magazine and got the idea this would be a good thing for the country. Prime Minister Blodgett spoke with Joseph over the phone just last week. *If England purchased the five or six planes they thought they wanted, and after paying all the overhead, Clint and I will be rolling in the dough*, Joseph thought. It would be a good week for the men.

*   *   *   *

Back at her home, Marie Claire received a phone call from Jeff Farthingworth. "Hello, Marie Claire," Jeff greeted her in quiet manner. Marie Claire knew something bad happened. "I have to see you right away. This pertains to your sister also. Is it all right if Dean and I come over in an hour?" Jeff asked her.

"Sure," Marie Claire answered. I'll put some coffee on. It's cold and wet today and you guys would probably enjoy some coffee." Marie Claire rambled, but she became nervous and knew it had to pertain to the murder and abduction. "Clint can't leave work, but I'm sure Jeanette will be here."

They finished their conversation and Marie Claire called Jeanette right away. "Come over right now," Marie Claire anxiously told her sister when she heard the phone pick up.

"Marie Claire, I have to work today!" Jeanette almost yelled. "I can't afford to be taking time off work all the time." It happened to be the first time since their reunion that Marie Claire heard her sister talk like that to her and she didn't like it.

"I'll pay you for the time you miss. Clint can't come home and Jeff and Dean will be here in an hour. They asked that you be present too." Marie Claire forcefully told her.

"Okay," Jeanette huffed. "I need to call in to work first and then I'll be right over."

"Thank you Jeanette," Marie Claire answered.

Mrs. Mulligan gave Jeanette the full day off. *That woman takes her job way too seriously,* Mrs. Mulligan thought. *She needs to lighten up - a lot.* The older woman knew the circumstances of the missing niece and the dead cousin, and she realized that this must be a hard time for the two sisters. Jeanette shared about the recent circumstances of Marie Claire's friends. If what one read in newspapers was to be believed, Jeanette's boss knew that this had to be very trying times for her employee and the sister.

Within the hour, Jeanette, Dean, and Jeff arrived and congregated in Marie Claire's living room. Dean, standing by the fireplace, stated, "They found Lisa Marie early this morning. The coroner concluded that Charlene walked in on a robbery. The Las Vegas office found footprints and fingerprints around the apartment complex and inside Charlene's room. They've matched the fingerprints of one suspect, who is involved in white slavery and is on the ten most wanted list. Apparently when they saw Lisa Marie, they decided to kidnap her. Charlene had to be murdered because she'd seen them and because she put up a fight to save her daughter.

"Where is Lisa Marie," Claire asked.

"She's at the Las Vegas Coroner's office right now. When he's finished, I've given a directive for her to be sent up here for burial. They're done with Charlene and I need to know if you'd like her sent up here also.

"Yes," Marie Claire answered. "I'll make the funeral arrangements today and let you know when that will be."

"Dean, Jeff," Jeanette quietly asked, "what happened to Lisa Marie and where did you find her?"

The two men looked at each other and Dean shoved himself away from the fireplace. Head down, shuffling the carpet with his left foot, and breathing out a heavy sigh, Dean said, "This is going to be hard for you both, but you asked and you deserve an answer. The officers found Lisa Marie in Reno, Nevada. She'd been raped, strangled, and thrown in a dumpster. The coroner will tell us of any more information he finds after he is done with his report. I can't tell you any more details, ladies, I'm sorry."

Due to the rainy day, it seemed a little chilly in the apartment. Marie Claire got up from her seat before Dean finished with his narrative and she stirred the embers in the fire. Her body shook so hard she could barely hold the fireplace tool that was held in her right hand, it shook so badly. Up to this point she'd been very quiet, but Dean saw how she held in the anger and hurt. With a look at Jeff and a flick of Dean's head, the two men flanked Marie Claire.

Marie Claire growled deep in her throat and catapulted back on her feet. Dean grabbed her from behind and held her arms to her chest in a hug. Marie Claire kicked and screamed. Jeff tried to get in there to help but she kicked him hard in the shin and he almost collapsed. *My leg is broken,* Jeff thought to himself, releasing Marie Claire as he stumbled to find purchase before he fell. Jeanette joined the fray. She grabbed Jeff's hands and helped him to sit in the chair where she had been seated. Jeanette pulled up Jeff's pant leg and procured an ice pack for him.

Dean's legs would be black and blue, but he still kept a bear hug around Marie Claire. In a few moments she tired of her kicking and screaming and calmed at some point.

"Are you done trying to maim and cripple me, Marie Claire?" At her slight nod, Dean turned her to face him and he still held her tightly as she cried harder than she'd ever cried in her life. The men knew how much she loved Lisa Marie, because the Bascolms had shared a lot with them about Marie Claire's life, finally asking him to help protect her from her former lawyer husband.

Jeff stood up again and, limping, he walked over and stood beside his onetime friend. He and Dean guided Marie Claire to the sofa and seated her a moment later. Jeanette brought her a hot cup of coffee, and it sat at her elbow on the end table.

"Are you going to be ok if we go now, Marie Claire?" Jeff asked quietly. "I wish Clint was here with you."

"I will be fine, Jeff, thank you." Marie Claire, now sitting stoically, felt tears flowing less heavily.

"I'll stay with her until Clint gets home," Jeanette told the men as she led them to the door.

"I'd like to see you when this mess is over, Jeanette, if that's okay with you?" Jeff stated, looking into Jeanette's crystal blue eyes. Her hair color, dark brown, was naturally curly. She wore it long, but in a cut that flattered her oval face. Jeanette stood 5'4", and seemed rather on the thin side. She was not beautiful like Marie Claire, but Jeff thought her to be a very pretty woman. "We can go out for coffee or dinner, whichever you prefer," he told her. "I would like to get to know you better, Jeanette."

"I have nothing on my calendar," she told him with a slight smile on her lips. She was not as in love with people, even family, as Marie Claire tended to be. "Friday night at seven, okay?" Jeanette smiled up into Jeff's green eyes.

"We've got a date Jeanette," Jeff replied. "I'm sorry about your cousins."

The two women, alone once more, quietly sat together, and Jeanette told her sister, "Why don't you go lie down for a while, Sis. You've had a bad time of it lately, and neither one of us needed this news on top of everything else."

"Thanks, Jeanette. I believe I will go rest for a bit. Wake me when Clint gets home, please." She squeezed her sister's hand, stood, and turned, holding her temples and massaging them as she walked away.

Jeanette liked to watch soap operas so she turned one on low while she straightened up the apartment a little. She heard her sister sobbing for a short time and then quiet settled in. *Marie Claire is a meticulous housekeeper*, Jeanette thought to herself, *but I think she goes a bit overboard*, as she noted the blinds and tops of the windows. No dust or dirt settled anywhere in this apartment.

Turning her thoughts back to Marie Claire, Jeanette pondered again, *Marie Claire was so close to Charlene and Lisa Marie. I hope I can find that kind of love with her someday soon. I know she's forgiven everyone who mistreated her, but am I someone worth loving?* This one thing, Jeanette would have to learn for herself.

Four hours later Clint walked in the door. Jeanette made a pot roast with a multitude of vegetables for dinner and the fragrance of dinner permeated the apartment. Marie Claire woke up at the sound of their voices. The smell never even fazed her.

"Hi, Sunshine," Clint said, as he kissed his wife and greeted her warmly. She wore a robe over her nightgown and walked into the kitchen where her husband and sister stood talking. "Dinner's almost ready. I understand you had a hard day, and I am so very sorry." Clint walked his wife back to the bedroom and lay beside Marie Claire as tears fell from his sad hazel eyes.

They lay there for a few moments, just holding each other and letting the tears cleanse the hurt away. Clint could tell by Marie Claire's puffy eyes that she'd been crying hard and often throughout the day.

"Dinner's on, you two." Jeanette called when she heard water running in the bathroom and she saw Clint come out with a robe on over his pajamas.

Marie Claire emerged a few moments later. She'd showered and put on her silver and white peignoir set. She had her black hair piled on top of her head in a chignon to keep it out of her face. Though devoid of makeup once more, Marie Claire was still a vision of loveliness.

*   *   *   *

The two sisters and Clint, along with Charlene's dad, Zane, attended the funeral two weeks later. There was a multitude of police and FBI agents there also. Their duty included attending murdered victims funerals and memorial services, in case someone unusual attended. Sometimes killers or perpetrators attended their victim's funerals, most of the time they didn't. Neither of the sisters nor Clint was upset at this. Coworkers from Charlene's office and a few friends of both Charlene and her daughter attended the services, but all in all the quiet ceremony went well.

Uncle Zane, though saddened, held a commanding presence. He spoke with Dean Manning afterwards. Clint and Marie Claire saw the men talking but they didn't interfere. Marie Claire had endured enough heartache to last her a lifetime, and Clint wouldn't let her get involved with anymore.

Chapter Twenty-Five

Two days later, Dean Manning called Marie Claire's apartment. "Ben's here with me, Mrs. Bellham, and he wants to talk to you."

Marie Claire answered him sweetly, "Please, call me Marie Claire. The other sounds too old! Can you hold a second? I have to get my cookies out of the oven before they burn. I'll be right back."

Clint left for work three hours ago, and Marie Claire was in the kitchen baking Gila Monster cookies. Everyone in her sphere loved these things. They were made with oatmeal, brown sugar, a little baking soda, butter, peanut butter, M&Ms, raisins, coconut, and chocolate chips. Marie Claire found the recipe in the Southwest Cookbook she purchased last year from the Mexican cooking section in the bookstore in West Seattle. Never being in the Southwest of the United States before, Marie Claire thought she could use a little experience with the recipes.

Dean, Ben Jackson, and Jeff tried the cookies one day last week when she brought some to their office. They couldn't wait for another platter of the goodies.

"You're trying to make my men fat, are you?" Ben asked Marie Claire, laughingly.

"No, just trying to keep a smile on their faces and working on my business," she quipped back at the FBI head.

Ben hugged the woman and kissed the top of her head. "If Tamara wasn't married to me, I'd have to grab you up and marry you!" Ben had to be at least twenty years older than Marie Claire so she was com-

fortable with his teasing her. She'd met Tamara just recently and she
really liked Ben's wife.

*   *   *   *

Today, Wednesday, Marie Claire received a call and she spoke with
Ben again. He asked her to come in to the office, as he needed to go
over something with her.

Marie Claire called Aerdinae and asked Clint if he could go with
her. "Handsome, I need to go see the FBI today. Would you be able
to come with me? I don't want to go alone."

"No, Sunshine. I can't today. We're very busy and Joseph needs
me here."

Next, she called Jeanette. "Hi. Clint can't get away and I wondered if you could come with me to see the FBI again. Ben just called,"
Marie Claire asked her sister.

"No, Marie Claire. I can't today. Can Jeff go with you? Call
Kara. Maybe she'd go with you." Marie Claire shared info about her
friends on Vashon. She felt that since she hadn't talked to the Mallorys
in so many years, she couldn't just drop this on Kara now.

I'll just have to go alone, Marie Claire thought. *I hate this. I wish
it was all behind me. I wish, God, that I was an only child, a single rich
woman, and had a gazillion acres and a million horses.* Marie Claire
wasn't serious, for she loved Clint too much to wish herself single, but
she really did want peace to last more than a week or two.

Marie Claire finished her cookie baking, packaged them up on a
colorful tray, and covered them with a towel she kept just for such uses.
She grabbed her purse and keys. Locking up, she went outside and set
the tray of cookies on the back seat. She then started the recently purchased Lincoln Towncar.

Thinking of how this car came to be hers and admiring the interior
for the millionth time, Marie Claire sat there for a minute. Clint gave the
Lincoln to Marie Claire as a surprise. He'd gotten a promotion to CEO
of Joseph's Aerdinae Aircraft Company, as Joseph decided to step down.
He would keep control of things, but not feeling well as of late, he and
Maggie decided he needed to retire. He'd taught Clint everything about
the company and the Fitzpatrick's knew they need not worry. Clint became, over the years, like a son to them, and they loved him deeply.

Clint arrived home that night after work and told Marie Claire what occurred in his day. "I want you to go buy yourself a nice car. You don't need to drive Francis' old Cadillac anymore. Get one of your own, or whatever you want," he told her.

The next day, actually just last Friday, Marie Claire went to the Lincoln dealership in Bellevue. She found a pearl white Lincoln Towncar with dark tinted windows, power door locks and seats, and a cassette player. Everything else that came in the standard package was just added perks for her. She loved all the gadgets like the on-the-door cup holder, console storage and cup holders, sunglass holder on the ceiling, a Kleenex storage compartment on the dash and automatic lights and mirrors. The outside mirrors were even heated to keep the snow and ice melted off. This car included dark gray plush leather seats and Marie Claire fell in love with it. For cash, they gave her a discount.

With a slight smile on her face, Marie Claire now drove her new Lincoln down the Alaskan Way viaduct to downtown Seattle. She parked near the entrance of the FBI offices. Taking her tray of cookies out of the back seat, she turned, locked her car, and proceeded up the steps and down the marble floored hallway to the elevator that would take her to Suite 614.

Marie Claire wore a lavender pant suit and matching heels. She looked elegant with matching lavender eye shadow above her long black eyelashes. Her bangs were trimmed to just above the eyebrows and the top part of her hair flowed back into a ponytail, the sides and back hung straight to her waist. She wore earrings with purple stones hanging from the post. Vanilla Bean perfume finished her ensemble.

The lovely woman would not have been more surprised if someone just handed her a million dollars. She stepped into the reception area and there in seats on her right sat Jeanette and Clint. She almost dropped the platter of Gila monster cookies.

"What are you two doing here?" she questioned.

"We were told not to say anything to you but we were summoned here," Clint smiled at her.

Marie Claire quickly sat down in a chair to her left. In a moment, Ben stepped into the waiting room and bid the three to follow him. He took hold of Marie Claire's elbow and led her into his office first. The first person she met was seated at Ben's desk. She saw this man at the Bascolm's funeral, but didn't remember him. Then she saw Jeff and

Dean, seated in leather armchairs near the window on the outside wall of the office. Mount Rainier commandeered the view.

"What's going on here, Ben," Marie Claire asked.

"Marie Claire, this is Troy Walden, the Bascolm's long time friend and lawyer. They've known each other for over forty years. He has something to tell you." Ben seated himself next to Clint after the introduction.

Mr. Walden entwined his fingers together and laid his chin upon the knuckles. Looking at Marie Claire, he said, "I was averse to Sam and Julia wanting to do this for you, not knowing you personally, but I gave in eventually. I have spoken with each of the people in this room, and the others I contacted through same. Because of what I heard and see before me, I agree with Sam's assessment."

"You have been dealt a great disservice, young lady, and I am here to rectify that," Troy said, as Ben handed her two letters. One came from Sam, to be read immediately, and one from Julia, to be read at a later time.

*   *   *   *

The others waited as Marie Claire read the letter from Sam. It brought tears to her eyes, but she felt a pleasant glow emanate out of her heart and it radiated from her beautiful brown eyes. The others sensed a change in her demeanor right away. They knew the letter held only good things regarding their beloved Marie Claire.

'Our dear Ms. Marie Claire,' the letter started, *'you have brought nothing but joy to Julia and me. We love you very much. We were never able to have children, but you gave us plenty of happiness, compassion, and pride. We enjoyed your shows, your endurance to keep going, and the beautiful way you handled yourself and your horses. We enjoyed every day we spent with you, be it in the hospital or out on a day trip.'*

'You must know that if you are reading this letter, we can no longer be with you here on Earth, but know that we will wait for you by the Pearly Gates, and you will be welcomed with open arms. You can expect a letter from your former pastor in North Idaho. He did you, and those of us who know the truth, a disservice. I set him straight on a few matters of importance, and he assured me he would be address-

ing his congregation as to their errors, generally speaking, of course. Gossip and slander should never be tolerated in the church, or anywhere else for that matter. We are sorry you had to endure so much pain because of it.'

'Marie Claire, Julia and I bought your ranch from the bank four months ago. We could have helped you out a long time ago, but we were waiting to see what you were going to do. It broke our hearts to see you bankrupt, but that was not all your fault. Francis did not treat you the way he should have, he did not support you as he should have, and then you had other responsibilities on top of what you already had. We were proud of you. You asked for advice, you've listened to what you were told, and you acted well with everything you were given.'

'We are very proud of Clint, also. Joseph has talked to us a few times, and we know what is in store for both of you. You both are worthy of love, admiration, and our support.'

'As of three months ago your ranch was worth four hundred fifty thousand dollars. Our house was worth three hundred fifty thousand dollars. Our bank accounts in total, equal nearly six million dollars.'

'Our friend and longtime lawyer, Troy Walden, has been well compensated for continuing to support you in handling your money from now on. Though he has not met you until today, we assured Mr. Waldon that you are willing to listen to his advice. We trust that you will continue to be the levelheaded young woman we have found you to be with us.'

'We would like you to take anything you want out of our house and make it your own. We also wish Clint to have our tractor, trailer, lawn mower, and anything else he wants. It's all yours anyway.'

'You are a very wealthy young woman now, Marie Claire, and we wish you all the best. Remember this, we love you and always will. We were never able to have children, which Julia will tell you about in her own letter, and you have far surpassed everything we could ever dream in our own children. Enjoy the rest of your life, live it to the fullest. Take care of your money, spend it wisely, but most of all be true and faithful to each other, both you and Clint. Be faithful to your Lord and Savior.'

All our love, dear one,
Sam

Marie Claire finished the letter and passed it on to Clint. When she looked up, tears stood in her lovely brown eyes. Mr. Walden picked up the Will to finish the reading. Most everything was covered in Sam's letter, but by law, a lawyer needed to read the actual document.

I, Samuel Clement Bascolm, and I, Julia Priscilla Bascolm, do hereby bequeath to Marie Claire Bellham, the following:

1)   Our entire holdings at 10234 Holden Way, Priest River, ID 57110, which include: a three-bedroom home, everything in the home, the outdoor and miscellaneous items in any and all outbuildings.
2)   A three-bedroom home at 11045 Priest River Way, Priest River, ID 57110, any and all miscellaneous items stored in the outbuildings.
3)   Any and all monies held in various accounts, of which Troy Walden, Atty. at Law, is in control and is directed to assist and portion out to Marie Claire Bellham at her request.

The sum six million nine hundred seventy-five thousand dollars ($6,975,000), to include all items above, now belong to Marie Claire Bellham.

The reading of the Will now finished, Marie Claire looked shocked, as were her family members. Mr. Walden hugged the woman he served, would serve from now on just as he had the Bascolms, and in turn, he hugged Jeanette. He shook Clint's hand and wished them all well.

"Marie Claire, I read that letter before I gave it to you, and I'm very pleased to say that they made a wise choice. I have spoken with your husband, your sister, and Jeff, and I hope you will put your trust in me," Mr. Walden told her. "I loved Sam and Julia, and like you, I will miss them very much."

Marie Claire could not speak. Clint and Jeanette thanked everyone for their time, and with wonderment, those two flanked Marie Claire and walked her out to her car.

Clint said, "Sunshine, I want you to follow me home. Jeanette will follow you, and we will see you back at the apartment." He knew she must still be in shock, maybe painful feelings still lingered also. He worried about her driving like this, but he didn't want the new car left downtown.

Marie Claire felt such a large lump in her throat that she still couldn't speak. She looked up at her husband with wonderment in her eyes, moist with unshed, presumably happy, tears, and nodded her head in assent.

Clint could not wait to get back home, but he turned to Jeanette, after Marie Claire settled in her seat with the door shut, and said, "Jeanette, when we get back home, would you mind going back to the flower shop and pick up two dozen red roses? You know what kind of card Marie Claire likes to receive from me, so would you mind picking one up and bringing it back with the flowers?" Clint handed her three hundred dollars.

"I will gladly do that for you, brother-in-law," Jeanette said quietly. She knew Clint was in shock and didn't want to leave Marie Claire. Jeanette didn't mind shopping for him. Clint and Marie Claire were very much in love, and respected each other. No one would ever doubt that.

Jeanette knew just what she needed to find for her sister. "Shall I get her favorite kind of pizza also?" Nearly four o'clock by this time, they would have an early dinner and then go over the day's amazing events. Everyone's minds were awhirl, thinking of the wonderful life Marie Claire could now have.

"That would be fine," Clint said. "You may want to call Jeff too, and ask him to come over to eat with us. Why don't you get two or three pizzas, one that you like and one that Jeff likes," and he handed Jeanette another one hundred dollar bill. Clint's wallet was now empty, and he didn't even notice.

The three of them drove home, each in their separate cars, thinking their own silent thoughts, dreaming their own private dreams.

Jeff arrived shortly after the others. Seeing Jeanette getting back into her car, he pulled in front of her and went to her window. "Are you leaving for home," he asked.

"No, I'm running an errand for Clint. Would you like to come with me?" Jeanette asked Jeff.

"How 'bout you come with me, my pretty, and tell me where I am to go!" Jeff teased.

Seeing Jeff's old but well cared for Mustang convertible with the top down, Jeanette said, "Sure, good lookin'. Let me grab my purse and lock my car."

Arm in arm, the two walked to the passenger side of the Mustang and Jeff helped Jeanette into her seat. He then walked around to the driver's side, wiping a bit of dust off the hood, sat in his seat, and turned his bright red head and winked at Jeanette. "Where to?" he asked.

Chapter Twenty-Six

MARIE CLAIRE sat at her window in her rocking chair as she read Julia's letter Tuesday morning, a week later. Marie Claire didn't think she could have handled anything else until today, so she'd put the letter in her dresser drawer for a later time.

As she sat there reading, she looked up and out her window far across the freeway at the green fields and Mount Rainier. *I can see why Sam and Julia wanted me to read this letter at my leisure,* Marie Claire thought to herself. What she read broke Marie Claire's heart for her dear friend and mentor, but in the end, Julia and Sam forgave Julia's attacker, and she knew they were in Heaven waiting to see her and Clint. Marie Claire couldn't be sad for their sakes. They had lived a blessed life, and now she would live one too. Looking at the writing once again, Marie Claire reread:

Dear Marie Claire,

Sam and I wanted to leave you our holdings en-toto. I want to explain that one night, years ago, I was leaving class. I was in college. Sam was working as an electrical engineer.

I was walking to my car when a man grabbed me. He forced me into his car and drove me to a secluded section of woods. There was a cement pad that had a grill, picnic table and benches, and a cover. He raped me.

The man was your uncle, Leroy. Remember, God is the judge.

Sam and I have forgiven, but I was always bitter until you came along. I could never have children since the man used a knife in the rape. I picked him out of a lineup, but nothing occurred afterwards because, I caught a ride home and showered before I called the police, and before Sam got home from work. There was nothing they could do to help me. I washed all the evidence away. The only evidence was the knife wounds, but even that couldn't help. It was just his word against mine.

Then you came along. You were the daughter I always wanted. Your mother showed me some pictures, and that's how I knew Leroy was your uncle. I took you under my wings because she told me some other things. You know the rest.

Enjoy your inheritance, dear sweet lady, and remember us with love. Don't mourn for long, because we will be watching, I will be watching, and I want you to be happier than anyone else on earth.

I love you to Heaven and back.

Always,
Julia- and Sam too!

Marie Claire folded the letter and stuck it away in her scrapbook of remembrances from North Idaho. It occupied a page of its own amidst a book full of horse mementoes, cards, and ribbons.

*   *   *   *

It took nearly a month for Marie Claire to come to terms with the changes in her life. Dean Manning and his wife Claudia would be here in a few minutes. Today, Saturday morning, Clint and Marie Claire planned to go to Priest River, Idaho with their new friends. Marie Claire would sort the things that she wanted to keep from the Bascolm home. Marie Claire promised Claudia that if she saw anything she wanted she could have it.

Dean had a fondness for the Bellhams, and he asked his wife to check on Marie Claire during the week as Jeff told him that she was still having a hard time of it. Marie Claire would be left alone every day, all day long due to her family's work hours, and so Claudia consented to watch over Marie Claire until she felt better. The two women had become quite good friends.

The Mannings arrived at the Bellham apartment shortly after their early breakfast cleanup. Grabbing her purse and new 35mm camera, Marie Claire followed the others down to the car. Clint admired the Cadillac Escalade as he and Marie Claire sat in the back. Dean, with Claudia in the front passenger seat, drove to Spokane, where they had lunch at noon, five hours later. The couples dined on fish and chips and their drink of choice was iced tea.

Forty-five minutes later they were back on the road. Clint had called ahead and Tom Horton, the real estate agent who handled the repurchasing of Marie Claire's home for the Bascolm's, waited at the front door with the keys to both homes. Marie Claire walked through the door first with Claudia right behind her. Marie Claire's heavy exhaled breath was audible to all of them, and a large lump formed in her throat that she swallowed. She took a few more deep breaths as she stood and looked around the house.

"This sure is a nice home," Claudia commented to no one in particular. They stood in the kitchen before Marie Claire walked around and opened all of the cabinet doors and drawers. Slowly she looked in each compartment, every so often pulling something out and setting it on the counter top. Claudia did the same, setting the things she wanted on the dining room table.

Clint and Dean gathered up all the boxes they could find, the ones they brought in from the car and the ones that were in the garage. Going into Sam's office, Clint pulled a felt pen from the desk. Together, they gathered all the newspapers that were piled up at the front door and setting by the sofa in the living room. Dean wrapped the item's Claudia wanted from the kitchen in paper and put them in boxes, marking the boxes as to content. Clint followed suit.

After checking the refrigerator, Marie Claire put all nonperishables in the box and everything else was thrown in the trash. There wasn't much here, but Marie Claire did not want to leave a dirty refrigerator. She checked the microwave and the stove and found that they were clean. She then walked to the dining room.

"Do you have need of this dining set, Claudia," she asked.

"I love the style, Marie Claire," Claudia answered.

"You can have it if you want it," Marie Claire told her.

"Claudia," Dean addressed his wife when she didn't answer, "would you like this dining set?"

"Only if Marie Claire doesn't want it," Claudia responded.

"No, you can have it," Marie Claire answered.

So the day went. The Mannings came away with quite an assortment of new furniture, pictures, and sundry odds and ends. Marie Claire recalled how Julia had wanted some of the furnishings that now sat in the home, how together, she and Marie had gone shopping for each piece. Marie Claire reminisced on the enjoyment she and Julia had gotten out of their days together, and how Sam teased them unmercifully when he felt they didn't need something.

"Jules," Sam would say to her, "do you know that we already have that!" Sam would tease, knowing that he loved to please, and tease, his wife and that he would let her have anything she wanted. *Oh, how their friendship would be missed*, Marie Claire thought to herself.

As she and Claudia went upstairs to clean out the two bedrooms and baths there, Marie Claire felt saddened once again. As she stepped into the bedroom she used when she sought protection, and Julia coddled her as she recuperated from a hospitalization, Marie Claire shook. The traumatic events that led up to her having to stay here in this room came to the forefront. Claudia, aware of Marie Claire's past, sidled up to her and gave her a one armed hug and a shake. No words passed between these two, but the comfort and caring carried through to Marie Claire's heart.

Walking into the bath, there lay the tube of toothpaste Marie Claire used, and her toothbrush sat in the glass by the faucet. Her comb and brush sat there on the vanity; and as Marie Claire looked into the mirror, she saw the sadness in her own eyes. *How will I ever live without my best friends? So much did they give me, do for me. So little did I give back. God, forgive me for my thoughtlessness.* Marie Claire picked up all her items and put them in a small sack she carried with her. She and Claudia turned and left these two rooms. Other than bedding, there was nothing else here. They cleaned out Sam and Julia's bed and bath. Claudia would take the clothing and pick out what she wanted to keep later. Dean could wear the nice suits Sam left behind. The rest of the stuff would be given to Goodwill.

Downstairs once again, the last room that Marie Claire wanted to go into was the large corner one that overlooked her old ranch from the picture window. Julia and Sam had called it their TV room, and they did indeed have their entertainment equipment in here, but they'd filled two walls with more of Marie Claire's trophies and plaques. Clint led Dean and Claudia through the doorway, but Marie Claire hung back. There were ribbons of blue, multiple grand champions, plaques received from rodeos and endurance riding, and dozens of pictures taken at a multitude of horse shows.

One picture in particular was a glass covered, oak framed four foot by four foot photo of Marie Claire. In her right hand she held the reins of a buckskin quarter horse gelding, bedecked in a black leather bridle trimmed in silver and on his back sat a black Western saddle, trimmed with large silver-plating front and back. A wreath of red roses hung from a solid silver saddle horn which, on the white ribbon streaming down from the roses were the words, Hell's Canyon Endurance Winner 1994.

In her left hand, Marie Claire held the reins of a sorrel and white paint mare. This horse too was bedecked in the same type of riding gear the buckskin had on. Instead of black leather, the mare wore dark brown tack with just as much silver as the gelding's. Both horses were well muscled and very tall.

"You must miss them very much," Dean said. "It looks to me like you had quite a lot of fun with your animals."

"Yes, I did." They could see the hurt and longing in Marie Claire's eyes as she answered Dean quietly.

Claudia put her arm around Marie Claire shoulders and walked her outside. Sitting on the front deck in the comfortable lounge chairs Sam had purchased last summer, Claudia turned to Marie Claire. "Hey," she said quietly, "you can have this all again, you know. You're still young, and this is all yours now. You can do anything in the world that you want to do, and you have a lot of people supporting you. Don't look back Marie Claire. Think and look ahead. I truly believe that someday you'll see your beloved horses again, but you need to make a new life. Let's go in and pack up those walls and go home. Someday you'll be happy to take those pictures and trophies out and put them some place so the whole world can see what you have accomplished. God's brought you this far and I know he wants to give you something better. I just know it."

Marie Claire looked at Claudia and said, "Thank you. I needed to hear that today. I just loved those horses so much, and I'll never forget them. I don't think I'll ever find another horse to match either one, but I can sure try can't I?"

Tears standing in Claudia's eyes for her new friend, she hugged Marie Claire. Brushing the younger woman's hair back out of her face, and cupping Marie Claire's face with her hands, Claudia smiled brightly and looked deep into Marie Claire's eyes. She kissed Marie Claire on the cheek before they headed for some more boxes.

Apparently Clint and Dean had the same mindset as Claudia because when the men got back inside, most of the pictures were wrapped and put in boxes. Clint decided to keep all of the entertainment equipment. He and Sam had gone shopping as Sam was not sure just what he wanted to purchase, being unfamiliar with most new-fangled equipment. Clint had an idea that he and Marie Claire were going to need the extras anyway.

After they were done at the Bascolm home, Clint called for the moving truck to come. The boxes were all marked and kept in the house, and now he would go through the outbuildings and pick out what he wanted to keep. Claudia wanted to see Marie Claire's old home, so with Dean in tow, they went next door.

Claudia commented on the beautiful kitchen. "This is quite similar to your apartment," she said to Marie Claire.

"I know. I think that's why I got the apartment. I just love it." Marie Claire smiled.

She showed them through the rest of the house, remembering how her French provincial living room set looked so good in here; and a matching dining set sat in the room just off the kitchen. Marie Claire still kept most of her furniture in storage. Pondering just what to do with the rest of her life, she hung on to most of her belongings, only selling off what she knew she wouldn't want to keep. She knew she wanted horses again, so she would keep her eye open in the Seattle area for another ranch.

Marie Claire took a moment, before crossing through the gate separating the two properties, to show the Mannings where Sam buried her horses. The moving truck was getting ready to leave as Marie Claire, Dean, and Claudia returned back to the Bascolm's.

"Clint," Marie Claire said, "I want to sell these homes. I can't bear to live here with Sam and Julia gone. I think I need to move on."

"If that's what you want," Clint said, smiling. It was just the thing he wanted, had hoped, to hear. He'd been searching all week in the Seattle area. Dean showed Clint a picture of exactly what he wanted, something he knew that Marie Claire could not walk away from, but he would have to make a phone call today. "Would you mind excusing me? I need to go in the house," Clint told his wife.

"You ladies stay out here. I'll be right back," Dean said.

"What are they up to?" Claudia asked.

"Oh, Clint's got something up his sleeve, I just know it." Marie Claire giggled. Claudia marveled at the younger woman's musical laughter.

Clint indeed had something up his sleeve, and Dean was in on it. Dean walked around the house, making sure the women stayed outside, while Clint made a phone call.

"Mr. Mason, this is Clint Bellham. I'm interested in buying that old ranch next to the dairy."

"Oh, yes. Dean and I are friends and he told me not to sell this to anybody until I spoke with you. There are three hundred twenty acres here, and a beautiful home. Dean's aunt and uncle own the place, but his uncle died several years ago. His aunt is elderly and she told me she needs to move back to be with her kids. I know she would give you a good deal."

Clint set up a time for the following day to preview the home.

Chapter Twenty-Seven

M ARIE CLAIRE sat in the divan on her deck outside the apartment. The morning was sunny, not too warm, and she enjoyed watching the traffic go by. She wondered what Clint was up to, telling her "I have a meeting. Be back soon." They got back home two days ago and Clint was always having 'a meeting.'

Oh, well. I'll find out soon enough I guess, she thought, leaning back and looking at all the wall to wall housing in this part of the city. This early in the morning, only seven, the traffic was already starting to back up on the main thoroughfare. *I wish I knew where I wanted to live*, she thought. *I love visiting Seattle. Living in this area of Midway isn't bad, but*, tears coming to the forefront, *I sure miss Tanny and Pride.*

She thought of her apartment to take her mind off the horses. Vanilla scents, vanilla flavors, and Vanilla Sugar perfume had become her favorite obsession. Her abode reeked of it, but vanilla, a pleasant scent, made her family and friends come to associate it with Marie Claire. *I guess I'll get another cup of coffee,* Marie Claire thought. She just started to stand up when the door chime rang and she bypassed her kitchen and ran to the door. *Who can that be at 7:30 in the morning*, Marie Claire thought. She became concerned because of the earliness of the day. She took a deep breath and opened the door. There stood Jeff.

"Oh, Jeff, you scared me. Is something wrong? Is Clint ok? Was there an accident?" Marie Claire again worried.

"No, Marie Claire. Everything's fine. I stopped to talk to you before work. Is it ok if I talk to you now, or do you want me to come back?" Jeff noted she still wore her peignoir set, and he saw through the dining room glass doors that a napkin and some fruit sat on the table where she'd been sitting.

"No, sweetie, come in. Would you like some coffee?" Marie Claire walked over to get another cup for herself.

"Yes, coffee would be fine. May I have some toast or something, too? I didn't have breakfast this morning." Jeff sat at the dining table.

Marie Claire noted that he looked anxious, worried wasn't quite the word, but she knew Jeff had something on his mind. While he sat there, she hurriedly mixed him up an omelet. She made scones last night so she took two out of the baggie in the refrigerator and warmed them as the omelet cooked.

"Would you like to sit out here with me?" Marie Claire motioned to the deck, as she handed him his plate of food. She went back to the fridge to get the blackberry and huckleberry jams. Marie Claire knew how Jeff liked her scones with the gooey stuff on them.

As they sat at the wrought iron table with the matching chairs on the lanai, Marie Claire steepled her fingers under her chin. She looked at Jeff, a happy glint in her eyes, and in the deepest voice she could muster said, "Spill it, young man!"

Jeff laughed, for he loved when Marie Claire teased folks. She'd never been this happy since her friends died in the plane crash. She'd never even seemed this happy at inheriting her fortune of millions a few weeks ago. Of course, she would never have expected to lose such a close-knit family as she, Sam, and Julia had become. He knew she still grieved, but she'd learned to go on with her life and cherish the memories.

"Um, well," Jeff stammered, unable to speak what he felt. He sat there crossing and uncrossing his legs and twiddling his fingers.

"Jeff, it's ok. Tell me what it is." Marie Claire thought something bad happened, or was happening to her friend.

"Well, you are Jeanette's only living relative, I guess, so it only seems proper to talk to you about it." Jeff kept his head down, unsure if he was doing the right thing.

"What about Jeanette," Getting a little antsy, Marie Claire snapped at Jeff.

"I'd like to know if you would let me marry her." There, it came out. He'd said it, but was he doing the right thing by himself, by Jeanette? They hardly knew each other after all.

Marie Claire heard something Jeff hadn't – her apartment door opening. She'd glanced over and saw Jeanette, back turned, shutting the door again. "Well, Jeff," Marie Claire said a bit loudly, "my sister is a spitfire, and you'll have to put up with temper tantrums and belligerence. Also, she is a bit young, don't you think?" Marie Claire was hamming it up. She loved teasing Jeff, and he got it, but Jeanette, standing beside the partially opened door didn't. She continued to stand there, tears rolling down her face. "After all, she just finished college not too long ago! I think she should work on her attitude and get a better job first." Marie Claire heard some sniffling, so after a slight minute she said, "Yes Jeff, you may marry her."

Marie Claire's chair almost tipped over. Jeanette jumped through the door and grabbed her sister in a bear hug. Tears streamed from the young fiancé's eyes, and she then grabbed Jeff, who had gotten up to stand behind Marie Claire's chair, waiting for Jeanette to acknowledge him.

"Um, Jeff," Marie Claire got the man's attention. "Have you asked for Jeanette's hand in marriage yet?" She had managed to untangle herself from her sister.

"No, I wanted to ask your permission first. Dad Ed taught me proper and I couldn't ask her before asking you." Jeff, always-honorable Jeff. Marie Claire knew he would make a fine husband for her sister.

Marie Claire, true to form, said to Jeff, "Get on your knees young man." Pulling Jeanette away from the table, Marie Claire positioned her sister in front of Jeff, kneeling there on his knees as directed. Marie Claire laid Jeanette's left hand in Jeff's left hand. "Now ask her proper," she said, trying not to laugh at his exasperated look.

"Jeanette, it would bring me great pleasure if you would consent to be my wife. I promise to love you forever, and take care of you always. I want children and hope you do too." From his shirt pocket inside his suit jacket, Jeff pulled out a solitaire diamond engagement ring.

"Yes, Jeff. I will marry you, gladly!" Gasping, Jeanette hugged her soon to be husband, tears still streaming down her face.

Jeff stood in front of Jeanette. He took the woman in his arms and kissed her for an indecent amount of time. They hadn't known each other very long, but there was a quality not unlike Marie Claire that drew Jeanette to his heart. Jeff, a Christian, knew that with time Jeanette would come to be a believer also.

Marie Claire finally just had to ask, "Would you like me to leave?"

The two separated and Jeanette, still starry eyed, turned towards her sister laughingly. "I have to go shopping. I have nothing to wear for my wedding!" Her voice held wonderment, her eyes shone with love.

"Finally, this spitfire answered without me having to throttle her. I almost gave up on you," Jeff said to Jeanette with a smile in his eyes. He intimated several times over the last weeks that he wanted her for his wife, but Jeanette had either ignored him, or told him to wait. Jeff needed to leave for work, and he kissed "his girls" goodbye.

Jeanette grabbed herself a cup of Marie Claire's vanilla flavored coffee and came back to sit with her sister on the deck. "I thought you might object, seeing as how you two have been friends for so long."

"I'm married to a wonderful man, Jeanette, my best friend Clint. How could I object to my other best friend, Jeff, marrying my sister? Now I can have him in my life as a brother-in-law. I get the best deal ever, I think!" Marie Claire was ecstatic. *Wouldn't Sam and Julia be very happy?* She thought to herself.

*   *   *   *

When Clint got home from work that evening, Marie Claire shared the day's events with him.

Clint had some news of his own. He would wait a bit, as Marie Claire was on the phone with her sister, again! They were done fifteen minutes later. Marie Claire turned to Clint and started talking right away, and Clint listened but he needed to get a word in too. "I'm going to take Jeanette dress shopping tomorrow. She's going to nee-"

"Time out!" Clint all but yelled. He had to talk to her.

Marie Claire, mouth agape, took a seat at the table and sat there looking at her husband.

"We've been invited over to Jeff's this coming Saturday to meet Ed Brown, of the Brown dairy," Clint told his wife. "I've been working on something. Jeff and Dean asked me to bring you over there."

"I remember Ed," Marie Claire said. "It's been years, though. How is he? Have you seen him? What have you been working on?"

"No, Sunshine, I've just heard about him. Apparently, his son, Oswald, left Ed by himself twenty years ago. Ed's wife died of cancer some years ago, and the son took off, saying he didn't want to be a 'milkmaid for a bunch of filthy cows.' The old man's not seen him since. Furthermore, I am not telling you what I've been working on. Can't a man surprise his wife sometimes?"

"Oh, how sad," Marie Claire empathized, thinking of the lonely old man. "You know I don't like secrets, Clint." But Marie Claire left it at that.

Marie Claire and Clint sat and talked about the wedding arrangements for a while. "I will buy the kids something for their honeymoon, Sunshine. You buy whatever Jeanette needs tomorrow. Don't spend too much!" He teased Marie Claire, looking into her eyes with a devilish glint.

Clint, with some business to attend, said abruptly, "I have to leave for a meeting. I'll be back in a short while." He left with a kiss to his wife.

Marie Claire watched a movie and then went to bed. She loved shopping and couldn't wait for the morning to come.

*   *   *   *

Jeanette told Marie Claire yesterday morning that they wanted to go to Vegas to get married, and Marie Claire passed that info on to Clint, who at that very moment was making all the arrangements for the couple.

"It's your job to keep Jeanette from doing anything! I already told Jeff that I would handle all the arrangements," Clint told his wife late last night. Clint wanted to give this gift as a surprise for Jeanette, so Marie Claire promised to keep her sister otherwise occupied.

When she and Jeanette were ready to go, Marie Claire drove over to pick her sister up. Ed asked Marie Claire to come into the house for a few minutes. As she stepped into the doorway leading to the kitchen, Martha, Ed's housekeeper, said, "Miss Marie Claire, Mr. Clint's on the phone for you." Marie Claire hadn't met her before.

Clint called Marie Claire at the dairy, missing her at home by just a minute. Martha handed the receiver to the younger woman. Ed talked with Jeanette alone in his den, and so Marie Claire was free to talk to her husband.

"Sunshine, I want you both to be done shopping and back to the dairy by six tonight. I talked to Dean and he let me know that Jeff is free for a honeymoon. He got the okay from Ben. Dean is calling everyone on the list I gave him. We'll have a wedding next Saturday night! I did the same with Jeanette's boss."

"Why the hurry to get back tonight?"

"I have a lot of work to do this weekend and next week so I can take several days off. I'll need your help too, so today is for shopping. We'll have dinner together, all of us tonight, and that should hold you until next weekend."

"Oh, Handsome! You are a wonderful husband, do you know that? I love you, in case I haven't told you lately! Thanks for everything you do for us."

They hung up and Marie Claire ran to the other room to grab her sister. "We have to go, Jeanette. Ed, is there anything I can get for you? Oh, Ed. I'm Marie Claire Bellham. Nice to meet you again!"

"I 'member you, young lady. Glad to see ya again. Welcome to the family!"

"We're going shopping." Marie Claire dragged her sister along behind her. They had only five hours to shop and get back.

Ed, of course, had known all along what was happening and he yelled back at Marie Claire, "No, girls. You have fun! Be careful. Them driver's out there can be mighty dangerous." Ed smiled at them and sent them on their way. "Oh Hey!" He called to them just as Marie Claire opened the car door. "Can you get me a box of them there See's candies? I haven't had any in a while. I'm outa my stash I used to keep in that drawer there," as he pointed to a bureau by the living room window.

"Ok, we'll get some for you!" Jeanette called back at him before Marie Claire pushed her into the front passenger seat.

*   *   *   *

Marie Claire took Jeanette to Bobbie's Bridals in the Southcenter Mall. Jeanette tried on several dresses, finally settling for an off the shoulder, satin gown in white with a veil trimmed in the same white satin as the dress. The wedding would be the following Saturday, so they didn't have much time to get everything done, since Clint had his own agenda for Marie Claire.

The shopping done, the two sisters went out for pizza and salad. "You have to work the rest of the week, don't you, Jeanette?" Marie Claire asked.

"My boss gave me today off. I told her I was getting married next Saturday, so she gave me a gift – three weeks off! Isn't that great?" Jeanette glowed, and it was obvious that she was very happy.

"Wow, nice boss you have!" Marie Claire told her sister, knowing Clint had worked that one to Jeanette's benefit. "Where are you two going to live?"

"Ed Brown is a swell guy. He's giving us the whole upstairs in his house. That's what our discussion entailed, that and Ed is giving me a monthly allowance. It's a huge home and it's beautiful. Isn't it just wonderful, great, stupendous?" Jeanette was almost delirious with happiness, "Jeff has kept up with the repairs and painting. Ed is so proud of him. He treats Jeff just like he is his own son. Did you know that Ed paid for Jeff to go to Quantico to learn to be an FBI agent?"

"Wow, no I didn't. That's great, Jeanette. I didn't know he and Ed were so close. Jeff was always there at the farm as a young man about my age when my college class went there for a lesson. I just thought he worked there, nothing more." Marie Claire's heart almost burst with pride for the life Jeff had made for himself. She felt thankful for Ed's mentoring and thoughtfulness, also.

*   *   *   *

Marie Claire and Jeanette shared a lot of past remembrances. Marie Claire sat with Jeanette as she enjoyed a manicure and a foot massage. The pampering continued when Marie Claire took Jeanette down the mall to have a stylish cut to her naturally curly dark brown locks.

They stopped next at Macy's where the two women indulged in a facial and a makeup demonstration. Each one experienced a makeover of foundation, blush, and eye shadow that brought out the highlights in their eyes. That took about an hour or so, and then they stopped for a latte.

Jeanette said, "You grew up the same as me, but even though you left home, I always thought you would stay the same girl. There is a big difference in you. Did you make something happen to change your personality?"

Marie Claire smiled, knowing that Jeanette was finally opening up to understanding her and maybe leaning a little toward knowing about Christ. "Jeanette, the difference is Jesus. I really came to understand him when I went through my divorce." Marie Claire shared her story of the breakdown in the parking lot. "Without Him, there would have been nothing for me to live for, but the horses, and that's no way for a person to exist. Having just animals in our life is not love. I would have had no hope without the saving knowledge of Jesus Christ. That is why we're here. To bring people to Christ, to bring glory and praise to Him for all things, be it good or bad."

"It's nothing I did, Jeanette. Ever since going to Bible school when I was little, maybe six or so, I always knew that there was one person in this world who loved me. His name is Jesus. If I hadn't learned who Jesus is, I probably would have chosen the same destructive things our family did –the drinking, the drugs, the perversions, you know the rest."

With thoughts of sadness in her heart for her parents and everyone in the world that didn't know better, didn't have the knowledge how much they are loved by God, Marie Claire shared what she knew with Jeanette. "2 Corinthians chapters 2-7, reminds us of a lot of things, but it shows the hardheartedness of the lost," and Marie Claire asked Jeanette to read that book at a later time. She did, however, give a shortened version of 2 Corinthians, as she understood it, ending with, "So, in other words," Marie Claire said, "there but for the grace of God go I!" With a sigh, and a slight smile at her sister, Marie Claire said, "I am indebted to Jesus for pulling me out of the miry clay typical of our family circumstances. I loved them all, and I am sorry I never talked to your dad, never told him he was forgiven. Did you know he asked forgiveness on his deathbed?"

"No, I didn't." Jeanette looked at Marie Claire with consternation. It was apparent that Jeanette seemed jealous. She had been abused also, but never received restitution as Marie Claire had.

Marie Claire looked back at her sister, steadfast and strong. "Well, he did. Grandma McCory asked me to go see him, to let him know she was praying, that she loved him, and she asked me to take a pastor, of the same faith as hers, with me. She wanted reassurance that her son knew Christ and asked forgiveness, and she wanted to know for a fact that he would be in Heaven. I found a nice minister and he consented to go to the hospital. Your dad looked me in the eyes and told me 'I'm sorry for what I did to you, Bones, but alcohol and drugs make people do things they wouldn't normally do to their loved ones.' I left the room in tears, but I know he reaffirmed his faith in Christ because the minister told me so. He asked me to come back to the room. I held your dad's hand for a bit, but then we had to leave. His doctor came in to see him."

After a moment, Marie Claire looked deep into Jeanette's eyes, a longing and a burning question of whether Jeanette would take that leap of faith, mirrored back at Jeanette. The two sat for a few seconds, just staring into each other's eyes. Marie Claire wanted her sister to know that she loved her, and she hoped Jeanette would really come to know Christ. Jeanette saw love and compassion in her sister's eyes. She knew Marie Claire wanted her to learn something from her today. She could sense the longing in Marie Claire, but knowing Jesus was personal, and she wasn't sure that He loved her, if she could take that 'step of faith' as Jeff shared with her once. She'd done drugs and alcohol, among other things in her life, and she felt unlovable and undeserving.

Marie Claire, giving Jeanette time to think about what she'd said, finally spoke what was in her heart. "I believe Jesus is the Son of the only true God, and I have accepted Him as my personal Lord and Savior. He is Lord of my life. I want everyone to know that, and to know they are loved." Marie Claire said quietly. She was playing with the straw sticking out of her iced latte.

"When I was eleven, nearly twelve, I stole some socks from the Burton Store once. I sinned, so I dishonored my Lord. When we have a crisis of conscience, it's His Holy Spirit telling us what's wrong, and we must do right in order to keep from rebelling against Him. I heard Jesus' voice, or maybe it was the Holy Spirit, but I did the bad thing, ignoring the Voice I heard in my head. I was told once some years later that we have a conscious. That conscious is the Spirit of God talking to us."

"So, you mean He makes you to follow Him? You have no mind of your own?" Jeanette looked as though she did not like this at all.

"No. It's like, say, you ask someone for something, your parents as an example, and you believe with all your heart that you will get it. It's nothing you earned, but a gift that has been promised. You love that person for their thoughtfulness and kindness. You do all you can to make that person happy. It's the same with Jesus. He has shown us how much He loves us by giving us beauty of sunrises and sunsets. Through a storm of desire for example, we want something, but know we shouldn't because it's not good for us, something we shouldn't watch, want, or do. Jesus continually watches over us. If we allow Him to, he shows us the way to go, if we know His will and follow His teaching. It's called walking by faith. You just believe and act accordingly, because you don't want to hurt and dishonor Jesus. It's hard to explain, but it's a metamorphosis where the Holy Spirit indwells the believer. Jesus won't do anything we won't allow Him to do. When we truly accept Him, we just have a desire to learn more about Him and follow His Will. The Holy Spirit indwells our heart and He is the voice of reason that we hear. It's all about Jesus, not ourselves."

"It seems hard, but it should be really easy then, right?" Jeanette asked.

"Well, I just always knew Jesus loved me. It was easy to accept everything I had been taught about Him. He lived to be a witness to us, to give us the hope we need as a lost world. He died as redemption for our sins, but then He arose to show that we will arise too and live eternally with Him in Heaven."

"What is sin, and how did it happen?" Jeanette asked another question. She seemed to Marie Claire to really be seeking understanding.

"Adam and Eve went against God's wishes not to eat of the forbidden fruit. When they became aware of their disobedience, they hid from God. But, God knew where they were. He wanted Adam to confess where his heart was when he went against God's command. Because of that, all men were cursed with a sinful nature. They needed to make atonement for their sins in the Old Testament. In the New Testament, God brought Christ down to become one of us. God knew man was not going to change and made mockery of the required rituals. Jesus lived, died, and rose again. It's all recorded for us. The Bible is the map for knowing how to find our way to Jesus' heart. Ultimately, as I understand it, the souls of saint and sinner alike will live forever. We can know without a shadow of a doubt that if we believe wholeheartedly in Jesus and obey Him, we will be in Heaven eternally instead of in the pit of fire."

After a moment of heart searching, Marie Claire shared something else with her sister. Tears came to her eyes, ready to fall, but Marie

Claire swallowed the lump in her throat and spoke. "I had been used by Leroy, then your dad, and I thought it was all normal, hateful, but normal. It wasn't until a few years ago that I read some passage in the Bible that got me really thinking. Francis used me, also, for his own gain. I told him many times he should have stayed married to Anne. I told him I didn't know why he wanted me! I knew in my heart it was wrong. I loved Francis in some ways, but not in the way a wife loves her husband. I hated him for marrying me. He took my childhood away. I realized that way too late. I wanted him to die, hoped he would have an accident or something.

Many times over the years, I have pondered on suicide. I devised ways to do it. But, knowing that murder is a sin, and thinking that I would not be in Heaven but in Hell, I couldn't carry it out, for there would be no way I could ask forgiveness. That's wrong thinking also, but it's just how I felt. I thought I would be dead, without hope - and I want to be in Heaven so badly. I know that suicide is not unforgivable, but it's still a sin and wrong! I still think sometimes that it would be for the best if I was gone, but I know that even thinking like that is sinful. Jesus knows my heart. He knows that I occasionally think of sinful things, but even though I don't want to do those things I hate, it's the sin nature in me, and I ask forgiveness and He's faithful to forgive. I have lost a lot in my life. My heart broke when my prize horses died, but you know, God gave me back more than I ever lost. So you see, God loves us. We just have to repent of our sin and allow Christ to lead us. God's grace is eternal. We can't earn it. God sent Jesus, so He could show us that He understands and will forgive us. As long as we know we are sinners and ask forgiveness, and accept Christ into our hearts and lives, we can be at peace. We'll never be good enough on our own to make it to Heaven, and God knows that. He wants us to come to Him because we know we are sinners and grateful for His abiding love. Ephesians 2:8-9 tell us that: For by grace you have been saved through faith, and that not of yourselves; it is the gift of God, not of works, lest anyone should boast."

Marie Claire grabbed a Kleenex and blew her nose. She wiped the tears of remorse and love that had escaped, knowing that crying wouldn't get her anywhere. "Well, I hope I explained without being pushy. I just know what I know and I want to share with all who will listen." As an afterthought, Marie Claire shared something else with

Jeanette. "What would be a good thing to do, is to read the Gospel of John. Do you have a Bible?"

Jeanette nodded her head in consent. "I have a family Bible that Grandma sent me. Where do I get one like you have on your coffee table at home?" Jeanette saw the study Bible Marie Claire kept on her coffee table. Jeanette needed time to think, and doing as Marie Claire asked would be a start for her to come to Jesus on her own terms, if she indeed came to Him at all. *That is a step I'll need to think about,* Jeanette thought to herself. *I don't walk into anything lightly.*

"Look past the center pages for births and whatnot. The New Testament starts with Matthew. Then there's the book of Mark, Luke, and then John. You'll get a picture of Who Jesus Is when you read that book."

Janette said, "I always thought men made up the stories in the Bible."

"Well, Jeanette. Men wrote the books of the Bible, but God ordained what would be written, by whom, and how many and which books would make up the Bible we know today. John, Jesus disciple, was the one who said, in John 21:25: *'And there are also many other things that Jesus did, which if they were written one by one, I suppose that even the world itself could not contain the books that would be written.'* There would be no book big enough, no world big enough to hold the writings of everything Jesus did, every miracle He performed. God chose the most important letters or books to be put in the Bible for us to live by." Amazement overcame Jeanette's face. Marie Claire hoped with all her heart that her sister would come to the saving knowledge of Christ Jesus.

Jeanette got up from her chair and hugged her sister. She held Marie Claire for a short while, rocking her, tears seeping from her blue eyes also. "No, you have a strong faith, and you aren't pushy. I do understand why we need Christ. No one else can save us. We can't even save ourselves. Jeff told me the other day that knowing Christ is a personal thing, but a necessary thing if we are to have any hope at all. I want to be in Heaven. I know you, Clint, and Jeff will be there. I'll think about what you've said. I want to come to church with you sometime."

*   *   *   *

Saturday came, and at seven o'clock that morning, a planeload of passengers all going to Las Vegas for the wedding of Jeffrey Farthingworth
and Jeanette McCory, took off into the wild blue yonder. The girl's uncle, Zane, and his wife Patricia, Ed Brown, the Bellhams, the Mannings,
various coworkers of all of them, Jeanette's boss, and assorted friends
were all in attendance. Two of Jeanette's close friends acted as brides-
maids. They arrived at the Vegas airport, deplaned, and caught taxis
that took them to the Excalibur Hotel and Casino.

The women congregated around Jeanette until she was deemed
ready to be seen by her soon to be husband. The men did the same with
Jeff, teasing and tormenting him until time to go to the chapel. Jeff
loved them all and took the joking in stride.

The wedding commenced at eleven that morning. Afterwards
Jeanette and Jeff changed clothes, and Clint gathered everyone for the
post wedding luncheon. "I propose a toast to the newlyweds," he said.
"Jeff, please open the envelope," Clint handed Jeff the item and then
he sat down beside his wife.

Jeff took a sip of his wine and then opened the brown manila
folder. He stuck his hand inside and came out with tickets and an itinerary. Jeff stood up, items in hand, and he pulled his wife up beside
him. There were two tickets with several destinations on them. Hawaii
was the first stop, where they would be staying on Maui for five days.
From there they would go to Bermuda for three days, and then on to
Italy and Paris for the rest of their stay. These are the places where Jeff
and Jeanette most wanted to go sometime in their life. Clint and Marie
Claire made it happen for them.

Lunch finally over, a few people stayed for the remainder of the
weekend, but the rest of them caught the four o'clock flight back to
Seattle. Ed, with Marie Claire and Clint, were playing some of the slot
machines in the hotel where the wedding had been held. They ran in
to Dean and Claudia, who enjoyed playing the slots also. This wasn't
something that was the norm for these couples, but they thought they
might as well have a little fun before going home.

"Fancy meeting you here," Dean teased Clint and Marie Claire.
Jeff and Jeanette stood by his side. "Nice to see you here with us, Uncle
Ed. I wasn't sure you were coming."

"Well, Jeff got terrible hurt when I telled 'im I was too old to
travel. I didn't like the disappointed look on his face, so here I is! Glad

to finally get to see Missy heah marry my fine son, actually," Ed spoke fondly of Jeanette, enfolding her around the waist.

"Clint, Marie Claire tells me that you instigated this whole thing. It was a lovely wedding, and we are so proud of Jeff. We're sure he and Jeanette will make a wonderful life together. They took to each other right away!" Claudia shared with the couple.

"Julia wanted me to do this for my sister. We talked a little bit about Jeanette and Jeff just the day before we left on our trip. Julia had given me some money just for this wedding, and Clint said he would be glad to help me with it. Aside from that most of the wedding was his doing, and I think he did a fantastic job." Marie Claire hugged her husband in appreciation.

"I didn't know Ed was your uncle, Dean." Marie Claire said.

"Yep, he is. I guess that makes Jeff almost a brother! It's good to have a big family." Dean was smiling, his white teeth visible and his eyes sparkling. Pleased that no one seemed to judge Uncle Ed's bad grammar, Dean winked at Marie Claire.

"Well, I guess we'd better catch our flight," Dean said. Stopping at a machine near the exit, they waited as Ed put a dollar bill into the slot. After pushing a button and watching the pictures go around in a circle, the spinning stopped and the machine clanged, banged, whistled, and dinged. A piece of paper slid out of one of the slots and Dean grabbed it. "Hmmm, would you look at this?" Dean smiled largely as he walked up to the barred booth, the other four close behind.

The cashier took the ticket from Dean's fingers and opened her cash drawer. With several bills in hand, she counted the money. Ed picked the bills up from the countertop and separated them. He handed five hundred dollars to Marie Claire, and he handed the other five hundred dollars to Claudia.

With a profuse 'thank you' all around, the five of them left the establishment. Laughing together, they got in a limo and left for the airport.

*   *   *   *

Instead of going to Ed's that evening, Clint and Marie Claire slept late into Sunday morning and then went to Ed's dairy for lunch. They arrived to see a very large home, painted white with dark grey porticos around the front porch. Walking up the steps, Marie Claire saw bougainvillea hanging every two feet apart around the roof line.

Clint saw Ed and an older woman in the kitchen and Ed introduced her as Martha, as she made them tea. Marie Claire helped her make chicken salad sandwiches to go with the hot drink. The four of them sat at the kitchen table and enjoyed two hours of food, tea, and talk.

"I remember you, young lady," Ed said pointing his finger at Marie Claire. "You was here in the early 70s when you was in college, and ya he'ped save one of my calves.

"Yes, sir, I remember that," Marie Claire answered. "Jeff has been here, what, twenty some years now?"

"Yeah, Missy, twenty-six years to be exact. I love Jeff very muchly, and it's unusual fer me to say things like that, but he's like a son ta me. I'm very prouda that boy," Ed reiterated. "His dad beat him pert regular, and when he was old enough he come here to work; I kep'im on, and he's been a terrible big help."

"Jeff's always been a nice person. We didn't see much of each other back then, but we dated off and on and we just became good friends," Marie Claire stated. "I'm glad he stayed with you."

Martha cleared the table and asked if she could show the couple upstairs. "This is a very large house." The woman said, "and the whole upstairs suite will belong to the kids and their children." Marie Claire thought it comical that these two called Jeff and Jeanette kids, and she adored them both for their kindness to her family.

I'll show you the Southside first, Martha told Clint and Marie Claire. At the top of the stairs going left, they walked into an enormous master bedroom. Three large plate glass windows were set in a wall facing the Cascade Mountains. One large window faced the south end where they could see Mount Rainier, and the southern part of Puget Sound. The wall facing west held an antique bed made of oak. A small window on each side of the bed and heavy oak nightstands stood underneath them. White chintz curtains were on all of the windows, with a chintz bedspread and pillow covers to match. The mattress was covered in cotton sheets, the color of the sky. A large walk-in closet at the north end of the room adjoined a remodeled large master bathroom. The walls were covered in a deep blue paint and a cream colored carpet covered the old oak floor.

From this room, past the stairs, there were four smaller rooms. The one nearest the master bedroom held a nursery, and the furnishings looked very old. This room, painted a light blue, held shelves on one wall where a train sat on tracks surrounding the upper part of the walls. Clint flipped the switch and the train started moving. A large picture window overlooking Puget Sound and the Olympic Peninsula and mountains beyond covered the far wall.

Clint flipped the switch again and the train stopped. Not speaking, they stepped back into the hallway and looked at each of the other three rooms.

"The kids will have plenty of room when children of their own arrive, let me tell you," Martha laughingly told the couple. " I can't wait to see them when they get home. Ed misses Jeff, and he's promised to talk with Jeanette. Oh, I'm not trying to be nosy, but that's what I overheard Ed say to Jeff the other night. I think he might have a surprise for Jeanette," Martha was near whispering so Ed wouldn't overhear her.

Clint and Marie Claire looked at each other smilingly. Marie Claire turned toward the big window at the north end of the last room they stepped into. What she saw took her breath away; for there before her sat the most beautiful house she had ever seen in her life; it was what she had dreamed of forever. The stately home resembled a plantation mansion with a wraparound porch, of which she could see three sides from her vantage point. Painted a pale blue with deep blue shutters, a matching metal roof of deep blue covered the structure. The windows were trimmed in shiny white paint and someone painted the porch a light gray color. It alluded to an inviting home.

As in this house, there were views of all the surrounding terrain. Marie Claire could see nothing for miles, it seemed, but green fields and mountains. Of course, I-5 lay to the west, but it was a long way from the houses, at least sixty acres separated them from the highway.

My dream is only that, however, just a dream, she thought. *No one would want to sell that beautiful place, but I wish I could buy it.* Clint noticed the melancholy look on his wife's face and exchanged a smile with Martha. Marie Claire let out a long sigh and turned to leave.

I know my sister will be very happy here. I would be happy here, too. I know just the thing for a homecoming for her, and I'll have to go tomorrow and shop! She shared her thoughts with Martha as the three of them walked downstairs once again.

"Clint," Ed said, "would ya like to come on out doors and I'll show ya the place?"

"Sure, Ed, I'd be glad to see the rest of the dairy. How long have you been doing this?" Clint assured the man. "Come on, Sunshine. Let's see the rest of Jeanette's new home!"

"Well, sir, I been here goin' on ninety years. My folks homesteaded this land before I's born in 1911. I think they was here in 1889. 'Course, the old house ain't here no more. I built this un when I got hitched to my Janie in 1933. We had our kid, Oswald, twenty years later. Janie had a hard time of it and we was unable to have any more kids. Janie doted on that boy, givin' 'im anything he wanted. He's a no good skunk and I ain't seen 'im for goin' on ten or so years. Good riddance to 'im, I say. He hit his ma and I near killed 'im fer it. He ain't been back since."

"May I ask why he would hit his mother?" Marie Claire, never afraid to say what was on her mind, asked her question. They reached the milking shed by this time, and Marie Claire already knew the workings of this area.

"Well, Missy," Ed answered her, "Janie wanted him to quit his drinkin'. He was about forty years old, spoiled rotten, and he got in with some bad company. He been helpin' me with the dairy runnin', but a few years afore this, he just plain quit helpin' me. Janie couldn't understand as there was so much to do, and she tried to talk to him 'bout his backslidin'. He told his mama that he weren't goin' to be no "tit squeezin', bull cuttin', land ownin' milk slave anymore. He was drunker'n a skunk on a three day free for all. She told him she would be obliged if he'd quit his whorin' and drinkin'. He hauled off'n slapped her so hard she fell on the hearth in the living room." Ed took a few minutes to breath. He cleared his nose. He'd had tears in his eyes by this time and they could see he had a hard time keeping it together. "I'd had enough of listenin' from the kitchen and was about to step in when I saw what he done to my Janie. I never once hit my woman, and I don't cotton to no man hittin' his wife. I was strong back then and I laid into Ozzie, that's what everyone called 'im, and he could barely walk when I got done with 'im. I drove 'im to the doc's, said my peace, and left 'im there. I ain't never seen him since. I come back here and took my Janie to the hospital. She was bleedin' and I didn't know what to do. She spent overnight, me sittin' there all night with her, but she come home with me the followin' day and she was fine 'til she died some years later of cancer."

Clint and Marie Claire didn't know what to say. They were pleased that Ed cared about them enough to share his life story with them. They knew Ed to be a fairly quiet, private old man, except with folks he cared for.

Ed showed them the outbuildings, but his pride and joy turned out to be the last one they had the privilege of seeing - an airplane hangar, and inside that hangar sat a Piper Cub airplane. Clint understood why Ed showed this to them last. It was a very special place for Ed, and held special meaning. Jeff gave this gift to the old man, who didn't love anyone as much as he did his new son.

Ed paid off all of Jeff's college tuition in the past, of course, Jeff wanted the schooling so he could become a police officer. After graduation, Jeff worked for a short while at the dairy, but Ed insisted he go on to be an 'important person'.

"I can't leave you, Pops," Jeff told him over and over. "You need help here at the dairy." Ed, after having gotten the ball rolling, soon adopted Jeff Farthingworth as his own son. He went by Farthingworth instead of Brown, because Ed wanted Jeff to have a 'classy last name'. It didn't make Jeff any less Ed's son, however.

A persistent Ed told his son, "I'll hire me a foreman to take your duties over whilst you're gone. You go on to school. Get an education, and come home when ya can." Jeff couldn't do anything else, and Ed wouldn't hear any more arguments, and so he enrolled and was accepted at Quantico.

The aging Ed became so stiff and sore after sixty years in the saddle, that he couldn't ride horses anymore. There were still a few horses here at the dairy for Jeff's benefit, but the airplane took over where those animals used to do the work. Ed couldn't ride the fence line anymore to check for damage. The one time he'd taken the truck out to check on his vast property, it got stuck in the mud. A neighbor came over with his tractor to pull the truck out and tow it back to the house. Ed would no longer drive except to town when he needed to go. Otherwise, Martha did the shopping and Jeff flew the plane.

Jeff offered to take some of his own savings and buy a plane so that he could fly Ed over the land, checking the fences and checking on the cattle, and if there were any problems, Jeff had a four-wheel drive and they used that to drive out to check the perimeters and make repairs. If there was a cow in trouble, or they saw dead cattle, Jeff would take the backhoe out and haul them back for vet care or bury them where they lay.

Ed made arrangements for the hangar to be built to keep the aircraft safe from weather and vandalism, and a runway constructed also. This proved to be a good investment, and Jeff would take his Pop up in the plane, and the older man got a kick out of it every time they flew. He'd offered to buy a helicopter but Jeff didn't think it necessary. He liked flying the airplane just fine.

When they got back to the house Ed called for Martha.

"Yes, Ed," Martha said. "Can I do something for you?"

"Yes, dear. Clint wants me to go with him. I'll be back in a little while."

Martha smiled at them all, knowing just what was going to happen next. She'd overheard that part of a conversation the other day, and she felt pleased that this wonderful young woman married such a wonderful, and rich, husband.

Clint, taking Marie Claire's hand, walked out the front door with Ed close behind.

Chapter Twenty-Eight

C LINT, AFTER checking that his wife and Ed were settled in the car, seatbelts fastened, drove down a dirt track.

"Wow!" Marie Claire breathed out. She'd seen this house from Ed's upstairs bedroom and she thought it beautiful then, but the view from the back was just gorgeous. Clint rounded a curve and she could see that the porch did indeed wrap all the way around the home.

"Who are we going to see?" Marie Claire questioned.

"I know the lady that owns this house," Ed commented. "Her husband died a few years ago. They had a very nice family and I miss Miller."

Clint stopped the car at the back porch steps, and he helped his wife and Ed as they emerged from their seats. There were several steps so Clint helped Ed to navigate them.

Clint, himself, never came over here until today, as he'd only spoken with Jeff and Dean, and Mrs. Montclair on the telephone. Awed at the size and grandeur of the exterior of the home, Clint couldn't wait to see the interior.

"Clint! Can you imagine living here?" Marie Claire excitedly asked her husband.

"No. I can't believe this place sat here in the middle of Seattle." Clint, himself, sounded awestruck.

Marie Claire wandered the porch, admiring the clean-cut flowerbeds that surrounded the stately home. Clint estimated the front and sides of the porch to be 10 to 12 feet wide. The house itself afforded pale blue vinyl siding, and two chimneys towered out of the roof.

"Hello, may I help you?" A small white-haired lady greeted them at the front of the house. "Oh, hello Ed. You must be Clint and Marie Claire Bellham! I'm Gertrude Montclair. My friends call me Trudi."

"Yes, ma'am, we are," the two said in unison.

"Well then, please, come on in. Ed said he wanted to come and visit. I'm glad he brought you both over also. I've heard so much about you from Jeff and Dean."

Inside the large living room now, Trudi asked them, "Can I get you some iced tea?"

"Yes, we'd love some," Marie Claire answered. "I will help." Marie Claire, awed by the home, was even more so by the huge kitchen. Twice as big as her kitchen in North Idaho, Marie Claire felt she'd spend her whole life in this room if she could, cooking. A stately oak pantry in one corner held canned goods, dry goods, and a host of other items every gourmet cook could need. Beside the pantry, sat a matching cleaning closet, which held a vacuum, broom, dustpan, and other assorted cleaning items.

A huge kitchen island with baking supplies on the shelves, and a countertop made of white, gray, and black multigrained marble sat in the middle of the kitchen. The stove and refrigerator were older models, but were clean and workable. Numerous cabinets than Marie Claire had ever seen in any one kitchen left the woman speechless, and the sink was of shiny black porcelain with stainless steel faucets. A large window over the sink overlooked the acreage to the North, and Marie Claire felt she could never tire of the view. She envisioned horses and cows, longhorns especially, wandering the vast acreage.

Trudi took them to see the upstairs rooms. Marie Claire and Clint commented on how the space was similar to Ed's home. Windows, similar to Ed's upstairs made for very bright rooms, which again were quite similar, but instead of carpeting, the dark oak floor was covered in white Persian wool in the master bedroom. The hallway and bath were oak, and the three smaller bedrooms were carpeted, each in its own color of dark blue, pale green, and red. Marie Claire thought it rather quaint, and felt she would not change a thing up here but the colors of the walls. She liked color, and all the walls were painted white.

Downstairs once more, Marie Claire finished the tour of the rooms. There was a mud room beside the kitchen, which contained a washer and dryer and a small bath off to the side, plus a door leading to the outside. There were two bedrooms downstairs, a master bedroom with its own bath, a smaller bedroom across from a main bathroom, and a large dining room, almost one wall taken up by a picture window overlooking Mount Rainier. The last room Clint led her to, the living room, had more windows around it and this is where they first come into the home. Clint seated her across from the fireplace on the large sofa. Iced teas in hand, Clint and Ed sat beside her and Trudi looked comfortable in her rocking chair.

Marie Claire looked around the room. Behind Trudi, a large window that overlooked Mount Rainier and Ed Brown's dairy took up most of one wall. Behind her was another large picture window, which overlooked the Cascade Mountain range. At the north end of the living room another window, just a bit smaller than the other two, found Marie Claire staring out at outbuildings, fences, and lots of trees.

Clint noticed that the windows were all thermal pane, and he commented on them.

"Yes. Dean, Ed, and Jeff came over a couple years ago and helped me fix some broken windows. A bad hailstorm came through and three were cracked by the golf ball sized hits. Ed told me I should get some new thermo panes put in. Dean set it up for me at a discounted price shortly after that."

Clint knew that Marie Claire was dying to have that kitchen, and he couldn't wait to see her face in a few moments.

"Wow, I'm glad you invited us over, Mrs. Montclair. I wouldn't have missed this for the world. I'd love to live in this place." Marie Claire looked around, she looked at her husband, and no one said a word. She did notice the wondrous looks on their faces and Clint looked a little askance at her.

Clint now had a smirk on his face.

"What? Did I say something wrong? What is going on, Clint?" Marie Claire asked coquettishly. She looked away for a second and then it hit her. "I am going to own this house, is that it? This is going to be mine, ours? Oh, Clint." Tears dripped down Marie Claire's cheeks. She jumped out of her seat and ran into the kitchen again and then back into the living room, and she sat down again and looked above the fireplace, which the hearth and mantle surround was made of pink Montana marble.

Everyone watched Marie Claire as she sat there looking up at a massive mounted longhorn steer head, complete with a seven foot set of horns. His mottled brown and white hide covered bony shoulders. Marie Claire hadn't seen this before. She sat there, mouth opened wide at the wonder of what she processed in her mind. She'd been taking in the mountain views and thinking her own private thoughts, not really seeing the living room closely. Then quietly, "Mrs. Montclair, would you mind leaving me your longhorn? I can't see him leaving this place. He looks so natural there and it would be a sacrilege to move him." With a hungry look in her eyes, Marie Claire whispered, "I'll pay you anything you ask."

Trudi had been looking into Marie Claire's eyes as she spoke. She then realized that Marie Claire, a lot like Trudi herself, had the same dreams and would cherish this place as much as she and her husband had at one time. "The story of that old boy is that we brought them here from Texas sixty years ago. I was eighteen and Miller was twenty one. We raised longhorns for a few years before my husband went in to horses. We bred and raised thoroughbreds. We raised cutting horses. Sam, the steer up there, was our practice animal. He died at the ripe old age of twenty-one. He was well loved by our children, and by Miller, my husband."

"We made it big in the races. We bought this place and started our own riding facility. I cooked for the workers here and my family, and Miller raised and showed his horses. We hired a trainer who was one of the best. We always won at the track, and Miller and a few good hired men taught riding lessons, as well as trained horses to cuts steers. He sold them for upwards of twenty thousand dollars for the best breeding stock."

"My children want me to move back to Minnesota to be near them. I would be pleased to see this place become a working horse ranch again," Mrs. Montclair commented a little wistfully.

"You must be sad to be leaving the only home you've known for so many years," Marie Claire commiserated. "I will love it here. I can see it being a facility for handicapped children, which has always been my dream."

The older woman looked into Marie's eyes. She saw compassion, love, laughter, honesty, and a touch of something that lingered in those brown eyes. Trudi thought she saw, just for a second, a bit of sadness lingering through the blessings. "Why don't you all have a seat, unless you want to check out the outdoors while I put on some tea and coffee?" Trudi Montclair scurried to the kitchen.

In the living room, Clint and Marie Claire were looking at each other. Clint told Marie about the terms of purchase. "Remember all those times I told you I had a meeting to go to?" Clint asked Marie Claire. "Dean is Mrs. Montclair's nephew by marriage, and Jeff has done all of the remodeling of this place. Ed has been good friends with the Montclair's for all these years. We've been talking about the two ranches, well the dairy and this place."

"Ed's been here a lot over the years, at first helping Mr. Montclair with repairs and whatnot, and now Trudi, and he knows the place. Well, he and I came up with a plan. With your home in North Idaho and the Bascolm's home both selling, we have just under six hundred thousand dollars between the two. The realtor called me just before coming over here. We have enough money to pay cash. What do you say? Do you like it? You'll be next-door to Jeff and Jeanette, and Ed too of course. My work is here." Clint didn't know what else to say. He looked into his wife's eyes as he waited, as they all waited, to hear what Marie Claire would answer.

"What say you, my dear? Shall we buy or shall we pass it by?" He bent at the waist and hovered very close to Marie Claire, hands straddling the back and armrest of the sofa where his wife sat, his voice very deep and menacing as he spoke, which got a gleam of delight from Marie's eyes and a playful punch in the stomach with her fist.

"I'll take it! Oh, Clint!" Marie Claire squealed, jumped off the couch. She grabbed her husband's neck and hugged him, and proceeded to dance around the room. Giggling like a schoolgirl, she ran upstairs and then back down a few minutes later to research the kitchen again.

"Show a little more enthusiasm, why don't you?" Ed said, laughing at Marie Claire, Clint and the others joining in.

Mrs. Montclair, who had been in the kitchen fixing everyone their drinks, placed one foot into the living room just as Marie Claire reached the breezeway into the kitchen.

"Excuse me," Marie Claire said as she stepped around the older woman and back into the kitchen. Handing out the tea and coffee-filled cups, the thoughtful Trudi could hear her pantry door open and close, and then the cupboard doors received the same treatment.

All was quiet for about two minutes and then, "I'm excited," a teary-eyed Marie Claire said, as she skipped into the living room and joined the people seated in front of the fireplace. Her eyes shone as Clint had never seen before. The excitement his wife exuded from her whole persona permeated the whole house. "I'm excited," she said again.

"Nooo. Really!" Clint teased.

Marie Claire's delirious laughter and trembling features brought joy to those who loved her; and enjoyment and appreciation for the younger woman, and the plans she had, shone out of the old woman's eyes.

Clint handed his wife a cup of tea, "Oh, really?" He asked laughingly. "No one could tell!"

Marie Claire, with shaky hands, laughed with the others over Clint's teasing her. It was kind of hard to stand let alone sit with a teacup in hand, unable to quit her laughing and crying, but when finally able to sit down on the sofa, she set her cup on the end table.

"Oh, Handsome! How much? Can we really afford this?" Marie Claire asked her husband, breathlessly.

Pleased as never in a long time, Trudi made her decision. She'd been thinking about it ever since this beautiful young woman stepped foot into her home. "How much do you have on you, Mr. Bellham?" Mrs. Montclair asked.

"I have a cashier's check here for five hundred thousand dollars, but looking at the barns and corrals, the forest land that seems to go for miles, I can see the place is worth probably five times that amount," Clint told the older woman.

"I'll take that and call it even," Mrs. Montclair said, reaching out her hand to take the check Clint held out to her. "I had the place appraised at well over five million dollars, but for you young people, I will take what you have on hand. I can't use that much money and my children are wealthy in their own right. They'd be more than happy to let me stay with them even if I was a pauper. Ms. Marie Claire, you may keep Sam the Steer. I'm glad you will make good use of this place, and love it as much as I have for so many years.

Do ya need ta give William his walkin' papers, Trudi, or will you keep 'im on here, Clint?" Ed asked.

"Who's William," Marie Claire asked.

"Oh, he's my handyman, and a big help to me," Trudi told them. "He's been here about seventeen years or so."

"Clint, shouldn't we keep him on? If he's a good worker, we may need him." Marie Claire felt she didn't want to make a man lose his job just because she bought the place from his previous employer.

"With me working every day, I suppose we'll need someone to help around the place too. I can't do it all and I don't want you worrying about what needs fixing or cleaned up. We'll keep him on."

"You need to go to the bank and get the paperwork transferred over," Ed told Clint. "They be closin' soon."

"I'll call the realtor. He gave the bank a one hundred thousand dollar down payment for me. That will give you six hundred thousand dollars altogether," Mrs. Montclair. "I know your asking price was four million nine hundred thousand dollars, and we appreciate you taking this check plus the hundred thousand," Clint told her, handing her the check

"Call me Trudi, please. This is more than I need, but thank you. Let me get my purse." Trudi Montclair stepped out of the room and Clint got on his cell phone. After the conversation ended, Clint told the group that they were to meet Ted Turner at the real estate office in half an hour.

Clint expressed appreciation for being able to park in front of the entrance when they reached their destination. This made it easier for Ed and Trudi to maneuver their arthritic bodies into the office. Within the hour the paperwork was signed, Trudi Montclair was in receipt of six hundred thousand dollars, and Marie Claire and Clint Bellham were the new owners of a 320,000-acre ranch. Clint took them all out to dinner afterwards.

Back at their apartment several hours later, the couple got on their knees. Marie Claire said, "God, you sure returned to me a thousand fold what was taken from me. Thank you, blessed Jesus, for your love and compassion!" Marie Claire prayed for a good hour.

The Bellhams, with so much for which to be thankful, Marie Claire knew she could never thank her Lord enough for his love and care.

Clint and Marie Claire turned in their apartment keys one week later. The paperwork for the ranch, after clearance with the title company, sat in Clint's hands and they were in receipt of the place free and clear. Insurance and taxes were a breeze, as they were lower than everyone first thought, and would be paid each June. Ed told them, before they bought the place, about tax breaks for certain land-use. Clint would speak with a tax advisor in the next week about what he should do about getting the breaks.

Clint marveled at his wife. The music of her laughter rang out, and her eyes shone with the love and wonderment for her Lord. After they got in the car to go back home, Marie Claire never quit praising God in song for his generosity to her. It did Clint's heart good to listen to her praises in her clear tenor voice.

Marie Claire, almost delirious with happiness, knew she never would have imagined living on a ranch again, let alone being able to do whatever she wanted with so much land. Marie Claire, Jeff, and various friends of theirs were looking forward to hunting this next fall. Marie Claire loved those Bambi's, but she wouldn't mind having some good tasting elk in her freezer. She hoped that Clint's brother, Gus, and his wife, Patty, would come for a visit. She'd met them at the wedding, and liked the joking between the brothers and the sweetness of Patty, whom Marie Claire felt would make a good friend.

That night, after walking all around their new abode, Marie Claire relaxed in her rocker that sat beside the big window overlooking Mount Rainier. Clint could see that calmness that settled over his bride, and he lay in bed admiring Marie Claire's serene look. He hadn't seen this side of her before, and he knew that moving here had been the best decision of his life – well, other than asking for Marie Claire to marry him, of course.

He watched as Marie Claire bowed her head in prayer and afterwards, she looked once again upon the big mountain and said, "Goodnight, dear Lord. Keep me in you care, please, and thank you again for this beautiful gracious gift you gave to me." She arose, laid her robe on the back of the chair, and walked around to the other side of the bed.

Marie Claire cuddled up to her husband, nuzzling his neck for a moment. Too excited, thus having a hard time sleeping, Clint and Marie Claire talked deep into the night.

Eventually, Clint rocked his wife to sleep as only he knew how.

Chapter Twenty-Nine

MARIE CLAIRE awoke at seven one rainy morning a month later. Not wanting to get up yet, she lay there thinking about horses, then Jeff and Jeanette. Her sister and brother-in-law had gotten back from their honeymoon a week ago, and were thrilled with Marie Claire's new home. Drowsily, she answered the ringing phone.

"Hello," she said in a scratchy sounding voice.

"Hi, sister-in-law. I need to talk to you right away. Sorry I woke you up." Jeff sounded stilted in speaking with Marie Claire. "I know it's early, but Ben called me in at five this morning. Can you come down to the office right away?"

Clint woke up and he could hear most of what Jeff said. Marie Claire, lying right next to him, made sure the phone rested near his right ear. He got up and grabbed some clean clothes. He proceeded to get ready for his workday.

"Yes, Jeff. I'll get dressed and be right down." Marie Claire hurriedly made the bed and padded into the shower.

"What was that all about?" Clint asked his wife.

"I don't know, Handsome. I'll call you if I need to later. Ok?" Marie Claire shouted from the shower.

"Ok. I'll make some coffee. Hurry down!" Clint answered his wife.

Clint called Joseph and told him he'd be a little late coming in to the office. He then fixed a light breakfast of bacon, eggs, and toast. He just finished setting down Marie Claire's coffee when she walked into the kitchen.

"Sit and eat before we leave, Sunshine. I can't imagine what Jeff needs you down at the FBI office for this morning."

Marie Claire looked up at Clint, a questioning glance showed in her eyes. "I don't know either, Handsome, but maybe they found out something more on the murders," Marie Claire shrugged her shoulders, not understanding the need either, "or something. I just don't know."

After a kiss goodbye, Clint rushed his wife out the door. He stayed behind to straighten the kitchen up before he left for work.

*   *   *   *

"Hi, Jeff. I made it. Sorry it took longer. Clint and I ate breakfast and I got here as fast as I could." Marie Claire rushed into Jeff's office and plopped into a seat next to his desk. "Why am I here?"

"Well, Marie Claire," Jeff breathed out. "Ben and Dean had me look through some old files that the Seattle police chief brought over. His office researched some cold case files over the last few days. Dean spoke with Margarethe Copeland and she and her husband came to see them yesterday. The Copelands said that their son Roy asked you to marry him. They know he went with you to see your mother and the Kingman's. They met him for dinner the night he disappeared, but they haven't seen him since. He told them was going to drive around the island and then go to work for a couple of hours, but he never made it there. Ben asked that we reopen this case." Jeff saw the sadness in Marie Claire's eyes, and he wished that he could take this hurt away from her. However, being a part of his job, he knew that he wouldn't try to get out of it. Dean found no one at the little paper shop Roy worked at who could remember the boy. His old boss died last year of a heart attack, and every other employee there never heard of Roy Copeland.

"Did anyone speak with you," Jeff looked through the pages until he found what he wanted, "regarding the evening of October 25, 1972?"

"That was the night that Roy disappeared, wasn't it?" Marie Claire asked.

"Yes, it was." Jeff continued looking through the paperwork on his desk. When he again looked up, he saw confusion and sadness in Marie Claire's eyes. Looking at her with compassion, Jeff asked,

"Can you explain to me again, the details of your last conversation with Roy?"

"Roy and I had gone to see my mother and then we went to the Kingman's. I finally decided to accept Roy's proposal. Roy, being the gentleman that he was, wanted to do the right thing by asking Mom and Dad Kingman for my hand in marriage. Francis threw a fit, and he kicked Roy out of the house. Mom Anne and I stood and watched Roy as he got in his car and waved goodbye to us. Mom said something about me eloping, but I could never do that. He drove out of the driveway, and that's the last time I ever saw him again. There was nothing untoward about it. It just happened to be a normal day in my life. But I could never understand why Roy never contacted me after that. He told me all the time that I was worth waiting for, and he kept coming back again and again. I think it was the fifth or sixth time that he asked me to marry him and I finally consented."

"Well, that's what we have in the paperwork too. We show Roy having dinner with his folks that night. Roy met his parents at the Spinnaker. He told them he was going to drive around for a while, and be home later after work. Mr. and Mrs. Copeland told us that Roy was very upset that evening, that driving helped calm him down. He told his parents he would be back before ten, that cruising in his car and thinking about his troubles helped clear his mind. The Copelands last saw Roy at six thirty, after dinner, and they got home around nine thirty that evening. Mrs. Copeland stayed up to await her son's arrival back home. However, at twelve thirty the next morning when he never showed up, Mrs. Copeland called his shop, and then went to bed without speaking with anyone. She never did see her son again."

A stoic Marie Claire sat listening to the words Jeff said. When Jeff finished giving her all the information he could, he stacked the papers neatly and put them back in the file folder in front of him.

"That's all we have for now, Marie Claire. I'll be right back. I just need to leave for a second and then I think you can go." Jeff stepped out no more than two minutes when he poked his head back in his office. "It's okay; we're done with you for now. Say good morning to Jeanette for me, please. She was sound asleep when I left, and when I kissed her on the cheek she never moved."

"I will do that for you, Jeff. Do you want me to kiss her too?" Marie Claire said jokingly. It gave Jeff's heart a lift, knowing that Marie

Claire wasn't brooding over the loss of her friend. But that was right now, and he felt pretty sure it would hit her later on.

"I don't think that's necessary," Jeff said to Marie Claire smilingly. "Just tell her I miss her."

"Will do," Marie Claire told her brother-in-law. "Maybe we can have pizza tonight," she commented as she walked out the door, her black leather purse slung over her right shoulder.

As Jeff watched Marie Claire walk across the street, he pondered their recent conversation. In a few minutes he would have to walk back to another office and sit down with Ben, where they would again go over the events that happened on that June night over twenty years ago.

A whole new can of worms opened up, and Dean expected Jeff to get this account closed.

Roy, where are you? What happened to you when you left the Spinnaker? How deeply did you love Marie Claire? Did you leave the island hoping never to return, did you leave against your will, or are you still there - somewhere?

Those were only a few of the questions for which Jeff would have to come up with answers. He knew he had his work cut out for him.

*   *   *   *

Marie Claire drove south on the Alaska Way Viaduct. She stopped at the nearest fast food joint to grab a large cup of coffee. She ordered one with lots of cream and a package of sweetener.

On the road again, Marie Claire's thoughts turned to Roy. She too asked herself the same questions that Jeff had asked, not coming up with any answers. She had known Roy pretty well back then, and she knew that if he were able to, he would have been back to get her. She did not want to believe it, but in her heart of hearts, she knew that Roy was buried somewhere on the island.

Clint came home early when Marie Claire returned to the house. He and Jeff sat at the kitchen table talking and drinking steaming cups of coffee when she walked into the house.

"What are you doing home, Clint? I just saw you at the office, Jeff. What brings you here this early in the day? I thought you had a meeting with Ben Jackson." Marie Claire looked with smiles at the two men in her life, grabbed a cup of coffee herself and added a packet of sweetener and some cream. She took a seat at the table opposite Clint.

"You must have stopped off somewhere and shopped! I made it here in the same amount of time as it takes everyday! Ben told me to come here and talk to you some more. What's your excuse?" Jeff knew Marie Claire liked to be teased, and he was giving it all he could.

"Smarty pants! I did stop to look at grain and check out tack and whatnot for when I get more horses. Clint and I have a few things to get done around here first and then I'll get my stock."

"Marie Claire, I spent my evening doing research on the Copeland case. I believe Roy was murdered. He proposed to you a few months after the school dance. You told him you wanted to finish high school first, in answer to his third proposal. He talked to his mother and she said it hurt her too, but she told Roy that it was probably for the best. Mrs. Copeland really likes you. She thought you would be the best girl for Roy to marry, but she told Dean last night, just as she told Roy years ago, that it was a wise girl who took her priorities into consideration first."

"He asked you to marry him several times, didn't he? Yet, it was the sixth time, I believe, that you finally accepted. You must not have been in love, am I right?" Jeff asked her softly.

"I guess that was part of it. I didn't really know at the time what real love truly consisted of. I never had any close encounters in all my life to show me what love meant, except with my grandparents and Uncle Zane. But, that's family. I didn't feel mushy or fluttery anytime Roy or any other boy came around. Roy was my only true boyfriend, until Clint. I know the difference now between true love and just friend-ship," Marie Claire commented casually, but thoughtfully. "I didn't even love Francis, not in the way a wife loves her husband. I always felt dirty with him. I missed Mom Anne and the kids. I wonder what happened to them all." Marie Claire became quiet. It was the first time in a long time that they came to mind, and she did wonder about them now.

"Well, it might interest you to know that Dean contacted them this morning. They're living in Florida, all of them. Anne married a swell guy named Al, and she told Dean he is good to her and the kids. He put the girls through college and set them up with places to live. Michael is a nuclear physicist and working at a major lab in Kissimmee St. Cloud, where Al works. Cathy married a pharmacist, and she's a hairdresser. She has two kids, a boy and a girl. Kaye has a horse ranch in Tallahassee. She graduated as a veterinarian's assistant. She's not married, but is dating a guy who is in the Air Force."

Marie Claire looked with wonder at Jeff. Her eyes were shiny with tears of happiness. "Kaye always did seem to worship me. I didn't want that, didn't expect that, but she was a sweet kid and I love her still."

"I'm sure you can get the address and write to them, Marie Claire." Clint knew how much his wife fell in love with people, and family was very important to her.

"You know, if they wanted to contact me, Mom would surely have asked. I'll let it ride for now. Maybe later I'll decide to get in touch, but not right now." Marie Claire got up out of her chair and walked to the sink. She rinsed out her cup, staring out the window at her acres of land, and then, with a wandering look, stared at Mt. Rainier as though to seek some kind of message from the snow covered giant.

Jeff, watching his friend, finished what he came here to do. "About a week before he last proposed to you, Roy went to see your biological mother on his own. She told him why you left home, and that you couldn't have any children. Roy didn't know that about you. You never told anyone else, did you, Marie Claire?"

Marie Claire turned to face the men. "Jeff, Clint, that was a terrible thing to happen to me. It was degrading, embarrassing, and it almost killed me. I wanted to forget. I never talked to anyone about what happened to me. I was eleven at the time of that episode. You can't know the hurt, the heartache, the pain a child goes through when they are violated. I can't talk about it. Why couldn't someone help me?" Marie Claire twirled back to the sink and stood there looking at the mountain, as still as stone. Clint knew his wife hurt though, as he watched her shoulders shaking. He and Jeff quietly flanked Marie Claire and held her as she cried.

*   *   *   *

A little while later, in control of her emotions, Marie Claire again sat with the men.

"Marie Claire, I agree with Dean's assessment. Roy would not have disappeared of his own free will. He seems to have been a happy young man, knowing where he was going and how to get there. His mother doted on him, and Roy doted on his mother. We have to add Francis to the mix. He's the only one with a motive. Where was he on the day Roy disappeared? You told us he threw a fit about the marriage proposal. Did you see Francis on that day and where was he, where had he been, what was he doing? What time did you see Francis? What occurred between you and him that day? Can you remember? What sort of day was it? Did he have mud on his shoes because it had been raining?"

"There is a lot to think about, a lot to remember. We need to sit and put the facts together. Will you help me, Marie Claire? Can you remember back that far? It's been, what, over twenty years. His mother remembers every second, but of course she would. She loved Roy like no one else in his life, other than his father. But, fathers aren't nurturing as mothers are." Jeff awaited answers.

Marie Claire had one question. "Why wait this long? Why didn't the investigation, and I know there was one, find out what happened that day? Why leave it for twenty years"

"The police could find no evidence of foul play, Marie Claire. They spent over two years researching, asking questions, and talking to everyone involved. No trace of anything – no murder evidence, no arguments with anyone, no blood anywhere. Everyone questioned had rock solid alibis. It just sat in the files until a new police chief researched cold cases. That's how Ben and Dean got involved. We're the "experts"! We were told to take the case over."

"Oh," Marie Claire nodded her head and looked at Clint, who could only nod back. Together, they sat back down so Marie Claire could finish telling her story to Jeff.

*   *   *   *

Francis received a phone call that same morning that Marie Claire was called into the FBI office. He answered the questions without flaw. He remembered the night of Roy's disappearance very well.

Ten minutes later, no one the wiser to the type of call he'd received, he left the office after notifying one of his partners he was going out for a few minutes.

"Larry," Francis greeted his associate, "I'm going to grab a coffee and go see a client for a little bit."

"Fine, partner. See you when you get back. Is there anything I can do while you're out?"

"No. I have my answering machine on, and I'm pretty much caught up with things right now. I'm still waiting on that Roybal case to come in, but the judge said that would be a day or so yet. I'll be back." He exited the office as quickly as he could, and drove to Alki Point in West Seattle to take in the sites and do some thinking.

*　　*　　*　　*

"I remember the night he proposed. We went to see a movie and then stopped for a burger. Roy and I went over to my mother's house, and we sat and visited with her for a little while and told her that I accepted Roy's marriage proposal. It was raining that day. Roy told me that he was going to go into the Naval Academy and then he proposed. Roy told me that he wanted me to be with him. I remember I was a senior, and I told him I wanted to finish school. No one else in my family had done that and I wanted to finish. An education is important if you want a good job, and I knew I wanted to go to college."

"I told Roy that I wanted him to see my parents, Mom and Dad Kingman. I asked him to ask for their blessing, and so we drove home. Roy helped me out of the car at the garage, and we went into the house together. Mom and Dad were sitting on the sofa watching TV, and holding hands, we approached them tentatively. Roy told Mom and Francis that he had proposed to me and that I'd accept if they gave their blessings. That's when Francis came unglued. Roy got in his car, and Mom and I stood there and watched him drive away. That's the last time I ever saw Roy again. He had the ring in his jacket pocket. I never even got a chance to see it, to wear it."

"By the time Roy proposed, I knew that I needed to get out of that house. I wanted my life to be normal, as it hadn't been for quite a long time. I wanted Mom Anne to have a chance to make things right for me. I think it was the first time that I ever rebelled against my father figure, and he became angry and refused to let anyone come between us. I should have known what was going to happen. He came downstairs, following me to my room. Mom Anne said something to him that I couldn't hear, and then I heard her fall to the floor. I just reached the last step, when Francis threw open the stairwell door and ran down the stairs to catch up with me. He dragged me into my bedroom, slammed the door, and pushed me onto my bed. He screamed at me, and when he was done with me, he ran back upstairs and he and mom got into an argument. Francis left shortly after.

Roy disappeared, I never saw him after that day, and I had no clue what to do. I thought maybe Roy went off and married Gidget, an old friend of Cathy's. They dated a while, but a few weeks later I saw Gidget in town and I stopped to chat. She hadn't seen Roy in weeks. Mrs. Copeland called me several times during those weeks, and I knew something was wrong. Roy wouldn't have taken off without letting his mother know what he was doing, where he was going. Thoughtful, kind, and smart is how a person could describe Roy."

Marie Claire thoughtfully pondered as she sat drinking a fresh cup of coffee. Her head bent downward as she fingered her cup. "I remember something now," Marie Claire stated, looking up once again. "I was in my room working on my math homework. I stayed there after Roy left our house. I ran upstairs to ask Dad Francis for some help, and Mom said he went to run an errand and left maybe an hour before. This was maybe seven or so. I did the best I could on the math as Mom couldn't help me."

"When Francis did get home, it was around midnight. He came downstairs to see my math. I guess Mom told him I needed help, or else he just came down to see how I felt. I showed my homework to him and he made a correction, and then he left to go back upstairs. He had never done that before, gone out and stayed out that late at night before. He usually sat with us to watch TV or visit with us kids about school, and around nine we went to bed." Marie Claire sat there for a little while longer, thinking her thoughts.

"You know, it takes a half hour to get to the Seattle end of the ferry from where we lived. From the house it takes twenty minutes to get to the Tacoma end of the ferry. It's a fifteen minute trip either way by boat. There would have been no time to get off the island. If Roy is dead and buried, it's a matter of looking on the island somewhere for his body."

Jeff's head jerked up at that declaration. "Marie Claire, we need to know exactly where the house is that belong to the Kingman's. Can you tell me that, and then I will talk to Dean and figure out some scenarios." Jeff exuded excitement that Marie Claire remembered this much. It was a lot when you thought about it. The timeline seemed right, and Jeff knew how long the ferry trips took because he went to the island before. His family went there for a reunion and a picnic at Stuart Park a few years ago. He'd gone there several times with friends and family just to enjoy the serenity that was Vashon Island, before moving in with Ed.

"In the morning, I'll take you over there and show you where the house is. My good friends live next door. A drug dealer bought the place from the Kingman's, but he went to prison a couple of years later. I don't know if anyone ever did buy it after that. I used to buy the island newspaper until Francis forced me to give it up." Marie Claire shared some of her remembrances of Roy Copeland with them.

Afterwards, Jeff got up to make some phone calls. Clint walked outside for a few minutes and then came back in when Jeff called him.

"Dean and Ben will be here at seven in the morning. I will let Jeanette know the scoop. She and Martha can stay together tomorrow. You two," Jeff glanced at both of them, "be ready to go. We'll take the Escalade so we can all fit. The guys said to say hello and that they are looking forward to seeing you again." With that and a 'thanks for the coffee and conversation,' Jeff headed home. He had a lot to think about.

Chapter Thirty

Two months after procuring the work force and talking to the governor, the construction of Rocking Acres Campground started. Governor Spacey, after making phone calls and sending letters, received word back that seven thousand trees were being delivered to 7 Bellham Lane, Midway, Washington, a gift from the State of Washington as a donation from the state parks who were clearing out old growth to make way for new. The fir trees were dug by backhoe, roots intact, and crews waited to be sent to the ranch to help plant in a manner respective of camping and horseback riding.

Bulldozers and other equipment had already started digging the one-mile long by thirty feet deep by one-mile wide lake. Natural underground artesian water sources, plus the yearly rainfalls, would assure the lake kept full year round. Cement trailer pads were constructed, and a clubhouse with an indoor pool, kitchen facilities, and assorted gaming tables had to be purchased and set in place for people wanting to play pool, Ping-Pong, and whatever else. Clint instructed a theater type addition be added to the back of the building so that folks could watch movies. He hadn't fully thought that situation out, but at least it was a start.

Clint and Tally Rodriguez, a foreman Marie Claire hired a few weeks ago to help with the longhorn cattle she'd purchased, devised the whole setup for the campground. The men, along with Richard, approached the governor about it and before a week was out, money had been donated from multiple sources to get the idea off the ground and into fruition.

"We need more campsites and tourist places closer to Seattle. This is a great idea, Mr. Bellham. Let me talk to my people here and in D.C. I'll have some news for you by the end of next week." Governor Spacey said his peace then had to get to work on his new legislature. That was three weeks ago. No one could believe that things would happen so fast.

*   *   *   *

A short while after they got up, before breakfast, Clint found Marie Claire outside walking the pasture. She had a large travel mug of coffee in her hand. "Sunshine, I want to show you some plans I have for the acreage nearest the road. Would you ride out there with me?" Clint had Jeff's horse, Saber, saddled up for Marie Claire and he would ride his dirt bike. She would follow him, since she had no idea what was going on. She'd heard big equipment since late last week, but she never sensed it had something to do with her property. She just walked this morning, enjoying the sunshine and the lowing of the cattle down near the trees leading to the forest service land.

Clint stopped at the fence line bordering I-5. "Ok, Sunshine, I'd like you to follow me. I have staked out where I want to put a lake. I thought a trailer park would be a great way to help our community and bring in some extra money, too. The section I have in mind has quite a bit of weeds and is underwater most of the year. It's really no good for grazing. This would be another way of utilizing some otherwise worthless land."

"Wow," Marie Claire breathed out, feeling the goose bumps on her back and arms. Clint sure knew ways to surprise her. "I never knew you had that thought in your head, Clint. That sounds great. Let's go!"

Afterwards, Marie Claire knew that her husband had a smart mind. There were trees where the construction was going on, so neither the Farthingworths nor Marie Claire saw the activity there on their land. Marie Claire knew she would have fun with this venture. They would have a clubhouse and acreage for parking. Marie Claire felt as excited as she'd ever been.

*   *   *   *

This morning at breakfast, back from their jaunt to the far pastureland, Clint told Marie Claire, "The campground, well, it's an early birthday present. I don't know anything about buying horses, so I had to leave that chore up to you. For now, that huge surprise I showed you this morning is for your benefit. I hope you like it." Marie Claire smiled at Clint.

She made a comment. "Can we afford all this? What you have planned here? It cost billions of dollars, doesn't it?"

"It's costly, I'll grant you that," he said, "but we have help with the finances through the government, and donations. I put money out to hire construction workers, Richard applied for the grant, but Governor Spacey helped with that. We'll have a full working campground here by the end of summer. What do you think?"

"I couldn't think of anything I'd like better! We won't have to travel to camp. We can just walk out our back door! This will be beautiful. I can't wait to see it reach fruition! Getting up to sit in his lap, Marie Claire kissed Clint and said, "Thank you, my love, for the gift. I know how much you like to camp, fish, and hunt, and just enjoy nature. I like the wide-open spaces and wildlife too. Oh, Handsome, I just love you! Thanks again."

Clint explained about the trees that were on their way to them, and that they would have to stock the lake with fish.

"Richard Hillman, Ed's dairy manager and foreman, will help me get the fish. He's researching types now."

"That'll be wonderful, Handsome. We'll have to buy a couple of row boats and rent those out, and we'll have something to do with our free time, too. I love sitting in a boat in the middle of a lake reading a book." In appreciation and because she thought Clint was the best thing to ever happen to her, she suggested going back to the house.

*   *   *   *

The next morning, being Friday, Jeff and the other agents showed up right on time. Clint and Marie Claire were ready to go, and Clint headed out to work while Marie Claire got in the car with Jeff. Clint, having taken two days off, needed to help Joe at the factory today. Everyone understood, and the other men assured Clint that they would watch over his wife.

Jeff drove to Denny's first, parked, and they all got out of the van and walked to the restaurant. A waitress led them to a large table by the back window. Everyone wanted to listen to Jeff's idea, and then make a joint decision where to start. Ben ordered coffee and sweet rolls for everyone, and they sat talking quietly until the orders came. Coffee cups full, their sweet rolls in front of them, Ben spoke first.

"We will drive to the island and go to Marie Claire's old home first, and then we will branch out from there."

"My friends, Rand and Kara Mallory, still live next door. I used to babysit for them. They had a big garden every year and the kids raised sheep and goats. Rabbits came along later and we all did 4H together." Marie Claire told the guys.

"I can hardly wait to see them again," Marie Claire told them excitedly, as she slapped her fingers on the table and squirmed in her seat, looking like she was dancing to a tune only she could hear.

Their meeting over, en mass they exited the restaurant, filled their cars once again, and caught the ferry to Vashon Island. It took a half hour to get to Sequoia, the area where the Kingman's once lived. The house still stood there where it always had, but it looked like no one had lived there for years. The barn and house showed wear from the weather. The roofs over all the buildings weathered the worst. A thick growth of vegetation clung to each one, as though a mossy green carpet lay there. The Kingmans used an oil based stain that weathered fairly well, but the cedar siding was just starting to show gray through the dark mahogany stain. The gutters were falling off the eaves, and two of them lay in the front yard. There had been no upkeep done to the yard or fruit trees, and everything grew wild. The siding on the house and barn showed deterioration, and the front door stood open from someone, kids probably, breaking in.

Tentatively, Marie Claire led the way inside. She could see that the once beautiful pine flooring was mildewed and scratched from not having any care. Jeff commented that they would find the reason for the mildew downstairs.

"Do you see the greenish black coloring throughout the flooring? The downstairs has to be very damp in order for the mildew to seep through the flooring above." Dean looked at Marie Claire. The men could see the sadness in the woman's eyes. The once shiny and multi-grained oak flooring now showed black staining throughout.

"Do you mind if we walk around up here first?" Marie Claire squeaked. There was a lump big as Texas in her throat. Her voice was taught with heartache.

"No, that will be fine," Ben answered her.

"This must be very difficult, Marie Claire. Many memories are held within these walls. I am so sorry to have to bring you here." Dean touched her shoulder, stopping her in mid stride. His right index finger tipped her chin upwards and the agent saw the pain and glassiness in those eyes. He truly was sorry, and nonspeaking, Marie Claire let him hold her.

Keeping a stalwart appearance, though everyone could see Marie Claire's torment, the woman gently pushed herself away, and led the agents through the dining room and into the kitchen. They followed her through the breezeway to the hallway. They saw the three bedrooms and the one bath, and then they were back to the open doorway.

Marie Claire stopped and took a deep breath. "This," Marie Claire said as she opened a door on the left into a large room filled with windows that let in lots of light, "is my old bedroom." Everyone could see the green-black mildew that permeated the pine floor in this room also. Marie Claire stood at the window overlooking the front yard and the woods beyond. The FBI agents looked through the closet and around all the window casings. Seeing nothing of interest, they followed Marie Claire into the living room on the left.

A massive gray stone fireplace commandeered more than half of the South end wall in this room. There were ashes in the bottom, covering the grate that had not been cleaned out.

"What hung here Marie Claire?" One of the agents asked.

"We had a black powder musket and a powder keg from Civil War times that hung from those nails," Marie Claire answered. "No, it didn't work!" she reiterated before anyone could ask.

The men walked around and searched every corner of the twenty foot square room. The large picture window overlooking the Olympic Mountains and the western passage was framed with oak, which now was steeped in mildew like the floors. Marie Claire led them through the adjoining dining room, where they again looked at every corner as well as the picture window in here. The six agents entered the kitchen, but Marie Claire held back. The agents searched every cabinet, corner, and under around and behind the old stove and refrigerator that stood there. Two of them pulled out the appliances, and every inch of floor space was searched. They did the same to the dishwasher. The window above the sink, and the larger window under where the kitchen table sat, also received scrutinization.

Marie Claire sauntered through the short hallway, where, on the right stood the door leading down the stairs, and Ben opened and closed that door and he opened the door on the left. Jeff looked through the empty broom closet and found nothing but dust and dirt that collected throughout the home. Marie Claire led them to the master bedroom, which was the door on the left in the hallway. She waited in the hall, while the agents searched the room with the adjoining bathroom. Floors, windows, doorways, everything received the same scrutiny as the rest of the house.

When they were done here, Marie Claire opened the door that once was Kaye's bedroom. Afterwards, she showed them the main bath. After about an hour, they were ready to head downstairs.

Ben led the way. The smell of mildew permeated this area. At the bottom of the stairs straight ahead and a little to the left stood an open doorway. This is where Marie Claire spent three years of her life. The once bright yellow paint on the walls had become a putrid smelling mass of dark green growth. The once shiny oak surrounding the window was now rotting wood. The window itself was blotched with green growth. Marie Claire watched as three men searched the large walk-in closet. The others walked around the room shaking their heads. Marie Claire went outside as she left them to research the rest of the basement. Standing under the outside deck, Marie Claire looked through the window to the stone fireplace, a twin of the one upstairs.

I remember the big pool table that used to stand there in front of the fireplace. Looking as far to the left as she could, Marie Claire thought, *the big old piano used to stand there on that wall, and I remember how Kaye used to practice and practice.* Walking through the basement door again, Marie Claire went to the basement kitchen. *I used to play my records while I churned butter in this room. At the sink there, I used to separate the cream from the milk. There stood the freezer that was full of little yellow plastic containers filled with fresh butter. And on that wall,* Marie Claire looked opposite the sink, *were the shelves that Mom and I and Cathy would stack with freshly canned vegetables.*

With the agents now done perusing the basement, the next and last place they searched was the kitchen. Agent Millford, a recent graduate from Quantico, was the first to see Marie Claire standing in the kitchen, tears running down her face. He signaled to Ben Jackson, who held up a hand to the others to wait.

Marie Claire turned to leave the room and felt embarrassed, even devastated, to see the others waiting for her. Embarrassed to the point of being mortified, Marie Claire covered her eyes with her hands and rushed outside.

"Jeff, go see to your sister-in-law." Ben signaled to Jeff and pointed to the door, speaking just above a whisper.

While the agents scrutinized the downstairs kitchen, Jeff hurried to get to Marie Claire. As he stepped outside, he saw the open gate and Jeff saw Marie Claire running to the woods just past the barn. At a fast pace, Jeff rushed to catch up with her. He had no idea that the acreage ended at the fence half way into the short area of woods.

Jeff came upon a stream that was maybe a foot across and not very deep. There on an old stump sat Marie Claire. Elbows bent, hands covering her face, Marie Claire wept. Jeff quietly and tenderly cupped both her elbows in his hands and bade her stand.

"I'm so sorry, Jeff. I guess my thoughts and my feelings collided. I wound up blubbering in front of everyone and I got so embarrassed."

"Can you get through this? There are going to be a lot of questions, but it needs to get done Marie Claire. I need you to be strong, as strong as I've ever seen you. I'll stay here with you, as long as you need me to." Jeff was gentle when talking to his friend. He understood Marie Claire, and he was sorry that he had to put her through this.

"I'm okay," Marie Claire said, "I'm ready to go up now. Please forgive me for being such a baby. The memories just roll in, and I hate it."

"No apology necessary, but if it helps, you're forgiven. Since I'm down here, I guess I'll look through the barn." Marie Claire showed Jeff the horse stalls, the milking stall complete with stantion, which kept the cow from leaving by way of a swivel board that swung up behind the ears and locked at the top. It was built as part of the haymow where the cow ate while she waited for the milking to be finished.

The old milk stool still sat in the corner, covered by thick dust and cobwebs. "Looks like no one ever used this place down here," Marie

Claire said to no one in particular. As in the olden days when Mom, Dad, Cathy, or anyone else chose to, at odd times of the day, be in the barn, Marie Claire looked out the window overlooking the hill up to the house, and she saw the five other agents coming down to the barn.

Jeff spotted some old straw like bales next to the milk stall, and he knew this used to be where hay would be kept. He walked through a closed door and found work benches. They were covered in mold and mildew, same as the house condition, and he knew that marijuana had been grown down here, too.

Marie Claire showed him the end room where Cathy helped Kaye raise baby pheasants and other fowl. This room, as before, was still dusty and fairly benign.

"Jeff, why is everything so moldy around here? The house, this workshop, the basement, everything looks moldy." Marie Claire tried to be brave, she put on a very hard front, but inside, Jeff knew she was hurting.

As the others joined them, hearing Marie Claire's question, Ben said, placing hands either side of Marie Claire's shoulders, "This was once a drug lords habitat, wasn't it? I believe Jeff told me that a drug dealer or someone like that bought the place at one time and then he went to prison." Marie Claire looked Ben in the eyes and nodded her head. "Well, marijuana was grown in almost every room in this house. Mainly downstairs, but we saw evidence in your old room upstairs and in the kitchen where plants were nurtured. Misting has to be done to keep the plants healthy and growing good. It's very moist in drug houses so the plants can grow rich and thick. That is why there is so much mold and mildew around the floors, windows, and door casings, and penetrating that beautiful wood. This looked like it was a beautiful place at one time. I'm sorry it's so run down."

"Thanks, Ben. I never was into drugs and never knew the significance of the signs before. I've learned something new, not that I needed to know about drugs and dealers, and everything else, but I don't think Francis was into any of that stuff. I'm sure he wasn't."

"I'm sure he wasn't either, my dear. He couldn't be a lawyer if he was convicted of any of that kind of thing."

Marie Claire moved away from the agents. She left them to look to their content at whatever they needed to. The young woman walked around the barn once more. The roof sagged. The lean-to where the animals used to come in out of the weather was torn down. The stall where One Dollar died was still intact, and the other one built for the second horse still stood too.

Lots of memories that Marie Claire would never forget swarmed into her brain. Lots of love had been here at one time. Laughter was plentiful as Marie Claire would say something the others thought funny, but she was included in the gaiety. They weren't making fun of her after all, only teaching her, and learning something about life themselves.

I remember that old rooster that used to attack us all the time. He cut Kaye's arm when he attacked her that last morning. We'd gone somewhere with the church that day, and we got home past dark. I remember grabbing a hammer as I went down to feed. There is the wall where the rooster sat sleeping every night. I remember hearing his coo as I stuck some hay in the cow's manger for morning. I lashed out with the hammer and hit the rooster as hard as I could. He fell. I ran to the house and called for Francis. "Dad, you need to check on that old rooster. I think I killed him," I remember saying.

"That bird wasn't hurting anyone," he said.

"I know, tonight, but he hurt Kaye this morning and would hurt somebody every chance he got. I told you I was going to kill him, and I think I did. You need to check and make sure, because I don't want him to suffer."

Dad Francis went down and finished him off. I hurt the chicken badly, but he was indeed suffering.

Marie Claire smiled at that remembrance. She'd gotten a good chewing out, and she was told that she needed to finish a job that she started, but, thank Heavens; she never had to kill anything else again.

Yes, life was sweet in the first days and months after coming here. The good times had been fleeting for her, but nevertheless, she knew that what she had endured here, only made her stronger.

*　　*　　*　　*

The seven of them walked back up to the house. After the agents were done scrutinizing everything to their satisfaction, they congregated in the driveway.

"Is this place for sale? Can someone find out for me, please?" Marie Claire asked quietly.

Jeff called information from his car phone. He contacted the realty in town. Turnbow Realty was open and yes, they had some information on the place. "The First State Bank owns it and it is not for sale, but the bank may be inclined to sell it," A nice sounding woman told Jeff over the phone. "Their number is 555-123-9845. Harold Blunte is the manager. Ask for him."

"Thank you so very much." Jeff told the woman. After dialing the bank's number, Harold Blunte answered. "If the agents can wait," he said, "I will be out in about a half hour."

"Yes, we can wait," Jeff told the banker, with a smile in his voice. Jeff hung up and smiled at Marie Claire, who knew that her question had been answered affirmatively.

The men sidled away; talking amongst themselves, leaving Marie Claire to daydream or think of Roy, or whatever it was she wanted to think of. They knew her life story, but there was no way they could know what was in her heart. Sadness warred with love, which warred with hatred, just like it did so many years ago.

God, please, let me remember the good times. Let me find Mom and Kay again, please. I love them. I know they don't know that, but I do. I always have. I want my mom and I don't know how to get her back! Please help me, father. Marie Claire stood there thinking, and then suddenly she felt like crying; Jeff wanted her to be strong for him, for them, and Marie Claire knew she was a wimp, but her heart was heavy, way too heavy, and she needed some release.

In about fifteen minutes, everyone saw a car coming down the driveway. A short, heavy set, balding man emerged from the Lincoln. What hair he did have left on his bald pate was light gray, nearly white. On his long thin face, he wore orange round glasses that helped him see through pale light blue eyes. He introduced himself to Jeff, who stood closest to him.

Hi, I'm Jeff. This is," and he introduced the agents to Mr. Blunte and then they walked over to where Marie Claire stood. Taking pains to wipe her damp eyes and appear to get herself together, Marie Claire smiled timidly at Mr. Blunte. The banker looked closely at the young woman as he shook her hand. He thought this young woman was a remarkable sight. He'd never met such a beautiful female in his life. Her bangs hung down to her eyebrows, and the very top and just a bit of both sides of her thick hair was pulled back in a ponytail. The bulk of her black hair shined like silk and hung loose as it fell below her shoulders to her waist. She wore a low cut, long sleeved, white cotton blouse tucked into the waistband of black designer jeans. Black boots adorned her feet.

"Hello Mr. Blunte," Marie Claire said after being introduced and shaking hands with him. "I lived here once. The place is a mess, and I wondered if I could buy it."

Mr. Blunte looked the woman over. She was very cordial and had good manners. He knew the Kingman's of course, but he'd never met this daughter. She was quite beautiful. She didn't look like either of her parents, but then, he hadn't seen them in years.

"I hold title to this house. Before your folks moved away, another man bought it from them for cash. I took over when the new owner was imprisoned for drug trafficking a few years ago. I can sell it to you for fifty thousand dollars. I know your dad built this house himself for thirty-five thousand dollars, but it needs a lot of work. I can give it to you for that. I guess you're thinking of moving back here?" Mr. Blunte rattled on.

"No, Mr. Blunte. I would never live here again. I would like to fix the place up and sell it to a nice family, someone who has a child interested in horses. I have a family in mind, and they have a handicapped boy."

*   *   *   *

Marie Claire stood there lost in thought as she thought back a few days, of the family she met recently through Martha, Ed's housekeeper. They got lost trying to find someone's home, and Martha, noticing the little boy's limp, inquired if they were looking for a riding facility. Of course, the couple was intrigued by what Martha was telling them of the Rocking Horse Ranch next door. They drove over and spoke with Marie Claire.

"Hi, I'm Jennifer, Jenna to most folks, and this is my husband, Maxwell, and little boy, Jared. He was born crippled and our house just burned down. We were looking for the Eastwicks, some friends of ours. We got lost. The nice woman next door, Martha I think her name is, sent us here. It would be wonderful if, after we get settled again somewhere, we lost everything we own in the fire, and, well, it would be nice to get Jared into a riding academy like you will be opening up, soon I think Martha said."

Before she could speak again, the woman's husband shook hands with Marie Claire. "My wife tends to rattle a bit, sorry. Yes, we would like to see Jared learn to ride. I heard of programs for handicapped children. It gives them a life they never knew before. Do you think you can help?"

"Marie Claire chuckled jovially, as she bent to ruffle the boy's hair. "We are working on the place now. I wanted to start lessons in two or three weeks, but I have to procure the horses yet and stock up on tack and special equipment needed for the children. We have bleachers set up in the arena and stations for seven children at a time to mount their steeds. We're in the middle of a trying time right now, so my plans are on hold for a few more months." Out of her pocket, Marie Claire pulled out a business card and handed it to Mrs. Stevenson. "Please," she reiterated, "call me in a month and I will let you know what I can then. I would love to have you and your boy come see me when it's convenient and I will go over my plans. It's never too early to round up my clientele, and I want to make sure Jared is on the list."

*　　*　　*　　*

That was just three days ago. A lot happened since then. Marie Claire, realizing she'd been daydreaming, didn't hear Mr. Blunte until he coughed louder. *Mr. Blunte must think me crazy for letting my mind wander,* when she finally realized she was being watched. She shrugged her shoulders and said, "Sorry. I was thinking about the little boy." She dipped her head, looked at her feet, put her hands in her back pockets, and looked up once again.

"Mr. Blunte, I can write you a check now, or would you rather have a cashier's check? I bank with First Federal Credit Union."

"Let me take your account number." Marie Claire handed the banker a blank check. "I'll be right back." Mr. Blunte quickly walked to his car and closed the door.

Jeff, half angrily, asked his sister-in-law, "Marie Claire, do you know what you are doing?" His hands sat on his hips, and she could see the concern in his eyes. "Have you thought how much it will cost to fix this place up? I bet the floors alone will cost thousands."

Marie Claire, brown eyes bright with mischief, smiled and answered him in a cheeky manner, "So, sue me, Jeffrey. I want to do this. I need to do this, and I will use some of the guys I know in my life to help me out. I will be taking advantage probably, but I know that I'm going to need your help." Staring into Jeff's eyes, adamant to make him understand, she continued speaking, but in a more serious manner. "You're handy with a hammer and nails and Clint is great with his hands, and if Dean and some of the others will help, that will save me a lot of money. I've been thinking that after the lake is done, and they have no more work to do there, I'll bring those guys over here, cook and clean for them, and get this place marketable. What do you say? Is that a deal? You know the Stevensons can use this place. He can get a job at one of the factories over here. We already have the saddling area, and I can tutor Jared until the ranch is ready for the other kids. I'll carry the mortgage contract for Max and Jenna Stevenson, and they won't have to worry about where to live. I can sell it to them for whatever it costs to repair, plus what I'm paying now to buy the place. They live with her folks now. It sounds feasible to me!" Marie Claire was done with her debate over her decision.

Mr. Blunte returned to the group. "The banking staff knows you very well. You seem to be well respected wherever you go. What did you do, win the lottery? The banking president said to take a personal check from you for thirty-five thousand dollars. "

"Thank you, Mr. Blunte," Marie Claire said, taking the check from his extended fingers, and filled it out. "Actually, my best friends, the Bascolms, were killed in a plane crash. They left me over six million dollars. My grandparents, Ruth and Matthew Hatley, left me an inheritance also. I have invested well. I will be sending notices over here when we're ready to open our campground.

Mr. Blunte again looked at the check Marie Claire handed him. "Oh, I read about you and your husband, Clint, regarding the state's plans to help you build a campground. It was in the island paper. How exciting. I can't wait to see it." Getting into his Cadillac once again, the engine purred like a kitten. "I have to get back to work. See you later, and congratulations on all of your ventures. What a pleasure it was meeting you!"

As the group waved goodbye, Mr. Blunte thought about the place he'd just sold, as he drove down the driveway. *Boy, am I glad to be rid of that house. The bank has hung onto it for over three years. I can see it was a beautiful home at one time, and I wish that young woman all the best. It's going to cost a fortune to make the place livable, and I'm just glad I don't have to hang on to it anymore. Even the land needs work. No wonder I could never sell it. No one wants to buy a drug lord's home that's as run down as that one.*

Marie Claire turned on her heel, and quickly walked up into the woods. The six agents followed. They found her sitting on top of a very large rock formation, quiet and staring out over the Olympic Mountains. Out of the corner of her eye, Marie Claire saw the men there, looking through the trees to the waterway and the mountains behind what could only be Southworth and the Olympic Peninsula. They were very impressed with the view.

Marie Claire said, as she turned to smile at the FBI agents, "I used to come here on nice days, when all my chores were done. I would bring my pen and notebook. I wrote poetry here all the time. Sometimes, I would play my guitar and sing or do recitations. No one was around but Jesus and I know he enjoyed my tribute to him. One time, I got off my rock and Francis was sitting there, listening to me. I never knew anyone was around. He had tears running from his eyes. I often wondered if God does that when one of his children pours their heart out to Him like I was doing. I'm glad that wasn't one of the days I would rant and rave about how life is so unfair. Francis would've killed me on the spot if he heard how I cursed him, which I did quite often upon coming here." Marie Claire giggled at that last remembrance. She had come a long way.

Chapter Thirty-One

A S THEY stepped out of the woods, Marie Claire noticed an older couple walking toward them.

"Rand and Kara, how are you two?" Marie Claire, in her excitement, yelled their names and, flapping her hands in the air, ran as quickly as she could to get and give hugs. "Oh, I have missed you so much! I looked over at your house when we were coming down the driveway, but I didn't see your car. I thought you might be out so we didn't stop in. How've you been?" Marie Claire was so excited; she fairly jumped all over the couple, and threw her arms around them. Hugging, she eventually remembered her manners.

"Jeff, Dean, Ben, Joe, Marv, and Quinn, this is Rand and Kara Mallory. Rand, Kara, these are my friends and FBI agents, except Jeff here is my brother-in-law and Dean is Jeff's uncle. Ben is the director and head of the Washington Federal Bureau of Investigation, Dean is the Assistant Chief, and Jeff and the others are agents."

Shaking hands and smiling at each other, the group got acquainted. Kara stood again beside Marie Claire, her arm around the woman's waist.

"Jeff and Jeanette got married. How nice. I never did meet your sister, though, Marie Claire." Kara looked the others over and turned to Marie Claire again.

Turning to Jeff, Marie Claire said, "I used to babysit for the Mallorys when I was a teenager. I have loved all of them forever, it seems!" The men gathered around Rand and they were all talking about

Francis and the years that the Kingman's lived here on Vashon. Kara walked away toward home, pulling Marie Claire along with her.

"I got your letter, Marie Claire. I was so glad you two got a divorce. You had every right to leave him. I'm sorry for all you had to go through. Don't worry about that now, it's over. If Rand and I had known, we would have done all we could to help you." Kara had always been concerned about children, and that made her very special to Marie Claire, who was treated like one of Kara's little chicks! Kara used to watch out for Marie Claire when she saw her with the horses, or riding. Kara was nervous around those "beasts," and she could never understand how Marie Claire could do some of the things she'd done with them. She and Rand were very proud of Marie Claire, and she deserved all the trophies and awards she'd received when showing or competing.

The Mallorys spent a weekend with Marie Claire some years ago. They all went to Canada via Highway 2 through Bonner's Ferry. Marie Claire, Rand, and Kara visited at the Kingman home, and Marie Claire shared with them her feelings and the goings on with Francis. The older couple had not approved of Francis Kingman, nor his treatment of their good friend.

"Well, you're remarried now, dear one, to a very nice man. We haven't met him, but are looking forward to that day!" Kara, being the motherly person she was, caring very much for Marie Claire, asked all kinds of details. Marie Claire could hardly keep up with the questions.

Laughing, Marie Claire hugged Kara and said, "Clint is wonderful. He and I see things about the same and he is kind, honest, gentle, and he would never, ever, ever knowingly hurt anyone, let alone a child. Everyone who meets him seems to love him."

"Why isn't Clint here with you today? He isn't working is he?"

"Actually, he was going to take today off, but his boss needed him. You got the last letter I sent, didn't you? I told you about Sam and Julia Bascolm and my cousins?"

"Yes, we did, and we were saddened by your losses. It's funny, you being involved with the FBI. Why are you all over here, anyway?" Rand and Kara became concerned upon meeting the agents, were still worrying but Kara stayed quiet so Marie Claire could explain.

"Well," and Marie Claire explained how the whole thing started.

They were seated in the Mallory back yard by this time, sipping iced tea and enjoying the shade of the virgin fir trees.

"You should have married Roy, Marie Claire. However, we did understand your wanting to finish high school. That was a commendable thing to do. It's just too bad, though, that the marriage never happened." Kara shared the couple's feelings about that with Marie Claire, and then filled her in about their own children.

*   *   *   *

About twenty minutes later, the men found Marie Claire sitting with Kara. They heard part of the discussion and were glad for some peaceful, comforting conversation. Rand hugged his wife as she sat there, and said, "I have an announcement to make to you." Kara turned her head to look up at Rand. "We are going to dinner. These gentlemen are buying." Kara looked at Marie Claire, who looked at Jeff and then back at Kara, and all she could do was to shrug her shoulders, smiling.

Chapter Thirty-Two

I N THE middle of Vashon, in the town square, was a nice Chinese restaurant, which had the best food to be found on the entire island. The owners also ran the sister restaurant in Chinatown in Seattle, the Pou Lei. They were an older couple, and their boy and girls were learning how to cook and run the business someday. Kara and Marie Claire were the only ones using chopsticks.

Marie Claire shared with the Mallorys that she purchased the old place this afternoon. Ben and Dean shared why they were all over on the island today. And Dean asked, "Would you, Rand and Kara, be able to tell us what you know and when you last saw Roy Copeland?"

Kara told her story first. "I saw Roy last when he and Marie Claire went to the ice cream parlor after a matinee one afternoon. He talked to me alone when Marie Claire went to the ladies room. He told me he was going to ask Marie Claire to marry him that evening, and that he hoped she would accept his proposal this time. He said he was taking his parents out to dinner the next evening, before work. He was going to the sportsman's club the next morning after that. He had an archery lesson. That's the last time I saw him."

"How did you come to meet Roy, Mr. and Mrs. Mallory?"

"Well, he was Marie Claire's boyfriend, and we saw them together all the time. She brought him over the first time he proposed, so we could meet him. She hadn't accepted his proposal that time. Roy's mother belonged to the garden club, the same one I attended every Tuesday in the spring. We got to become good friends."

What information she gave to the agents aided them with a clue they hadn't had before. "Thank you for that information, Mrs. Mallory." Ben told the woman. "Jeff, I want you and Quinn to go to the Sportsmen's Club right away and obtain what information you can from them. Ask around about Roy, and if you see Francis Kingman there, leave. Don't let him see you. I know he doesn't live here, or hadn't, but we don't want him knowing our business. Got that?" Jeff got directions from Rand.

Their dinner finished and tea still sitting on the table, the two men left. Dean and Ben put their money together to pay the bill. Looking at the Mallorys, Ben said, "You two have shared quite a bit with us today. It was quite useful information at that. We are very thankful, and this is the least we can do. Besides, without your care and concern, where would our girl here be?" Ben gave Marie Claire a smile. The waitress took the money and tip away, refilled the tea cups, and they sat there for a while longer enjoying conversation and the ambience of the dining room.

They had all been about to leave the restaurant when Jeff came back inside. He motioned with his head toward Ben, turned on his heel and went back out the double glass doors and waited for the others to come out.

"Boss, I think you need to call and talk with the manager of the club. He's with Quinn who is writing down more information, but he has to leave for Seattle. He said to call him at this number," Jeff handed a slip of paper to Ben, "and he said he can meet with us in the morning. Marie Claire, you know this island. Can you take us around to all of the out-of-the-way places where things could be done without being seen from the road?"

"Yes, I can. I've ridden or walked just about every mile of this island."

"Thanks. I'll go get Quinn now." Jeff went to pick the other agent up and they would meet back here. There was a patio in the back of the establishment and the others found a quiet corner to talk. The waiter brought out glasses of iced tea for them all and then he went away.

"Kara and Rand, I need you to keep quiet about what you heard today. Please, you could hurt the investigation if you talk to anyone. Don't even say anything about Marie Claire working with us. She is going to be very helpful to our case. She is working undercover for us, and she is to be incommunicado. Got that?" He looked back at Marie Claire, and then the Mallorys.

"Oh, about Marie Claire's purchase of the house next door to you. She told you, but that has to be kept quiet also, for now. " Dean mentioned to them.

Ben looked at Dean, and then commented, "We didn't tell the banker to be quiet, so word has probably spread by now. We didn't say anything to him about Roy, I believe, so it's probably okay, but I wouldn't say anything unless there is a question."

"I did buy it to fix it up, Marie Claire said. I want to give it to someone who really needs it. I have a family whose son will be coming to my Academy, and they just lost their house to a fire, which was due to faulty wiring, I believe. I'm going to talk to them and if they are willing to come over here, I'll put in a good word at the factories and hopefully he can get a job. Jared can still see me and the family will have a home again," Marie Claire stated in a hopeful tone.

"I heard the tractor factory is hiring again. They pay fairly well. If the man can do mechanical, or work with soldering and chemicals, he should be able to get on there," Rand told her. The ski factory left the island, but there is a chemical treatment factory here now. There isn't much left here but real estate offices, banks, and those two factories. We have a small hospital and three medical and two dentist offices.

"If I lived here, I'd probably get on with the sheriff's department. I suppose it's called a police station now. Seems like the farms are all but gone and citified folks live here! I can't stand the streetlights that are seen all up and down the roads over here now." Marie Claire shared her feelings with them. "The boy's dad can get on there, maybe. He used to be a security officer."

"There are nearly twenty thousand people living here now, Marie Claire. Our house is paid for and we want to move," Rand sadly told his friend.

"We searched all the cities and towns where we might like to live, but there is no place we can afford. Even if we sold here, there would be more gas expenses, state income taxes, and the list goes on," Kara explained more of their quandary.

"Would you two like to come and spend a few days at my place? We have lots of room. Clint would love to meet you both. You can come see where we live and what we're doing with the place." Marie Claire hoped they would acquiesce.

"That's right. You mentioned you were looking to move back to mainland Seattle." Kara commented to Marie Claire.

"Has it been that long since I've written?" Marie Claire was aghast that she hadn't corresponded with her dearest friend since over a year ago.

"Well, we did get a post office address two years back. If you wrote since then, we never got the letters. The last we heard from you is that you'd been in the hospital and were thinking of divorcing Francis. We heard that you'd since gotten a divorce. You talked about the Bascolms and the help they'd been to you."

"Oh, wow," Marie Claire expostulated. "I wonder why my letters didn't come back."

"I don't know, gal," Rand said. "Maybe the post office lost them, or they're sitting in a dead letter file somewhere as undeliverable."

"You hadn't written or called in so many years, but we figured Francis had something to do with that," Kara sadly told Marie Claire.

Marie Claire's face showed a look of remorse. They knew it hadn't been her who shunned them, but she'd had to tow the line with her then husband. They knew all about that situation.

"It's ok," Rand said to Marie Claire. "Don't worry, Kara. How about we go to Marie Claire's and meet this husband of hers, and maybe we can stay for a few days with our girl here. Would you like to do that? Do you feel up to it?" Kara suffered a heart attack last year but she didn't want to worry Marie Claire with that problem. She hadn't said a word about it to anyone, fearing word would get back to Marie Claire.

"Rand, that would be lovely. Yes, let's do it! It's been such a long time since she and I have spent any time together. I've missed her so much," and looking at Marie Claire, she held out her arms to the woman and together they hugged and kissed cheeks. "I love you, dear girl," Kara whispered in Marie Claire's ear.

"I love you both, so much. I'm sorry it's been so hard for us to correspond. Thank you for understanding."

"Tell you what, can we follow you home tonight, or do you have to stay and work on the case?" Rand asked Marie Claire.

Dean looked at Clint's wife, chin cupped in his upraised fingers, elbows on his chest, thinking, and then he said, "We men were thinking of researching as much as possible here. We'll get a motel room and stay until we're done."

Listening to his agent, Ben said, "When we're ready for you to show us around, Marie Claire, we'll have you come over here then."

"Well, I guess, whatever you say guys. It doesn't matter to me." Marie Claire stated.

"You're not going to find a motel or even a hotel over here," Rand told them. I'll give you a key to our home. We have five bedrooms and three baths. Kara and I will go home with Marie Claire and then she can come back here when you need her. How does that sound? Ok with you, Kara?" This idea made everyone happy. "We'll run home and pack a bag, then take off with Marie Claire."

The agents followed the Mallorys and Marie Claire. They parked in a line in the circular driveway, and entered the house. Kara handed her house keys over to Ben. Make yourselves at home. I changed all the bedding this morning. I hope you're comfortable.

Ben said to the Mallorys, "Here, we'll give you some money. He handed Rand seven hundred dollars. Thanks for the offer. We'll take care of the place for you, don't worry about anything. We'll use your phone, but we'll pay your bill for you. We'll set up more phone lines in here tomorrow, but don't worry. You won't even know we've been here when we leave!" Ben and Dean shook hands with the Mallorys.

They all hugged Marie Claire and Jeff kissed her on the cheek. "Take care of my wife, will you? Tell her I love her and it's ok to tell her what we're doing. She won't say anything to anyone. Thanks, sister-in-law, my friend. Take care."

Marie Claire called ahead and told Clint to expect her two friends from Vashon Island. In less than thirty minutes the three were on their way to the Rocking Horse Ranch. Marie Claire had an idea and she pondered it all the way home.

Chapter Thirty-Three

A S A surprise for Marie Claire and the Mallorys, Clint called Martha and asked if she could help him.

"Martha, my wife and her two friends from Vashon are coming home. Marie Claire said they'd be staying here for a few days. Would you mind helping me with dinner? I'm making steaks, but they'll be here within a half hour and I'm afraid I won't have everything done."

"Oh sure, Dear. I'll be right over."

"Thanks, Martha. Jeanette and Ed can come over too, if they haven't eaten." It was nearly six thirty and Clint heard Martha talking to the other two people in the room with her.

"Oh, fine, Clint. We'll all be right over. I was just getting ready to make dinner myself. This will be a welcomed break."

Clint set out dishes and the best china. Martha bustled in a few minutes later with Jeanette and Ed trailing behind, and she set to getting the dining room ready while Ed and Clint went to the back yard to get the grill heated up.

"Jeanette, please check on the potatoes that Clint has in the oven baking. I'll fix the vegetables if you'll help me with the salad." So the next half hour was taken up with food preparation.

Marie Claire pulled into the driveway at seven fifteen. The air smelled of succulent steak. Her stomach growled, and Kara chuckled at the sound. "I think someone is hungry! Those steaks smell delicious. We can't wait to eat, can we Rand?"

Marie Claire led them up the front steps and Jeanette met them at the door. "Hi, I'm Jeanette."

Marie Claire introduced Rand and Kara to her sister, and then they went into the house.

"Martha! What are you doing here? It's so good to see you," Marie Claire hugged the older woman and introduced her to her two friends.

"Ah, but this lass has some fine people in her life, I can see that! It is a very great pleasure to meet you both. Would you like some iced tea or water?"

"Martha is a dear friend to us, and the housekeeper for Ed, our neighbor and Jeanette's father-in-law." Marie Claire explained the relationship, not sounding as though Martha were anything but family.

"It's nice to meet you too, Martha," Kara said as she wandered into the dining room. "Oh, dear girl, what a beautiful place you have here, and this dining room is just gorgeous. Martha, you didn't have to go to all this trouble." Kara admired the fine bone china dinner plates and the clear crystal goblets and gold plated dinnerware that sat on a silk lace tablecloth. The lavender irises with green stems in the center caught her attention. The scalloped edging was of deeper lavender with gold trim on the rims of each placement. Martha placed gold charges under each dinner plate, and a coffee setting sat on a gold tray at one end of the table.

Clint came in the back door, through the dining room, and set the platter of steaks on the kitchen island for Martha to tend. He turned and went back into the dining room where Ed stood while Marie Claire was finished introducing Ed to the Mallorys.

"Dinner's on," Martha called, setting the plate of cut up steak on the table. Everyone was seated, and Marie Claire told Martha, "Sit with us, Martha, please. I'd like to have you sit here, next to me on this side." The older woman had sat with family before during a meal, but at Marie Claire's insistence, she set a place for herself beside Marie Claire, opposite Kara, and Clint said grace for the meal.

Later, over after dinner coffees, the boisterous conversation that had gone on during the meal waned to a more sedate tone.

"I'm so glad you guys are staying a few days. We have so much to show you!" Jeanette struck up a friendship with Rand and Kara, and she enjoyed hearing from them about Marie Claire during that time of her life.

"Marie Claire told us about you and your brother. She worried about you so much. I'm sorry we couldn't have met sooner. " Rand was a kindhearted man, sincere, and he wanted to assure Jeanette that they cared about her, too.

Thus, conversation carried through the midnight hours.

Chapter Thirty-Four

CLINT AND Marie Claire woke up to the smell of coffee, sausage, and pancakes cooking downstairs. They rushed into the bathroom to shower and dress before heading down to the kitchen. Marie Claire panicked when she looked at the time. It was nearly ten o'clock! She never slept past six. Pulling on some black slacks and a white western style shirt, Marie Claire hurriedly dressed, combed her hair, and rushed downstairs.

"Oh, Martha! Good morning! You didn't have to cook for us this morning, but thank you very much. This is wonderful." Marie Claire reached down to give the dapper woman a kiss on the cheek and a hug.

"It was no problem, dear. Master Ed told me to spend some time over here to help you out, so I got up at eight and fixed coffee and toast for Master Ed and then I came over here. I enjoy having family to cook and care for. I am beholdin' to you for your kindness."

Marie Claire looked at Martha with a glint of mischief and laughter in her eyes. "Master Ed?"

Giggling, Martha nodded her head. "Yes, dear. You see, Master Ed did not want me calling him Mr. Ed, too much like the horse on TV don't you know! He didn't want me calling him Mr. Hollingsworth either. He said it was too much of a mouthful, so I said, fine, sir; I will call you Master Ed out of respect for you, and do not tell me you don't want to hear that, either! 'Well', he said, 'I guess Master Ed is fine, since you won't just call me Ed. Thank you, Miss Martha, I'm honored.' Therefore, he calls me Miss Martha. Isn't that just the jolliest predicament?"

Marie Claire laughed and just as she was going to kiss Martha again, the phone rang.

"Good morning," Marie Claire answered joyfully.

"Hi, Marie Claire. Can I come over?" Jeanette had gotten a call from Jeff and she didn't want to be alone today, so she was heading over to the Rocking Horse Ranch. Jeff would be on the island with the other agents for a few days at least.

Martha had made plenty of food, so she set five place settings.

*   *   *   *

Kara and Rand slept in the corner guest room upstairs, overlooking the vast property that made up the Rocking Horse Ranch. Last night, they stayed up and sat in rockers in front of the window facing the west. The moon shone brightly last night, and the couple enjoyed looking out over the Olympic Mountains and watching the lights twinkle from the shore to the passageway of Puget Sound. The view from upstairs was something they had never seen before. They saw bats flying outside, catching bugs in midair, and one settled on the screen of the window opposite where they were sitting. Coyote cries were heard on the still night air, and they caught a glimpse of a snow-covered mountain. They stared at Mt. Baker to the north, finally realizing the peak, and they noticed some elk roaming the fields of the Rocking Horse Ranch. They talked until they got so sleepy they finally called it a night.

Upon awakening this morning, Kara again looked out the window and saw a massive construction project underway. The lake that Marie Claire had told them about was filling up with water. "Rand, come look at this! What is that they're doing?" Rand came to stand beside his wife.

"Well, looks to me like our girl is going to have herself a mighty big campground. Those cement slabs there are for setting up trailers, and those trees with the paths through them are for riding trails I imagine. I suppose Clint is going to have tent camping around there somewhere, and that truck over there," Rand pointed to a small semi filled with camping grills, tables, and benches, "is full of stuff to set up individual camping sites."

"Marie Claire sure did fine by herself didn't she? God has truly blessed the dear girl." Kara was proud as any mother could be of a child, and Marie Claire, Kara felt in her heart, was just another one of her own children. They had known Marie Claire since she was fifteen, and that was more than thirty years ago now.

Rand and Kara joined everyone in the kitchen after they finished their conversation. They all sat down for a filling breakfast. Afterwards, Kara asked Marie Claire to come upstairs with her.

"I love the view from this room, Marie Claire. It's beautiful. I see a hill where it would be great to have a house."

Marie Claire sidled up to Kara and asked, "Where?"

"Right there. See the tree with the crooked top? I'll bet Mt. Rainier could be seen from the windows of a house set on that hill." Kara made sure she pointed out the right place to Marie Claire.

The two of them walked down the stairs and then Marie Claire said, "I have been thinking, and I spoke with Clint this morning. I have something I want to show you, Kara, if you will come with me! Clint and Rand can spend some time together. Jeanette is going to help Martha clean up." Marie Claire peaked into the kitchen and said, "We'll be back shortly." Marie Claire included everyone but Kara in her look. She led Kara out to the car and they drove down the driveway and stopped at a little knoll, still on Bellham property, but it was an area that Marie Claire thought she could never use for anything.

Marie Claire parked so as not to block the drive. She and Kara walked to the top of the hill, and the two of them surveyed the hills and the property from the peak. Marie Claire saw the stream that flowed from the waterfall barely visible high up on the mountainside. Mt. Rainier stood majestic behind. She showed Kara where the RV Park would be.

They saw the ranch house and the vast property beyond and around. Kara knew this could be a wonderful home site, and she looked up at Marie Claire. What do you have in mind dear one? Marie Claire only laughed and ran back down the hill to the car, and Kara followed at a more sedate pace.

Kara tried, all the way back to the house, to get Marie Claire to talk about her thoughts. "No way," Marie Claire said jokingly. "You'll just have to wait!" So, wait Kara did.

Chapter Thirty-Five

Back at the house once again, they strode thoughtfully inside, Marie Claire with her mind on her idea, and Kara knowing that Marie Claire had a surprise but she wasn't spilling it!

The phone rang as they stepped into the kitchen and Martha answered then handed the receiver to Marie Claire. "Hello, this is Marie Claire."

"Hi, Marie Claire. This is Dean. I need you to come to the island. Bring Clint with you, if he can get time off work."

"Ok, give me an hour." Marie Claire knew better than take time asking questions. She ran outside to catch Clint before he left for work.

"Handsome, I have to go to Vashon. Dean asked that you come too. Can you get off?"

"I'll be with you in a minute. Let me call my guys."

Clint tried to contact his floor manager to no avail. He did get his assistant manager, Kevin Stillwell, and Clint told him, "I will not be available for a few days. An emergency has come up and I'll be out of town. I couldn't reach Dave Mackey. Will you call him and have him call me at this number -" Clint read out the phone number at the Mallory's and then he said, "and have Dave call me at the FBI number that's on my desk if he doesn't reach me at the other number. It's Dean Manning's phone, but I'll be with him. Tell Dave that the two of you have to take care of business until I get back. Call me with an update every night, ok? Thanks, pal. I'll give you some time off when I get back." Clint hung up and went inside to collect toiletries and a change of clothes.

Kara finished first and she was cleaning the bedroom and bath. She found the cleaning supplies in the bathroom closet. She didn't want Marie Claire to have to do it.

"Where did Marie Claire take you, Kara?" Rand asked his wife.

Kara told him about the conversation with Marie Claire, and the comment about that hill being a great home site, "She must have something up her sleeve. She never said anything to me at all about the trip out there."

"Well, it would be a perfect place for a house. I'd live there if I owned this property." Rand dropped the subject and finished dressing.

In the car and on the way to the ferry nearly an hour later, Marie Claire dropped her idea onto her husband and Kara and Rand. "You're going to have to get a manager, aren't you Handsome, for the RV park?" Marie Claire innocently ask Clint.

"I suppose so, when the time comes. Why?" Clint inquired. He knew his wife, and he never put anything past her.

"Weeeellll," Marie Claire said, drawing out the word, "How about in exchange for being our RV Park managers, Kara and Rand build the home of their choice on the acreage including that hill?" Turning in her seat, Marie Claire looked at the Mallorys. "What do you say, guys! We'd be a real family! There is an acre or more there, I believe. I can have it surveyed if you're interested. The land will be yours."

Dumbfounded, Kara's eyes got teary as she held her face in her hands. Rand could not believe what Marie Claire had proposed. He loved camping, and right now, he was a supervisor at the largest aircraft company in Seattle. He was due to retire in lieu of a lay off soon, and the opportunity really hit home. "Wow," Rand breathed out. "This is quite a surprise. We'll put our house on the market today and I'll meet with an architect for a plan." He looked at Kara, and not finding any consternation or hesitancy on her part, Rand agreed to be the park manager.

"We'll give you a stipend, of course. We can't have you working for free. Kara can maybe help me out some, too, but only if she'd like to do that. When the academy gets up and running, I'll be pretty busy. She'd get a wage too, of course. Kara and I can go places and do things together like we used to, and go to the mall and eat out!" Marie Claire was as excited as she'd ever been, and Clint was chuckling. Rand, still thinking about the prize he and Kara had just been given, ignored the women.

Clint finally put a stop to the ramblings. "Let the poor people think, Marie Claire! You're enough to drive a person to drink!" Clint teasingly sounded exasperated with his wife, and Marie Claire knew that. She stuck her tongue out at him and pretended to pout.

"You're so mean." Marie Claire told her husband in a whimpering voice, and her lower lip stuck out. The others laughed so hard, Clint almost drove off the road. Marie Claire grabbed the steering wheel just in time to turn into the ferry dock.

"We can't take advantage like that." Rand said to Clint, looking at that man in the rearview mirror, laughter still shone in the man's hazel eyes. "How much would you want for that corner of the property?"

"We'll deed it over to you. We wouldn't want you paying for it, Rand. If you choose to be our managers for the park, that's only fair. You can sell it back to us if you decide to move sometime, or you can rent it out if you move but have plans of coming back. We'll be your managers if you rent the place out. Whatever you want, just let us know." Clint had said his piece and the rest of the ferry ride went quietly.

After debarking and heading for the Mallory home, Rand said that he would contact a realtor right away. "We can find out what our place will sell for and get it on the market. If it sells before our new place is built, can we rent a room from you two?"

"No, you may not rent a room! You can stay with us anytime, for as long as you want. We will not have you paying rent." Marie Claire stated in a determined and defiant voice.

"Thank you both, so much. We appreciate your kindness. We are both very proud of you, Marie Claire. Thank you for giving your heart so easily. We love you, too." Kara reached forward and squeezed Marie Claire's left shoulder.

Clint looked in the rearview mirror and saw tears welling in both the Mallory's eyes. *My wife is a jewel,* he thought. Clint loved Marie Claire so much. *I wouldn't want to live without her.* He reached over and picked up her left hand and held it in his, playing with the ring that never left her finger. Marie Claire looked over at Clint, and he gave her a wink and a smile that melted her heart.

Chapter Thirty-Six

WHEN THE four friends reached the Mallory home, several more cars sat in the driveway. Marie Claire parked at her new old house and they walked over to see the FBI crew.

Jeff met them halfway, as he watched Clint's car drive by. "Hi, all. Sorry to call you over here on such short notice."

"Oh, that's all right," Clint answered in return. "It gives us something to do today!" Jeff chuckled with them over Clint's remark.

"I'm sure the gals would rather be cleaning out the stores on this chilly wet day!" Jeff remarked.

"Oh, quit picking on us, Jeffrey." Marie Claire told him in a mock angry voice. This brought more chuckles, because Marie Claire balled her fist and hit Jeff lightly in the jaw with it. He pretended to fall backwards and almost did land on his fanny.

"Ok, quit clowning around. We need to see Dean." Clint was a bit serious. He really didn't like having to come over to the island because of the serious matter before them, but it needed to be finished and Marie Claire was the only one who really could help at this point.

"Spoil sport," Jeff and Marie Claire said in unison.

Arm in arm, the five walked the twenty feet to the Mallory home. There, on the deck, sat seven agents. Dean stood as the women approached. He pulled out some more chairs and Rand and Kara sat with them. Marie Claire sat on the railing, looking at Ben and wondering what they found, if anything.

Robert Sorbian, another FBI agent and forensic specialist, and

Toby Mitchell, his assistant, stood while Dean introduced them to the newcomers. "Nice to meet you both," Marie Claire and Clint told them.

Dean held some files in his hands and from these he pulled out a few sheets. "Kara, Rand," Ben addressed the two homeowners. "Robert here would like for you to pack everything you will need for a lengthy stay at the Bellhams."

"It may take a couple of hours or so. We will pack our truck and leave as soon as we can." After spending a moment talking to Clint and Marie Claire, Rand and Kara turned to go into the house.

"I'll help you pack the truck, if I may," Clint told Rand. "Marie Claire probably doesn't need me anyway."

"Clint, it might be nice if you came along with us. Marie Claire may need your shoulder," Jeff commented. "I'll help you pack up the truck when we get back."

"Good idea, Jeff. You two can take your time packing. Don't load the truck yourselves. We'll pitch in when we return. If you're not done before we get back, we'll cover more paperwork details until you're done," Dean told the Mallorys.

With all the major details out of the way, Clint and Marie Claire joined Jeff, Ben, and Dean in the official car. Marie Claire sat in front with Ben and Clint. She would direct the way to go since she knew the best places a body could disappear easily.

Earlier in the day, Dean called the three mainland federal precincts to see if a body had ever been found floating in the sound or washed to shore. Never in the last hundred-year history had an unidentified male body ever washed up on a beach anywhere near the Puget Sound vicinity. The feds called other areas of interest. No other bodies were found in the waters between Canada and Tacoma since 1970. The few before that time had already been identified and taken care of.

Ben drove to the Copeland's, after verifying the occupants would indeed be home. They made it there in ten minutes. They didn't live too far from the old Kingman place.

When Ben parked in front of the Copeland's front door, Marie Claire saw the multicolored rhododendrons and azaleas. They were thick and colorful as always. Mrs. Copeland loved her flowers and beautiful yards and gardens. Mrs. Copeland stood out the front porch, and Marie Claire walked up to the older woman and they hugged.

Mrs. Copeland cried for the days long past. She couldn't believe how beautiful this lovely girl had grown. Her still waist long black hair glistened in the dim sunlight of this cloudy day. The only change the older woman could see was Marie Claire's eyes. Now they were bright and shiny, where once they were sad and dull.

Marie Claire's figure may be a little fuller, but she stayed lithe and athletic looking. She stood tall and Mrs. Copeland could tell that Marie Claire wasn't proud and arrogant, but rather exuded confidence and stature.

Margarethe Copeland was very proud of this young woman. She wished now, more than ever, that Roy and Marie Claire had been able to marry. She could imagine what the grandchildren would look like, how they would grow up to be as beautiful as their mother was for sure.

The agents and the Bellhams sat with the Copeland couple for a while. They talked about Roy and the past years without him. Mr. and Mrs. Copeland shared some stories of Roy and Marie Claire, and how they themselves wished for things to be different.

The Copelands watched Clint and Marie Claire together, how they seemed to be happy together, and how kind and attentive he was to her needs. They were glad for her sake. Neither Marie Claire nor the others mentioned the bad years with Francis, but then, Mrs. Copeland touched on it after a long while.

"We heard some things about Mr. Kingman and you. We are so sorry, Marie Claire. We would've helped you had we known," Mr. Copeland told her.

"I know. I did seek help, but no one believed me. I just lived my life as I had to. I was sorry for getting involved with Francis, but I had no one to turn to. It's hard knowing that everyone said the same thing, that I was a 'tramp', and not realizing that there really were those who would've helped. It was so embarrassing and I was such a weak person, that I couldn't come to you or the Mallorys. I never shared anything with Roy. I knew you all loved me, but I didn't want to lose that love." Marie Claire explained the best way she knew how. Sadness crept in where happiness once was.

Mrs. Copeland brought that happiness back. "Marie Claire, it's over," she said. "You have grown into a beautiful young woman. We can see you are admired by these agents, the Mallorys, your husband, and you are admired by us too. We can tell just by looking at you that you are a worthy individual. We read the papers also! There was a write up in the island paper about you when you received a big inheritance and starting building up that riding academy for handicapped kids. One of your old classmates is head of the paper and he wrote it, because you are always going to be a part of the people here. I saved that article. Would you like a copy?" Margarethe asked her.

"I would love the article," she answered. "Do you have a copy machine?" Marie Claire asked happily.

"Yes, we do. Come on in and see what we've done with Roy's room." Marie Claire and Clint followed Mrs. Copeland to the back of the house. She made space in Roy's old bedroom, and set up her own personal office.

The agents followed, and after asking permission, Jeff collected hair from a brush on Roy's dresser. Mrs. Copeland kept Roy's things in his room, moving the larger items to make room for her equipment. She kept some semblance of normalcy around her. It wasn't a shrine, but neither was the room totally transformed into what was now her office.

Marie Claire remembered the yellow orange color Roy loved. The walls stayed the same, as well as his Explorer trophies and high school memorabilia. His boat curtains still hung on the windows, and a sailboat depicted on the rug placed on the dark Oak flooring remained right where it used to be, in front of the closet. The woodwork was still pale beige. Aside from the desk and stand Mrs. Copeland used for her office, Roy's room hadn't changed one bit. Marie Claire remembered so much, and the memories flooded her brain.

"I remember when a little girl disappeared from kindergarten. The principal called Roy away from class to help search for her. He found her huddled in the bushes behind the cemetery." Marie Claire recalled. The girl was found a day later, tired, cold, wet, and very scared. She never told how she came to be lost like that. She was miles away from the school and no one had ever seen her leave. They never knew if someone took her or she just walked away. I remember she never could talk after she was found.

"Did you hear if she ever said another word? Does the family still live here?" Marie Claire asked curiously.

Mr. Copeland told her, "The girl eventually said a few words. She committed suicide a few years ago. Her devastated family moved away to another state. They never could figure out some of her ramblings. She wasn't right in the head after that incident. When Roy found her, he took her to the doctor's office in town. She'd been hurt by some man, if you know what I mean, and they didn't have DNA back then."

Marie Claire did understand. Children were missing on the Seattle streets, and it was on the news nearly every day. They all wondered if it was related, but decided it probably wasn't since this case was so old.

After another cup of coffee, Ben told them, "We better get moving before it gets dark." They said their goodbyes and took off toward Maury Island.

Marie Claire knew of an old antique graveyard Roy and a friend found while Juniors in high school. They talked some more about Roy and his family. Marie Claire shared some more of her memories of him and her, what they used to do, and where they went when they were together. She met Roy when he was a freshman and she was in eighth grade. They were best friends and did a lot of things together. He was always a nice boy.

Chapter Thirty-Seven

FRANCIS DIDN'T know what do at this point but keep his cool and act as though he knew nothing. He drove back to the office after two hours of thinking on the situation. Francis never worried about getting caught at anything. He was wily and cunning. Thought and perseverance is what got him where he landed today. He was rich, a lawyer, and he had the world at his fingertips. His latest squeeze happened to be a voluptuous blonde that knew how to please him. He felt on top of the world. This was no time to come apart now.

Back at his desk, he searched the police computer records to see what they had on Roy Copeland. Forewarned was forearmed, and he would be ready for questions when the time came, and he knew his time was coming.

Closing down the system, Francis walked down to Seattle's Finest Coffee shop and grabbed an extra large Hazelnut latte. Back at the office, he closed the door and sat at the window overlooking the Seattle Center, watching the kids play in the fountain and people travel up and down the elevator of the Space Needle. A girl sat on a bench sketching some children sitting across from her, playing with blocks and giggling, as their parents sat nearby watching people walk by and enjoying their cold drinks. Lost in his own thoughts, Francis sat there long after the sun set.

*   *   *   *

October 25, 1972 – 7 p.m.

It was mid winter and the sky was very dark at seven o'clock in the evening. Roy left Marie Claire's home yesterday and never spoke with her at all today. He stayed overnight with his friend, Chris, and only today felt able to talk to his mom and dad. He went to the Spinnaker to eat dinner with his parents.

"Mom, I want Marie Claire to marry me. She wanted me to talk to Francis Kingman, and I did. He threw me out of the house. He was irate and irrational. Marie Claire's mom told me to come back and take Marie Claire away to elope." He loved Marie Claire deeply, and his mother saw it in her son's eyes when he looked at her. She saw the tears he held back, and she knew his heart was breaking. "Mom," Roy pleaded, "that's not what I wanted to do. Sir," Roy said as he looked towards his father, "what should I do?"

Over the meal, Roy told his parents what happened, what Anne told him regarding taking Marie Claire away, and he wanted their opinion. Roger didn't think he should pursue her anymore, but it was Roy's decision. They would go with the couple if Roy wanted to meet Marie Claire somewhere with whatever belongings she could grab, and they'd have a decent wedding in California, or wherever they wanted to go.

Roger Copeland sat sipping his wine. He looked into his son's eyes and saw the same love his wife did. "Son, let's talk about this. We don't think eloping is the right thing to do, either. You will both regret that decision. Marie Claire deserves a nice white wedding, not a hurried, justice of the peace thing." He spoke with his wife for a little while, and Roy listened.

"Roger, how about Roy see Marie Claire when Francis is gone? They can collect some of Marie Claire's things and we'll take them to California. We can have a nice wedding down there. Or maybe there's someplace else the kids would like to go!"

Roy, with a lot on his mind, decided to drive around the island, trying to get these next plans in his head. He kissed his mother' cheek, and shook hands with his dad. "I'll be home around midnight or so. I'll drive around a bit, and then I'll catch up a little at work. I'll be home later. Thanks for dinner. I love you both."

Roy did a lot of thinking. *"I'll take Mrs. Kingman up on the idea of taking Marie Claire away from here. I'll get her horses; let her do*

anything she wants if she'll just consent to marrying me. I don't care.
I just want her as my wife."

October 25, 1972 – 9:08 p.m.

Roy was on a very dark back road, not knowing how he got here. A bare fifty feet sat either side of the potholed paved road. It was left over from the county building the main highway further out in order to make the highway straighter. The kids used this area periodically for make out sessions in the spring and summer. Otherwise, it was a barren place, surrounded by trees, where garbage sometimes got dumped. Someday the county may build something here, but for now, it was just a place to drive through on your way to nowhere.

A black car skidded to a stop in front of Roy's car. Roy barely missed hitting it with his white BMW. His dad would be very angry if anything happened to the twenty thousand dollar car. Roy stepped out onto the pavement after pulling off to the shoulder of the road. He approached the driver's side window of the Mercury Cougar.

Roy never saw the gun that fired the shot that killed him. Francis Kingman waited for the right time. When Roy leaned down to speak, that's when Francis pointed his 38 and shot Roy right between the eyes.

A cap covering his hair, gloves on his hands covering his sleeves nearly to the elbows, Francis loaded the boy's body into a large tarp then carefully placed the tarp-wrapped boy in the back seat. He made sure there were no blood spots anywhere. He'd loaded his trunk with a shovel, branches, five gallons of gasoline and water, plus other items before he left home. With the gas and water, he washed the little bit of blood away that puddled there on the cement. The water ran into the dirt and into a hole Francis dug there in case hair happened to have landed around the scene of the crime. He then filled the hole in with more dirt.

Deeming that area free of evidence, he covered the body with boxes and sundry items he'd carried in the trunk. He periodically heard traffic, but no one bothered to come down this road. He worked quickly, so as not to be caught, just in case. He did such a good job placing the items over the tarp that no one could tell anything else was there unless they looked deeply. He locked up before leaving his car on the side of the old road.

Francis drove the BMW deep into the woods to hide it until he could come back to destroy that as well. He was very adept at espionage, being a former navy seal. He would never be suspected of doing this thing to a young man such as Roy.

Francis drove around the island in the Mercury Cougar, a car he stole from an old man who lived near his house, leaving his car there at the end of the drive. The old man was a drunk and everyone knew he must be a hermit. He only used that car on occasions, when he needed to fill up his liquor supply and after having bought groceries to last a month. Like most people, keys were kept in magnetic boxes stuck to wheel wells. This old man had been no different.

Francis drove to Inspiration Point. He pulled in with his lights off. He didn't want anyone from across the way seeing anything. They wouldn't be able to tell what was going on anyway, it was so dark. Those homes were miles away across the Sound, and forest grew up around this area. Francis performed his movements very carefully. He carried the body to the most southwestward corner of the parking lot. The trees were very dense here and due to the steepness of the incline, normally no one bothered to climb down for any reason. Francis brought enough of the right equipment, to be sure that Roy's body would never be found.

Vashon Island is as dead as a doornail during the weeknights, and this night is no different from any other, Francis thought, glad for the circumstances. He hadn't seen a car at all this evening. He'd only heard two or three over on the main highway. He stopped the Mercury by his Jaguar and transferred the equipment to his vehicle, then proceeded to return the Mercury to where he found it. He walked back to his own car. Checking that no one was coming, he pulled out into the road and went back to Roy's car. He parked the Jag and walked into the woods where he had hidden Roy's BMW. He started it up and drove to the road. Again checking that no other car showed in the vicinity, he drove out onto the highway. He attached the Jag to the BMW with a chain and a tow bar. He towed it to the road they lived on and down the hill to the waterfront. These were summer homes only and the places were all deserted now since it was nearly winter. With lights off, Francis unhooked the Jaguar and moved it out of the way. He knew where a large motorboat was moored just two houses down. It sat in a covered garage on a pier, but the end was open. He ran to get the boat he found there earlier in the day. He jimmied the starter and the motor started up. The boat pulled out into the channel. He drove the boat in front of the BMW and dropped the anchor.

Francis had already donned his diving suit before going for the boat, and he swam to shore. He grabbed the tow chain out of the trunk, attached the other end of it to the BMW, and then swam out to the boat. He attached the chain to the boat rigging, pulled up anchor, and drove until the chain became taut. He swam back to shore.

He had attached a strong bracing earlier in the day so the boat wouldn't be damaged. The owners of the boat would probably just assume they forgot the brace was ever there, since they were gone nine months out of the year. It would leave damage if taken off, and Francis couldn't risk that. This family, Francis knew, stayed from June to August. Everyone on the island was so trustworthy it was ridiculous. However, Francis had been thankful for the unsecured boat, as it suit his purpose.

He swam back to shore, put the car in neutral and let it go. He quickly swam back out to the boat, revved it up, and towed the car out as far as he felt safe enough to let it sink. It would have to go undetected for years, if not lifetimes. This maneuver had to be perfect. The waters of the strait were frigid and only occasional sailboats or fishermen were out here.

No one had seen the man and his maneuvers. No lights were used. Francis just knew where everything was, as he'd done his research. Nothing had gone wrong so far, and with his luck, nothing would.

After he finished his cleanup, putting the boat back in the mooring from which it came, Francis ran back to the car and drove home. He used lights this time after turning the car around. No one would suspect anyone had come this way and was now leaving again. He would never return to the two places of his crime. Many guilty parties did that and that's how they'd gotten caught.

Francis got home around midnight. He walked quietly down the stairs to check on Marie Claire. Not being able to sleep well for a few years, Marie Claire heard the last step squeak. She turned her bedside lamp on just as Francis stepped into her room, which was downstairs.

"Hi, Marie Claire. I came down to check on your homework." Francis kept his voice very low, barely a whisper.

"It's on the desk there on top," Marie Claire whispered back.

"This?" he asked, holding up three sheets of her math homework. "Yes, that's it."

"Go back to sleep. I'll check it over and leave you a note." He turned on her desk lamp and Marie Claire turned her bed light out. She was asleep again in seconds.

Francis checked all the homework on her desk, made a couple of corrections on her math, and then turned the lamp out and crept back up the stairs.

He took a shower and went to bed. No one woke up, as he was always very quiet. Even Anne, sound asleep, never heard anything, nor did she feel him crawl into bed beside her. He fell asleep in seconds.

Chapter Thirty-Eight

MARIE CLAIRE asked Ben to stop at an intersection of the highway and an out-of-the-way driveway that was not used anymore. She didn't know how she remembered this, but it was a big find when Roy and his friend Christopher found the old graveyard in 1970. Walking through the weeds, Marie Claire tripped over the old fence line that the county used to mark the area. Clint helped her up and brushed the weeds and dirt off her back.

The gravestones all dated back before the 1900s. Other than someone keeping weeds down and the grass mowed, there was no newer looking dirt movement or grave marker. Roy was not here. Twenty years or less would show if this area had been disturbed in any way, it seemed to Marie Claire, and it had not been. They would have to keep looking.

Marie Claire and Quinn continued past the men, through the outskirts of the gravesites, and into and around through the trees. Jeff did the same thing, except in the opposite direction. Neither one found anything. Clint watched attentively as Joe, Marvin, and Quinn did a thorough search inside the fencing of the graveyard. They found nothing and they looked under every rock and around all the gravestones.

In a half hour, everyone met back at the van. Marie stood there thinking for a moment and in the van once again, she took them to within ten miles of the Mallory home. Marie Claire remembered an old out of the way parking area where young people used to gather. It was on a secluded road near where she grew up. An old van had been dumped there on the hillside years ago.

They got to the area within fifteen minutes. Marie Claire and Jeff slid down the hillside. Ahead of them, they could see the skeleton of an old 1950s black Chevy van. It resembled the newer PT Cruiser of today, only larger. The men above started to spread out as they descended the hillside. Joe, Ben, and Quinn searched the grasses and weeds in the surrounding area of where Marie Claire and Jeff searched. They covered the entire circumference of the area, even ground Marie Claire covered before. They found nothing.

There were several plastic baggies in Jeff's pocket. He and Marie Claire made a circle of the area. Lower down the hill from the others, they made their way toward the van. Jeff found a watch, expensive, and old. He picked it up with the pen he had in his pocket and put the watch in a baggie. He would add this to the other baggie in the evidence box that held a clump of Roy's hair.

Closer to the old relic, Marie Claire found a piece of old cloth. She didn't touch it, knowing she might damage evidence. She called Jeff over there. He picked it up and put it in a separate baggie via a pair of tweezers he carried for that purpose.

In amongst the skeletal remains of the car, a bottle of Rainier Beer had been tossed. Pieces of the bottle were intact enough to see the numbers. It was dated 1972. Jeff picked up a piece of the glass, even though Marie Claire said that neither Francis nor Roy ever drank alcohol. They never touched alcohol or any other substance.

Everyone thought maybe they would find something here, but there wasn't anything to see. There was no skeleton, no body, and no clothes. Marie Claire sat on a piece of the old car frame sticking up out of the grass. She was thinking of where else she could have them look. Inspiration Point came to mind. She couldn't fathom anyone wanting to go down that steep hillside, however.

Hmmm. Marie Claire thought, and she thought hard. *Maybe that would be a good place to look. No one would want to traverse that hillside. It is very steep, steeper than this place. There are lots of trees. Maybe, just maybe, that is the next place to look. God forbid Roy was left there all these years, but where else could he be? If we can't find him, we will look at the Springer Trail. Horses and cars used that a lot twenty years ago.* Springer Trail went through the woods between the cemetery and Marie Claire's old home. It had been one of Marie Claire's favorite riding places.

"Jeff, Dean, Ben, I may have an idea. Let's go back to the van. I'll take you to the old parking area for lovers and visitors, Inspiration Point."

*　　*　　*　　*

"Clint, please talk to me about something. I cannot be thinking of the past or I will cry. I want to keep the tears at bay," Marie Claire petitioned. Clint felt sorry for his wife, but sorrier for the parents who lost their son so long ago and did not have a clue as to his whereabouts. For the next ten minutes, Marie Claire's husband kept her occupied with memories of places they have been and things they have done.

Marie Claire asked Ben to stop the van at the cement boundary separating the parking area and benches from the hillside that dropped almost to an 85° angle. Much more of an incline and this would be like sitting on the edge of a cliff that dropped straight down to the Sound.

The afternoon turned out clear and sunny. Mount Rainier stood tall and proud, her snow-covered sides showing rock formations a quarter of the way down from her dormant volcanic crater to the bottom of her rugged sides. The fir, pine, and cedar trees were dark green and nearly black in the shadows, and they hid her snowy base. Her majestic beauty was a remarkable sight.

"Marie Claire," Clint said, taking in a deep breath of awe, "this view is spectacular. Mount Rainier is a remarkable sight! I've never been here before."

In front and below them, the inlet that was Puget Sound was flowing from the North end, between the Seattle mainland and Vashon Island on the east side, and then circling the southern end of Vashon and meeting with the Tacoma mainland. The waters flowed south. The inlet between Vashon Island and the Olympic Peninsula had all but disappeared around a bend to the west side inlet, which flowed from the Juan de Fuca Straight to the Seattle area, and down between the two pieces of land on the west.

Those gathered could see the two smoke stacks that towered over an area that people knew as the Tacoma flats. They would eventually be torn down to make way for different commerce, according to the news last night. Marie Claire felt sad knowing that one day this old piece of Tacoma history would be gone. She still remembered the putrid smell of them on very hot days. It had been hard to enjoy the beach on the south side of the island due to their stench.

They could see the south end of the Olympic Mountains from this vantage point, and the Cascades off to the east. Tears slid down Marie Claire's cheeks. She loved it here. Everything that God made for her, as a child to dream about seeing someday up close, was here for her enjoyment. It brought tears to Clint's eyes too. He could see why his wife loved the island so much. He enjoyed God's beauty, and he had never seen anything this spectacular .

"I think, if you were to go down this hillside, something might be found here. It's very steep, as you can see, and it would make a very good hiding place." A choked up Marie Claire was determined to get her point across. "If I were to make someone disappear, this would be the ideal place as no one can walk down there. Nothing would hit the water - there are too many trees. I think this would be the most logical place, but then, you guys know more than I do. This is just my gut feeling."

The men knew that a lot of times it was someone's 'gut feeling' that got them on the right track. They listened as Marie Claire spoke.

Chapter Thirty-Nine

Now that they had found another place to look for the body, they had to decide the best way to go about traversing this hillside. The trees were very thick, and there was hardly any room to squeeze between, from the looks of it up here.

"What about a helicopter?" Clint asked the men. "Could you maybe take a flyover of the trees, get an idea of denseness, or look to see if anything is noticeable from the air? Maybe clothing or something is still visible."

Ben thought about Clint's suggestion. "It might work to just fly over the area once or twice. Dean, call headquarters and ask for a climbing team, say maybe four people, and get them sent over here right away. Call for a chopper while you're at it with two extra people. You know what we need."

Dean called Michael Zwieback. They spent fifteen minutes on the phone, and then afterwards, Dean reported to Ben. "They can fly a chopper here, but their people are already busy and one is out sick. My friend, Maurice, is the best lookout man on the Seattle police force. Michael contacted him. Maurice is flying a chopper here now, but Jeff will have to fly it while Maurice does the combing."

"That's fine by me," Ben said, "but I hope he gets here soon. We don't have all day." Ben looked all around him and all he could see was trees and water. *This is a revolting situation,* Ben thought to himself. *If we don't find something here, we're going to get mighty sick of trees. This island is full of them.*

Dean saw the look on his chief's face. It was a daunting situation, and it would take weeks to search this whole island if they didn't find anything here. Dean, too, hoped that they would hit pay dirt soon. Within twenty minutes, they heard and saw the whirlybird flying toward them. There was just the FBI van here and they moved it to the side of the road so the chopper could land in the center of the park area.

A tall tanned blonde man jumped out of the pilot's seat. His long legs, brought him over to the group waiting for him in just a few strides. His eyes were stark blue.

"Hi, I'm Maurice Combs, at your service." Standing before Ben he said, "Ben Jackson, isn't it?" he greeted the Chief with a wave at Jeff and Dean. "I've heard so much about you, and I'm pleased to meet you," he said, shaking Ben's hand, a toothy smile on his face.

After the introductions, Ben got down to business. "Jeff will fly the chopper. I need you, Maurice, to do the best you can to find something, anything, on this blasted hillside. I've been thinking. If someone didn't want to be seen, this area from the center here," Ben walked over to the edge of the western side of the barrier, around to the eastern side of the barrier, "to this side, would be the best bet, so the perpetrator wasn't in the street. Who looks this way or could see anything here anyway if someone parked here? In case a car came around the corner there, or anyone was driving up the hill from the other direction, they couldn't see anything, as long as the incident happened in this range." Ben again drew an arc with his arm to clarify his thoughts.

"Morrie, if you see so much as a dead fly I want to know about it. I know, you know what to do, but I want this area all along here searched thoroughly. If you see something, clothes, bones, anything, let me know right away. Here's a remote that works hand in hand with the ones we have here," Ben told the man as he showed him the equipment they'd brought along with them.

"We've sent for a team of climbers, but we want to get the layout first. Fly over the area a few times then go back and start your search, ok?" Dean told Maurice and Jeff.

"Gotcha, Dean, Ben. Jeff, take care of my birdie. She's a beaut and I don't want her hurt." Jeff and Dean knew Maurice very well. They took the kidding in stride. The man really had no worries, and he knew it.

In a few minutes, Jeff, in the driver's seat, got the blades whirring; and Maurice, binoculars and handheld telescope in hand, felt the smooth glide up as the chopper rose into the air. The glassed-in two-man crew were ready for action, and Maurice was one of the country's best trackers and field research agents.

Out over the Sound, Jeff dropped the helicopter to just above water level. They took a swing around the directed arc and then flew upwards a bit to follow it back the opposite direction. They made four arcs this way before swooping again down to just above water level. The bystanders at the top watched as Maurice, binoculars in hand, homed in on every tree and the ground beneath. He never missed one spot or tree as he focused on the job at hand.

It's amazing what one can see from the air with binoculars. Little wild strawberries, wild primroses, and snakes and lizards lived in the loamy soil. Everything but a body or evidence of a person was seen along the lower edge of the dense woods. Jeff flew the bird up higher, turned, and flew back again to start fresh from the opposite end. This made it easier due to not having to move the equipment, and Maurice could have the whole passenger side free to look to his heart's content, and without any obstruction.

They already searched about twenty feet from the shoreline up-wards along the whole length of the area. They moved up some more and went over the same ground, plus a few feet higher.

Jeff and the onlookers at the Point watched the boats come in to see what the chopper was doing. Jeff had to take the bullhorn and tell them to back away. The boats were carrying onlookers and very soon, they got an eyeful as four men, complete with mountain climbing gear, arrived on the Point. The boat pilots knew something to do with the law was happening and they did back off several feet and they sat in the water to observe.

Terry Gilford, the sheriff of Vashon, arrived shortly after Jeff and Maurice took off. He just finished setting up road blocks one thousand feet either side of the Point, as the boats and onlookers on the road ar-rived. He couldn't do anything but ask the Coast Guard to oversee the waters. Three Coast Guard cutters came in quickly to Terry's request. Jeff was free to do his job without watching out for the boaters.

A few television choppers flew over the island, catching what information they could on their cameras. They would have to wait for interviews if, and when, their boy was found.

Again, Jeff moved the chopper up and over the area again. Maurice perused the next several feet upwards, as well as the area they just flew past. This was taking a lot of time, three hours so far, but the trees were so dense that the men were willing to stay as long as it took to do the job right.

*   *   *   *

Marie Claire drove to the mercantile in Burton to get some lunch for everyone. It was the store where she had stolen those socks so many years ago. Mrs. Frazier was no longer alive, but Marie Claire had a bittersweet feeling and knew she would always be grateful to the woman for the major life lesson. Marie Claire never did steal from anyone again.

She parked near the door and walked into the mercantile and up to a young cashier behind the counter. The young woman had silver studs in her ears, and Marie Claire thought she saw one on the girl's tongue. *What a long way we've come. I hate how these new age kids look. I never was into that scene when I was younger. It's worse today.*

Marie Claire must have been in another world. The young woman asked, "How may I help you today? Is there something you want to purchase?"

"Oh, sorry. I haven't been in this store for years and years. I grew up here. I'll just get some sandwiches and sodas. I think I'd like some chips too. I'll be right back." Marie Claire grabbed some sandwiches from the deli, freshly made by the older woman behind the glass counter, and she took some sodas and iced tea out of the refrigerator compartment. She put these in the basket and headed toward the counter when she saw the chip aisle. She picked up three big, different flavored bags of potato chips, and a couple packs of cookies.

"There you go, ma'am. Have a nice day," the young girl said to Marie Claire. "Ma'am, are you all right?"

Blinking her tear-filled eyes, Marie Claire looked at the girl and said, "What ever happened to Mrs. Frazier? I know she died. Do you know why? Is she buried here on the island?"

"Yes, she is at the cemetery. She had a heart attack several years ago. I think I was seven or eight. Did you know her well? My name is Amy."

"I'm Marie Claire. Nice to meet you, Amy. Yes, I did know Hazel

well. She was in my church. We kids used to tease her a lot. She wasn't
well liked, but I know that she may have had a good heart. She was
strict and seemed mean." Marie Claire went on to explain other things
she knew of Hazel also.

Giggling, Amy said, "I'm her granddaughter. Grandma was different. She had been an abused wife. When Grandpa died several years
before I was born, Mom said that Grandma vowed never to remarry.
She hated men. She was rather strict and set in her ways."

Marie Claire knew just what Mrs. Frazier had endured in her
lifetime. She now understood the older woman better. Unlike Marie
Claire, Hazel had let life scar her. She became a bitter and hardened
old woman.

Amy reiterated, "Grandma did have a heart of gold though as far
as I was concerned. Most people never saw that side of her. That was
a shame. I graduated from high school a few years ago. I start college
in the fall. I wanted to take some time off before going back to school.
Where do you live now?" Chatterbox Amy caused Marie Claire to
smile. She was one of those girls that liked to talk a mile a minute.
Actually, Amy had to be in her twenties if Hazel died when Amy was
a grade schooler.

Marie Claire told Amy about the riding academy she hoped she
could open up soon, and the location in Midway. Marie Claire even told
Amy about the sock incident. Amy understood.

"Grandma used to talk about you after church. We would pray
for you. I was just a little kid, but I still remember. She remembered
you too, and always kept praying for you. She ranted and raved about
your parents and how you were always bringing in notes for cigarettes
and stuff. She didn't agree with that." Marie Claire needed to leave, but
Amy had something else to tell her.

"Grandma would be happy to know how you turned out. She
can see us, I'm sure. Jesus is with us every second, so I have to believe
Grandma is watching too. "

"Thank you, Amy, for sharing with me. I really have to go now.
My crew is waiting for me. I'm glad you're doing well and had a grand-
mother you could love, and who loved you. I did too. That makes life a
little more precious. Take care." With that, Marie Claire left the store.
She was smiling and then laughing at Mrs. Frazier and all she repre-
sented to the kids of her day. Tears came to her eyes and she breathed a

prayer of thanksgiving for knowing such a wonderful woman. She felt she would see her in Heaven someday because Amy was a wonderful young woman, and shared so much good stuff about her grandma.

*   *   *   *

Marie Claire spent so much time talking that she hadn't paid any attention to the time. She'd been gone almost an hour. She rushed back to the Point where the men still searched for Roy. Jeff flew near the top now. He had just a few more feet to go. Dean and Ben called the two in and so they landed in the center of the Point and jumped out of the chopper. Everyone, including the sheriff and the climbers, took the goodies handed out by Marie Claire. A few cement tables with benches sat here and there around the perimeter of the small lookout park, and they all found places to sit.

Marie Claire passed out plates and napkins that Dean kept in a box in the FBI van. She and Clint sat with Jeff and Dean. Everyone sat quietly as they took their first bites, just enjoying the view from the highest point on Vashon, until Clint asked a question.

"Tell me about your trip to the store, Sunshine. Did you meet anyone you knew there?"

Marie Claire told about meeting Amy, Mrs. Frazier's granddaughter, and about the stolen socks. She shared about her life as a child, and she didn't leave anything out. When she finished her history, Marie Claire sat back and took a deep breath, realizing that she didn't have tears or remorse in her heart.

The men seemed to all talk at once. "What a horrible childhood. My cousin lived like that." Another said, "Marie Claire, you should write a book. You could help so many." And even another one said, "My sister and I had the same kind of upbringing. That's why I decided to be an FBI agent." On and on the comments went.

The men admired Marie Claire for her courage, her faith, her willingness to let the past be past. They admired her for being loving and kind, caring and forthright without being hurtful to others. The courage and willingness to share something as personal as her story of stealing those socks made them admire her even more. Marie Claire knew they all understood her. All of them shared stories of their youthful escapades too.

Ben, realizing that the time was flying by, gathered up his garbage and stood to take it to the garbage bag Marie Claire set out. The others followed suit.

In the helicopter once again, Maurice and Jeff took off, headed back to the eastern end to comb some more of the hillside. At the end, Jeff was about to turn around and call it quits. They'd been searching for another hour and never saw anything, until now. He thought he saw something - *was that a pair of jeans or something else?* Jeff thought to himself. Then, he turned around so Maurice could use his binoculars and search closer. Jeff maneuvered closer to the trees that covered the hill on the western point.

Hovering near that end of the parking lot, Ben's remote system blared. He took his radio off his belt and pushed the intercom button. The loudspeaker came on for all to hear. "Did you guys find something?" Ben asked.

"Yes, Sir. There's a pair of pants just west of where you're standing. Come my direction," Maurice said as he watched Ben walk the direction indicated. "Move a bit to the right, now down. We'll shine a red strobe light on the area. Have the climbers descend there. The pants are about fifteen feet or so below you."

"Good job, men. Thanks. Come on in. We'll get out of your way. The climbers are on their way down." Ben said, after the climbers had taken stock of the strobe of light and threw a marker down towards the site of the body. They secured their ropes quickly for the descent and headed down before Jeff and Maurice landed.

*   *   *   *

Joe descended and called, "Down here!" The other three climbers, including Robert Sorbian, Toby, Sorbian's assistant, and Maurice, descended and followed Joe's voice and the marker line down the hill. "I've found something."

"Oh, I wish I were down there too," Jeff said to no one in particular.

Robert Sorbian, the forensics specialist for the Washington FBI, kept his eyes on the hillside. He hated heights, couldn't stand climbing down or up hills, and he just wanted to get this job over with. His team needed him here so he never complained. He also knew to watch for items of interest on his way down.

Toby looked at Robert and knew the man was not coping well with this hill, but he admired his boss for not wavering in the climb down. He didn't say anything for fear of reprisal, however. Toby, Robert noticed, looked out for any sign of evidence around the area, and for that he was grateful, because, he thought, *I don't feel able to do much of anything but keep myself from getting killed, so I'm searching close to my person. I don't want to slide down this hill. I'll die of a heart attack for sure!*

"Maurice is with them. He'll catch anything of interest that the climbers miss. Also, Robert is one of the nation's best, he'll keep the area pure and do his best job when the body is brought up," Ben told Jeff.

"I know. I just miss being in amongst the action."

Ben and Dean both put their arms around Jeff's shoulders. "You did real good today, buddy. Take it easy for a while. Your turn's coming." Dean told his agent.

Joe climbed up the hill, past Robert and Toby. When Joe reached the railing, Clint, Dean, and Jeff grabbed his arms and helped the man over the railing and across the cement wall. Joe held something in his hand.

"What did you find, Joe?" Ben asked.

"It's a jacket," Joe told him. "I carefully took it off the body it was covering, and rolled it up so that I could carry it to keep anything that might be in the pockets from falling out. It blends in with the terrain, so it was harder to find. Jeff and Maurice made those three swipes over the hillside just in case they did miss something. It's a good thing they did. We need to send a stretcher down there so we can bring it up," Joe requested softly.

"Would you open it for me please?" Marie Claire asked the man. "It looks like one of our old high school jackets. Our colors were green and gold." Joe did as Marie Claire requested. Tightly wound, Joe now unwound it.

Marie Claire looked her fill at the now opened letterman's jacket. Joe held up the front and then he turned it to the back. Dean saw something sticking out of the right front pocket. "What's that?" he asked. Joe reached in and took out a little box. What he held in his hand, made

Marie Claire turn white. The tears she held back when she first saw the jacket, she now let fall.

Marie Claire looked questioningly at the FBI chief, and with a nod of affirmation from Ben, Marie Claire reached for the little red velvet box. Joe released it to her. Marie Claire opened it up, and there lay the ring Roy would have given her, had they been able to marry. Dean took the ring back, but he would be sure to return it to her when he was able.

Marie Claire didn't swear, ever, but now she let it all out. The anger, the hatred, the pain of so much death in her life came forth. She hated Francis Harlan Kingman with a passion. She knew he had done this horrible thing to the only love she'd ever had in her younger life. Marie Claire hurt for the parents who had doted on their son. Roy had been the best thing to happen to her before she met Clint Bellham.

No one dared touch Marie Claire right now. They understood her very well. They let her have her whirlwind mad, and when she finished, they knew she would be apologetic and upset over the outburst. Marie Claire deserved this time, though. Ben motioned the others to walk with him as they left Marie Claire there, beating on a tree trunk with a thick branch she picked up under a tree, crying, screaming, and growling out her anger. When she was ready to talk, the men would be there for her.

*　　*　　*　　*

Technically, they didn't know for a fact that Roy was the one they found, but gut instinct left them feeling that they worked with the remains of who they had been searching for.

The climbers were taking a much-needed break until they got the rest of their equipment The men assembled the needed tools to bring the boy's remains up. Robert would perform the forensics investigation of the crime scene after the others left the area. Right now, he was working around the bones, gathering as much information as he could find.

Toby and Maurice hadn't climbed back up either, but stayed behind to film the sections of the site and do the preliminary workup. The skull lay there, partially hidden, but they took pictures showing the bullet hole. The investigators knew the young man had died of a bullet to the frontal lobe. Roy probably never saw it coming.

The three climbers returned down the hill pulling the gurney behind them. Piece by piece, the bones that fell loose were turned, magnified from top to bottom, each side, end and shaft captured on film. The whole skeleton that wasn't in pieces would be kept intact as much as possible. It would be sent to the pathologist, along with the other bones and clothing pieces found on the scene.

It took about two and a half hours for Robert to do his job. When he finished, Maurice and Toby helped him gather the skeleton onto a plastic sheet and together, they set it on the gurney. No coyotes or wolves inhabited Vashon, so aside from some small animals chewing the fascia that held a few leg and arm bones together, the skeleton was almost totally intact. A femur and a few smaller bones from one arm lay loose, *but at least*, Robert thought, *it appears there are no missing parts.*

"Robert," Maurice said, "here's the bullet! Looks like a 38 caliber."

Scooting over to Maurice, Robert took the bullet out of the man's fingers. Toby bent over to see also. "It sure is, buddy. Lots of 38s around."

"Toby and I will head on up the hill. We'll see you when we see you, Robert." Toby and Maurice knew the drill. They climbed up the hill first, taking with them one end of the rope pulley that one climber attached to the gurney by the other end. When Toby and Maurice reached the top, Ben and Dean took hold of the rope and when they heard, "Go ahead, pull," from Robert, they pulled the rope and kept it taut as they drug the gurney upwards.

The three climbers followed along to make sure the gurney remains stayed intact. Once, the stretcher hit a tree and stayed there until it was pulled away. The climbers used their feet and hands to pull themselves up the hill, occasionally putting the stretcher in front of them on the right course. In no time at all, they reached the top and were thankful that job was done.

Robert stayed down at the death scene for another two hours. By that time, the sun, nearly below the mountain peaks, created an eerie darkness in the deep woods. Being able to see no more without his flashlight, he felt he covered everything but would come back in the morning to finish up his research. He then secured the area and climbed up the hill.

Someone had brought a camper for the climbers to stay in. They would stay the night, and take turns guarding the area. They didn't need unwanted visitors coming in.

*   *   *   *

Jeff radioed the Mallorys. "No one will get there in time tonight to help you guys load up your stuff." He had taken Clint and Marie Claire back to the Mallory place a few hours ago, and Robert Sorbian and Maurice would stay the night there. Dean and Ben went back to their homes in Seattle, as did the three other agents, whose services were now ended here.

"That's ok," Rand told him cordially. Clint and I did most of it together. "We'll finish in the morning. We need your help with a few items that are heavier. Did you find what you needed, there at the Point?"

"Yes, we did. We're calling it quits for tonight. Robert and Maurice will stay there tonight, but the rest of us are heading back to the mainland. I'll be back in the morning, as will Dean and Quinn."

Talking to Marie Claire for a moment, Jeff started to ask her about how she was feeling, but Marie Claire cut in. "Jeff, I can't talk about it right now. I'm ok. I won't say, haven't said, anything to Kara and Rand. I want to wait until tomorrow. I'm sorry for my tirade." Jeff could barely hear her. Marie Claire's voice was very quiet and he had to concentrate to hear her. He figured she didn't want her friends to know anything.

"It's ok, Marie Claire. I do understand. We agents have tirades too, mostly when it comes to children, the innocent ones. Try to sleep, love. Jeanette and I love you very much. I'll see you in the morning. Say hi to Clint for me, ok."

"Jeff, thanks. You're a peach. I love you too." Marie Claire smiled, the first one in hours. Clint smiled back at her when she glanced his way.

The Bellhams spoke softly with Maurice after the Mallorys and Robert went to bed later that night. Marie Claire had a hard time sleeping, and she needed to talk, to apologize for her outburst. The three of them talked deep into the night.

On the way home, Jeff thought of Marie Claire. They had been such good friends years ago, and he thought of marrying her once, but never asked her. Jeff understood Marie Claire almost as much as Clint did. He loved both of them more than he'd thought possible. Clint was the big brother Jeff never had. Jeff couldn't thank Marie Claire enough for bringing Jeanette into his life. He knew his wife worried about Marie Claire, and he wanted to hold Jeanette all night long. This case hit his very soul, hard, and he felt nearly as bad about Roy as Marie Claire did.

Chapter Forty

A T FIVE the next morning, Robert and Maurice were back at the scene of the crime. They found more hairs and clothing fibers again this morning. Other than the body and the ring, and the little bit of tarp that lay under the boy's remains, nothing else was evident here. Yesterday, Robert dug a narrow trench around the body's resting place, but there was nothing there to be found, and nothing was buried in this area.

It took another three hours, and after having searched every square inch of the area, Maurice and Robert knew they would not find anything more. Above them, they heard cars pull in and the motors turn off. The other agents had arrived.

The climbers helped Maurice up and over the railing. Robert followed and they did the same for him. Together, they showed Dean and Quinn the packets of evidence procured. Hair, blondish, belonging to Roy, according to Marie Claire, was the only hair samples they found. The clothing fibers and pieces came off the clothing Roy wore that day. The majority of the tarp that Francis first wrapped Roy in, unknown to the agents of course, had not been found. They knew Roy had been thrown down the hillside, from the steepness of the climb. "The body could have slid down that far, probably did slide that far, and only stopped when it hit the tree where it did. That's a good sixty feet, I'd say," Robert reiterated. "We searched every square inch for a total of fifty feet diameter, starting where the body was found, going out each direction from there in a circular pattern. There is nothing more we can find. There is no disturbance of the ground under or around the body. The tarp was made of a plastic covered canvas, green and white, and the wind and weather must have carried most of the rotting material off somewhere. The slickness of the tarp allowed the body to slide until it hit that tree where it lay."

"Robert," Dean said, "I thank you so much for all your help. Maurice, the autopsy started last night. The coroner, which happens to be your pal, Terry Piloni, didn't wait on this one. As soon as the body arrived he came in and got started on the details right away. He's good friends with Mr. Copeland, too. I imagine, since you did such a great job here, you'd like to take a rest. Go see Terry. Maybe you can learn something about cadavers while you're at it." Dean was joking of course. He did feel the guys all needed a break. Dean knew that working side by side with Terry, though, would give the young specialist more knowledge. Maurice loved it when he could, after doing field forensics, sit in on the hows and whys of a murder with Terry. It helped him better understand the cases that they worked and the how of why a murder happened. Robert was getting on in years, and Maurice was a promising candidate for becoming the next King County Medical Examiner.

*   *   *   *

Marie Claire, Clint, Dean, Jeff, who had returned within the last hour, Maurice and the climbers, who had cleaned up the area and were done with this case also, went together to the Mallorys, where lunch was promised. Maurice went home to the mainland afterwards, the climbers went to explore Vashon some more. There were lots of hillsides leading down to the water, and they wanted to have some fun before going back to Seattle. "The views from this island are to die for," one of them commented.

The Mallory house was on the market. "We signed up with a big realty on the island. Our house was appraised at four hundred thousand dollars. We have room to negotiate that way, too. The house is paid in full, has been for years, so we have, free and clear, whatever money that ends up being." Rand told them. Marie Claire seemed happy at that. She beamed a big smile and squeezed Kara's hands.

After lunch, Clint, Marie Claire, Jeff, and Dean visited the Copelands. They drove there and were met at the door by Mr. Copeland.

"Did you find anything?" Roger Copeland asked, as he seated the group in his living room.

"Mr. and Mrs. Copeland. We came to tell you that we found a body. The coat we found is with the corner. A red velvet box holding an engagement ring was in the pocket." Margarethe gasped. "We'll let you know more after the coroner is done with the forensics." That seemed cold to Dean, but he couldn't put the term in a way that would be any more pleasing to the boy's parents. "It may not be your son, but we need to be sure. We are keeping this under wraps for now until the coroner is done with his report. We will be sure to let you know when we're finished. If it is Roy, we'll let you take him for burial at that time," Dean spoke to the Copelands as calmly and quietly as he could.

Mrs. Copeland, tears in her eyes, thanked Dean. She then turned toward the others and took them in with her eyes. When she touched on Marie Claire standing there, she broke down. Marie Claire took the older woman in her arms.

"I just wish you had married my boy. He wouldn't be dead now. You two would be across the country and out of harm's way." Margarethe was beside herself.

Sick to death of crying, Marie Claire said, "I'm sorry. So sorry. I didn't know what to do. I wanted to finish school. I didn't know what to do. Francis would have maybe killed Roy anyway. I'm so sorry."

"Margarethe, it's not Marie Claire's fault," Her husband, Roger, told the woman as he took her in his heart arms and led her to the rocking chair she loved.

Clint, angry that the woman blamed his wife, cradled Marie Claire as she sniffled. Dean and Ben stood either side of the younger couple and they talked to Marie Claire, making her realize Margarethe didn't mean what she said. They knew Marie Claire didn't hold any grudges, but they had become attuned to comforting those to whom they carried bad news.

Marie Claire's eyes were dry when she looked up at the men. She turned and walked outside. Letting his wife cry, Roger walked outside, took Marie Claire in his arms, and lifted her face so he could see her eyes. "Marie Claire, Margarethe didn't mean what it sounded like; nothing would've saved our boy. I knew a man like Francis Kingman before. Nothing can keep a man like that from doing what he's going to do. Maybe Francis didn't kill Roy. We'll not blame you if it turns out he did. It's not your fault." The older man enfolded Marie Claire in his arms and rocked her like a dad would rock a young child who had fallen down and skinned his knee.

Marie Claire looked up, and she hugged Roger Copeland and thanked him for his support." I know we don't know that Francis did this," she said," but I have a feeling he did. I will do all I can to help the FBI find the killer. I'm so sorry for Roy. He didn't deserve what happened to him."

"Are you so sure it was Roy they found, then?" Roger Copeland asked Marie Claire.

"Mr. Copeland, Roy gave me a ring to look at when he proposed to me. I gave the ring back. He was going to ask for my hand again after he spoke with my parents. Then he disappeared. The ring and box was in the jacket pocket when the climbers found the coat on the hillside at Inspiration Point. I have no doubt it's him, but I know the law states we can't assume until the autopsy report comes back. The FBI has the ring right now. They'll give it back to you." Marie Claire had a glimmer of tears in her eyes at this point, her voice tremulous. "Do you want the ring, or may I keep it?" she asked the older man.

"If your husband doesn't mind your having the ring another man was going to give you, you may keep it. Ask Clint first, however. It's the right thing to do."

"Thank you, sir. I will." Marie Claire hugged Roger Copeland again.

"Yes sir, no sir, I will sir," Roger Copeland mimicked. "He was a good boy. I won't ever have another. My grandchildren are all girls. My daughters never had boys. Roy promised me a grandson. I guess I'll never have one to carry on my name." Now his eyes shined, wet with unshed tears.

"I know. I remember you and Roy talking, and I remember he admired you."

Roger cupped Marie Claire's chin in his large right palm. "Roy always told us how beautiful you were. You still are, maybe even more so now than then. You chose a good man to be your husband. I enjoyed visiting with him. may we take you to dinner later? It will be my treat!"

"I think that would be great." When Clint looked in Mr. Copeland's eyes, he smiled at the man and then at Marie Claire. "Roy meant the ring for you. Marie Claire, you may have it, it's up to you; I don't care if you keep it." Clint had overheard everything regarding that conversation. His heart hurt for the pain Marie Claire and the Copelands had gone through so many years ago, and more so for what they were going through now, would be going through for a long time. It was terrible when something this life changing happened. Clint didn't envy anyone the loss of a child.

Marie Claire hugged her husband and, joyful tears filled her eyes."Thank you, Handsome. I love you. More than anything or anyone!" She held Clint's face in her hands, her thumbs softly ran, back and forth across his lips.

"I know you two want to go back to the island and get your friends settled in. you'll come back tonight?" Roger asked Clint.

"Yes, we'll be back about six." The time was close to eleven by this time.

"I want to go to Inscription Point where you found our son. Will you allow us to follow you there?" A while earlier, Margarethe walked outside to stand beside her husband.

"Of course we'll go there with you." Marie Claire smiled at Margarethe Copeland.

Back at the Point once more, Marie Claire hurried over to the railing where the men looked for Roy yesterday. With everything cleaned up this morning, no evidence remained showing that anyone had been here, and no evidence remained that anything horrendous had ever happened here.

Marie Claire stood at the railing, looking down where Roy's body once lay for these many years, and she said a prayer. "Father, I'm sorry for what occurred so many years ago. You know I have hated myself for succumbing to Francis pleasures. Thank you for your blessed forgiveness. I pray for Margarethe and Roger, for their understanding and love. Give them peace, Heavenly Father. Please, I beg of you. They didn't deserve to lose such a wonderful son. He was so kind to me and we loved each other. Forgive me for my part in this thing that happened. If I had run away with him, maybe he would still be alive.

The older couple stood together for a few moments before taking a spot near Marie Claire at the edge of the hill. The couple wanted to talk to her, and so they walked near to Marie Claire. When they heard her praying, they stopped, closed their eyes, and prayed along with her, silently. When she finished, she rested on her elbows, looking down the hill. "Roy," she said, "you are in Heaven now. I think you know we found you. Please forgive me for not saying 'yes' the first time. I loved you and always will. You will always be my first love. Say hello to my niece, Lisa Marie, and to my best friends, the Bascolms. I love you all."

Margarethe Copeland opened her wet, gray eyes. Tears ran down her rosy cheeks. Roger Copeland didn't cope much better. He cried, something he never let himself do. He had almost cried once before, just after Roy disappeared. He now swallowed his pride and allowed the hot, wet drops to fall as they would.

Marie Claire turned and saw the older couple there in their distress. She sauntered over to them and enfolded both in her arms. She had cried her fill. Now was the time to comfort Roy's parents.

"Marie Claire, we have always cherished you as Roy did. He loved you so much. We're all sorry for his disappearance. Roger and I don't blame you, and we've told you so already. We are just reiterating that, okay? We love you. We're very happy that you have Clint in your life. He's a good man," Margarethe Copeland told the younger woman.

The couples went their separate ways. The Mallorys met the Bellhams at the ferry dock. Carol drove their car and Rand followed in the truck towing the trailer that carried their furniture. Looking forward to their new life, Kara and Rand sat with Marie Claire and Clint in a window seat upstairs as they drank coffee and watched the island of Vashon grow smaller behind them.

Chapter Forty-One

THE MORNING dawned bright and sunny. At seven, Martha came over with Ed, Jeanette and Jeff, and she and Jeanette prepared a breakfast of hot cakes with fresh strawberries, scrambled eggs, and sausage. The tantalizing aroma drifted up the stairs. Kara and Rand had awakened a bit earlier, dressed, and headed downstairs. Clint and Marie Claire lay in bed stretching not wanting to get up yet. However, they heard the couple moving around next door, so they decided they had better get a move on.

They were all seated at the dining room table and Ed gave thanks. After the day the Bellhams and Mallorys had yesterday, they were still a little tired.

"Moving is a big job," Rand said. Clint and Jeff promised to put the Mallory's belongings in the shed for safekeeping until the contractors finished building their house. The building was due to commence in the next two weeks.

Rand needed to meet with an architect later in the morning, and Kara would be working with Marie Claire to procure the information on a well, electrical setup, and phone line. She and Rand hadn't slept much due to the excitement of their new venture. Marie Claire, just about as excited as anyone over her best friends moving in, talked to the Mallorys incessantly. Rand again expressed his appreciation for the new home site. "I'm looking forward to seeing how the campground pans out for you two! Thanks for the opportunity to work as the overseer. I think I'm really going to like it."

Ed, listening to the conversation between the Bellhams and Mallorys, he wanted to say something too. Marie Claire saw the expectant look on Ed's face and created an opening so he could speak.

"It looks like you've got something on your mind, Ed!" Marie Claire said to the old man, smiling at him.

"Yes, Missy, I do. I been thinkin' bout splittin' my property. I'd like to give half of it to you all to have a bigger pond. I'm gettin' tired and been thinkin' what to do with the place. I can't run no dairy no more, and I wanna retire. Jeff and I been talkin' and we gonna give you two hunderd more acres. That'll leave the kids here," pointing at Jeff and Jeanette, "jest about half'n that fer farmin'. They wanna grow vegetables and have some ponies fer when they got kids."

Marie Claire's eyes grew bigger than saucers. Rand and Kara sat back in their chairs and stared at the Bellhams, mouths open in surprise.

"Whatsa matter? Cat got yer tongues?" Ed asked, chuckling at the surprised looks on their faces.

Clint, the first to recover from the shock, said, "We're going to have to see what area you're talking about, Ed. The camping sites are up, cement slabs are about done, and they are almost done with the lake digging."

"Oh, Clint, doncha worry. Jeff and I's been talkin 'bout this fer a long time. When was the last time you was down there lookin' at the job site?"

"Just the other day," Clint told the older man.

"Well, ya betta go on down there today and check it out. I have a notion you's gonna be mighty surprised." Ed drank from his coffee cup and started in on the rest of his breakfast.

Clint, pushing his chair back from the table, stood up. Taking Marie Claire's hand, he said, "Please excuse us. We have something to check on." They rushed outside, to the barn, and Clint pulled out his motorbike. Marie Claire went to the tack room, pulled out a bridle and her saddle, and was going to walk over to get Jeff's horse. She didn't get that far. From the far end of the stalls she heard a whinny. Clint heard it also.

She dropped her tack and ran over to Clint. By that time, she heard Jeff yell at them. "Wait," he said, running over to the couple. Jeanette, Ed, and the others were close behind.

"Ed and I have something to show you. It was going to be an anniversary gift, but you can have it a little early." Jeff, a bit breathless, smiled at his in-laws. He led them into the barn once again and down the row of stalls. There in the last one stood a beautiful black and white horse. A tall Clydesdale, his brass halter plate read "Buster," nickered when he saw Marie Claire.

"What -" Marie Claire cried. "Oh, Jeff, Ed. Where'd you get him?" Marie Claire walked into the stall and kissed Buster on the side of his mouth. The big old horse nickered at her and rubbed his head on her arm.

"Oh, he's beautiful. Is he really mine?" Marie Claire, tears of joy standing in her eyes, looked at Jeff, then Ed, then at her husband and sister. "Thank you so much."

"I had nothing to do with this, Marie Claire," Clint told her, his right hand waving in the air. "I didn't ask for any hay burner."

Chuckling, Jeff commented, "Oh, Clint. You'll enjoy him. Follow me." Jeff led them out the end door and around to the back of Buster's stall. Sitting there was an old chuck wagon that Ed kept in one of his barns. It needed a little work, but it was in great shape for the age of it, thanks to the storage that kept it protected.

Clint looked at the wagon, then walked all around it. Marie Claire, after giving Buster a flake of hay, ran around the barn to see what the excitement was all about. She'd heard Kara exclaim surprise, and then laughter and joyous conversation. She gasped when she saw the chuck wagon.

"Ed! Where did you get this? Oh, it's wonderful. I love it!" Marie Claire covered her face with her hands and then walked over and gave Ed a big kiss on the lips.

"Hey, hey, now, none a that, Missy. I's jest glad ya like the old thing. My Janie and I, we used that a lot when we was workin'. This land used ta be mine, and Janie and I and baby Oswald would come out here and feed the punchers when they was roundin' up the cattle. We had beef as well as milk stock in them days. Boy, what a lot a fun we had back then. I figured you'd wanna use it too. You's a cowboy's woman, Missy, and I wanted to give ya a gift you would really love. Buster there belonged to a friend a mine who died last week. You was over on that island and I got the news. His daughter told me to come and get the horse, so Jeff and I brought 'im here fer ya. I give ya the wagon so's you can take the horse to pull ya around. No more of them new fangled contraptions they call motor bikes. I hate them noisy things."

Ed said his peace and he turned and walked back to the house. "My goodness," Marie Claire said, surprise in her voice. "I didn't know all that info. Why didn't you tell me that Ed owned all this land at one time, Jeff? I thought the lady we bought the place from bought this from someone else. Wow, the questions I could ask and the fun facts Ed will give me! I can't wait to sit down and talk to him! Wow. This is great. A real old west ranch. Man, this is exciting!"

Clint laughed at Marie Claire, he laughed at his good fortune to have such a wonderful family, and he laughed, hugging each one in turn. Clint was happy to be loved as much as those around him expressed.

Jeff put an arm around Marie Claire and Clint in turn, and together, with the Mallorys, they walked to the barn. "Dad showed me how to harness Buster. Shall we do it?" He squeezed their shoulders and then walked to the stall next to Buster. There, he picked up the harness and carried it out to the wagon. Marie Claire looked on with awe.

She haltered the horse and led him outside. "Back him up, Marie Claire," Jeff instructed. He then showed her and Clint how to harness the horse. When Buster was hitched to the wagon, he then asked everyone, "Get on board you guys! Let's go for a ride." Ride they did. Right down to the construction area. The fencing between the dairy and the Rocking Horse Ranch was gone. In its place was another half mile of lake. Water filled the depression now, and Richard Hillman, the dairy foreman and overseer of the construction of Clint's campground, rode over on his three-wheeler dirt bike.

"What do you think?" Richard asked Clint.

"I don't know what to say," Clint said, shocked amazement showed on his face. "I never expected this big of a lake. Ed just deeded this property over to us. Can you believe that?"

"Well," Richard said, "I've known for a while that he wants to retire. He's not been feeling well. He loved the idea you had for this area, and he wanted to contribute. He loves hunting and fishing, and you are helping your community. I guess the state gave him some good information about what you're doing."

"Yes, Clint. Dad and I went a month ago to check on deeding this over to you. It's a good tax break for both of us. I hear the governor is going to donate fish from around the country to stock this lake. That was going to be a surprise, but I needed to tell you in case you had other ideas."

Again, Clint couldn't believe how blessed he and Marie Claire were. He never dreamed that someone would donate fish. "What kind," Clint asked.

"There will be bass, trout, and I don't know what all. You'll find out as soon as they get here, which should be in about a week."Richard told him. "I have to run. There's a guy coming to help me with something. I think I just saw his car pull in."

Richard mounted his bike and Clint said, "Thanks, Rich. I appreciate everything you're doing."

Rand needed to go too. He had a meeting in an hour with the architect. "Are we ready to go back? I have to leave in a few minutes."

"Sure," Clint answered, helping his wife and Kara up onto the hard wagon seat, as Jeff helped Jeanette. As Clint drove back to the house, Marie Claire asked Jeff about Roy,

"I'm sure it's Roy we found. Are you, Jeff?" Marie Claire asked her brother-in-law.

"The facts so far lead me to believe it is indeed Roy Copeland. Until proven different, though, we aren't allowed to assume or even act as though it is him. That's the way it is with any case. Everyone is innocent until proven guilty. No one is dead until the proof is there, or enough time has elapsed."

"What about the case of a disappearance and the wife eventually gets her inheritance, or vice versa," Clint asked.

"Well, in cases like that if no evidence is proven of a death, and for seven years if no proof of life is there, then the inheritance goes to whomever it is supposed to go to. The IRS keeps track of social security numbers. If the dead person's number is not used for seven years, then it's supposed that the person is indeed deceased."

They then spoke of the Mallorys and the move they were making, the house they wanted to build, and plans Rand had for running the campground. "I think we should have an opening ceremony with a big barbeque and horse and boat rides. Wouldn't that be fun?" The conversation turned to that topic until they reached the house.

*   *   *   *

Marie Claire heard the phone ringing when she hopped off the wagon. She ran into the house and picked up. "Hello, Marie Claire Bellham speaking."

"Hello, Marie Claire. How are you? Is Jeff there with you?"

"Hi, Ben. I'm fine. I'll get Jeff for you." Marie Claire set the receiver on the countertop and then she went to the door. "Jeff, " she called, "Ben wants to talk to you!"

Jeff took the receiver from Marie Claire's hand. "Hi, Ben." Jeff greeted his chief.

"Can you come in to the office? We'd like to talk to you. It won't take long." Ben told his agent, his voice sounding reserved.

"Sure," he answered, "I'll be right there." Ben and Jeff finished their discussion and then Jeff assured Jeanette he would be back in time for lunch.

Clint and Marie Claire put the horse in the pasture. The wagon, Clint put in the spare building that was being used for storing farm equipment, and there was just enough room to house the chuck wagon. Kara and Rand left for town and Jeanette went home. Martha had cleaned the kitchen earlier and left before everyone else got back.

Arm in arm, Clint and his wife walked sedately to the house, thoughts of the new developments in mind. Clint picked Marie Claire up in his arms at the front door. She smiled at him with a surprised look on her face. "Just what are you doing, Handsome?"

"I'm carrying my beautiful bride over the threshold. We're finally home, Sunshine. Thanks to those loved ones around us, we have everything we could ever need or want. God has truly blessed us, my dear." Clint opened the door with one hand and gingerly stepped over the threshold. He set Marie Claire on her feet as he locked the door behind them. He kissed her passionately, then together, they walked upstairs.

*　　　*　　　*　　　*

It was starting to rain as Jeff made his way through the Saturday traffic on I-5. *People are either traveling,* as he spied a few out of state licenses, *or going shopping at one of the many malls that make this area popular,* he thought to himself. Jeff arrived at the office in about forty-five minutes.

"What's up, boss?" Jeff queried as he walked into Ben Jackson's office. Dean was seated there, along with Quinn and another agent.

"The coroner just finished the autopsy and research. We did find Roy Copeland. I wanted to give this ring to you for Marie Claire. I would like you to go with Dean to see the Copelands. You may take Marie Claire with you. We don't want to inundate them with a bunch of people, so that's why we are sending the two of you. We didn't want Marie Claire to know until we talked to you." After a moment, "Be sure she gets this ring back. She's a wonderful lady," Ben seemed, to the others, to really care for Marie Claire as he spoke quietly. The men saw the forlorn look on Ben's face, and knew he was thinking of the ring's recipient. Jeff did appreciate the man's respectfulness to his family.

"I'll head home then and get Marie Claire. I'll tell Jeanette I have to work, and then catch the earliest boat I can to the island. You did check to see if the Copelands are home today, didn't you?"

"Yes, Jeff. They are expecting you this afternoon. They'll be there. Dean will break the news to them. I just want you there for support." Ben looked at Jeff and then at Dean, and he knew his directive was not being questioned. "Before you leave, Jeff, you need to know something else. Francis Kingman was the murderer. We asked Dr. Wilcox's nurse to call Francis in for a physical on the presumption that Dr. Wilcox needed him to give an up to date blood and urine sample. It's something most every company is randomly doing now, to check their employees for drug use. Dr. Wilcox supplied us with Francis' blood for DNA testing against our hair sample from the barn. They matched, as well as a hair sample found at the Point."

"I didn't know you found some hair at the Point." Jeff was surprised.

"We sent Robert Sorbian before anyone went there to look for Roy. We just didn't want anyone to know we'd done that in case word leaked out. Kingman was crafty, but there were some hairs found near the railing where Roy went over. Some were from people not in the database, a few from people who were, and two were from Francis Kingman. We did a process of elimination of who was most likely to have motive. Kingman won out. There's an APB, all points bulletin, out on Francis Kingman now."

Jeff, like Dean did before him, sat up straighter in his chair and thought, *this is unorthodox.* "The evidence can be thrown out of court!

How can you do that, have the guy to come in and give blood like that? Under false pretenses?" Jeff didn't want this creep to walk, and he was not very happy with how this procedure went over.

"Mr. Kingman knows that, sometimes, the DA can get things done that no one else can. If the evidence is brought into question, we'll have the DA cite the ruling that he or the next of kin can obtain and hand over evidence. This is not far from the truth. Marie Claire may have hair in something she has of her ex-husband. We do have a right to ask a physician for any and all medical records on file. If blood is on record, we can petition for that too. It's covered, Jeff. Don't worry." Ben put his agent's mind at rest."

"There's a warrant out for Francis Kingman's arrest at this time, right? " Jeff asked his superiors.

"Yes, there is. We know where Kingman lives. We visited his office and home. We just don't know where Kingman is right at this moment. He was not at either place this morning, and his office says they haven't seen him for almost a week. He is supposedly on vacation somewhere, but no one knows where that 'somewhere' is!" Dean told Jeff.

Chapter Forty-Two

JEFF MADE it home in time to tell Jeanette that he had to go to the island. He looked apologetically at his wife. Jeanette, ready to leave for the mall and very disappointed, said, "I planned pizza for dinner, but I forgot it's Ed's birthday tomorrow. I need to get something for him and wanted to go to the mall."

"Don't wait dinner for me. I don't know how long this will take. I'll be with Dean Manning. He may have dinner plans. You know how it goes, Honey."

"I guess I'll ask Marie Claire if she'll go with me, then. She and I can eat out and enjoy getting a break from home. You're gone so much and she has all the chores to do over there, it seems. I get bored without you, Jeff." Jeanette complained.

"Marie Claire will be going with us, Jeanette. Go have some fun. I'll fill you in when I get home." Jeff reasoned with his wife. She was important, more important than the job, but she needed to realize that this wouldn't be forever. It was his work, and he had to do it.

Jeanette reached up and pulled Jeff's face downwards. She kissed him sweetly on the mouth. "Don't mind me, Sweetheart. I haven't been feeling well today. I'm sorry to be so cranky."

Concerned, Jeff pulled gently on Jeanette's long locks and tipped her face up to his. "What's wrong, Babe? Do you have the flu? Is it a cold coming on? What?"

"I really don't know. I just had been a bit nauseated and woozy earlier today. I'm so tired. I feel bored now that I'm feeling better and I wanted to go out for a bit."

"Well, I'll be home as soon as I can. Take care. I love you, Jeanette."

Jeff drove over to the Rocking Horse Ranch. Marie Claire answered the door in a few seconds. "Hi, brother-in-law." Marie Claire said. "What can I do for you this afternoon?"

She looked at him for a second and then it hit her. "They found Roy, didn't they?"

"Marie Claire, I have to go to the island with Dean. We need to see the Copelands again. Ben asked me to check to see if you wanted to come with us." Jeff, always smiles and fun to be around, looked a bit demure when he answered.

"Let me call Clint at work and then I'll come. If Clint wants to, may he come with us?"

"I know we don't want to inundate the Copelands with people, but I think they'd be ok with both of you. I think it would help to have Clint along." In turmoil, Jeff acquiesced . He knew this would be hard for Marie Claire to hear, let alone Roy's parents. His sister-in-law had a tender heart, and when she loved, she loved with everything she had in her heart to give. He knew why Ben wanted Marie Claire along. She would be the best support available when the Copelands received the report about their son. The three of them would hold each other up.

"Let's hurry. I have to pick Dean up."

"Ok. Just let me call Clint first," Marie Claire said as she hurried back into the house. A minute later, Jeff heard Marie Claire as she called to Rand and Kara, "I have to go to the island with Jeff. Make yourselves dinner and I'll be back as soon as possible. Clint's going with me. We'll eat out most likely. Bye. Love you!" With purse in hand, she ran back outside, shut the door, and hurried to Jeff's Lincoln.

Just as Jeff touched the key to start the engine, his phone rang. "Jeff Farthingworth. What's up?"

"Jeff, Dean. Meet me at the ferry dock. My wife and I are going to the ocean for a couple of days after we leave the island. I'm dropping her off in town there and pick her up on the way to the ferry."

"Will do. Clint is coming with us. We'll call and have him meet us there, too."

Marie Claire called Clint on his car phone. He left work shortly after her call earlier, and he said, "I'm on my way, Sunshine. I'm almost to Midway now. Can you wait? If not, I'll park at the Fred Meyers store and you can get me there. Bye."

"Jeff, what ferry are we catching? Clint will meet us at the Fred Meyers beside the freeway just before the Midway exit." Marie Claire asked.

"The next one, 1:45, if we can get there in time. Ok. Hang on." Jeff uncharacteristically sped down the driveway, going at least fifty.

It's a good thing Clint had this drive blacktopped. I can just see the days it would take us to clean the dust out of our house, Marie Claire thought to herself.

Within ten minutes, Jeff and Marie Claire pulled into the store's parking lot. Clint parked near the front and they saw him waving at them.

"Hi," Clint greeted the two as he sat in the back seat. Marie Claire said she would sit in the back, but Clint ignored her.

On the way to the Seattle dock, Clint carried on a conversation with them. "I called and talked to Maxwell Stevenson this morning. I told him of Marie Claire's plans regarding the house on Vashon. Max said they would be more than willing to move there and help with the repairs too. Apparently, they have some savings they set aside for dire emergencies. He called the John Deer Tractor factory over there and he has an interview tomorrow. He goes for one after that with the police department."

"Sounds like everything's working out for the Stevensons then, doesn't it?" Jeff pulled up to the tollbooth at the ferry dock to purchase their tickets. Dean came out of the terminal to let them know where they were sitting in line.

"We'll meet you upstairs, Dean. We'll find you. Doesn't seem to be too many people traveling to Vashon right now." Jeff commented to Dean before that man turned to go back to his car.

"Commuters are working at this time. The ferry usually gets busy after four in the afternoon and before seven in the morning." Marie Claire, knowing this area very well, gave the information. "My uncle Stan used to work the Southworth to Vashon to Seattle runs every day. Sometimes, he captained the boats. I sure miss him." She retreated into her corner of the front seat, memories flooding into her head threatened to choke her. She loved so many in her life who were now gone.

When she pictured the Bascolms and the last time she saw them, tears threatened to choke her.

Clint, sensing the melancholy change come over his wife, enfolded her from behind the seat. He whispered in her right ear, "I love you, Sunshine. Always remember that. Think of me when the sadness overcomes you. You are a brat, you know, and I wouldn't want to live without you!" With that said, Clint settled back into the seat again and breathed a sigh of remorse. He loved the Bascolms. Clint thought they would have been, should have been, around for a long time, but life throws curves sometimes that we can't avoid.

In a moment, cars were in gear, their engines purring, and then the cars rolled, one by one, onto the deck of the ferryboat. Marie Claire watched as Dean's car pulled up to the front right and stopped at the yellow line. Jeff drove to the front and stopped on the left side, and then the two deckhands pulled massive chains across the lines of automobiles. The chains, one forward and aft, were there to secure the deck as they skimmed across the Sound.

Not having time to dally, looking at the life preservers and fire extinguishers hanging on the walls surrounding the stairs to the top decks, or to watch the seagulls as they glided on air, Marie Claire followed the other four upstairs.

Seated at a table on the south side of the boat, the two couples and Jeff sat and talked, periodically looking up to see Mount Rainier. The sun was out today, and the mountain was brilliant white. It never lost its snow covering, and some of the bare rock formations gradually were disappearing as the rain on the land meant snow on the mountain. Even the Olympic range was pure white once again with snow.

In fifteen minutes, the horn blew and the passengers had to head back down as the boat was about to dock. Walk-on passengers stood in front, letting the wind blow their hair behind or around their faces. The smell of salty sea and fish permeated through the breezeway that was the car deck. Waves hitting against the sides of the ferry blew spray up and through the round portholes, and the passengers watched as a lone gull mistakenly flew through the center of the big boat. It was a windy day, and Marie Claire wished at that moment that she could stay on the island forever. But again, she pictured the new life she had in Midway, and thought about the day when her dreams for that place reached fruition. She smiled, looked up to Heaven, and said a silent prayer of thanksgiving.

*   *   *   *

On the road again, heading for Sequoia, Jeff talked about their findings a little bit. He wanted Marie Claire to get a picture of what he would talk about when they saw the Copelands.

Marie Claire sat, stoically, not speaking at all. She saw some riders along the road outside of town, and they peaked her interest. Two of the kids, about twelve or so, looked familiar. *Probably grandkids of one of my old classmates,* Marie Claire thought.

In less than thirty minutes, Jeff parked in the Copeland's driveway. Roger was waiting outside on the porch. He met them as they exited the cars. "Hi, Marie Claire," he said first, giving a hug to his onetime almost daughter-in-law.

"Hello, Sir." Marie Claire stepped away from him just slightly. She looked up into his gray eyes and pictured Roy standing in front of her. She imagined he would look just like his father now, had he lived. Tearfully, she turned away to walk up to the front door.

Marie Claire took in the heavy teak enclosure. The door had a beautiful oval lead glass window in it that inset just inches from the very top to the level of the lock. In the center flew a hummingbird with its beak buried in a deep pink hibiscus. The window's gold trim matched the gold of the deadbolt lock and the thumb release and handle below.

The men shook hands and quietly carried on a conversation Marie Claire couldn't, maybe didn't, want to hear. Margarethe met her, pulling the door open and waving her into the home. Marie Claire looked back at Dean's silver El Dorado, remembering that Claudia wanted to tour the town of Vashon, so stayed behind.

"Is your wife with you, Detective?" Roger asked Dean.

"No. She's in town. This is business, and she never wants to be part of it." Dean meant that telling people about their dead loved ones was not Claudia's forte, but out of deference to the older couple, he did not want to say that.

"May I have a glass of water, Mrs. Copeland?" Dean asked the woman.

"Of course. I have some iced tea poured. Let me get a glass for you." Dean followed her into the kitchen.

As Dean drank the iced water, the others sat themselves around the living room. Dean finished the water just a moment later, and Mrs. Copeland set a glass of tea down beside each chair, Dean's included.

Marie Claire remembered from the last visit that the paint was the same color as always. White Persian carpet filled the dining and living room, contrasting to the deep mahogany of the doorframes and mantel in this room. A mounted rhinoceros head commandeered the wall above the fireplace, and here and there around the room were scattered stuffed and mounted African antelope, zebra, and lion and jaguar heads and skins. Pictures of African wildlife and scenery hung on the walls of this room, and the theme carried over into Mr. Copeland's den just off to the right of where they all now congregated.

The many windows were inset, and beige miniblinds covered each. The large fan overhead turned clockwise, slowly, and the teak blades shone, as well as the brass fittings and chains that hung down. Crystal pulls ended in gorilla motif. The Copelands traveled to this country every year to help with famine relief. Apparently, from some of the travel itinerary and plane tickets that lay on end tables, they continue in their mission. Ferns in animal planters adorned the room.

Marie Claire had not taken the time to appreciate the interior when she came here the other day. She used to enjoy coming into this room when she visited in the past. Roy's sisters lived here then, and though quiet, they were gentle and kind girls. Marie Claire asked about Sylvia and Denice now.

"They are doing just fine, thanks, dear. They are both due to have children again. That will be two for Sylvia and three for Denice. She wanted to try for a boy this time, but we'll see."

Chapter Forty-Three

Dean cleared his throat. He stood in front of the clean, quiet fireplace. The day was temperate so no fire was necessary, but by evening, the embers would be glowing and the flames high, and crackling of branches and twigs would be heard. The room seemed to turn a bit chilly presently, however, as the other five people looked to him. He turned his tape recorder on and set it beside his chair.

"The other day," Dean started out, "Marie Claire showed us places where bodies were the best likely to disappear on this island." He reiterated where they had gone, what they had done, finally coming to the final place of rest. "The last place we looked was Inspiration Point. The hillside is extremely steep on one side. We had climbers come over to assist us in our search. Jeff flew the chopper, and our agent, Maurice Combs, was the lookout. After six hours ten minutes, he found what we had all been searching for." Dean had a debriefing session with all of them there. Not one question would be left unanswered.

He explained about finding the clothing and bones. He explained how the climbers carried out their duties. He finally ended with saying, "On that body was a jacket, gold satin numbers and letters on green wool, which Marie Claire told us was the high school colors back then. They still are green and gold, according to our research."

"Inside the pocket of that jacket, a red velvet ring box was found, which contained a yellow gold one carat diamond engagement ring. Marie Claire assured us it was the one that Roy had presented her with when he proposed over twenty years ago." Dean explained how they collected each and every bone and piece of fiber, whatever they could find there. "The remains of Roy Theodore Copeland now reside in the King County Morgue, where they can be procured by his parents." Dean got through his whole spiel without breaking down. However, at Margarethe and Roger's tortured facial features, he broke down. "I hate giving people this kind of news. I'm sorry." And with that, he walked out the front door and closed it quietly behind him.

After several minutes, Dean came back inside. The Copelands cried for their lost son. They hugged each other, rocking and clinging. Marie Claire felt sick at heart, but went to the kitchen to get some water. She found more iced tea in the fridge and fixed a glass for herself. Jeff and Clint came in, and Dean left his wife's glass inside the sink, shaking his head as a refusal for a refill. Dean turned toward the bay window and stood staring outside at the azaleas, rhododendrons, and iris in bloom in a long bed that contained the red, orange, pink, crimson, and purple flowers.

After a little while, he turned toward the group of people now sitting quietly around the large room once again. The women still dabbed tissue to their noses, and periodically wiping away tears that still fell, of their own volition, from their eyes. Clint sat on one side of Marie Claire, with Jeff on the other. Each had an arm around Marie Claire's shoulders, and her wrists and hands received squeezes and rubs occasionally. Jeff knew what was coming. He'd shared a little with Clint earlier, so they were available in case Marie Claire felt a need to explode and vent.

The Copelands sat together. Roger held his wife close as Margarethe sat there in his arms, still and quiet.

Dean turned and stood in the center of the seated group. He cleared his throat of the lump that lodged there, and then he just said what had to be said. "The bureau's chief investigator, Robert Sorbian, Michael Zwieback, King County Prosecutor, and forensic specialist Maurice Combs have all concurred with the Washington FBI that Francis Harlan Kingman was the murderer of Roy Theodore Copeland." Marie Claire gasped, grabbed her chest, and since she couldn't jump up with four arms and hands holding her, she sat staring at Dean, eyes clearly registering anger and a demented and tortured soul. Tears fell slowly, but Marie Claire remained stoic. "They came to this conclusion when DNA from hair and blood samples found at the scene and on the jacket, and from the former home of the Kingman's, was verified."

Margarethe and Roger sat with tears running from their eyes. Dean tried to remain aloof and determined to get this out of the way, he continued. "Roy probably never saw the shot that killed him." He heard gasps coming from the women, and he felt sick for having to be the one to bring such heartbreaking news. Dean pulled some pictures out of a manila folder he'd laid on the coffee table earlier, and he handed them to Jeff. "If you don't want to see the photos, you don't have to look at them, but these will show how Roy was killed."

"The gun was a small caliber 38. We are trying to find Mr. Kingman. We have no clue where he is, or how to find him. His office hasn't seen him in nearly two weeks. He went on vacation, supposedly, but no one knows where. He hasn't been home, according to his neighbors. If you see this man," Dean handed the most recent photo of Kingman around, "call us right away." He dropped some bureau business cards on the table where the folder once sat.

"Sir," Roger Copeland stood, red faced, with tears in his eyes. "When do we get to have Roy back? Can we have his jacket back?"

"The jacket is old and has been through the weather, but I'll bring it in. It's in my trunk. You can go to the morgue Monday morning and work out the details of burial and whatnot. The coroner will give you his full cooperation. I'll be right back." Dean bowed his head after speaking with Roger, turned on his heel and walked out to his car.

"Marie Claire, thank you for helping find our son. We'd like to reward you for it." Mr. Copeland held Marie Claire in his arms for a second.

"No, please. It's all I could do for Roy. I was glad to help. I needed to help. I don't need or want a reward. I'm just so very sorry for what happened. So sorry." Marie Claire turned to leave the room, but Clint stopped her and held her to his side. She glanced at Margarethe, and she too stood beside her husband.

Dean stepped into the house as Marie Claire said her piece. He stood silently so as not to disturb the conversation.

"Clint, take this." Roger Copeland directed Marie Claire's husband to take a check he was handed. It was for the amount of fifty thousand dollars. "We know, through speaking with the Mallorys and with Dean here, that you can use this money for your riding academy.

You've come a long way little girl, and we want to assist you in this important venture. You are very deserving of our appreciation. "

Mrs. Copeland, her crying under control, stood and walked over to the Bellhams. She took their hands in hers and said, as she looked into their eyes, "Thank you. We will always love you. Roger and I want to help you in your mission to help children. We understand the facility and lesson attendees list is growing. We read the newspaper article, and Roger had lunch with the governor last week. Roy would be very proud of you."

The Bellhams, very appreciative of the money, hugged the Copelands in turn. Clint shook Roger's hand and asked him, "Do you and your wife like to camp or fish?" he explained a little more about the campground. He told them about the small lake that with the help of Ed, became nearly twice as large as planned.

Roger laughed and commented, "I love to sleep out under the stars, but my wife's idea of camping is hitting the spas and making sure the hotel is five star rated!" Clint, Dean, Jeff, and Marie Claire laughed with Roger.

"Well, I have a great idea. How about you men camp out, fish, have a guy day or two and leave us women to enjoy some fun time away from you," Marie Claire glanced sideways at Clint with a sly look. She knew just how to tease him.

With a sideways look back at Marie Claire, Clint groused play-fully, "You're cruisin' there, woman!"

Dean knew that Clint and Marie Claire were trying to lighten the mood, and they had done a good job of it. The Copelands laughed at the camaraderie between the two, and then Dean added his two cents worth, "These two took a fairly nice place and made it beautiful. Marie Claire has a horse that pulls a wagon, and I understand the horse is comical. My nephew and uncle gave her the chuck wagon. It's fun to ride on. You should really take some time to visit the ranch and see what they've done."

Marie Claire's smile reached her shiny brown eyes. "Did Jeff tell you about Buster, Dean?"

Marie Claire went out before leaving the house to come to Vashon. She meant to feed her horse, and he pawed the ground, pranced in place as she collected his feed, and he nuzzled her neck as she tried to place the hay in his feed rack. He playfully nipped at her, which was a little disconcerting, when she put grain in his feeder. What got Marie Claire giggling the most, is the pawing he did, letting her know he needed fed. He nickered and his eyes looked somewhat sad, as though to tell Marie Claire that he was starving.

"Yes he did my dear. Claudia and I would love to see his antics sometime." Looking at his watch, he said, "I really need to go, unless you and your wife need anything else, Roger."

"No, we'll be ok. Thanks for telling us the truth. We'll go over on Monday and take care of Roy." Roger hugged his wife. Letting her go, Margarethe walked over to Marie Claire and Clint and hugged them both. "Thanks, you two. We'll come over Monday when we get done at the coroners. Is that ok?" turning to Dean, Margarethe hugged him and said, "I hope you and your wife enjoy your weekend. Thank you again." She left the room and Marie Claire knew Margarethe had gone to the couple's bedroom, by the direction she took, *probably to pray and cry some more,* Marie Claire thought.

Dean left and Roger asked Marie Claire and Clint to stay a few more minutes. Jeff remained seated on the sofa, where the other two sat beside him. Roger stood at the fireplace, bereft of a fire, looking thoughtful.

Looking at the older man, Marie Claire hadn't realized before just how much these two people meant to her. *I would love to have Roger and Margarethe stay a week or so with us. They need to have some newness in their lives. It's time I gave some love back to them. They didn't get it from Roy all these years, and he did love his parents. I know how much they must have missed him. Roy meant a lot to me at one time, as a friend. I just wished I had felt more love for him, had married him, but then, Francis may have killed both of us.* Marie Claire would never know, could never know, as she sat there waiting for Roger to speak. She didn't know why he'd asked them to stay. They heard Margarethe in the back room, and Marie Claire excused herself to go to the heartbroken mother.

Roger sat beside Clint when Marie Claire left the room. "I didn't want you both to leave yet. I want Margarethe to spend some time with Marie Claire. I want to spend some time with you, Clint. The governor and I are good friends and I know a lot about what is going on at your ranch. I am so glad Marie Claire had such good friends as the Bascolms. You should not let her ever forget them, not that she would.

Nevertheless, with time, memories fade. Maybe she needs something to remember them by, something regarding the campground – a plaque or something. I have an idea."

The two men sat and talked for some time. Marie Claire and Margarethe, now quieted, spoke softly together as the afternoon wore on.

Chapter Forty-Four

Back at the Rocking Horse Ranch on Monday, Clint took the day off so he and Marie Claire sat on the front porch with the Mallorys. The couples played Skip Bo as the clouds cleared away from a drizzly morning to a partly sunny afternoon. Clint, an avid card player, was teaching the Mallorys how to play the game as they went along. "Beware," he said. "My wife cheats! She has no heart when it comes to this game." Clint told the couple emphatically. Laughing, joking, playing the game, the foursome had a great time.

"I do not cheat!" Marie Claire emphatically emphasized. Marie Claire won the game and Clint reiterated that she did it by cheating. He was teasing of course, and they all had a good laugh over it anyway.

At three o'clock, the Copelands drove up and the other four went out to the car to greet them. Clint took three bags out of the now opened trunk. As Marie Claire introduced the Copelands to the Mallorys, Clint excused himself and took the bags to the guestroom upstairs that used to be him and Marie Claire's room. They fixed the downstairs bedroom up for themselves and now used it as the master bedroom. It was identical to the one above. The Mallorys stayed in the guestroom at the opposite end of the upstairs. Their house construction was now underway and within two months, they would have their own home.

The others were in the dining room, Marie Claire serving iced tea, when Clint came back down. They sat and visited for the rest of the afternoon. They eventually went out for a steak dinner and came back and visited some more, until one by one bedtime called and Marie Claire and Clint were left to go to bed themselves.

*   *   *   *

It had been a fun and busy week. Clint worked, and Marie Claire took the others on a tour of her ranch. Buster nickered loudly whenever he heard Marie Claire outside, and he kept it up until he saw his mistress enter the barn to feed him hay or apple flavored treats. Once in a while, Marie Claire had an apple or some carrots for her new best friend. Buster pranced happily when Marie Claire pulled the harness out so he could pull the wagon. He loved to please Marie Claire.

The friends took walks in the woods or up and down the driveway everyday for exercise, and sometimes, Jeanette met them at the bisection of the dairy driveway and the connecting lane to the Rocking Horse Ranch. It was on Friday morning that Jeanette met them, excited as Marie Claire had ever seen her sister. "What's up, Jeanette?"

Looking at the group standing there, Jeanette blurted out tearfully, "Marie Claire, sister dear, what would you say if I said that you were soon to be an aunt?" Tears of happiness fell from Jeanette's eyes.

The women, typical of news like this, exclaimed excitedly, "Oh that's great! Wonderful news! Is it a boy or girl? When is the baby due?" and other questions of course were asked, or congratulations were poured out. Jeanette joined the walkers and took a stroll this bright and sunny morning.

"I don't know if it's a boy or girl yet. I don't know when I'll find that out, but the doctor said in a few months we can do an amniocentesis to check."

Marie Claire beamed with happiness. "I'd love to have a niece or nephew to leave the ranch to someday. I hope you'll allow me to teach the kids to ride?"

"That would be wonderful. I'm sure, like you, one of our kids will be horse crazy. Mom was. It must run in the family!"

Jeanette enjoyed the laughter and camaraderie she found on the early morning walks, and today was no different. She just felt today was extra special with Marie Claire's friends joining in on Jeanette's good news.

And so the day progressed. Roger and Rand being the odd men out, decided to stay behind when Margarethe and Kara mentioned going to the mall so they could all look at baby things.

"I'll bring the van over, ok? All of us can go together. It will be so much fun! I'll see if Ed wants to come visit, Rand, and then you guys will have some company."

Jeanette jogged down the driveway. The others watched her as she fairly hopped up the steps and into her house. They then sauntered back to the ranch.

Marie Claire called Clint and gave him the days' activities. "I'll be back sometime. You guys fix whatever if we're not home in time to fix dinner. Oh, Ed's here now, too. Love you." Ed and Jeanette had just walked in the door when Marie Claire hung up the phone. Together, the women got into the van and left the three men playing cards.

The women didn't return until nearly eleven that night.

Chapter Forty-Five

RICHARD KNOCKED on the door at eight o'clock that Saturday morning. Margarethe was in the kitchen fixing breakfast. The clan were going to take Buster and the chuck wagon out to the lake.

"Come on in and have some coffee," Margarethe told the dairy foreman. She hadn't seen Tally behind Richard, but she expressed happiness at seeing him again and bade the two to sit and drink coffee with her. Tally was in the barn Monday when Marie Claire showed them the horse and tack. The Copelands met him there and had expressed their happiness that Marie Claire did so well with her inheritance.

They had a chance to go with Tally to see the fifteen head of longhorns Marie Claire and Clint bought a few months ago. Unbeknownst to anyone else, Richard, Tally, and Clint built a wagon that sat sixteen people. Four seats in all, the front floorboard afforded heavy hide covering an attached footrest to the slightly slanted front floorboard. They wanted to show the new contraption to Marie Claire before she hooked up the chuck wagon, which was no good for hauling more than three people; unless folks wanted to hang on as they sat up top of the cook's area, which wasn't comfortable at all.

Soon, Marie Claire traipsed downstairs with Clint and the others. Roger, Rand, and Kara followed behind. Jeff and Jeanette walked in just as Margarethe and Kara were setting places at the dining room table. "Take a seat, everybody. Breakfast is on." Margarethe said.

Margarethe and Kara had done some grocery shopping the day before and Margarethe set heaping plates of pancakes, waffles, and fresh strawberries on the table. Three kinds of breakfast meats, scrambled eggs, and orange juice sat there too.

Jeff said grace and they dug into the food before them. The talk was jovial and they all enjoyed the food and good camaraderie as they consumed the rather large breakfast. Marie Claire wondered, *I think I might get fat one of these days. I can't eat all of this. Please God, give me the energy to burn it all off!*

*   *   *   *

They finished eating breakfast, and the cleanup got underway by the women, who listened through the open window as the men talked on the front porch, where they seated themselves on the dairy side of the deck. They were discussing the woods beyond the property. An area snaking through the trees that possibly could be a waterfall caught their attention, and the men wondered if taking a walk there would prove them right. The six of them decided to start on making a trail through the woods, tomorrow after church.

The women came out and joined them, seating themselves on the railing or steps. Richard and Tally arose a bit before the women showed up, and they wandered around the front of the house to the barn. Marie Claire figured they were hooking Buster up to the wagon, and she wondered, *how are we all going to fit on that chuck wagon?*

Marie Claire didn't wonder long. She thought that what came around the end of the porch was a figment of her imagination. Here came Buster pulling a buckboard instead of a chuck wagon. She closed her eyes and looked again. She saw the same thing. Clint smiled as he watched his wife get off the stoop and take a good hard look, closing her eyes again and opening them back up, she realized she saw the real thing, and she turned to Clint. "What, how," and Buster gave a loud, shrill whinny when he came within sight of Marie Claire. She ran inside, grabbed the remainder of the carrots, and ran back out to her horse. She dropped the carrots on the ground at Buster's feet, hugged his neck, and ran around to see the new wagon. The new oak seating shone with spar varnish. The sides and back and front did too. The wheels looked original, except they were new, not rusted.

The others came over to take a good look also. They were almost as awed by the workmanship as Marie Claire seemed by the idea of having this in her midst.

"Great job, guys," Rand said. He'd watched off and on as the men built this surprise for Marie Claire. Looking at her, Rand knew Marie Claire appreciated and loved her new toy.

With happy tears in her eyes, Marie Claire said, "May I have a ride in it?"

Clint chuckled and helped his bride up into the front seat. He then motioned the others to follow. The men helped the women up and sat beside them. Richard and Tally took the very back seat. Clint drove. He chucked the reins as he had done when a small child on the farm in North Dakota. They ambled down the driveway, Buster's shoes clip clopping all the way.

*   *   *   *

"Clint, take the dairy drive. We'll pick up Ed and Martha and head on down to the lake at this end," Jeff told the driver.

Clint stopped at the house, and Ed helped Martha up into the back seat beside Tally and Richard. The seats were sort of cramped with four adults sitting there, but not too badly. The men had built it mainly for Marie Claire to enjoy with the children when she got her academy up and running. Richard took the reins of Saber, Jeff's horse, as Ed had saddled him and now Richard rode beside the wagon, leaving Tally and Ed and Martha sitting in the very back seat.

Jeff and Richard, they were told, had taken tractors and made a somewhat smooth track for the wagon to ride on as they rode to the lake. Richard had a big surprise for everyone, but he kept mum about it until the time was right.

The water of the lake, when they reached the southern end, was filled to the top. A beach all the way around had been made with sand. The trees surrounding the lake seemed to have grown four feet in the short time the Bellhams owned the property. It wasn't so, but the lake made everything around it look different, bigger, more inviting. The trailer pads were finished and electricity and water spigots stuck up beside the pads at each site. A cable for TV and radio was being placed as they sat here and watched. At the north end of the lake, smoke drifted up on the breeze, and Richard galloped Saber that direction.

"Well, what do you think, Sunshine?" Clint asked Marie Claire.

"Oh, my love. This is beautiful." Marie Claire looked around her and then at Clint, tears of joy and bewilderment in her eyes. They could hear the freeway traffic, but the thick trees growing on that side kept the noise down to a dull roar. No one could see this area from the freeway, and anyone camping here couldn't see the mess that was the freeway.

"The governor said to me the other day that he will have a sound barrier of brick and mortar built all along this property line. People who camp here will rest better without the noise around them." Tally told Clint, as he looked on both sides of the lake. "The trailer dumpsite is at the far end. As campers leave here, they can dump their tanks." Clint nodded his head in understanding.

The east side showed more campsites and the clubhouse loomed large at this end of the lake. The entertainment building was there too, and Clint looked forward to seeing the finished insides. He knew that inside the clubhouse awaited a swimming pool and five showers. A kitchen and seating area with tables and benches awaited diners and visitors alike. Several vending machines should be there too. *I'll come back and check it all out later.* Richard hadn't said much about this building, but as the overseer, Clint knew that whatever Richard promised him, had been done to provide the best possible enjoyment for the consumers of the campground.

Clint chucked the reins once more and Buster headed to the north end of the lake. Smells were wafting the wagon's direction and they knew a big barbeque was going on.

It was nearly one in the afternoon and everyone felt hungry again. This was the grand opening of the Rocking Acres Campground, and Marie Claire saw a plane fly overhead. She pointed up at it and her friends saw "Rocking Acres Campground, Grand Opening" on a banner that flew behind the plane.

Marie Claire, busy with finding Roy, didn't hear about this surprise. Richard kept in touch with Clint on the progress and final inspection. This happened to be the day of the grand opening, and Clint knew about it, but he wanted to surprise his wife, and the others.

Amazement lit up their faces as the owners and friends alike watched children and adults stream from the trees and run down to the lake. Clint stopped the horse and wagon at the barbeques and everyone climbed down from the padded seats. "That was rather fun, Marie Claire, Clint. Those seats would be hard if not for the leather padding you put there." Rand told Clint.

"That was a good idea. I remember the hard seat of the wagon as a kid. I used to drive the team as mom worked with her hand tools in the garden. I didn't want to deal with that discomfort again." Clint answered drolly.

Richard came over to Clint and he asked everyone to take a seat in the front of the many picnic tables and benches that were set up in rows just for today. Someone had set up a sound system and dais between the lake and the benches. Richard had a quiet voice, but everyone heard him clearly as he stood at the microphone. "Please, everyone take a seat here in front of me. Please hurry. We have a guest speaker today and I'd like you all to listen to him."

The front seat occupants watched as the adults and their children, about three hundred in all, took their places behind. They watched as several cars drove down the blacktop road that ran thirty feet parallel from the tree line all the way around the lake. There were tables set up on the east side of the dais. Tally pulled the ribbon off from around the area, and from the cars and buses erupted men and women, Governor Spacey leading the way. All in all, after everyone took their seats, there were four hundred fifty personnel, community and state visitors, and the governor himself.

Governor Spacey stood at the podium. With microphone in hand, he stated, "Your host and hostess, Clint and Marie Claire Bellham, had two wonderful friends who were killed in a plane crash on their way back from the Bellham wedding. They left Marie Claire a tidy inheritance. With the State's help," Governor Spacey said, "this campground became a tourist attraction. In honor of Marie Claire's best friends, we are about to present a statue in honor of Sam and Julia Bascolm."

"Oh," was all Marie Claire could say, as she held her hands to her face, tears rimming her eyes. "Thank you," she said, as she stood and walked up to give the governor a kiss. He hugged her in return and then she sat back down, bewildered and happy at this honor to her friends. William and Richard uncovered a white marble base that held an inset plaque near where Marie Claire sat. There in gold letters on black marble, was the name *Bascolm Lake*. Out of the marble base depicting a sandy shore, brass cattails arose. Among the reeds, wedding rings on their left ring fingers, sat a couple on a bench looking at six ducks that flew above their heads. *Oh, someone got a picture of Sam and Julia,* Marie Claire thought. *The hair, the glasses, the rings, everything looks just like the Bascolms.* She stared for a moment or two. Then it hit her. *The picture of us at the zoo! That's where this is from.* Marie Claire felt proud as she could be, and silently, she gave thanks to God for his many blessings to her.

Clint, knowing that the Copelands had this planned, gave Roger a picture he found on Marie Claire's vanity mirror. Roger also had a smaller statue of his son in the clubhouse, but Marie Claire hadn't been in there yet. *Marie Claire will always remember Sam and Julia now. She'll never be able to forget them, and she'll always be able to see them through an artist's eyes. Thank you, Lord Jesus, for your love. Bless this place. Bless the artist. But most of all, Jesus, bless my wife. Thank you for her, Father.*

Governor Spacey asked everyone to stay seated and to listen to the next proceedings. A truck carrying containers arrived beside the lake, and the dais was taken away. Richard held the microphone in his hand as they watched the containers being placed on the lakeside.

Out of nowhere it seemed, William and a few other men, using dollies, lugged five huge plastic crates over to the northwest tip of the lake where everyone seated could see the proceedings. The men opened the lids on each crate. William, standing on a ladder and using a net on a very long handle, dipped the net into the first crate. He pulled out a large rainbow trout. He held it up for a few seconds for all to see. He put it back in the crate. William moved the ladder in front of the next crate. He again dipped the net into the open crate, holding up a brown trout.

Governor Spacey took the held-out microphone from Richard's hand, and he turned and faced his constituents. "My cabinet and I asked the farm in Carnation to donate one hundred trout to the Rocking Horse Ranch for the lake," Governor Spacey told the crowd. Four men released the two crates into the lake, both containing the trout.

William moved to the third crate, and from the top of the ladder, he dipped the net in, and pulled out a large catfish. Governor Spacey replied, "We have fifty catfish here. They were donated to us by the Crystal Springs Catfish Farm in San Antonio, Texas." Again, the four men released that crate into the waters. "I heard that Marie Claire especially loves blackened catfish. We are pleased to say that we asked for these specifically in her honor. Without her, we would not have this beautiful camping resort."

William set the ladder between the fourth and fifth crates. He stood at the top of the ladder, and dipped his net into each crate pulling out a fish. Last but not least, the governor said, "We have one hundred bass. Some people love this fish so we wanted to be sure these were donated by Griffith's Bass Farm of Moline, Illinois. I called several weeks ago and they assured me that they could accommodate as many as we could use. The mayor of this great city helped donate the money for the venture here. We want to thank him for his generosity." Mayor Garfield, who had been seated in the bleachers, stood up and waved as he walked to the front.

"Clint and Marie Claire Bellham, we wish to thank you for bringing this camping resort to our city." Mayor Garfield now stood at the microphone. "Through your foresight and willingness to help our city grow, Clint, you helped us achieve something that we hadn't thought of before. A new intervention that would bring in tourism, thus, more revenue. Richard and William, the foreman of the dairy and the ranch here, assured us that Clint and Marie Claire secured a knowledgeable and responsible man to oversee this campground. Rand Mallory, would you please come up front."

Some of Rand's coworkers sat in the crowd, and they stood and cheered. A red-faced Rand took the microphone, turned, and he looked at Marie Claire and Clint. "Governor Spacey asked me to fax over a list of clientele that are signed up, for the next eight months, to use this campground. Altogether, we have secured," and Rand read off a monetary figure that startled everyone sitting there. It was much more than Clint could ever imagine. They were assured that the campground would be filled with campers, every spot, for a long time. "I will be at the clubhouse for those of you waiting for a camping date. We are filled up until next August. I guess that's fortunate for us, but we're sorry there aren't more spaces to fill."

"Thank you, Rand. This is wonderful news for both you and for Midway." The mayor now had the microphone in hand as Rand stepped away to take his seat again. "I would like to ask Clint and Marie Claire Bellham to come up now." The couple walked up to the lectern next, at the governor's bidding. He shook their hands and asked them to say a few words. Clint took the microphone first." I don't know what to say. Thank you, so much, to everyone who made this possible. Our governor had the trees donated to us when the forest service was clearing for firebreaks. You can see they are doing very well. The fish -- well, we had no idea anyone had procured the fish yet to fill the lake. From here, we can't see the ending of it as Ed Brown, my brother-in-law's dad, donated enough acreage to lengthen the lake from one mile to one and a half miles. We won't have motor boats on the water, but we have procured twenty rowboats and a few rubber rafts for those who would like to rent them for the day. The building there," Clint pointed to a window fronted building on the west side of the lake opposite the crowd, "is where you go to rent a boat. The cashier's cage, you can see, is where you pay. The boat will then be pulled out, by someone, for you. The docks along here are for the boaters to use, and so we ask the kids not to play on them. If you're sitting and fishing, that's fine, but we don't want people to be inconvenienced in any way. I'll now give my wife time to say something." Clint handed Marie Claire the speaker as she stood by him. Clint held his arm around her waist as she spoke.

"I cannot express my astonishment, my thanks, and the love I feel for all of you who donated or helped in some way. Not only a thanks to you who helped us in this venture, but also a big thanks to those of you who came here to spend your time at our new facility. What a blessing we have been given. In this place, all of us can find some solitude, some natural beauty, and enjoyment away from crowded malls and movie theaters, whatever. This is a special place to me, and I hope all who use it get satisfaction and relief from their everyday lives. Thanks go to my best friends, who are now waiting in the Great Beyond. They gave me hope, love, and the means to help accomplish this great goal of my husband's. I didn't even know of this until recently. He kept it as a surprise for my birthday, which happens to be tomorrow." Marie Claire bowed her head, a bit embarrassed to say that. Clint and Marie Claire heard laughter coming from the people, and then *happy birthday to you*, resounded from the audience. Happy tears appeared in the Mallory's and Copeland's eyes, and their faces glowed with love for the couple standing up front. Richard whispered something to Marie Claire and when all was quiet once again, she spoke.

"The lake is thirty feet deep and there are no shallow places except at the ends here," she pointed to the very ends of the lake, "so don't expect to wade anywhere else. Parents, watch your kids closely. There are warning signs on the posts here, and I will be hiring a lifeguard this week to oversee swimmers. We've been so busy with other things that we didn't have time to oversee that chore. Thanks again. I want to tell you that we will be showing a movie tonight. Richard just told me about it! It starts at seven." She saw Richard and William, who wanted to speak again. She handed the mike over to William.

"If I can get the men to oversee moving the tables and benches around the lakeside, we'll go ahead and get a line going for the barbeque." He explained the food awaiting them and told them where the garbage cans sat. "We expect you to clean up your own dirty plates. Thanks for the patronage and have a great time."

After grabbing a quick lunch, Marie Claire loved on the horse. Before anyone got done eating, she remembered something she forgot to say in her speech. She walked back to the microphone and turned it on. "I forgot to tell you all an important announcement. In the spring and summer months, horses will be available for trail rides. We'll be working on these trails this fall and by spring, we'll have a pony ride corral set up for the littlest of the children. I will be procuring horses for the riding academy in the next couple of months. Some of the horses will be kept down here near the lake for the campground to use. Most of them will be up above for the handicapped children. I will be helping anyone wanting to take riding lessons, but those days will be only once or twice per week, and yearlong. Handicapped kids will be weekends through October and three days per week during the spring and summer. See William at the Rocking Horse Ranch barn, up above, if you want to sign up. Please, let everyone you can, know about my facility. Thanks again. If anyone has questions, please see me before you leave. I'll be around here, and the clubhouse for the rest of the afternoon." Clint noticed the faraway look on Marie Claire's face before she stepped off the platform. She didn't say anything at the time, however.

An hour later, everyone finished eating. The governor and mayor sidled away to walk along the lake, deep in discussion. Their aides surrounded them. They each held a large cup of iced tea.

The other men had all picked a table to move, and that was now in progress.

*　　*　　*　　*

Roger and Margarethe Copeland walked up to Marie Claire. "Would you like to go into the clubhouse with us, Marie Claire? Clint says you haven't been in there yet!" Roger asked.

"Sure! I'd love to see what my husband did with the place. I love the statue, Sir. Thank you so very much." Marie Claire looked at each of the Copeland's, hugging them in turn.

The couples had gone up to the clubhouse, talking all the way. Once inside, Clint led his wife over to the pool table. Clint turned Marie Claire back to the door through which they came. There, near the wall holding several of Marie Claire's trophies and the couple's picture, sat a pedestal made of black and white marble. Atop the pedestal sat a bust of Roy Theodore Copeland. Marie Claire again felt tears come to her eyes. She slowly walked over to take a better look. The same artist who fashioned the memorial out by the lake, also created this beautiful piece of artwork. A gold plate bearing Roy's full name was affixed to the base of the bust.

The artist caught every facial aspect of the real man. The eyes bore the same wondering glint in the brass bust. The dimples that showed slightly around the smile brought a strong remembrance to Marie Claire's mind. Her heart beat faster at the wonder of seeing Roy here in front of her.

"I want you to know, Marie Claire, that Margarethe and I wanted to thank you in the best way we knew how. You helped find our boy, and we wanted him to be displayed here so everyone could have something to remember him by, as well as bring awareness that you were the instrument God used to find him for us. For that, we will be eternally grateful."

"Thank you," was all Marie Claire could get out before running out to the Bascolm's bench and kneeling there to pray. When the others reached her, they helped her up at the appropriate time, and she looked into the eyes of her husband, her friends, and her sister. "I love you, and again, I am so sorry for Roy's being lost to you both," speaking to the Copelands. "I can't thank you enough for your love."

Clint wanted to get a picture so he asked for everyone to get closer. Marie Claire stood between the older couple. Kara and Rand stood behind and Clint took a picture of them there by the lakeside. Jeanette took the camera from her brother-in-law and she said, "get in there between Mrs. Copland and Marie Claire, Clint. I'll get a picture of you all." Jeanette looked through the lens. What she saw made her eyes moist. There were Marie Claire and Clint enveloped by the Copeland's hugs. Rand and Kara stood looking over Marie Claire's shoulders, one at each side. The smile on each face would almost outshine the sun, and then Jeanette snapped the picture. The Bascolms sat on the bench behind them all, smiling and looking toward Heaven.

Chapter Forty-Six

E ARLIER, MARIE Claire thought she saw a familiar face in the back of the crowd as she spoke the last words to the people seated there before her. She stepped down from the dais where she stood to get a better look at the man, but she'd lost him. The nervous feeling kept at Marie Claire, but she said nothing about it as she was caught up in visiting and the picture taking. She was now walking alone with Kara, and she thought she saw the same face again, over by the boat ramp.

Before they left her house this morning, Jeff fitted Marie Claire with a wire. She could talk to him without doing anything but speak. All she had to do was push the button on the transmitter in her pocket. The beep would alert Jeff and Dean that she needed them to listen. They would push their buttons to confirm they were listening. She could talk all she wanted without doing anything else.

"Dean, Jeff, can you hear me?" she heard the returning click letting her know they heard. Jeff knew what she was doing, but Clint, sitting on the bench beside him, did not. Jeff calmly told Clint to walk with him and Dean, who had showed up in shorts and a T-shirt.

"I hear you, Marie Claire. What's up?" Dean answered.

"I think I saw Francis in this crowd. He was in the back of the picnic area earlier, now I think I saw him by the boat ramp. What do I do?" Marie Claire sounded nervous. Jeff walked a little faster, catching up with Marie Claire, Clint by his side. Jeff asked Jeanette, as he passed her, to head for the clubhouse; and a few moments later, he didn't see her anywhere, so assumed she'd made it.

Marie Claire had been walking and talking with Kara, but she asked the woman to go up to the clubhouse. Marie Claire wanted Kara out of harm's way. Kara looked at Marie Claire, saw the scared look on her face, and walked quickly to Rand. She whispered something to her husband and then they walked toward safety. Clint put his arm around Marie Claire shoulders. Clint touched her forehead with his and kissed her there.

"Keep walking," Jeff said to them, before he and Dean sidled away to speak with Ben.

"The Channel Four news crew has been here all afternoon. I wonder if they have a picture of the crowd. Ben, would you mind checking with them? You know what Francis Kingman looks like?"

"Gotcha, Dean. I'll radio back to you after I speak with them." Ben headed toward the KOMO News team standing on the dock, watching the fish swimming around. Smelling a story, two of the three walked towards the van with Ben.

The governor had been alerted, by Rand, of the trouble brewing. A car awaited beyond site of the campground. Mayor Garfield walked with Governor Spacey as though nothing untoward had happened. They reached the Lincoln around the bend of the trees just beyond the clubhouse. "At least those two are safe," Dean told his friends there with him, knowing they would be awaiting them at the ranch house.

Marie Claire was shaking. Clint could feel this and he knew she had to be scared. Marie Claire tripped and fell right then. People moved out of the way. Some stopped to see if they could help her, but Jeff moved them on.

Dean and Jeff kept the looky loos moving. Marie Claire pretended to cry. She kept her head down and rubbed her ankle, her eyes moving in every direction, trying to get a glimpse of her former husband. Clint then caught on to what she was doing, what was happening.

He helped Marie Claire to sit on a bench they came to, and together, Dean, Jeff, and Clint looked at her ankle. "Did you see Francis, Marie Claire?" Clint asked. Marie Claire nodded her head. "I thought I did once, but I wasn't sure it was him. I think he's a little bit ahead of us. I don't think he saw you fall. He was just in among several people that appear to be a group of family members or friends." Clint told them.

"Where are the two horses?" Marie asked.

"Richard has them," Jeff told Marie Claire. "In fact, look behind us!"

Looking back, Marie Claire and Clint saw Richard and William, one driving the wagon and the other riding Saber, who was trying to keep up with the Clydesdale. Marie Claire laughed.

"Let me go to Buster. He's going to wear Sable out." Marie Claire ran back to the wagon. Buster stopped when Marie Claire reached him. "Buster, I'm not going to leave you. You don't have to hurry to try to catch up to me," Marie Claire playfully kidded her horse, rubbing his face. Marie Claire jumped on Buster's back. The horse turned his nose and sniffed her pant leg. She nudged him with her knees and he walked sedately alongside Clint. Richard sat in the seat of the wagon behind her and she could hear him giggling. Marie Claire stared straight ahead, but her eyes were moving. She spied who she thought was Francis. He stood a ways away from the crowd. "Dean," she said looking like she was talking to Clint, "Francis is at ten o'clock, ahead of me."

"Does he have a white hat on his head and a green long sleeved shirt?" Dean asked.

"Yes, that's him," Marie Claire answered.

"Thanks, Marie Claire. We're onto him."

"If Francis has a gun, he could kill you, Marie Claire!" Clint was not so much angry as scared for his wife. Frantic now, Clint quietly pleaded with his wife, "Please get down from there. Francis could shoot you and nobody would necessarily see him do it."

Marie Claire jumped off the big horse. Afraid for the horse, she ran to Buster's head and away from him. She acted out of character as she grabbed Clint and kissed him long and deep. Her back was towards the lake. Jeff walked toward the couple, and he saw the exchange and smiled, but then knowing the Bellhams, he knew this was not normal in front of so many people.

He'd been talking to Richard, not paying attention to the conversation between Dean and Marie Claire. He realized his mistake, but not too late, as he took the pistol out of his waistband, and held it inconspicuously. Marie Claire became concerned when she noticed Jeff's movements, but she didn't say anything. She just pushed away from Clint and sidled near to Jeff.

The birds sang, the fish jumped up out of the water to catch flies, and the bass swam near the edge of the lake, watching for bugs. Someone had seen a boat on the water. They said there was a man in it. The people around them could be heard saying, "Let's do that later.

Let's do this or that. Let's go." Marie Claire voiced her concerns and Ben sent an agent over to the boat shop to delay anyone from getting on the lake with Francis.

Francis Kingman, from what Jeff could see, was in fact in the boat and coming their way. He relayed the information on to Dean and Ben.

There were people again at the barbeque area, and that was a good thing. Jeff and the others with him meandered toward the southern end.

Jeff noticed a watermelon-eating contest at one table, and someone else tested the waters to see how cold the lake water felt. Some man tried his best to keep some kids from shaking the pop cans and squirting the fizz all over everyone standing around him, and a three-legged race with several teams was underway across the lake.

Jeff didn't take time to further peruse the area. He needed to make absolutely sure that Francis indeed sat in that boat. No one had really gotten a positive look at him, just presumption. *Marie Claire only thought she saw Francis, but we need to make sure.* He jumped on Saber and ran the horse to the woods. He looked back to see Francis rowing, but not noticing what was going on around him. The man had Marie Claire in his sights and he kept the boat gliding, slowly, in her direction. Jeff ran the horse through the wooded area, around to the opposite side of the lake. He stopped Saber close enough, and he got a good look through the small binoculars he borrowed from someone in the crowd, and stuck in his pocket. It was Kingman all right. In his hand, now, he held a very deadly gun. It would take out a grizzly bear from the boat to the tree line, which was over a thousand feet away.

*   *   *   *

"Dean, Ben," Jeff spoke. His voice carried over the airwaves to the wired men. "Confirmation positive. Francis Kingman is sitting near the shore and he has a gun in his hand." The news crew spread out, still filming some more of the lake and campground amenities. A few campers and visitors smiled as they gave interviews and opinions of the new camping center. One of the agents dressed in shorts and no shirt meandered down to Marie Claire. He spoke with her and Clint.

He looked around and seemed satisfied that there were a lot of people, some of them fellow agents, gathered around the couple.

Police officers moved into the woods to join the FBI and, discreetly, they spread out, guns ready to pull out should the need arise. After dropping the governor and mayor off at Clint's home, some of the secret service came back to join the FBI and police officers as they tried to control a murder. They knew with all the people here today, someone else might be hurt, or killed.

Richard, after speaking with Ben and Marie Claire, moved the wagon out of sight of the man on the lake. Richard grabbed the reins and led a reluctant Buster to the northwest corner of the woods. They took the cleared trail along the fence line opposite Kingman's location.

Francis Kingman neared the lakeside. He looked for Marie Claire a few times, saw her still surrounded by a group of people gabbing at her, and thought, *I wish those people would get away from my wife. She needs to come with me and they're in the way. I can't get her attention. I guess I'll have to get out and make her come with me.*

Jeff kept up with Francis' coordinance and relayed it to Dean and Ben. Jeff said now, "Looks like Francis is going to go in by force and take Marie Claire. He's at the shoreline and getting ready to tie the boat to the dock."

"Come on down, Jeff, and do whatever you have to for Marie Claire's safety. I'm on my way," Dean told his agent.

"Marie Claire, come with me. I don't want you hurt. Please, let's go home." Clint saw Francis tie the boat and he was now getting out onto the fishing pier.

"Clint, I can't leave. I have to see this finished. That man killed my fiancé. He almost killed me several times. I want to see him fall. How can someone be so hateful?" Marie Claire was angry, but not at Clint. She was tired of running, tired of looking behind her, and most of all, tired of Francis.

A resigned Clint just kept Marie Claire close to his side, watching Francis, and hoping the man would get caught soon. *What a way to start off a new venture,* Clint thought to himself. Marie Claire felt Clint shaking a little. She looked up at him and saw the worry on his face.

"Clint, why don't you go home, or go into the clubhouse. Francis wants me, but he's not going to get me. Look around; there are at least fifty agents and police here. It'll be fine." Marie Claire spoke quietly, and her stature and strength buoyed Clint.

"No, Sunshine, I'm staying right here where I belong. You're my wife," Clint stressed 'my' and he stayed there beside Marie Claire.

They heard a helicopter landing and a news anchor ran over to see what they had going for the opening ceremonies of the campground. When they heard about a possible killer on the loose and who may be here, who may have been sighted here, they went crazy trying to get the story.

*   *   *   *

Being Saturday, people would be watching the first of the season home football game on television. Francis' coworkers and partners were no different. Everett Wyant, senior partner of Kingman, Louis, and Bates, held a party at his house this Saturday. His wife had just brought in a big bowl of popcorn and another case of beer when the game, interrupted by a breaking news story, disappeared. A musical tune accompanied a red, white, and blue flashing screen. Then, a banner came across the screen that read, 'Channel 4 News Live Broadcast. Breaking News Live.'

The anchor came on holding a large microphone, and a look of concern showed on her face. "This is Maria Kostas talking to you live from the Rocking Acres Campground. Today is the grand opening of this new travel center, and a situation has arisen here, causing grave concern. We've been showing the footage of the festivities, and we were told, just a moment ago, that there is a possible killer in the area." News cameras spanned the entire campground, and they rested on the man on the lake.

Francis acted nonchalant and very cool as he got back in the boat and rode out to the center of the lake. The wagon was gone and he couldn't see the governor either. He figured there were agents in the trees. It would behoove him to keep a low profile. *She took everything from me when she left. I have to show her that I love her, that she can't treat me like this.* Anyone could see how unstable the man seemed. Francis, the egotist, just could not see it himself. He still owned the law firm, but his partners were getting tired of his tyranny. He wasn't the same man with whom they had entered the partnership. They'd wanted to have a talk with him, but hadn't gotten a chance yet.

"Our mayor and Governor Spacey were here earlier," a brief image of both showed them speaking at the dais. "We are told that the governor and mayor are at an undisclosed location to keep them out of harm's way."

The newscast showed a close-up of Francis Kingman in the middle of a lake. "Howard, is that a gun in Francis hand?"

"Oh man, I see it. They said the governor was there and that he fled the scene. What does Francis think he's going to do? Doesn't he know the FBI is there, probably up in the woods and in that news van? There's some agents in amongst the crowds. I recognize some of those guys." Howard was dismayed and disgusted, and Wyant said, "I knew Francis was losing it, but this totally shows he has lost his mind."

Howard and Everett sat together watching the newscast. Speaking together, they devised a plan, and Everett called Detective Michael Zwieback. They had been friends for quite some time, and he told Michael what was happening at the Rocking Acres Campground.

"I just turned the news on, Ev. I have two guys on the way, as well as an ambulance and fire truck." Michael explained a little bit about Francis Kingman, what he perpetrated, and Marie Claire's involvement with Francis. "We'll get him. You might want to think about taking over the agency yourself. I'll support you if you want to do that. Francis Kingman will be in prison for years, if he lives that long."

"Yeah, he's not well liked. I don't know what happened to him. He was a swell guy, but one day – poof – he turned into someone we don't recognize." Everett never did figure out the change in his partner. Francis had so much going for him. "I think he must have broke when his wife divorced him. I can't imagine anyone being so devious and fanatical as Francis has become." Everett thanked Michael and they finished their conversation and then hung up.

"The game's back on. News 4 will interrupt again when they have more to tell," Howard told Everett when he sat down once again. Howard shared a little of the conversation with Michael as they waited for a good move from the home team.

A few minutes later, Howard called Michael Zwieback again. "Hey, Michael. Can you get a hold of the FBI there on the scene? Everett and I have been talking, and I thought what I would do is call Francis. I'll ask him if he's busy and would he please come into the office. I'll tell him we have a problem with the Mason case and we need some help.

You can get someone to come and arrest him here. Can we do that?" Howard questioned. "I know there are FBI and policemen there, but with all those spectators around I'm afraid someone will get hurt."

"I will page Dean Manning. I know he's there. You make your call. I'll see if Dean will pull his agents back so we can get Francis there to his office. Call me back." *The idea might work*, Michael thought to himself, and he picked up the phone once again.

*   *   *   *

"Hello." Francis answered his cell phone, as he sat in the middle of the lake wondering how to get to Marie Claire.

Hello, buddy. Are you busy? Can you come into the office? I have a major problem with the Mason case. We have to go over the terms of the settlement again. Mrs. Mason has decided the sum is not good enough. She's asking for more and she'll cause her husband more grief. She's again threatening to sue us. I cannot get her to see reason.

Disgruntled, Francis acquiesced. "I'll be there in a half hour or so. I've been fishing. I'll leave right now. He rowed to the dock, tied the boat to the mooring, wrapped the gun with the beach towel he'd used earlier to hide the weapon, and headed for the car. *Man, I had no chance to get to Marie Claire today. I'll have to find some other way to talk to her. At least I know where she lives, and I'll devise a plan, maybe for tomorrow.*

Dean and detective Manning were able to stop the arrest at the lake. That probably would have been a bad thing for the Bellhams anyway, but no one thought of that at the time. They just hoped to stop another murder from taking place.

"Michael," Howard said, on the phone once more. "He's on his way in."

"Good deal, Howard. I'll send some officers your way. We'll meet you at the office."

Detective Zwieback was at the parking garage with some other law enforcement officers. Michael Zwieback held the search warrant in his hand. When Francis arrived, they were waiting.

"Francis Harlan Kingman, you are under arrest for the death of Roy Theodore Copeland. You have the right to remain silent. If you give up that right, anything you say can and will be used against you in a court of law. Officer Holbert cuffed the man and led him to the patrol car.

"What are you talking about? I never killed anybody. You have the wrong man. Do you know who I am? I can sue you for false arrest!" Francis was jabbering, and through the whole trip to the precinct, he never shut up.

The detective searched Francis' car and found the 38 under the seat, wrapped in a towel. They didn't find any other evidence, but Michael felt sure that the bullet would match the ballistics. After firing it once in the officer's practice range, he took the gun, along with the bullet he pulled out of the backboard where it lodged, to the forensic lab. Sure enough, the scratches on the bullet found in Roy's skull, matched the marks on this recent bullet, and inside the barrel and firing pin of the gun. The FBI and Seattle Crime Lab knew they had found the killer of Roy Copeland. There would be no denying that.

Francis Kingman will never again be able to hurt Marie Claire or anyone else. I'm so glad I can finally rest. This case nearly did us all in, Michael Zwieback thought as he left the precinct.

Chapter Forty-Seven

IT TOOK two months, four days, and five hours for the jury to find Francis Harlan Kingman guilty of first-degree murder. "May God have mercy on your soul," the judge said. "The many men you have sent to the prison will be after you. I don't suspect you will live long. I would have given you the death penalty if the state still subscribed to that sentence. You have been a child predator and maniacal lawyer. I hope to never again see another like you, sir. Think hard and long about your deeds. Seek forgiveness." With that, the judge banged his gavel and dismissed the court.

Sentenced to life in prison without the possibility of parole, Francis left the room a very dejected looking man. Anne, Kaye, and Michael sat there as they watched Francis. He stopped once beside the seat where his once long ago family now sat. Anne's present husband, Al, sat there beside her.

Francis looked at the four of them, and then with a backwards glance at Marie Claire, pursed his lips as though throwing her a kiss. Without a word, he walked with the officers flanking him out of the courtroom door.

This was the same judge who handled the Charlene and Lisa Marie Busche case. He felt sorry for Marie Claire, but he was happy to see that she seemed so well adjusted and at peace now.

Clint stood there with his wife. He saw how relieved she appeared. Jeff and Jeanette were there also with the Mallorys, the Copelands, and the Mannings.

Marie Claire stood next to the seats where Anne and the others sat. Anne looked once at Marie Claire and then, taking the hand of her husband, they got up. Together with Michael and Kaye, they walked the other direction away from Marie Claire.

Marie Claire exhaled a very loud sigh. Clint felt her tensed muscles loosen. He hugged her to his chest, but amazement overcame her features when Kaye turned and ran back to Marie Claire.

"I understand, Marie Claire. It was nice to see you again. Thank you very much for the mentoring you did with me." Knowing Marie Claire knew about her horse ranch, because her mother shared the phone call from Dean Manning with her, Kaye didn't say anything else.

Marie Claire told her, "I am very sorry for what your dad did to me, to all of us. I'm sorry too, that he did what he did to Roy."

Kaye smiled slightly, touched Marie Claire's hands, and ran back to her mother, who stood at the door, anxious to leave. Anne waited for her daughter, never once acknowledging Marie Claire. Kaye was crying by the time she got to her family. She turned once and waved at Marie Claire, then they disappeared through the doorway.

Marie Claire stood looking at the exit as the others came up to her. They all placed their arms or hands on her as though to protect her from an enemy.

"Are you ok?" Kara asked Marie Claire.

"Yes, Kara." With bowed head and another big sigh, Marie Claire turned her tear-filled eyes toward the older woman, who enfolded her with warm arms and a kiss on the cheek.

"Remember this, dear girl," Kara stated quietly. "It was not your fault, anything that you went through. Anne should know that, and maybe she does feel some guilt. I don't know, but look at these people here! You are loved, and God has forgiven your past. Look up, dear girl, and hold your head up high. You deserve love. If Anne hasn't got it to give, just know that Rand and I are here for you. We love you like one of our own. Keep your chin up and don't worry about anything. God's got you in His hands, and He'll never let you go. That's more important than anyone on this earth. Ok? You understand?" Kara received a big smile and a kiss in return from Marie Claire. Kara knew, just by looking at Marie Claire, that she would be all right. This young woman that came in to their lives so many years ago had finally grown up and realized the importance of her life now, that she'd come home and she was needed.

Kara felt proud as Marie Claire said, "Thanks, Mom. I will always love you, too."

*   *   *   *

Every one of their friends encircled Clint and Marie Claire with their presence, and Clint asked, "Where shall we all go for dinner?" It was five in the evening and everyone felt, and heard, hunger pangs.

"Let's go to Cooper's," Rand said. "I'm ready for prime rib and a salad bar."

"Sounds great," Jeanette commented. "Besides that, the view is to die for! It's a beautiful night."

The fancy waterfront restaurant is where they all ended up, seated at a huge window seat overlooking the Olympics. The blood red sunset and multicolored blue, green, and orange hues settling on the snow capped Olympic Mountains and around the billowing gold lined clouds appeared breathtaking. They enjoyed cocktails while discussing the case and watching the sun go down through the window that covered the whole wall from corner to corner.

It was winter now, and one of the days that it hadn't rained for hours on end. Marie Claire, very happy when the verdict came in, smiled, "You want to know something?" She asked in a moment of silence, her voice slurred. Just one glass of wine did that to her. She hadn't eaten in hours, and she fought hunger pangs. "My head is telling me that it would have been better to see Francis shot through the gut by Rand, kicked in the rear end by Buster, and his male anatomy bitten off by our resident cougar. But knowing he may not last long in prison is good enough for my heart to deal with." Marie Claire missed her chair as she tried to sit. She landed on the floor. The others tried not to laugh, and there was no way Clint or Kara could help her. They were teary eyed from keeping the laughter at bay.

Marie Claire got up, lifted her glass of wine, waved it to all those around the table, and said, "Here's to me." She hiccupped very loudly. Marie Claire thought she would have to call an ambulance for the lot of them. They were cackling so hard that she thought they would die of excessive laughter. *They all sound like they're laying eggs,* Marie Claire thought. *I don't know what's so funny!*

Clint got a kick out of his wife. Just one small glass of wine held enough alcohol to make her tipsy. They had saluted their wedding vows on their first evening together as a married couple. They had been watching *Sleepless in Seattle.* She drank one glass of wine, too quickly actually, and the next thing he knew, she stood naked and then danced for him. He remembered picking her up in his arms and putting her to bed to sleep it off. She had been very embarrassed the next morning. Clint served her breakfast in bed that day and made everything all right. He remembered his promise to never to let her do that again. *Well, I guess this celebration is special. She deserves a moment of inebriation today. Forgive us, Father, please!*

He made her drink coffee now, so she wouldn't further embarrass herself in front of her friends and family. By the time their meals arrived, Clint had served Marie Claire two cups of strong coffee and brought the conversation around to the Mallory home. The others still giggled in remembrance of Marie Claire's indiscretion. It was all in fun, however.

"Now that your new home is about finished, are you planning on having an open house, Kara?" Clint asked.

"Marie Claire and I were talking about that last night before we went to bed. She wants to have a luncheon open house for all of us here, and the dairy and ranch hands. We'll probably have it next weekend. Marie Claire doesn't sit around. She gets things done!" Kara said.

"How well I know," Clint said. "She makes me dizzy sometimes with her plans and doings. She's busy in the church and still manages to take care of her family."

"I love that view you have from your kitchen, Kara. What a neat floor plan, you guys came up with," Marie Claire commented, very excited to have her friends there so close. She now sounded herself once again, though her cheeks were red.

"We are happy to be living there. We can't thank you enough for your generosity," Rand said in return.

"I wanted to have the same views you have from your upstairs rooms. The first night we stayed with you, we fell in love with the scenery, the sounds, and the whole area." Kara held Marie Claire's hand and smiled into her eyes, showing how happy she was to be Marie Claire's best friend.

"You know what?" Kara asked Marie Claire. "Now that the princess has her prince, Rand and I have you back in our lives, and we have a new venture going, how about Rand and I take you and Clint to Hawaii for a week!"

"Wow, what a surprise!" Claudia and Dean said. The others inserting their opinions also.

Marie Claire looked at Kara and thought, *Thank the good Lord for friendship.* She looked at Clint and the others seated at the table.

So many new friends and family! Marie Claire thought her heart felt lighter than it had in a long time. Her soul seemed happy, no worries or second guesses about herself there. She smiled at each person in turn.

She took her coffee cup in hand, stood, and gave a heartfelt, much-needed salute to her loved ones. "I have never told any of you that you are much appreciated. I remember the person I used to be. I hated myself. I have many people to thank, but the few of you here with me now are the ones who deserve the most praise." Marie Claire demurely smiled and tipped her head. Looking back up a few seconds later, she smiled her toothy smile. "I remember Clint's proposal, and then his mortification when I received that huge inheritance. He worried that I wouldn't want to stay married to him. He's probably sorry that he did marry me!"

"Sometimes," Clint teased, smiling at each in turn before he turned his gaze on his wife. He was very proud of her and it showed.

Marie Claire laughed with the others, and then she continued. "I wouldn't want to live without him, though, and he knows that." Marie Claire became serious once again.

"I remember the first time I asked Jeff and Dean if I could be an undercover agent. It regarded Charlene and Lisa Marie." She looked at Dean. "I didn't do anything, yet you said you were proud of me. That was the first time I ever realized what that word meant. You explained the life I had lived through, how others aren't so fortunate, the things I planned to do with my life, where others go into drugs, alcohol, etc., and you told me that I thought of others before myself. I feel sorry for those people. They just don't realize they have voices, wills of their own, and so they get stuck in their assorted ruts. Kara and Rand, remember how shy I used to be and how much your friendship meant to me, how insecure I always was?" Marie Claire recalled a lot of things, many times that her life was not as it should be. She reminisced with her friends and family, everything that mattered, everything that was wrong with her past life, and how, with God's help, she got to where she is today. They listened - all of them. They let her get the past out of her system. She needed to be free of it. She needed to go forward with no more thoughts of her former life to interrupt what could otherwise be a pleasant experience in whatever comes her way.

A few knew her back then, and others could only imagine. "I know most of that past life was not my fault. It was the way I was raised. You," pointing to each one seated there, "helped me grow. You helped me become a woman respected and loved. I thank you for your friendship, love, and care. I owe a debt to you all, and I just wanted to thank you for the most wonderful ride of my life."

"I feel I have been on a roller coaster. Some of terror, some of fun, most of confusion and sadness. I have landed now. I wanted to share my thoughts with you. If I can ever help you in anything," she waited a second, "with anything," she emphasized, "please come to me! I'll be here for you at any time."

Clint stood and said, "My sentiments exactly. We love all of you, and thank you for your friendship." Then he sat down.

Marie Claire stood once again. "I want to share one more thing with you, because of who I was, who I am, and who I want to continue to be. Everything you appreciate me for, everything I have come to appreciate, and the duties I know I have to carry out, is because of the Christ Who willed it for my life. I have not done anything of myself. I am nobody special. I want to make that clear. I chose to follow God's call for my life, and I choose to always follow my Savior's leading. I may stumble, and I will make errors, but it's not because of anything but the sin that is me, in all of us, that makes things like that happen, if we truly put our faith in Christ Jesus. I don't wish to cause ill feelings, do grievous acts that hurt others, but sometimes, because we don't think or act the way we should, we will hurt others. Because we as Christians believe in the saving grace of Jesus and what He did on the cross for the redemption of sins, and we know that is what saves us. I'm digressing, but I hope you all know that I mean well. I just want everyone to realize that it is Jesus Christ, the ruler of all, creator of everything we see, creator of us humans, who should be praised when we love and accomplish things through His will. I love each of you because you accept me, love me, for who I am. Thanks again for your guidance, acceptance, and love."

Marie Claire lifted her glass, filled with crystal clear ice, a lemon wedge, and water, and the others raised their glasses of wine. "Here's to love and friendship," Marie Claire said, a lovely smile on her face. With her eyes shining, she looked toward Heaven. With her glass raised high and a large smile on her face, Marie Claire said, "Thank you, Sam and Jules. I will always love you. I hope I did well by you." Glancing back at the others seated at the table, who were smiling proudly at her, Marie Claire said, "Salute!"

The End

Philippians 4:11-13: Not that I speak in regard to need, for I have learned, in whatever state I am in, to be content. I know how to be abased, and I know how to abound. Everywhere and in all things I have learned both to be full and to be hungry, both to abound and to suffer need. I can do all things through Christ who strengthens me.

Afterword

ONE THING that the author didn't write about in her last two books is the fact that often over her lifetime she pondered on suicide. A lonely and battered soul such as hers once was feels bereft, abandoned, unloved and unlovable.

"God, I want to die. It would be better if I hadn't been born. I can't wait to get to Heaven." Marie Claire had these thoughts, and sometimes, when she is in pain, still lashes out with these words. But in the scheme of things, in the end, suicide is not an option. She knows many youngsters and adults have taken this way out, but murder is not an option. Suicide is murder, and not to be a part of one's life. There are things to do, medicines to take, people to talk to who have the knowledge to help people talk about their problems, their feelings, and they can overcome the feelings that push them to suicide.

Marie Claire has had years of counseling, years of loving God, and He, she says, is Who has kept her from committing that final act of rebellion. She knows that the ones left behind face terrible strife. They wonder what they themselves did wrong. They question why and what was so bad that their loved one had to kill them self. Suicide is a terrible thing to do to family and friends. If you love them, you will find help for the pain you are undergoing. You could seek counseling, adopt a hobby, read books and talk to a minister or loved one. Marie Claire knows the heartaches of losing family members at the hand of suicide. She had family members who committed this act. She has met others who lost a child, a parent, a cousin to similar tragedies.

Marie Claire believes that if she keeps praying and keeps her faith, shares her life with others and stays open to listening to people, then her life will have been worth all the pain she endured in the past. She knows her reward is on the other side of this world, and she keeps her eyes on The Prize.

RESOURCES

King James Version of the Holy Bible

Women's Aide Institutes at various websites online

Medical Offices throughout the country have in-house poster boards

Children and Women's Shelters Throughout the world

Rape Crisis Centers in every city in America

Police, Fire, 911 – each have information to help in family disputes, crises, and domestic violence

Battered Women's Shelters throughout the country

These are just a few of the places I researched to put my past two books together in a way that anyone can understand. I hope that someone, somewhere, will find my information useful.

END NOTE

D ON'T TELL, Baby is written for the screen. The script is in the process of consideration for the big screen. The subject matter, though
difficult to fathom, is nevertheless true for many in this country, and
around the world.

Before The Music is another story that will be made into a screen-
play. The author's dream is to bring awareness, and safe havens for the
many who are enduring violence at home. Home is no place to fear.
Home stands for safety and nurturing. If this isn't the case with you,
dear reader, please, seek help. There is always a time and a place to
run.